CANTICLE

CANTICLE
First published 2018
Turas Press
6-9 Trinity Street
Dublin D02 EY47
Ireland

www.turaspress.ie

British Library Cataloguing Data
A CIP catalogue record for this book is available from the British Library

ISBN: 978-0-9957916-3-3

Cover Image by Jordi Forniés *The Permanent Side viii*
Cover design by Reads

Interior Typesetting by Printwell Design, Dublin 3

Printed in Ireland by SPRINTprint

CANTICLE

LIZ MCSKEANE

Turas Press

Monastery of San Gerónimo, Madrid,
Seventh day of January in the Year of Our Lord, 1616.

I did not ask for this commission, I do not want it and yet, here I am. I still do not understand what has persuaded me or whether, having agreed to carry it out, I have committed an act of wisdom or folly. It certainly appears to be an act of advancement, as I now find myself in this majestic office, a privilege granted by my new superiors.

I confess, such grandeur does not reassure me. High-ceilinged, oak-panelled, this room is graced with fine, broad windows that frame a pleasing view of the monastery's walled orchard to the east and open countryside beyond. If I crane my neck I can glimpse the meadows around the convent of Atocha in the distance, to the south. A few days ago, when I received the sudden order to come to Madrid, I was sure that Our Lady of Atocha was my destination, being a renowned hermitage and place of refuge for troubled, and troublesome, Dominican friars.

Instead, I find myself lodged in one of the most important monasteries of the kingdom, enjoying the hospitality of those illustrious Hieronymites, gentleman monks who are famed for their table, their herbarium and their skilled apothecaries. And, not least, for their intimacy with the king. I am told he is a frequent visitor to the royal apartments adjoining the eastern wing of the chapel, that he might hear Mass through the wall of his chamber. Of course, I do not expect to see him, my own living and working quarters being perched high above the western cloister. But at last, I am at the centre of things – a great reversal of fortune for a simple Dominican novice master with a suspect past and no future.

"Take heart," Fray Boniface advised me three years since, when first I arrived in the obscure little convent of San Salvador, fresh from the humiliation of being voted from my professorship by my own students. I still choose to believe that they were browbeaten, bullied and bought by certain of my colleagues in Salamanca. For reasons which I am determined to forget.

"At least they did not throw you in gaol, as they did Luis de León."

But Fray Luis de León had actually broken the law when he translated the Bible directly from Hebrew into the Spanish tongue. And it was reckless of him to have distributed his own version amongst his students. However superior to St. Jerome's twelve-hundred-year-old translation it may have been – and I am prepared to believe that it was – Jerome's is still the single version authorised by the Council of Trent, whose lengthy deliberations sought to recover the authority stolen from our Mother Church by heretics such as Luther. The decrees of the Council were devised not only to root out wrongdoing and abuse, but to guarantee consistency of dogma and practice.

So. One Bible. One translation. One story.

Still, at least Fray Luis de León got out in the end and regained his position at the university, which I never will.

Such recollections unsettle me, reminding me that I, too, am risking much in committing these thoughts to paper, all the more that they are in the Spanish tongue. Even so, it is a great comfort to set down these words in my own voice, in my native Castilian, to indulge in the nuances and flourishes that are so alien to the precise, arid Latin I am obliged to use every day. Perhaps it is simpler than that: no more than a small rebellion, in private defiance of the discourtesy I have endured from Prior Ortiz since my arrival. It seems that I, a former professor of Theology, from one of the oldest universities in Europe, am hardly deserving of good manners, and that any questions I might pose concerning my commission are regarded as little more than an impertinence.

"Excellencies." I cleared my throat, not yet sure how I should address my new colleagues: the Archbishop, small and squat, seated behind an enormous carved desk; his companion, Prior Ortiz, tall and angular, standing to one side. "Without a clearer idea of the purpose and the intended readership for this study, I fear I may not be in a position to draw conclusions and make my recommendations with the confidence and authority you will require."

Ortiz actually snorted in response. "We are the readership, Fray Martín. Archbishop Crespo, whom you see here, and myself. No one else."

I raised my eyebrows. I know, and he knows, that Crespo, as a diocesan Archbishop, has no formal authority over me, a friar of the Dominican Order. Nor, for that matter, does Ortiz himself, who is prior of a Carmelite convent somewhere in the kingdom of Toledo, I believe. We are all three of us guests of the Hierony-mites. The thought that neither Ortiz nor Crespo belong here any more than I do emboldened me.

"And the form of conclusions, recommendations..." I persisted.

"Recommendations? We are not interested in your opinions, Fray Martín. Keep to the facts."

At that, Archbishop Crespo looked up from his desk and surveyed me with interest. He could not have failed to notice the flush that crept over my neck and face, accompanied, as always, by my silent cursing of this fair skin, which unfailingly reveals my feelings, my distress. I reminded myself that perhaps it was not so, that in my burning cheeks and glittering eyes Crespo might just as easily have observed anger as the shame I struggled to conceal. I refused to meet his gaze and instead lowered my own, pondering the faded spirals and lozenges traced on the carpet where I stood – for they had not invited me to sit – its many worn and threadbare patches a testimony to costliness and great age, the intricate work of Arab craftsmen, their descendants now gone from our land. Evidence, if any were needed, that great learning, art, even piety, are as nothing before the imperatives of power.

Still, one consequence of the expulsion of our Arab and Jewish brethren is the continued existence of the Holy Office of the Inquisition, bloated by an endless supply of cases: investigations into Arab and Jewish families whose forefathers had elected to convert to Christianity – their only recourse if they wished to remain in the country. Many of the *conversos*, strangely enough, being rich merchants accused of practising their old Jewish ways in secret, of corrupting good Christians. Therefore, a threat to the state. Of course, the Inquisition is permitted, indeed required, to confiscate the assets of the guilty, so the richer they are, the better.

Ortiz has a cousin who is a procurator fiscal of the Tribunal of the Holy Office in Toledo. I must remember this.

I looked up suddenly and, in anticipation of the request I was about to make, took a single, not very decisive, step forward. Immediately, the air in the room was charged with tension. Ortiz actually flinched. Perhaps it is true that the slightest of our external actions can produce an internal metamorphosis that is communicated to others without our willing it. Perhaps he, or more likely Crespo, had perceived the conflicting responses warring within me since I had been summoned to appear before them: gratitude, though reluctant, at my apparent elevation; anger that my own Dominican superiors had seconded me to the Carmelites for this as yet ill-defined task, as though my services in the convent of San Salvador were so easily dispensable. At that moment, in spite of my vow of obedience, anger was gaining the upper hand.

"I would like to have my associate Fray Boniface named as my secretary. There is also an old assistant of mine from the university, Diego Clemente…"

Ortiz did not trouble to waste his breath on pleasantries. "Absolutely not. No secretary. And personal servants are out of the question." There was nothing to be gained by correcting him. Diego was not my servant. Rather, he was attached to the university in some undefined capacity, charged with tasks the regular servants could not or would not perform. A man who did me a great service. I am in his debt.

Even now, I am unsure how far my vow of obedience obliges me to take on this commission. Perhaps a confrontation with my Dominican superior in San Salvador would be preferable to my current situation.

Crespo surveyed me. He had read my thoughts and for some reason decided that sullen acquiescence on my part would not suffice. "You will have no need of such services, Fray Martín. All reports, all notes are for our sight only," he stressed, the gravity of his deep, resonant tones softened by the hint of a smile that carved furrows around his hooded, deep-set eyes, their whites tinged an unhealthy yellow. "Informal, rather than formal, nothing to labour over. But in your own hand. And in Latin."

Lest my musings be found by some servant or peasant, no doubt. As though written Spanish would be any more comprehensible to our servants and peasants than written Latin. In truth, I have no need of a secretary nor of a servant, but I should like to repay Diego, whose loyalty and cleverness saved me from a dungeon in one of the Inquisition's many gaols. Or worse. But it appears that I must bide my time.

"And my queries concerning the terms of reference?" I glanced at Ortiz. His long, bony face was pale as milk, his thin lips pursed. It was his turn to examine the carpet. Crespo ignored him and leaned towards me, arms extended over his desk, palms raised, as though to invite my embrace. The folds of skin around those hooded eyes crinkled once more and this time, the smile reached his lips.

"Fray Martín, you have raised some reasonable questions. We do have need of the disinterested eye of an outsider, yet one whose work is renowned for precision and intellectual rigour."

I answered with a half-smile, which I hoped conveyed graciousness rather than gratitude.

"You are perhaps not aware that some initial research concerning the life of Fray Juan and the miracles attributed to him has already been conducted quietly during the past ten or twelve years," he said.

I was not. But this intelligence did not surprise me. During the last decade, numerous visits from Vatican inspectors have been occupied with investigations into the life of Teresa, in preparation for her beatification, which took place last year. That a similar process should be set in motion for her most famous associate and friend, considered by many a saint in his own lifetime, is to be expected. Yet, none of this explains my presence here.

"Your Grace. If such searches have been carried out already, I do not understand the need for another investigation. Are you not asking me to repeat a task that has already been completed? One which the Vatican inspectors will no doubt conduct again, on their own account, when the preparations for Fray Juan's beatification commence?"

Crespo's eyes swivelled away from me and fastened on Ortiz's face. For a moment, no one spoke. I heard my own breath ebbing and flowing like a tide. Crespo's basalt gaze returned to my face where, for a few uneasy moments, it rested. At last he nodded. "You are quite right. Up to a point. Nevertheless, you know the kind of thing they look for."

I do indeed. Miracles. Evidence of sanctity. A certain kind of background, proper to those considered pious. Thus are the lives of the saints made qualitatively different from the lives actually lived by the men and women who become saints. Certain traits, events, subjected to a little embellishment. Others, such as a stain on *limpieza de sangre*, quietly ignored. Yet who can make claim to absolute purity of blood when half of the royal courtiers have at least one Jewish grandparent? Not Teresa. Not even Torquemada, my fellow Dominican, Queen Isabella's first Grand Inquisitor.

While Crespo continued to study me, I distracted myself with these and other thoughts, determined that I would not allow him to discomfort me further. After a time, though it may only have been a matter of moments, he planted his palms on the desk and lumbered to his feet, those sharp little teeth bared in a semblance of a smile. Crespo's smirks perturb me far more than Ortiz's scowls.

"Prior Ortiz will furnish you with the witness testimonies that have been gathered informally during the last thirteen years. Much of this material requires clarification and verification. It also needs to be edited and summarised, to provide a resource for the Vatican inspectors when they arrive at the beginning of next year. At the moment the files are in some… disarray."

One Bible. One version. One story. Is that what Ortiz and Crespo are about?

"We believe that your status as an outsider to our Order, your long experience of research, of languages and theology, equip you uniquely for this rather complex task."

"Will my investigations be based purely on this documentary evidence?"

Ortiz shook his head vigorously and two pink stains appeared high on his papery cheeks. Perhaps he was annoyed at being silenced. "There is as yet no certainty concerning the veracity of these testimonies, or that they constitute evidence at all. Therefore, we will furnish you with a list of witnesses, carefully selected, who will be able to assist you in reaching a judgement concerning the reliability of the facts presented, filling in any gaps and summarising the whole in a useful manner."

So. It seems that they do want my opinion after all.

"There is also the question of Fray Juan's papers," Crespo added as an afterthought. "You know that he was an accomplished poet."

And a famous one. His writings are already widely known and admired in Spain and even beyond. France, Italy, England, Portugal. I believe I may have read one or two of his poems. As far as I recall, I thought them rather strange.

"The originals have never been found. He was known to have recited some from memory and his words were often transcribed as he spoke. It is certain that notebooks also exist – or existed – although these have never come to light. Likewise, his other personal papers: letters, minutes of meetings – he held many positions of importance in the Discalced Carmelite Order, the reformed branch of the Carmelites which, as you know, he helped to found. It is known that he also wrote instructions on spiritual guidance for the sisters and laypersons he confessed. Commentaries on his poems. That sort of thing. They could all be relevant."

Relevant to what? And for what purpose? As I pondered these questions, a heavy, expectant silence descended. Raindrops pattered on the window behind Crespo's desk, glittering like jewels in the low winter sun. My own shallow breath ebbed and flowed as the two continued to regard me, both frowning in concentration, as though gauging my willingness to support their endeavours.

Did I make some sign of assent? A nod, a smile? I must have done so, for at a certain instant, the tension broke, Crespo waddled out from behind his desk, arms extended to receive my embrace, while Ortiz continued to intone instructions, insisting upon the need for discretion and circumspection in all matters concerning the investigation. Though how he can expect hermetic silence when thirty-one witnesses will be summoned, I do not know.

"We must remember that Fray Juan de la Cruz is at present one of the most venerated men of the Church in all of Spain. Perhaps a little too much so," he added, "given that the Church has, as yet, accorded him no official sanction."

Despite my distaste for the man, I understood his argument. In the absence of the formal blessing of the Church, such devotion on the part of the common people may fall into practices that are little short of idolatry, most difficult to control and almost impossible to stamp out. I said as much.

"Not only amongst the poor," Ortiz agreed. "The king himself insisted on having a part of Fray Juan's finger when the remains were on the way to Segovia. Or rather, the remains of the remains," his lips curled in a sneer, "of what was left, after his devotees had got hold of the body. Which wasn't much."

I had heard this story before, about the king and Juan's finger, but had always thought it a yarn. So his reputation for piety really had reached so high, in spite of the resistance, the scorn – the hatred, even – unleashed on him by some of the princes of the Church and by many of his fellow friars. Already I had learned something curious, even though my work had barely begun.

As part of my office furnishings, I am now in possession of a large desk, ancient and worn, scarred with many scratches and stained with the ink of a multitude of other owners. It boasts several compartments of irregular size and it would not surprise me if one of them concealed a secret space where my private papers might be stored. But I believe in not settling for the obvious solution. I must survey this entire room, and also my sleeping quarters, in search of a place where I might conceal my own confidential documents.

Against the far wall, beneath the south-facing window, stands an ancient oaken chest. I am sure it was not there yesterday. I approach it and run my hands across the pock-marked lid. Though badly worn, it is a fine piece, edged with a delicate interlay carved in the intricate *mudéjar* style of Arab craftsmen and embellished with an ornate brass handle. I prise it open.

Dust rises from a jumble of parchments and papers, some of them numbered and ordered but most in disarray: loose pages covered in tiny handwriting, letters, accounts, scraps of prayers and lists, all written in different inks, only a few gathered into rough, random bundles. Not Fray Juan's personal papers, of course – rather, the confused records of fragmented inquiries conducted with neither method nor design, over a period that spanned more than a decade. I will need at least a month to sift through this muddle. Also, I may have found the hiding place for my personal papers.

But I suspect that Ortiz is right. The reality of Fray Juan's life, his works, miracles and death, will not emerge from the mass of papers crammed into this fine chest. The evidence contained herein, if evidence it be, will lead me only so far. Then it will be time to take to the road. I have one year to accomplish the entire task. Whatever the wider intention of this work may be – a purpose which eludes me still – this is an opportunity, and a handsome one. I must be sure to make the most of it.

Ciguela, Kingdom of Toledo,
Twenty-first day of January in the Year of our Lord, 1616.

The innkeeper runs his calloused palm along the counter and raises both hands in a gesture of mock offering, as though to display his abode and livelihood for my pleasure rather than his own pride. It is a sturdy dwelling, handsome enough for this part of the country, which is remote and harsh. The roof has been reinforced with wooden beams, new doors have been fitted, there is a fire in the grate and scented rushes are strewn upon the floor.

But the rough comfort of the place, the complacency of the man and, most particularly, his air of familiarity, all conspire to irritate me. Too late, I realise he has misunderstood the friendly earnestness of my demeanour, as I impress upon him the importance of his recollections of that dark night, almost forty years past. My soothing tone, intended to assuage his unease and loosen his tongue, has instilled in him an excessive sense of confidence.

"We reached home after midnight, padre, and a snowy, freezing night in midwinter it was. We brought him to this very room, to this inn that I inherited from my father after he went to meet his maker, fifteen summers past. Though we have greatly improved the place since those distant days."

I resolve to maintain my air of neutral interest. It is my experience that people speak more freely when they imagine that their meanderings, however irrelevant to the question asked, are of interest to their interlocutor. In this case, I have little choice but to humour him for I believe the events leading up to Fray Juan's imprisonment to be of great significance – even if Ortiz and Crespo do not agree. This bumptious innkeeper may be the only person left alive who was present on that dreadful night.

"You remembered it was snowing," I prompt.

"It was. The memory of Jaime de Echeverría, born here in Ciguela full fifty-three years ago under the sign of the Lion, never yet has faltered and is at your service."

Now he really is annoying me. I frown slightly, set my jaw and fix him with a look, under which, I am gratified to notice, he starts to quail. With reason. The Holy Office of the Inquisition requires little motive to inspect the premises and accounts of potential heretics, especially those with prosperous livelihoods, lucrative properties and an apparent interest in Judaic astronomy. Even without such inducements, it is never too difficult to find an unsavoury character in the family tree – a *morisco* uncle-by-marriage or some *converso* cousin suspected of practising Jewish rites in secret – sufficient to guarantee you a place on the pyre at the next *auto-da-fé*.

In spite of the fire blazing in the grate, the room is not warm, the flames having failed to dispel the winter's chill. Yet Echeverría has begun to sweat and his florid complexion has turned pale. I have never been aware of a desire to provoke fear or even discomfort in others and for the first time in my life, I notice a pleasing warmth in my gut as I watch him flounder and gabble, trying in vain to retract his indiscretion. Now he is frightened. I recall Crespo's silences and understand my compulsion to fill them.

"The night you brought the prisoner here." I allow him a reassuring smile and soften my regard. He is of no use to me if he is babbling and incoherent. "The truth, please, only the truth and you will come to no harm."

As though the truth were to be found in the words of this florid, fat little father of girls. As though it could be found at all in these fragments of paper and scraps of stories. Yet stitch it all together I must, into some semblance of coherence. Echeverría hesitates, then appears to compose himself.

"I was little more than a boy. It was deepest winter and yes, it was snowing." He draws his chair closer to the fire, perhaps wishing to dispel the chill that my glare has instilled in his bones and for a few moments, he contemplates a shadow that the weak winter sun has cast across the mantel. It is a fine piece, carved from pale grey stone and too ornate for this room. It must have been transported at great cost, for I know of no quarry closer than El Escorial.

"I am a man of Castile myself," I soothe. "I know these harsh winters as well as anyone."

Still troubled, he continues to inspect the light and shade dappling the stonework, as though reading a portent in those veins and whorls. His attention is contagious and I am almost inclined to reach out to touch it when, in a hoarse voice, he speaks. "It was early in December."

"How can you be so sure?" I am aware, though, that he is correct. According to some of the records I retrieved from Crespo's wooden chest, Fray Juan and his captors lodged here around the third or fourth day of December. Nevertheless, I wish to know not only what he remembers, but how. I observe his features soften as he casts his thoughts back to that night.

"Because we had just started to sort the pigs for the slaughter. Which that year, we began later than our custom, the days since the feast of San Martín being much warmer than the usual."

My own name day, November eleventh, when the weather is cold enough to salt and store the meat. An important date for farming families.

"Yes," I murmur. "To every pig arrives his San Martín." I intended no hidden meaning, for that refrain echoes down the years from my own childhood. My little sister would chant it from the moment I awoke until our mother, laughing, would bid her cease. Yet Echeverría looks up at me, startled. He divines some threat in my words – that sooner or later, he will pay the price for some transgression. "It is my name day," I point out, aware that this is but a poor explanation, but I have no intention of sharing my memories with a witness, an unauthorised one at that. I raise my eyebrows. Echeverría takes a deep breath and favours me with a grimace that is not quite a smile. I wonder what guilt weighs on his conscience, to have perceived such menace in my words.

"It was my job to mind the pigs, and my little sister Maribel had the task of feeding the chickens and finding the eggs they sometimes hid. My father told us to kill two or three birds and Maribel wept because she had learned that her favourite, an old scraggy thing she had even named, was for the pot. Henny-penny! That was it! 'Henny-penny's going to meet her Lepanto,' my father laughed, and poor Maribel wailed for the rest of the day. So when he found a different job for me, to travel to Ávila and accompany three guests from the convent there, all the way back to our inn, I was glad of it in spite of the harsh weather. I had rather braved the snow and ice for two days there and two days back, than endure the blood of slaughtered pigs and Maribel's weeping. I was fourteen or fifteen years old." His lips move as he counts silently. "Fourteen. This was seventy-seven, in the reign of his Majesty King Felipe the Second, the noble father of our present king. And His Holiness Pope Clement," he adds, for my benefit.

"Tell me, how was the prisoner taken?"

"That I cannot say, Fray Martín. In fact, I did not know that I would be meeting a captive. Only that we were to have three guests and that I was needed to guide them here and assist them on their journey. I had thought to help with carrying their packs but they had none. Only a cart, which they wheeled across the bridge and hitched to my horse. The older friar and his assistant travelled in the cart, I rode my horse, and the other little friar rode behind us on a mule."

"Did you observe them apprehend him?"

"No, Fray Martín. How he was taken, I do not know, for I met them outside Ávila city walls. Two men in black habits approached me in darkness, while the moon was covered by a cloud. They ordered me to wait at the bridge over the river Ouro while the older man, who I later learned was Prior Maldonado, accompanied by many others who melted back into the darkness, led the little friar out through the city gate. They treated him roughly and it was only then I became aware that this was not a guest, but a prisoner, and that Prior Maldonado and the other friar, whose name I never knew, were his captors. I particularly noticed that the small friar wore a threadbare tunic and no shoes, only those flimsy sandals, even though the ground was covered in snow."

I sigh deeply and make some effort to steady my breath. I must not allow my excitement to show, lest this frightened, impressionable man remark my keen interest in what he has just said. I have become aware, from my own unhappy experiences in Salamanca, how certain people may adjust their answers to suit the questioner's desires, or what they imagine those desires to be; and that their responses may seek to support, or oppose, the position of the questioner, depending on the esteem in which the interrogator is held. I care not whether Echeverría likes or loathes me but I do not wish him to distort his memory, so I affect a nonchalance I do not feel and proceed with a question to which I already know the answer.

"You are sure that Prior Maldonado was part of the company?"

"Yes indeed, *padre*, because the prior insisted that the little friar should ride behind us, with a rope around his neck, secured to his own wrist. The prior's wrist, I mean. I recall that particularly, for it made me think that the little friar must be a dangerous man, guilty of some terrible wrongdoing."

It is certain, then. Maldonado himself, the prior of the Toledo Carmelites, apprehended Fray Juan. He travelled from Toledo to Ávila, in order to seize him, have him dragged behind a cart, transport him in the deep of the night to the Carmelite monastery in Toledo, a journey of almost thirty leagues, in the depths of winter.

"My mother did not like him," Echeverría ventures, sensing that he is straying close to the boundary of propriety. Other interrogators would judge this comment irrelevant or an impertinence: the witnesses' private impressions are not on the list of permitted questions set out for me by Ortiz and Crespo. But then, Echeverría is not on the list of approved witnesses. Besides, I find this an intriguing nugget of information, all the more so for having lodged in the mind of a fourteen-year-old boy who remembers it almost forty years later.

"Your mother did not like Fray Juan? The prisoner?"

Echeverría shakes his head. "No, his captor. Prior Maldonado. He reminded her of Gregorio, my father's steward, a very trusted lackey who was most valuable to my parents for his work in the fields and the outbuildings. But not a friend," he added. "He never ate at our table. His family were not of equal status with ours."

Thus, even the common people make the finest distinctions between their castes and the privileges and powers of each, differences in rank as finely wrought as those of the very Grandees of Spain. Who may wear a sword in the presence of the monarch, who may speak first or must wait to be spoken to, who may retreat without permission – the faintest of nuances, hard-won in bitter struggles for the right to wear a plume in a cap without applying for the permission of the king. Even in this most barren part of Castile, such distinctions exist and are enforced with as much bitterness and passion as at the royal court.

"My father did not like Gregorio to be near the beasts at slaughter time. 'He enjoys it too much,' was all he would say. That night when the little friar arrived, freezing and hungry, Prior Maldonado instructed my mother on how the captive must be treated. When the prior left the room she whispered to my father, 'He has the look of Gregorio about him.' They exchanged glances and said no more, for they saw I was listening.

"The little friar was listening too, with great interest, as he sat by the fire sipping his soup, uncomplaining and serene, showing no sign that he had been dragged across half of Castile in winter. Instead of securing his hands after he had eaten, as the prior had ordered me to do, I left them unfastened. Even though I was just a boy, it was clear to me that the little friar had not seen what my mother and my father had seen in Prior Maldonado: that is to say, something of Gregorio, something deep and dark. Just the opposite, for in some strange way he seemed to trust the prior, in spite of being dragged by him through the night and the snow."

"Did your father know that you left the captive's hands unbound?"

"Of course. He told me to put away the rope as soon as the prior had left the room. But my father thought him a half-wit."

"Prior Maldonado?"

"No, the prisoner. You see, much later, my father came in and told me to go to sleep because he would keep the vigil. That was another condition that Prior Maldonado insisted on, that the prisoner should be watched throughout the night. All pretence that he was a guest had disappeared. I lingered at the door and heard my father speak to him. 'They are asleep and have had plenty of wine, so they will not awake until daybreak. I have made ready a mule laden with fleeces and food, hidden in the barn. There is a cave in the mountains not two hours' journey to the south. The boy will show you the way. Wait there until we send word to your people.' But the little friar simply thanked him and said no.

"'Unfortunately, these are my people,' and he gave a little laugh. 'I must face them sooner or later and the time has come.'"

I listen to all of this, trying not to show my puzzlement. Could this be true? Did Fray Juan guess what they had in store for him and yet decline the opportunity to escape? "You mean, he refused your offer of assistance? Did he think, perhaps, you were laying him a trap?"

Echeverría gathers his cloak around him and shivers. "Who knows?" He shrugs. "I did not think so at the time. At first, I wondered if he feared to visit upon us the wrath of the prior, even the Inquisition. After all, my father did not know for whom Prior Maldonado was acting, only that he was from a Toledo monastery and required discreet assistance with a traveller. My parents had first thought I might be required to transport an important personage, someone from the Vatican, even. Instead, it was a frail, ragged man, not much taller than my little sister and not half as sturdy as she."

Unable to conceal my consternation, I stand and take a few turns about the room, Echeverría falls silent and regards me, his brow furrowed, as though fearing that I doubt his account. I do not, for the detail and fluency of his memories convince me. That Maldonado himself would make the journey to Ávila to apprehend Fray Juan shocks but does not surprise me. After all, agents of the Carmelites of the Ancient Rule, perhaps even some of those friars, had kept Fray Juan under surveillance for weeks before the events of that December night. Had he not been under the protection of the townspeople, who organised patrols to watch over him, the abduction might have occurred even sooner.

And he could never have predicted the suffering that awaited him as a consequence of his refusal to escape. That is, if Teresa's letters may be believed and she does not overstate the torments that Fray Juan endured in Toledo. But those stories, at this point in my work, are no more than rumours which I must verify with the testimony of other witnesses.

Echeverría observes my doubts but misinterprets their source and hastens to demonstrate his perceptiveness. "One thing my father did not understand was the little friar's reference to his own people. They were taking him to the Carmelite monastery in Toledo, that much was clear."

I nod. "But in fact, there were two Carmelite convents in Toledo, were there not? I thought that Prior Maldonado was the head of the other one. Their tunics were black, not brown. And they never walked unshod. So they were not his people."

This Echeverría is sharper than he looks. But then, the conflict between the two strands of the Carmelite Order – the Mitigated or Ancient Rule on one hand, and Teresa's reformers known as the Discalced on the other – was well known, even to the common people. For at that time, these were still indeed two branches of the same tree, only granted the status of separate Orders many years after the events of that snowy night.

How could people not have known of this struggle? Open displays of dissent left no room for doubt that relations between the reformers – the Discalced Carmelites – and those of the Mitigated Rule, were beyond bitter. I myself as a boy, without understanding what I was seeing, witnessed the disgraceful public disorder provoked by Teresa's arrival to take up her position as prioress of Encarnación. Could this hostility explain why Maldonado and his agents dragged Fray Juan from his little house beside the convent of Encarnación, all the way to Toledo, through the snow and ice? A neutral observer might conclude that the two Carmelite communities detested each other more than they hated the infidels.

Yet knowing all this, Fray Juan chose not to escape when the opportunity was offered.

Echeverría continues to intone his memories. "I thought that he may have wished to protect me. To spare a boy the burden of leading him to a place of refuge. But he did not explain himself. That is why my father thought he was an idiot, so clear it was to him that whatever awaited the little friar in Toledo, it was not warm soup and succour for his frozen feet."

Indeed it was not. But the details of Fray Juan's imprisonment in Toledo are as yet fragmented and uncertain in my mind. I must learn more of that time in his life. But Echeverría cannot help me with this.

"Did you see them leave?"

"Yes, they set out not long after daybreak. Prior Maldonado was in the cart, his assistant too. The prisoner rode behind them on his mule, with that rope around his neck. Like a beast from the fields."

So there really was no measure too low for Maldonado and his agents in their attempts to humiliate Fray Juan. Worse was to follow, if the worst I have heard may be believed. But what is it, this quality I have seen time and again, that persuades these innocents to be led to abuse and sometimes slaughter? To endure beatings, the greatest humiliations, even the pyre? Is it fear alone? Or perhaps a secret wish for martyrdom, to suffer these torments on earth that they might gain eternal salvation?

I think not. I believe their acquiescence arises from an imperfect perception of the nature of others. Incapable of such treachery and brutishness themselves, they are unable to see into the hearts of those whose capacity for brutality they can never imagine, and are therefore blind to the dangers that menace them. I have seen it so many times. Neighbours denouncing neighbours as secret *conversos*. For personal gain. To avenge a slight. Sometimes, simply because it is within their power. Often, their victims anticipating nothing. It is a quality that accompanies many a tragedy. One I must take care does not befall me. Again.

Echeverría falls silent and I find myself lost in a daydream. We sit by the window, the agreeable view of the plains of La Mancha and the winding road that brought Fray Juan here almost forty years ago, the landscape not much changed, the inn a little improved and the boy who tried to help Fray Juan now a jowly grandfather. So many changes. Yet so many things that do not change, or only on their surface. I look at the man, and see the boy. The deepest things – the rocks, the inner workings of the heart – remain the same, no matter what embellishments or decay time casts upon the outer shell. The thought should fill me with peace but instead, a great sadness floods me.

It is time to leave. I stand, bless my witness and thank him, as he bows his head. He parades his children before me, all girls, women really, one great with the second grandchild and I bless them, too. I have already mounted my horse when he looks up at me and raises a beckoning finger. I lean forward.

"There was one more thing." He scratches his head, smiling a little slyly. "A piece of advice the little friar gave me before I went to bed that night, after he refused our offer to help him escape. Though how he found himself in condition to give anyone advice after what he had suffered, I never knew. Still, his words have stood me in good stead – though I have never told them to another soul." Although impatient to be gone, I am curious. "He thanked me for my kind offer of help, a mischievous glint in his eye. He lowered his voice to a murmur, as though to share an important secret that only a chosen few might hear. 'Love your enemies.' Well, I already knew that. It is a message known to any small child who kneels to say their prayers at night. But then he gave a little half-smile. 'Love your enemies – and thus inflict upon them greater torments than forty legions of devils.'"

Echeverría bursts out laughing. "I looked at him, not understanding a word. And then, just before I bade him good night, he bowed his head, half-turned towards me and – I could swear that he winked."

At that, Echeverría falls silent. We look at each other. Perplexed, I shrug and turn away.

As I urge Caminante onwards, my witness calls after me. "I heard he got out later, though. Escaped."

I nod and turn my face towards the road to Madrid but his final words follow me, carried on the wind: "I suppose they got him in the end, though?"

Indeed they did. They always do.

Monastery of San Gerónimo, Madrid,
Ninth day of February in the Year of Our Lord, 1616.

I was sure that such an elderly alumnus of Salamanca would know nothing of the rumours concerning me that have lingered in the university cloisters since my departure three years ago. Even so, I anticipated this interview with apprehension. Almost as though they expected me to resist it, both Crespo and Ortiz insisted on the old prior's importance and bade me question him on the circumstances of Fray Juan's first acquaintance with Madre Teresa.

As though to press the point, Ortiz stressed how few people there are still living who knew Fray Juan in his youth; and how Prior Andrés would illuminate his pious companion's early life. Of course, it had not occurred to me to exclude old Prior Andrés from the investigation. Such an action would far exceed my authority and serve only to draw attention to the one subject I wish to avoid.

Ortiz nevertheless perceived my discomfort. "Do not be concerned, Fray Martín. Prior Andrés has lived almost a half century in the mountains of Asturias and has rarely travelled to

Madrid. And never, in these past fifty years, to Salamanca. He will have no opinion of your situation."

I kept my eyes fixed on the pages before me and continued to scrutinise the list of thirty-one witnesses written in Ortiz's barely legible hand. Each name was accompanied by a terse phrase summarising the nature of the individual's acquaintance with Fray Juan or their connection to him. My heart began to pound. I had to remind myself to breathe, else I would have bellowed the response which Ortiz's comment merited, which he perhaps wished to provoke: that there is no situation and never was. Nothing but innuendo, false accusations, none spoken aloud, only vile calumnies murmured in secret and therefore, immune to challenge. To refutation.

Yet there is one fault that is mine, and mine alone. An error of judgement whose consequences have haunted me these three years past and will, I fear, follow me to the grave: to have been persuaded to withdraw my demand for a formal retraction and public exoneration; most of all, to have been convinced that the high rank of the people who accused me would arouse the interest of the Inquisition, and not in my favour. To these counsels, against the urgings of the inner voice that I so often, and always to my cost, discount, I acquiesced. At the crucial moment, my courage failed me. For that, there will be no absolution, ever.

I raised my head, favoured Ortiz with a mild smile and had the satisfaction of seeing his left eyebrow twitch in irritation.

"Then I regret having summoned a man of his advanced years on such a long journey, most especially in this inclement weather," I answered. "I could have travelled to Oviedo myself."

Ortiz placed a companionable hand on my shoulder, his bony fingers pressing a little too firmly. "I think not." That grip, held a fraction too long. "Your time is limited, you must judge which journeys are essential and which witnesses you can more efficiently interview here. Besides, Prior Andrés can take advantage of the journey to meet with family members whom he has not seen for decades."

The old prior awaits me in the anteroom to my office. In spite of his great age, his frame is large and has retained much of the girth of the burly man he must have been in his youth and middle years, not much run to fat. He surveys me with a bright blue gaze set in a square, wind-browned face that suggests years of manual labour, although his family were not farmers but weavers in the city of Oviedo. A coincidence, as Fray Juan's mother and father were weavers, too, they in Medina del Campo and in Hontiveros, Fray Juan's birthplace. Unlike Fray Juan, however, who rarely remained in the same posting for more than a few years after his graduation, this aged friar has spent the greater part of his life tending the fields and orchards around the Discalced Carmelite convent close to his home town.

"May I ask what you studied at the university, Prior Andrés?"

"Arts. Philosophy. Theology, of course. The study of those disciplines was a new idea in my time, handed down from Trent, the intention being to ensure that we priests and brothers of the Church were properly educated. It was considered important to foster a high standard of intellect and – how may I put it? – ethical conduct, amongst those of us in positions of leadership, however humble our posting after graduation." He regards me narrowly. "Ethical practices were not always the norm, as you may know."

Perhaps he has, after all, caught a whiff of the rumour that clings to me. I thrust the thought from my mind and nod.

"Hence Luther."

"Exactly. You are too young to remember, but improving the education of the religious orders formed part of a strategy. It was one of the policies adopted by Trent in the middle of the last century, intended to restore the reputation of the Church. Which, I need not tell you, was almost destroyed by the heinous acts of our unholy brethren. Their practices tainted us all and fuelled the rebellion of those northern heretics who defied the Pope himself."

The old man's voice is shaking and his eyes are moist. I understand his anger and sorrow better than he knows. It is not easy, after a lifetime of virtuous conduct, to be blackened by the wrongdoings of others. I murmur a non-committal reply. It is true that Prior Andrés, having lived through the Council of Trent's eighteen-year deliberations on the future of our Church, has first-hand knowledge of that time, whereas I was born just a year or two after the final sitting. Even so, my experience in Salamanca has convinced me that participation in events does not necessarily produce a firm understanding of their meaning. I am well aware that the old prior's account of the causes of the schism in the last century is much simplified.

I refrain from pointing this out and indeed, I do agree that the measures enacted by Trent came not a moment too soon. By the time that Council was established, the mad English king's break with Rome was more than a decade gone, and almost thirty years had passed since Luther published his ninety-five theses. They, and men like them, were as much driven by personal ambition and hunger for power, in defiance of the authority of the Church, as compelled by disgust at the decadent ways of the priests and bishops they denounced.

Yet I do not excuse the disgraceful conduct of many of our own people: the selling of indulgences, the violation of vows of poverty and even chastity, fiefdoms created around well-placed bishops, sin rife amongst those priests whose calling ought to have inspired piety in the common people, corruption that incited the rabble-rousing of Luther and those other heretics who succeeded in separating the northern countries from Rome. I will not debate any of this with my interlocutor, who is immersed in memories of his youth that our meeting has enkindled. A hint of nostalgia colours his words.

"What greater way to develop the critical faculties of the mind, than to study Philosophy, the Arts and Theology at the most illustrious university in all Europe?"

A stab of regret pierces me. The old prior speaks with the pride and yearning of a man who is recalling the most vibrant and carefree days of his life. All at once I am overwhelmed by a wave of grief at how much, through no fault of my own, I have lost: work, security, the respect of my peers. But I must not wallow in self-pity. The Salamanca conspiracy cost me my professional standing, it is true, but Diego, my loyal assistant and in the end, my saviour, lost his livelihood on my account. I must not waste time on regrets.

In an effort to steady my emotions, I cast my gaze around the room and concentrate on admiring its beauty: wood-panelled walls adorned with a few fine paintings; delicately worked cornices; gleaming floors, warmed by the low winter sun; this handsome desk. I am well situated here, on the edge of the city, where I may savour the light, clean air of this noble quarter, enjoying the elevated position, surrounded by meadows and greenery and the estates of high-born neighbours. To the north, lie the palace and lands of the Duque de Lerma, and the domain of the Conde de Olivares just a little beyond. But my struggle is futile. No matter how much I insist on the good fortune that has brought me here, far from the dirt and clamour of the narrow streets of the capital, thronged day and night with beggars and homeless wretches, this tide of melancholy refuses to subside.

Prior Andrés is so immersed in his memories, he barely glances up. If he did, I fear my countenance would betray me.

"It was not a luxurious posting – the convent was located in a rather unpleasant part of the town." He names a *barrio* that is well known to me.

"I know, I was a student there myself. And a professor," I cannot resist adding, and straight away regret it.

"Really? Then you know well what a wonderful place Salamanca was in those days, the ambience brimming with scholarship and learning, the town squares thronged with students in their gowns, having great arguments or debating questions of philosophy in the bookshops and the taverns…"

"…not frequented by young Carmelite friars, I hope."

Prior Andrés chuckles. "I cannot speak for other Orders," he says. "Some of those Dominicans were rascals."

They were indeed. It is a matter of shame to our Order that the first religious brethren whom Luther accused of selling indulgences were my fellow Dominicans. But I am sure that the prior's intention is jocular. I choose to interpret it thus, though my laughter sounds forced, even to me. Enough. It is time to press on. "The Carmelite practices were always especially austere, were they not? Even before the reforms introduced by Madre Teresa and Fray Juan?"

He shrugs. "Perhaps. At that time, I was too inexperienced to judge whether or not the demands of the Carmelite Rule were harsher than those of other Orders. The Discalced Carmelites, as you know, did not yet exist."

I nod. How, and why, the Carmelite reform came into being are questions I am keen to discuss with witnesses who were present at the time. I resolve to adopt an oblique approach. "But you enjoyed those days, when you first became acquainted with Fray Juan?"

"Indeed, yes, in spite of the strict regime, which was very rigorous indeed. We were not permitted to leave the college alone, for example. Wherever we went, we were obliged to walk in pairs, on pain of whipping. Or expulsion."

"Harsh measures."

He nods. "But this rule presented us with no difficulty, for we were four companions. Fray Juan, myself, and two other young friars whose names, it pains me to admit, I no longer recall. During our final year, we four attended the weekly discussions, the *tertulia* which Fray Luis de León moderated. You may have heard of it."

"I have indeed."

The gatherings held by the great theologian and poet were legendary, in spite of the chequered reputation of their host. I am curious to hear more about them and the nature of Fray Juan's participation. "Given the strictness of the regulations, how did it come about that you were permitted to attend Fray Luis de León's evening *tertulia?*"

"Because Fray Luis de León invited us," Prior Andrés answers with a touch of pride. "It was a great honour to be asked."

"I understood that you had duties in the hospital."

"Fray Martín! I see that you have investigated me!" the old man exclaims. "You are not a lawyer, by chance? They say a man of the law never asks a question to which he does not already know the answer!"

I find myself tolerating a levity in my visitor that I would not be inclined to accept from a person of lesser years. In fact, he is right. These last three weeks of sifting through the documents crammed into that wooden chest have not been wasted. My research has even suggested several potential witnesses not on the list furnished by Crespo and Ortiz. Time permitting, I may decide to interview some of those individuals. I also found a crumpled sheet of paper listing dates and duties assigned to Fray Juan and his companions at the Hospital of Santa María la Blanca, where patients suffering from the Gallic disease and such illnesses of the dissolute life, received treatment. That is interesting. As a youth in Medina del Campo, during his various unsuccessful apprenticeships in the Colegio de Doctrinos, Fray Juan worked as nursing auxiliary in the Hospital de la Concepción, which was dedicated to those afflicted by the same disease.

"We received special permission to delay our duties for two hours on one evening each week. At that time – and I am referring to the autumn of fifteen sixty-six when I was a young man of twenty-four and Fray Juan de Matías..."

"...Fray Juan was known thus, at that time?"

"That is correct. He took the name of Fray Juan de la Cruz some years later."

"And Fray Luis de León was your tutor?

"Indeed he was. At that time, Fray Luis was not only professor of Theology, he was also the vice-rector of the university and much renowned as a man of piety and great learning. And also as an accomplished poet."

From time to time, Fray Luis would invite chosen members of his final year Theology class to read and comment on his writings, that they might exercise and hone their critical faculties. As a teaching method, it was considered effective and helped to shape some of the finest minds in the whole of Spain. As a political strategy, somewhat less so.

"Did you read and discuss your own work?"

Amused, the old prior raises his eyebrows and shakes his head. "Mostly Fray Luis's. And other texts of interest to his current projects. Which were sometimes...surprising. I will never forget the silence that descended during our second meeting, when he had finished reading aloud selected verses from the Old Testament. We were all struck dumb."

I suspect I can guess the text of which he speaks but I would like to hear it from the man himself. I would also like to know how his fellow students reacted. "You were struck dumb from timidity?"

"Yes. But not for the reasons you might think." Prior Andrés is enjoying himself. I cannot resist helping him along.

"Why so, then?"

He takes a deep breath, leans forward, plants his elbows upon my desk and launches into his story. "Well, partly because his work-in-progress was a translation of a section of the Bible that is not often read. I am sure you know it," he inclines his head, "or at least know of it. Fray Luis presented it to us in a rather casual fashion, insisting on the confidential status of his work, but at the same time with a demeanour that was far from anxious.

"This translation was but a small project he was engaged in, he said, a favour for a young cousin of his, a nun, who had a great desire to read the Bible for herself but knew no Latin. This was a private manuscript, created in a hurry, which he wanted us to critique. And he had translated it – wait for this – not from the Vulgate, the Latin version approved by Trent, but from the Hebrew *Tanakh!* Imagine! Flouting the law on two counts by translating into our Castilian tongue, and from a source other than the only permitted version!"

"Did any member of the assembled company comment on these infractions?"

"We did not. To tell you the truth, until we read the actual passage, we were flattered. One of the most famous teachers in the university, in all the land, asking for our opinion! It was a literal translation at this stage, he said, which he was thinking of rendering into a more poetic format, *ottava rima*, perhaps. But before he embarked on that more challenging task, he wanted to know what we thought of the work-in-progress."

"And what did you all think?"

"Nothing, at first. We were too shocked. Even more when we heard him read the text aloud."

"No one spoke?"

"No one. Not until the silence lengthened and became unbearable – as silences do, you know."

I do know. The faces of Crespo and Ortiz, and others whom I wish I could forget, crowd into my mind's eye.

"After some time, a general opinion was expressed that what the vice-rector had done was extremely interesting."

"That must have pleased him."

Prior Andrés chuckles. "Not at all. Just the opposite. Fray Luis rose from his bench, stalked over to the window and stood there a while, with his back to us, gazing out over the courtyard below. 'Are you acquainted,' he asked in that clipped way he had, 'with the work of the Florentine, Dante? His *Inferno*?' We all four murmured assent, a little wary, if I am truthful.

"'Well,' and at this, he turned and swept back to his bench, 'Dante reserves a special place for people like you. Even worse than the seventh circle. Do you know where?' Fray Juan spoke up. 'At the gates of hell,' he answered. He was laughing, which I thought rather bold at the time. Before Fray Luis could object, Fray Juan recited the entire passage that explained his answer:

> '...the melancholy souls of those
> Who lived withouten infamy or praise.
> Commingled are they with that caitiff choir
> Of Angels, who have not rebellious been,
> Nor faithful were to God, but were for self.
> The heavens expelled them, not to be less fair;
> Nor them the nethermore abyss receives...'

"'Inferno,' Fray Luis agreed. 'Canto the Third. They were too bad for heaven and too good for hell. So Dante condemned them to sit at the gates of Hell, to be stung by horseflies and tormented by buzzing wasps, for all eternity.' We four sat looking at him, and he at us, in silence, until he tired of our dullness. 'By which I mean: abandon neutrality. Express an opinion. Take a position. If you haven't got one, acquire one. And never base your judgement on the eminence of the speaker. Consider every question on its own merits.'

"Well, as you know, these ideas did not do him any good, in the short term at least. There were those who considered him fortunate to have escaped with his life, that four years in a dungeon was a light enough punishment for actions and pronouncements that were considered very close to heretical at that time."

Even today, Fray Luis de León's activities would be considered unorthodox. How much more shocking must they have seemed half a century ago, when the young Fray Juan was a student, Trent having adjourned only three or four years earlier. Of course, the Council re-affirmed – insisted on – the fundamental role of priests and bishops in the interpretation of scripture and the sacraments as the only channel for mediating the Word of God. Thus, Trent would reclaim the authority of the Church and vanquish the followers of Luther and their ilk. In that climate, even to suggest a role for personal interpretation, or multiple versions of the sacred texts, was foolhardy. All things considered, Fray Luis de León was very lucky indeed.

"The idea of translating the Bible into our native Castilian was already alarming enough to attract the attention of the Inquisition. Moreover, the text that Fray Luis chose was quite a challenge for four young men, not yet twenty-five, who had taken vows of chastity. The *Song of Songs*. No doubt you are familiar with its – human – content."

I am indeed. It is one of the books of the Old Testament that has always attracted the closest attention, of a clandestine nature. So that young men who have embarked on the spiritual life are reduced to reading it in secret, like guilty schoolboys.

"Then you will recall why texts from the *Song of Songs*, read in our native tongue, unmediated by the intellectual barrier of the Latin language, were considered frankly dangerous. As they are openly…"

Even in his advanced years, the elderly prior is incapable of saying the word. No wonder Fray Luis got irritated with them, the intellectual elite of Spain, young men who had never seen a woman naked and never would.

"Erotic."

There. He has said it. Perhaps he is afraid that I will faint. Or report him to the Holy Office. I reassure him that I have no interest in the Index of proscribed texts and he brightens up.

"So, you know how it goes." And, eyes closed, he begins to recite:

"How beautiful are thy feet with shoes, O prince's daughter!
The joints of thy thighs are like jewels, the work of the hands of
a cunning workman.
Thy navel is like a round goblet, which wanteth not liquor;
thy belly is like an heap of wheat set about with lilies.
Thy two breasts are like two young roes that are twins.
How fair and how pleasant art thou, O love, for delights!
This thy stature is like to a palm tree, and thy breasts to clusters of
grapes.
I said, 'I will go up to the palm tree, I will take hold of the boughs
thereof."

Good Lord, he appears to know the entire thing by heart. I am sure he is observing me from beneath those fluttering lids. "It is difficult to believe that this is part of the Holy Bible," he declares. "Yet it is. Nothing to be shocked about," he adds, head tilted, appraising me. I suspect that he aims to provoke. The privilege of age. I cannot hide my amusement.

"Was Fray Juan shocked? Did he disapprove of the licence taken by Fray Luis de León?"

"In fact, he did not. Which surprised me at the time, for we were very aware of the exceptional piety of young Fray Juan de Matías. The extreme austerities he practised were not widely discussed but they were well known and if I am honest, somewhat intimidated those of us who did not have the physical or mental discipline to endure such privations. Indeed…" He hesitates.

"Go on." I am curious to hear random details and impressions from one who shared Fray Juan's life at close quarters at that early stage. Even more so if they depart from the conventional picture we have formed of him.

"It was not through prideful boasting that we knew of his practice of austerities. But on different occasions, when washing, for example, I saw scourges on his back. His skin was always red and sometimes quite raw, irritated by the burlap shirt he wore next to his body. Then there was the knotted girdle he wore tight around his waist. Twice I found ragged *disciplinas* – scourges – bloodstained and obviously much used, in the refuse pit at the end of our laneway."

"Was that all?"

"I first arrived at the college a day or two after the others. By then, all the rooms were allocated. Fray Juan had chosen the most uncomfortable part of the house for his sleeping quarters. It was an alcove, with a bed consisting of rough boards and a little straw crammed in, and a block of wood for a pillow. I know for certain that he took very little sleep, for if ever we arose in the night to perform our necessities, he was awake, in silent contemplation. And by day, he was either in class or at work in the hospital.

"Yet in spite of these self-imposed trials, his demeanour was ever modest and humble. Therefore, I am sure that there was no pride in his practice of austerities. Rather, a genuine desire to emulate the sufferings of Our Lord Jesus Christ and to share in them. Perhaps that is why he elected to change his name from Fray Juan de Matías to Fray Juan de la Cruz. No doubt he wished to mortify his own flesh when its stirrings threatened to interfere with his progress towards spiritual fulfilment. Which, in youth, can sometimes happen."

He gives me that sideways look again. Is he inviting a confidence concerning my own trials in Salamanca? I say nothing.

"We often fell silent when he spoke, or even when he entered a room. His own quietude had a contagious quality; it made us aware of the frivolity of our usual conversation and inspired the desire to return to inner reflection."

Prior Andrés rests his chin on one cupped hand, his sapphire eyes gleaming, undimmed by the years. "If I had expected that anyone would object to some of the very frank images in Fray Luis de León's work, such as those I have just quoted, it was

Fray Juan. In fact, another young friar, Fray Bartolomé, I remember now, took Fray Luis at his word and launched into a long speech on the dangers of vocabulary that describes forbidden aspects of female anatomy. 'Surely there are no forbidden aspects of anatomy, female or male?' Fray Luis remarked. 'For we are all human and incarnate, as Our Lord Jesus Christ became incarnate. Why is that shameful?'

"But Bartolomé insisted that the use of certain words stirred the senses, just as the words of the poet Ovid did – a charge which the Inquisition directed at the work of Fray Luis de León just a few years later – because they stir the blood and inflame the lusts of the flesh, he said. 'Very well,' Fray Luis answered. 'Perhaps we could edit out the reference to 'breasts.' I could call them 'loves' instead. The Hebrew word is close enough. Perhaps no one will notice. Would that do?' Bartolomé agreed and, to my surprise, Fray Luis did make that change. It surprised me that he would substitute something that was correct for something that was wrong but he must have thought young Bartolomé had a point after all. That wasn't enough, though. It didn't stop the Inquisition from throwing him into prison for several years."

Four in total. For the sake of a translation. Unless it was simply that the colleagues who testified against him wanted his job.

"How did that discussion about the *Song of Songs* end? Do you recall?"

"I do. Fray Juan did not say much, but his demeanour was most alert. There was a glint in those deep brown eyes, as though a new idea had just gripped his attention. 'This girl is the soul seeking her bridegroom in a marriage with God,' he said. I remember those words often. As you know, he used that very image in his most famous poems."

I hesitate before answering. Generally it does not trouble me to acknowledge ignorance of a subject but in this case, I feel that this is something I ought to have known. "I am not well acquainted with Fray Juan's poetry," I admit. "I have read only one or two pieces, of which I have little recollection."

Prior Andrés slaps his thigh and beams in delight. "Then I have the very thing for you, for I have in my possession many copies of Fray Juan's poems. A wonderful experience awaits you and it would give me great pleasure to make you a gift of my archive. Where should I send it?"

I look over at the bundle of papers strewn on my windowsill and think of how many others are crammed into the open chest beneath, hundreds of documents awaiting my attention. Even so, my pulse quickens at the old man's words. It is just possible that unknown to him, amongst the many copies of Fray Juan's poems... Not wishing to alert him to my excitement, I nod without further comment. The notion that one or two originals of Fray Juan's poems could be in the possession of this elderly friar distracts me from our conversation. I find that I have heard enough and am anxious for him to be gone, back to his convent, to fulfil his promise. In fact, Prior Andrés has little more to say of Fray Juan and nothing at all about how he became acquainted with Teresa.

"Did Fray Juan have any further contact with Luis de León after his graduation?"

"I do not know, for by then I had returned to my convent near Oviedo."

The old man has begun to tire, but I must be sure. "Do you know anything of the circumstances under which he became acquainted with Madre Teresa? When he joined her in her mission to reform the Carmelite Order and follow more rigorous practices than those of the Mitigated Rule?"

He shakes his head again. "I know only that they met in Medina del Campo, where he grew up, either just before or just after he graduated and sang his first mass. By which time I had graduated myself and had no further business with the world of the university. Nor have I had since."

As we stroll through the shaded cloisters into the vestibule where I will take my leave of him, I continue to prompt his recollections. "Were you present on the day Fray Luis de León returned to his position at the university after being released from prison?"

"No. When the Inquisition arrested him, I had already graduated. But I have heard the story many times from old friends who were fortunate to have heard that first lecture he gave on his return…"

"'*Dicebamus hesterna die*… As we were saying yesterday…'"

Such legendary wit and resilience. I do not know which I envy more.

I am sure that Prior Andrés has given me all the assistance he can, and at least I have gained some insight into Fray Juan's early religious disposition. It is a pity, though, that the old fellow cast no light on that first meeting with Teresa. Crespo will be disappointed.

A strange unease interrupts my train of thought, a hollowness in my gut, as though I were peering over a cliff from a great height. The sense that an important thread of the tapestry is within my grasp hovers in a corner of my mind, beyond my perception but present and close. I take my leave of Prior Andrés and make my way through the herb garden and the cloisters, back to my office, pondering my discomfort.

Monastery of San Gerónimo, Madrid,
Twenty-second day of February in the Year of Our Lord, 1616.

"It was rumoured that he arrived by night, blindfolded, having endured six days' circuitous travel between Ávila and Toledo, which more than doubled the journey from thirty leagues to almost seventy. I do not know if this is true, for I was not present when he arrived at our monastery and therefore, have no evidence that such was the case. Besides, I do not think such proof exists, for all those who were party to that sad journey are gone from us now. These general recollections are all I can offer."

Fray Angelo raises his shoulders and spreads his hands, effusive gestures that I dislike and mistrust. This little friar knows very well that I require a factual account of Fray Juan's fate after he arrived in Prior Maldonado's monastery in Toledo, and not these uninformed musings on the route. In any case, not all those who accompanied Fray Juan on that journey are dead: Jaime Echeverría, the florid innkeeper of the *mesón* where the travellers broke their journey, has already provided me with many details of that night, none of which I intend to share with Fray Angelo.

But I cannot believe that Fray Juan's captors would have troubled to cover a prisoner's eyes, much less wander the byways of Castile in midwinter, in order to conceal from him his destination. I suspect that that part of the story is indeed rumour. One more link in the chain of events that I may never understand.

"Nevertheless," Fray Angelo turns his pale blue gaze upon me, reading scepticism in my raised eyebrows, "it is true that our superiors were keen to ensure that the… visitor… would have no knowledge of his location. For we were instructed to remove many items from the walls of the oratory and the refectory and from any other part of the monastery where he might pass."

Now, this is interesting. Fray Angelo mistakes my furrowed brow for puzzlement and begins to explain, as though to a small child. "Such as, the coat of arms of the dignitaries of the town, past and present, who had bestowed their bounty on the monastery. Portraits. Engravings on church pews, which were covered. Likewise, stained glass and any other embellishments that might identify the place. It took three of us almost a full day."

"What was the date? Can you recall?"

The little man shakes his head, eyes lowered, as though he would prefer to have forgotten it all, not only the day of Fray Juan's arrival, but the whole dreadful tale that followed. No doubt, the terrible events that took place that year in the Carmelite monastery of Toledo were the most distressing ever to have occurred, then or later, in the otherwise sheltered life of the plump, smooth-skinned little friar who sits by my side. I must also remember that almost four decades have passed since those events. At that time, Fray Angelo was a young fellow of about twenty or thereabouts.

"Twenty-two," he corrects me, without meeting my eye. A light flush suffuses his neck and face. "Young, yes. But old enough to know better."

He dabs his moistened eyes with the hem of one sleeve, gripping the cloth with such ferocity that his knuckles have gone white. I hope I will not be obliged to drag the facts out of him with sympathetic words. I am in a hurry and wish to finish here and send him on his way. Besides, he was, by his own admission, twenty-two years old, not twelve. If he had thought the actions to which Prior Maldonado exhorted the community were so abhorrent, he was of an age to resist, even if he lacked the stomach for open rebellion.

I must curb this urge to rush to judgement. Not because the judgement in itself is mistaken, but in this case, revealing my distaste for the man may put him on his guard. If I allow Fray Angelo sight of my ill will or bad grace, he may hesitate to share his more unpalatable memories with me. He could even suffer some kind of collapse. So I set my features in the semblance of a sympathetic mien and search for a platitude.

"It is easy to be wise after the event."

He gazes at me in relief. "Yes," he breathes, as though I have given him absolution for the most heinous of sins. Which in a way, I have. At any rate, my words have the desired effect: to loosen his tongue. "Prior Maldonado was very insistent about other things, too. We were not to refer to the name of our monastery or the town or even the province, in the presence of the prisoner. We were forbidden to speak with him, call him by name or meet his eye. All these most firm exhortations made us uneasy."

Such measures do not embody the demeanour one would expect the prior of a contemplative order to encourage amongst the members of his community. I nod and do my best to empty my countenance of expression, resolved to conceal my disquiet.

"Most of us felt perturbed," he continues, "even before Fray Juan arrived. It was clear that something unusual was afoot. Nevertheless, I do not think any of us believed that the Rule of the Carmelite Order or the law of the Spanish empire could justify treating a man of God as Fray Juan was treated whilst amongst us. No matter how grave his deviations from our laws."

Fray Angelo seems never to have heard of the Holy Office of

the Inquisition, whose functionaries specialise in imposing the greatest torments on people, many of them men and women of God, suspected of deviation from orthodox beliefs. But I do not remind him of this. In spite of my dislike of the little man, in this respect, at least, I share his puzzlement. I struggle to understand why such great hatred was visited upon a man who had the reputation, amongst the common people as well as his brothers and sisters in Christ, of being the most pious and unworldly of creatures, uninterested in power or personal advancement. His greatest crime, so far as I can tell, was his determination to eschew the less rigorous – though far from soft – life of the Mitigated Rule, and to support the reforms of Madre Teresa by returning to the austere practices of the Desert Fathers of Mount Carmel, hermit ancestors of the Carmelite Order who lived on that remote mountain so many hundreds of years ago.

I begin to suspect that the most important facets of this whole story – or rather, of these various stories, for I see a web of tales that strain and pull on each other – are interconnected. Though I cannot yet see the picture in its entirety, I believe that such a seamless tapestry does exist, and if I persevere and follow each strand, sooner or later the threads will cohere and the entire will be revealed. The truth of this matter is neither simple nor accessible, as Crespo and Ortiz led me to believe. It must be discovered, perhaps created. Whether they will accept this view when I present my first progress report, I do not know. But that cannot be my concern, not yet.

"The first day I saw him I did not recognise him. Padre Maldonado had not told us the identity of the friar who was to come within our midst. As you know, the Carmelite monastery in Toledo is perched high on a cliff above the rushing waters of the river Tagus, close to the old Alcázar."

I do know. In fact, I intend to see it again very soon. However, that is a journey which I do not plan to discuss with Crespo and Ortiz.

"Our monastery was once a Moorish fort, before our Catholic monarchs routed the Moors and banished them from our land. But I tell you, Fray Martín…" The little man can barely speak, for now his tears are flowing, unchecked. To my horror, he leans across the arm of his chair, reaches for my hand and, before I realise what he is about, clutches it in his clammy palm. I have to muster all my self-discipline to suppress a shudder. Unaware of my discomfort, he withdraws his hand and rubs his eyes before continuing.

"Fray Juan could not have suffered any harsher treatment than the torment he endured in Toledo, at our hands. All on the instructions of our Prior Maldonado who was, he insisted, acting on behalf of the representative of the Vatican, Padre Tostado, one of the highest-ranking princes of the Church. Padre Tostado himself told us that we were duty bound to protect our Carmelite Order from fanatics who wished to drag us back to the distant past and impose upon us the greatest austerities, practices that our Pope Eugenius the Fourth had mitigated more than a century before, to allow us to eat meat from time to time, and suchlike."

I begin to understand the source of the dispute. The rigours of daily living imposed by the original articles of the Ancient Rule of the Carmelite Order – solitary living, prolonged silence, detachment from the world, lengthy periods of fasting and strict abstinence from meat – were practised by the earliest Carmelites, more than four hundred years ago, in imitation of the contemplative life of the prophet Elijah. Those first Carmelites lived high on the slopes of the mountain for which their order was named, surrounded by the desert and in sight of the sea. In modern life, once the order had been forced to flee to Europe, these rigours could no longer be sustained: hence the need to adapt and combine contemplation with an apostolic mission in the world. Of course, there are always people who resist change and cling to the ways of the past.

I am not about to debate with Fray Angelo the fine detail of the Mitigations to that Ancient Rule granted by various popes. Passions have always run high on the merits or otherwise of those changes: the demands of daily solitude were relaxed somewhat, a less severe fasting regime permitted, the friars allowed to live in community. Blessed Teresa and Fray Juan were not alone in their desire to turn away from these lenient ways. Many considered that these changes encouraged a certain worldliness in the conduct of some Carmelite friars and nuns. And there is no doubt that the more relaxed conditions of the Mitigated Rule were sometimes abused.

I must remember that my own opinion on such matters is of no relevance. For the purpose of my investigation, I only need to know whether the Carmelites who followed the Mitigated Rule were willing to use physical force to suppress their opponents, those who, like Fray Juan and Madre Teresa, supported a return to the Primitive Rule.

Judging by Fray Angelo's continued rant, at least some of them were more than willing. "A reform of that nature was madness in these times, Padre Tostado declared when he addressed us later. Worse. It was the work of the Devil. It would divide and destroy our order. Those who urged such measures were agents of Satan. Each of us, he insisted, had a duty to play our part in suppressing such evil. Only thus would we fulfil the will of God."

When I hear those words, a chill enters my bones and I must draw on all my resources of concentration to meet Fray Angelo's frank, open gaze without flinching. I am not easily shaken but the account of those orders, recalled by this mild-mannered little man, make my head swim. I am peering into an abyss within whose depths lurk all the repressed anger and hatred that lie dormant in the human heart, ready to erupt at the right provocation. And fulfilling the will of God is the most powerful motivation of all. Prior Maldonado has much to answer for, not only in the torments he unleashed upon Fray Juan, but in the grievous wrong he visited on his own friars in inducing them to inflict such agonies upon him. Concerning Padre Tostado, who supervised Fray Juan's reception in Toledo, I know little as yet, except that he was Portuguese, had been appointed the papal nuncio's representative in Spain and previously had held some position of high standing in the Vatican.

"You said you did not recognise Fray Juan at first. So you were acquainted?"

"Yes, indeed. When I was a young student in the new college in Alcalá de Henares, Fray Juan had been my confessor and spiritual guide for a year. He was a little stern in those days but always kind. He never spoke to me of austerities or encouraged me to practise them, although he was known to do so himself. Hair shirts, bloodied whips, that sort of thing."

I am sure that such was never Fray Angelo's sort of thing. Nor mine, if truth be told.

He seems to read my mind. "I think that this may have contributed to my decision to turn from the Discalced Carmelites and take the black robe in place of the brown. That is one reason I did not recognise him. He was wearing our black robe, for his captors had taken the habit of the Discalced Carmelites from him, their brown tunic which is fashioned out of harsh brown cloth, somewhat rougher than the usual.

"The Mother Foundress had designed that robe to convey the principles of poverty and simplicity. She wanted to distinguish the Discalced brethren from those of us who wore the black, flowing robes of the Carmelites of the Mitigated Rule. Madre Teresa said that voluminous garb created a sense of vanity and superiority more fitting to the aristocracy than to friars and nuns. That is why the brown habit of the Discalced reform is rather poor and mean, more like a beggar's shift under a white cowl and scapular, to show that the wearers are men and women of God."

"Was his unusual garb the only reason you did not recognise him?"

The little man shakes his head. "When I first saw Fray Juan in Toledo, stripped of his brown habit, he was a wizened little creature who looked to be near sixty, though he could not have yet seen forty years."

Fray Angelo is correct. On that December night in fifteen seventy-seven, when Fray Juan arrived as a captive in the Carmelite convent of Toledo, he was barely thirty-five years old.

"There was an odd atmosphere in the refectory that day. Our preparations indicated an important visitor was expected but the strangeness of our tasks had cast a pall of unease over the community. Of course, we were silent during meals and did not discuss any of this.

"Just after our food had been served, the door swung open. The brother reading the chapter of the day paused and looked towards the outer corridor. Padre Tostado swept in, followed by our prior. As the Reverend Father approached the lectern, we heard strange noises behind him, out of sight, sounds of shuffling that accompanied the thud of our superiors' footsteps on the stone floor.

"The two men came to a halt in the middle of the room and looked around. The shuffling ceased. A thick silence descended upon us, as heavy and dense as the snow that covered the plains of Castile outside our window. Before us stood a pitiful figure in chains. Only when Padre Tostado had finished speaking did I recognise the prisoner: my old confessor, Fray Juan de la Cruz."

It is a large room, high ceilinged and chilly, starkness unmitigated, neither comfort nor warmth in the feeble flames that flicker in the grate around a bundle of damp twigs. The window frames a picture of the city walls on the far side of the Tagus, surrounded by fields and hills, powdered white. Dark clouds, laden with yet more snow that will deaden the plains this night, brood low in the sky. The quiet tapping of forty-two spoons beats a staccato rhythm as the friars eat from rough wooden bowls. The fare is simple: gruel, a little bread, a sardine or two placed on the tables where they sit, side by side, on rows of benches.

Two places closest to the lectern are unoccupied. Prior Maldonado has not been seen for some days; nor has his Portuguese visitor, the Padre Jerome Tostado. The light, pleasant voice of Fray José, to whom this day has fallen the duty of reading aloud whilst the others eat, soothes the ambience. He will take his meal when his companions have finished. He is coming to the final verse. Today, the reading is from the *Book of Job*.

The young friar leans forward, about to place a kiss on the page, when a commotion erupts in the corridor behind him. The door bursts open and Padre Tostado, with whom their prior had been in conference for days before they both absented themselves for most of the previous week, strides into the room, Prior Maldonado close behind. The prior motions Fray José to move so that Padre Tostado might approach the lectern unimpeded. Scowling, Prior Maldonado positions himself beside the door where he stands, granite-jawed, surveying the company.

Every man present raises his eyes to the newcomers, spoons halted halfway to mouths, morsels of bread clutched in hands suspended in mid-air. The friars exchange glances but those who dare meet Tostado's eye look away, for that gaze immobilises everyone it touches. How long does it last? One minute? Less? Perhaps only a few seconds. To the forty-two friars paralyzed by that stern regard, it is an eternity. Something is about to happen.

It begins with a sound, a dull stain on the silence. A few friars have resumed eating, their troubled eyes cast down as they spoon up one, two, mouthfuls of the thin gruel. Others remain immobile, their eyes fixed on the open door. A gust of wind whistles down the corridor, the door shifts a little, hinges groaning. Something or someone approaches. Metal scrapes on stone, dragging along the corridor, accompanied by a whisper, as though a broom were sweeping up dust. Silence. The rustle and the clanging resume as the source of the noises draws closer. Forty-two friars watch the door, dreading they know not what, hairs prickling their arms, the back of their necks.

Swift, impatient footsteps and something shuffles – no, tumbles – through the open doorway, as though propelled by a push or a kick from an unseen hand or foot.

It is a spindly figure clad in a ragged black tunic, the same tunic which the friars who look on in horror are wearing themselves, but filthy and rent, tied in the middle with a bit of string, covering bones and little flesh. The face is emaciated, eyes large and dark and hollow, the skin grey, smudged with the beginnings of a beard. The prisoner is unshod. Discalced. A rusted shackle fastened around one ankle attaches the foot to a chain which weighs the captive's every step as he drags it along the stone floor. One foot is free of restraint but both ankles are red and bleeding. This chain has bound the prisoner's every movement, in waking, in sleeping, and has been removed for a very little time, perhaps to improve his gait. If that was the intention, it has failed, for he is barely capable of staggering to the centre of the U-shaped configuration of benches.

Forty-two friars behold the wrinkled face of a little monkey that bears the swellings and abrasions of one who has had a bad fall or perhaps more purposeful encounters. But his eyes are undimmed. They sweep once around the company and that lightning glance catches the gaze of every friar in the room. They all stare, transfixed by this half-corpse, swaying before them.

"Kneel." From his position by the doorway, Prior Maldonado's voice thunders into the silence.

The prisoner drops to his knees, his gaze fixed beyond the window on a place somewhere high above the raging river Tagus, deep in the landscape, as though pondering for the first time a fresco of fields and mountains and city walls illuminated by a strange light, the colours of hallucinations and bad dreams.

Tostado begins to speak. His voice, his bearing, his posture, dominate the assembled company more than his words. At first he speaks in measured, rhythmic tones, through gritted teeth, his breathing controlled. He demands that the captive renounce Teresa's reforms. He orders him to leave the convent where he is father confessor to Teresa's nuns. Little by little, his voice swells to a roar, punctuated by shivering silences that strike terror in the souls of his listeners. "Disobedient."

The prisoner raises his head a fraction.

"Contumacious."

Words from Piacenza, the Council assembled a year ago, whose conclusions forbad the expansion of the Discalced Carmelite reforms. And more – sought to suppress those already enacted.

"Pursuer of fame and personal ambition. Conspirator. Betrayer of the true Carmelite Rule."

Edicts issued by the Council of Piacenza carry the full weight of law. Every friar present now understands why the prisoner is here, the nature of his offences and the reasons for the screamed insults that follow.

"Rebel. Traitor." Tostado is trembling with rage. He punctuates his words with frequent pounding on the lectern, upon this ancient bible bequeathed to the convent almost a hundred years before. Fray José has just finished reading from it and Padre Tostado may be in danger of destroying it, if he has a mind to fling it across the room. The silence and immobility of the figure kneeling on the hard stone give him no satisfaction.

"Agent of the devil."

But he does not call him a heretic. Once that word is uttered, the prisoner becomes the property of the Holy Office of the Inquisition. And Tostado wants this one for himself.

All at once, the rage drops away from him, just as a wind

abates and sends leaves swirling, fluttering, tumbling from the sky. His forehead beaded with sweat, Padre Tostado leans forward, elbows planted on the lectern, and passes one hand across his face. The friars glance at each other, one or two even dare to whisper but Tostado does not notice. He has stepped down from the lectern, he is approaching the prisoner, he is going to strike him, perhaps kill him, he may be capable of anything.

Fray José, who occupies the bench closest to the prisoner, rises from his place, one hand outstretched, pleading or warning but Tostado waves him away and approaches the captive, looms over him, his sturdy black shoes not a finger's breadth from the prisoner's feet. A golden crucifix dangling from a chain on his breast almost grazes the captive's cheek as he bends down to whisper. Tostado has regained his calm and is quiet, even pensive. He lifts the golden cross dangling on his breast and holds it out between finger and thumb, in front of the prisoner's face. This is a valuable piece, solid gold, no doubt. He is offering it to the prisoner. How can this be? The flicker of a smile plays on the kneeling captive's lips, his gaze steady, directed beyond the glimmering candlelight into the gloaming, for dusk has fallen while Tostado has been ranting, the friars' gruel has gone cold, congealed in the bottom of their wooden bowls, smoke is rising from the few twigs in the grate, the room is icy now that the last fingers of the wintry sun have disappeared.

Tostado looks straight into the captive's eyes.

"Feed him."

The order is so unexpected, so contrary to what has gone before, that for a few moments no one moves. Fray José is the first to compose himself. He rises again, takes two steps towards the prisoner, holds out a bit of bread.

"Not like that!" Tostado's bellow fills the room.

Fray José hesitates, looks from his prior to the prisoner, then over his shoulder to one or two of his brother friars, a question clearly etched on his dark, handsome features: has their guest altogether taken leave of his senses? But Tostado nods towards Prior Maldonado, who snatches the morsel of bread from Fray José and casts it to the floor. It lands about an arm's length in front of the prisoner.

The room sighs. It is the collective breath of the brother friars, some gasping, some holding their breath. All watch while the prisoner, continuing to stare straight ahead at the snow glittering in the dark, spares not a single glance for the bit of bread lying on the floor, just out of his reach.

"Feed him, I said."

Tostado, who has by now returned to the lectern, thumps again upon the ancient bible. The friars keep their heads bowed while their prior walks up and down alongside the tables, which he raps as he addresses his friars.

"Feed him, feed him now."

There is an open murmuring of discontent, a shuffling, a moment charged with resistance that endures until Prior Maldonado halts in front of each of the forty-two friars, looks each man in the eye, saying not a word. And there is no one present who does not flinch or lower his gaze, not even Fray José who remains standing, hands empty but thus absolved, at least for this evening, from casting the prisoner's food to the ground from where he will retrieve it, for many days, during the next nine months.

After Maldonado, who is the first to cast Fray Juan's food upon the ground? Impossible to say. Perhaps it is not one single person, perhaps it does not matter; for, whoever has acted, acts for them all. None objects or refuses. Not one, having endured Prior Maldonado's grim stare, stands in silent resistance.

After the first crust is cast upon the ground, the rest follows. The head of a sardine. A spoonful or two of cold gruel. Still, even yet, no one, except the prior, believes that Tostado will really ask the prisoner to eat from the floor. A minute, perhaps two, and the last morsel has been cast. Some, flung hard by the over-zealous, have struck the prisoner. The silence is absolute.

Then, a whip crack. "Eat."

The prisoner leans forward, steadies himself with one hand and slides the other along the floor – he has perhaps suffered bruising to the ribs – until his fingers close on a bit of black bread. He brings the morsel to his broken lips, presses it into his swollen mouth, begins to chew, eyes never leaving that spot in the darkness where his attention is fixed. There is something insolent in that swift, uncompromising obedience and while he eats, Tostado watches him, hands on hips as though sizing up an adversary, his weight, heft, girth, balance, before deciding where to strike.

All at once, Padre Tostado turns on his heel, his shoes clack against the stone as he strides the length of the room. Keys jangle and though his back is turned to the assembled company, they know which key he has selected and what that cupboard contains. He marches back up the length of the refectory and holds the whip out to the prior.

"Two lashes."

Fray José stands. "Padre Tostado. Prior Maldonado. Please."

The prior looks hard at him and continues to stare as Tostado takes hold of the whip and, gaze unwavering, calls out to the rest of the assembled friars.

"From each of you."

It may not be widely known, but acceptance into the orders of our holy Church is subject to rigorous assessment of the postulant, concerning not only his intellect and family background – this last, I suspect though cannot prove, may have impeded Fray Juan's admittance to at least one other religious order – but also, the quality of the spiritual vocation of the person, his physical robustness and, in particular, his strength of character and mind. The religious life is not an easy one, and this may attract persons who crave discomfort for its own sake, or worse, have a taste to inflict discomfort on others; and also those who imagine that it is a path free of the worries of domestic or family routine.

Individuals who have unfortunate tendencies of this kind are often identified during the first weeks and months of their novitiates. It is one of the chief, if least vaunted, duties of the novice master, one that I fulfilled myself in the little monastery of San Salvador for almost three years. A few disturbed minds do slip through but for the most part, we can expect that our brothers and sisters in Christ are at least as healthy and compassionate as our brothers and sisters in the world outside the convent walls, if not more so.

The Toledo Carmelite monastery where Maldonado was prior during that year of fifteen seventy-seven was home to forty-two souls, pious men who had left their families, chosen a life of hardship and contemplation and endured many privations. They were not criminals or ruffians. What, then, could induce grown men to subject this frail being who was known to some of them, perhaps even loved by them, to the torments that Fray Juan endured that day and during the months of his captivity that followed?

Fray Angelo moves his chair closer to the fire. "We used to believe that evil arises from wickedness of heart or from demonic possession. Those nine months during which Fray Juan remained with us in Toledo, those weekly lashings, the scraps of bread and sardines he was forced to claw from the ground, changed my mind. What power in heaven or on earth can transform a community of friars into a baying mob and set them on the most fragile of men who, nonetheless, proved himself the strongest of us all, capable of the greatest feats of endurance and mental rigour?"

I follow Fray Angelo's train of thought better than I like. Are we so obedient to our superiors? Is a stern order – perhaps accompanied by a threatening look, such as the shrewd little eyes of a Maldonado, appraising who is and who is not compliant in embracing their dark duty – sufficient to unleash the beast within? The thin, pale countenance of my great-uncle Ginés returns to my mind's eye and I repress a shudder of disgust at those vile words that made him famous. And worse, at the notion that such blood as his should course within my veins. I drag my thoughts back to this room and the creature hunched on the chair at my side and murmur to myself "How could Maldonado live with this?"

Misunderstanding, Fray Angelo thinks this is a real question I am addressing to him. "The promotion must have helped."

"What promotion?" Through my shock, I realise I have been expecting something of this nature.

"I'm not sure. I think he was made a provincial not long after. Or something else. Some higher office."

How any community, any individual, could ever recover from having inflicted such brutalities, I cannot imagine. This, at least, is one question I have not been called upon to answer. Perhaps it is the most important question of all.

I cannot help wondering if Prior Ortiz, perhaps doubting my innocence of the accusations made against me in Salamanca, decided to test me by appointing such a comely young novice to help in the administration of my work. Unless he simply wishes me to think so, and thus increase my discomfort. If that is the case, his efforts have failed, for Fray Francisco's handsome countenance is matched by a frank and sunny temperament which, combined with his efficiency, makes him an ideal assistant.

I admit it, I miss Diego's rough, sometimes surly, ways. Diego, whose learning was, mysteriously, far superior to that expected of a simple handyman; Diego, who did not often observe the proper conventions of communication between master and servant, his demeanour assuming an equality of status. At times his bearing strayed close to the boundary that separates familiarity from impertinence, yet never quite crossed it. Still, he was my most loyal and clever ally when all others had turned against me.

Fray Francisco, in contrast, is blessed with impeccable manners: hence my surprise when he raps on my door and enters without waiting for a response, especially as I had asked not to be disturbed. His cheeks are flushed and he is out of breath, as though he has been running.

"Beg pardon, Fray Martín. You have a visitor."

I do not look up. Without answering, I tap the shaft of my plume against the edge of my inkstand, open the top drawer on the left side of my desk and remove a cloth which I draw across the tip of the quill, taking care to avoid staining my fingers or the sleeve of my habit. When I am sure that all excess ink has been removed, I place this favourite writing implement of mine in the silver dish I keep at the centre of my desk.

"I most certainly do not have a visitor, Fray Francisco. This morning I must revise the summary of my findings for Prior Ortiz and Archbishop Crespo. It is needed for next week. You know this."

The young man shifts from one foot to the other, opens his mouth, closes it again and gazes at me in desperation. Do I really inspire such terror in my subordinates? The gaunt image of my great-uncle Ginés sitting by our fire, expounding his odious theories, flashes before me. "Well?" I cannot suppress my impatience. Whenever I provoke distress in others, my immediate response is to soothe, often followed by an opposing desire to crush, in the way that some people cannot resist the urge to aim a kick at a cowering dog. No doubt an effect of the bad blood gifted me by my illustrious ancestor.

"I am sorry, Fray Martín. He insists. It is…"

I get up from my chair and stand, a satisfying head taller than this young man. "Insists? Fray Francisco, people come to this office at my invitation and my invitation only." I resume my seat, toss the ink-stained rag into the open drawer and slam it shut.

"It is Doctor Enrique Naranjo, Padre. The *procurador fiscal* of the Holy Office of the Inquisition in Toledo."

Ortiz's cousin. I feel the blood drain from my head and a slight dizziness comes over me. I must have turned white, for

Fray Francisco's frightened brow reassembles into an anxious furrow of concern. A light sweat breaks out between my shoulder blades. I reach for the cup on my desk and take a sip of water. This hand seems to belong to someone else but at least it is not trembling. "Thank you, Fray Francisco. You were right to interrupt me."

As he turns to leave, I call him back.

"May I get you something, Fray Martín?"

I shake my head. "I apologise for my harsh words a few moments ago. It was wrong of me to speak to you thus." The young man's fair complexion turns a deep pink, which I affect not to notice. Eyes cast down, he turns to leave. "Before you go, Fray Francisco, there is something you can do for me. But only if it is not too difficult."

"Anything, Fray Martín."

"Try to delay Doctor Enrique. Just for a few minutes. While I get these papers into some kind of order." I spread both hands across my desk. "Offer him refreshments, perhaps."

"I will do my best, Fray Martín," the young man promises and scampers off.

I make no attempt to arrange the documents strewn across my desk. These reveal nothing of the several unauthorised interviews I have conducted in recent weeks, for I did indeed spend the morning reviewing my notes from the fourteen meetings I have conducted with official witnesses, those named on the list supplied to me by Ortiz. This is swift progress, representing two, or even three, meetings each week since the beginning of February.

Casting my eyes over this disordered collection of notes I hesitate, stride across the room and open the door a crack. No echoing footsteps approach. There may be time, just, to review the rough scribblings that will form the basis of my next progress report and thus refresh my recollection of the information I have gathered during these last weeks. Even though I have no intention of allowing this Doctor Enrique access to it. I return to my chair and, elbows on my desk and head in hands, I survey the results of the morning's work.

My reflections on this dry-as-dust summary of Fray Juan's life give me some satisfaction. Not because the account is adequate, but for the opposite reason. Set out thus, in the manner demanded by Crespo and Ortiz, it is obvious that my first instinct, mocked by Ortiz, was correct. The most significant aspect of Fray Juan's life is not what happened to him, but why; not the events but rather, the reasons behind the events.

Why, for example, was Fray Juan in particular singled out for such ill-treatment at the hands of the opponents of the Discalced Carmelites, during the early days of their reforms? And why, in the later days, did his own people turn against him, strip him of his office and banish him to the most remote part of Andalucía, a posting which most probably contributed to his death? There are many other puzzles which, I believe, my own chosen witnesses – not identified for interview by Crespo and Ortiz – will help me to illuminate.

Yet none of my work so far has revealed why my masters have engaged me in this task. Perhaps they are preparing a case for the Vatican inspectors who may need this information, in order to advance Fray Juan's beatification. After all, Madre Teresa was made Blessed last year, only after a long period of research and scrutiny of her writings and her life. Or they might wish to put meat on the bones of an authorised biography of Fray Juan; or oversee the writing of a prologue to a published edition of his poems. These last possibilities could explain Crespo's interest in recovering Fray Juan's original papers.

Glancing up at the door, I finish reading my summary of the main events in Fray Juan's life. It covers less than two pages and I see nothing here at all that might interest a *procurador* of the Holy Office of the Inquisition. But this brief review of my recent work has calmed me. I am now ready to receive this Inquisitor on my home ground, only a little disturbed by the sudden recollection of my recent visit to Fray Angelo and my plans to visit Toledo next week. The door swings open and I arrange my features in a bland smile. As I receive the Inquisitor's weak and bony embrace, I resolve to volunteer no information at all.

Doctor Enrique resembles so many other officials of the Holy Office I have seen from afar: long-limbed, thin, the same physical type as my father's uncle. A high, old-fashioned collar covers his wrinkled neck; glittering eyes exude the hard, intense sheen of basalt but soften to hazel, almost green, when he turns to scrutinise me. The taut, papery skin of his cheekbones is a little flushed and his lips are pursed in a thin line. He is not pleased that I have kept him waiting and makes no effort to hide his irritation.

"Your secretary insisted on providing me with food and drink I did not want," he snaps, without introducing himself. I do not yet know if this man is my enemy but I resolve to take the advice that Fray Juan gave the innkeeper Echeverría as a young boy, and love him all the same; at least for the next half hour or so.

"Fray Martín de Sepúlveda at your service." I lead my guest to the most comfortable chair in the room, which I have placed beside the south-facing window that looks out over the cloisters and the orchards, towards the hermitage of San Blas and the convent of Atocha in the distance, a vista which I always find to be a pleasant distraction. "Please excuse Fray Francisco, Doctor Enrique. He was acting on my instructions. I felt sure that you would be in need of rest and refreshments, after your journey from Toledo."

"I did not arrive from Toledo by coach. I came on horseback and spent last night with relatives near Madrid. And I have little time to spare."

So he left Toledo the day before yesterday and lodged with Ortiz's family for his second night on the road. A long journey for such a brief visit. I nod, taking care to display only mild interest. "Then I must beg your pardon for the delay, Doctor. I had no idea you were in such a hurry."

He glances up, alert to any sign of anger or discomfort on my part; he must be well aware that I had no idea he was coming at all. I smile.

"A misunderstanding. I am delighted to make your acquaintance. I have heard much of the excellent work you and your colleagues are conducting in Toledo." I take a few minutes to summarise details I have heard concerning the most prominent cases that have come before the Inquisition in that part of the country: a Jewish family whose grandfather converted but aroused the suspicions of a neighbour who noticed them avoiding the consumption of pork. The family were discovered lighting candles, preparing unleavened bread and intoning strange incantations on their Sabbath. An elderly woman – in an unrelated case – who endeavoured to persuade her young serving girl, also of *converso* stock, to return to the Jewish faith.

"It is difficult to believe," I muse, gazing out over the cloisters, "that there remain in our land, Jews – former Jews – who have not fully embraced their conversion to Christianity and who will persist in taking such risks."

Doctor Enrique does not wish to discuss his historic cases, no matter how productive or how vaunted his successes. "You are greatly burdened with this investigation concerning Fray Juan de la Cruz, I believe. And you are no doubt aware that Prior Ortiz is my first cousin."

"I am busy with the case, it is true. I would not say burdened. And indeed, I believe I did know that Prior Ortiz had a relative in the Holy Office but not specifically who that was." I look him straight in the eye. "The prior has been of great assistance to me in my work these two months past."

"He informs me that you have assembled a draft report of your findings."

"Not quite, Doctor. The full report only becomes due when I

have completed my investigation, which will probably be in the early autumn. I am currently working on a progress report," I point to my desk, glad of the disarray, "which will give a factual outline of my activities to date."

Doctor Enrique's eyes flicker across the jumble of papers strewn over my desk. Leaning back in his chair, he slips one hand into the folds of his habit and draws out a tiny, leather-bound notebook, complete with pencil attached to a fine silver chain. His hands are soft and white, the nails unappealingly tended. Pencil poised, he opens the notebook at a blank page. "Perhaps you could give me a general overview of what you have learned so far."

I shrug. "Alas, Reverend Doctor, I am still at the assembly stage, as you put it. With nothing coherent enough to share. In any case," I hesitate, as though wondering whether I dare continue when, in fact, I have been longing to launch this barb from the moment I understood what he wanted, "I am afraid that I am not empowered to discuss my findings with anyone other than Prior Ortiz and Archbishop Crespo."

His slender fingers move to the chain of office of the Inquisition seal on his girdle. "Prior Ortiz is my cousin, Fray Martín. As I have already mentioned."

I spread my palms, open my eyes wide in distress. "If the decision were mine, I would not hesitate to discuss this with you informally. However, both Prior Ortiz and Archbishop Crespo are most insistent on my following correct procedures. They have set out a comprehensive process." Feigning an energy I do not feel, I stride over to my desk and move a few papers around. Miraculously, the one I am seeking comes to hand. I scan the text, murmur a few phrases aloud, all the while failing to notice Doctor Enrique's outstretched hand. "My instructions are clear. I am sorry."

To my surprise, he yields. "Very well. I understand your position. Your reticence is commendable." When I make no reply he lowers his head, pinches the brow of his nose and regards me from beneath hooded lids, a glint – could that be humour? – in his eye, tracing a bony index finger on the air while speaking. "Perhaps, instead of your giving me an account of what you have learned during the last two months, if I were to give you an account of what I have learned of the subject during the twenty-five years since Fray Juan's death?" His voice falls to a murmur. "At least, the salient parts. And you would be free to question me. Would such an arrangement be of interest to you?"

Of course I understand his game, for I have played it myself, many times. Careful observation of the kind of questions I ask would give him some insight into what I know and do not know. And yet… if he is so well informed, surely his cousin would have included his name on the list of witnesses? Perhaps Ortiz does not know that he is here. Most certainly, I should decline this offer.

"That sounds very fair, Doctor Enrique." A half-smile flickers over his thin lips as he returns notebook and pencil to the folds deep in his tunic. "But I confess to some surprise that you should be so well informed on this subject. I did not know that Fray Juan was of such great interest to the Holy Office of the Inquisition during his lifetime, much less a quarter of a century after his death. Was he ever actually arrested by the Holy Office? Or even interviewed?"

His smile fades, or rather, mutates as he regards me, eyebrows raised. "I am afraid I cannot answer that."

"Because you do not know, Doctor Enrique? In which case I can consult the public records and find the files."

"You will not find them. They have been…lost."

I am almost speechless but instinct tells me not to pursue this topic further, at least for the moment. This is something I can verify at a later time. "Yet, detained or no," I continue, adopting the mildest of tones, "it seems that the activities of Fray Juan were of interest to the Holy Office. Or perhaps only to you?"

While I am speaking, the Reverend Doctor leans forward and with a little grunt, slides a worn leather satchel out from beneath his chair. "To both. To the Holy Office, and also to me personally." He lifts the satchel and balances it against the arm of his chair. "Fray Juan was a very fine poet whose reputation has increased significantly since his death." With great care, he opens the satchel and withdraws a cylindrical object that I estimate to be about twenty fingers in length, wrapped in a heavy shawl of undyed wool. He nods towards my desk.

"May I?" I move the bulk of my papers to one side and clear a space where the old man places the bundle. Gently, one fold at a time, he unwraps the shawl as though peeling layers from an onion. The object revealed is something I have not seen in quite a while. "A scroll of the old type," I breathe. "Parchment." The translucent fabric is coiled around two wooden rods designed to roll and unroll the document for reading in the early style, in the days before our codex pages became the norm.

"Vellum," the Doctor corrects me. "Much more valuable." He moves to the other side of my desk so that the rays of the late morning sun fall on his narrow back and not on the bold strokes and subtle tints which appear, as he unwinds the scroll to reveal a remarkable composition. It is a most beauteous harmony of images and written text, both formal and ornamental in style, which almost completely covers the entire length and breadth of the vellum spread out before us. Delicately tinted drawings illustrate successive scenes in a narrative of the most arresting type, one I am surprised to find in the hands of a *procurador fiscal* of the Holy Office of the Inquisition.

It is a love story, the progression of a courtship, starting with a solitary, lovesick young girl who is shown wandering and searching *by mountains and rivers... through pastures and fountains* in search of her Beloved, as she begs the forests and flowers and the wild beasts she encounters on her journey to say *if he has passed that way.* And when, *in the silent music, in the sonorous solitude of daybreak*, he finally reveals himself to her, they are united, the Bride resting in the sweet arms of her Beloved while he watches over her, *that the Bride may safely sleep*. Hovering above these most exquisitely wrought images and words, a shimmering golden light bathes the whole in a heavenly glow, the upper border of the vellum adorned with a single word, formed in fine-spun majuscules:

CÁNTICO

For a few moments, we contemplate this magnificent document in silence.

"Have you ever seen the like of this?"

I hesitate, uncertain of how best to answer. Especially if this is what I think it is.

"Not in this exact form. It is quite remarkable. Perhaps a few of the lines…"

"It would surprise me if you had not already encountered at least some words from the pen of Fray Juan de la Cruz."

"This is his *Spiritual Canticle*." I endeavour to keep my tone flat, both a statement and a question. The Doctor nods, silently tracing the line of the story along the length of the page, his long fingers not quite touching the surface of the vellum.

"One version of it. This is the Bride, that is, the soul, in search of her spouse, who is God. These are the places where she seeks him, amongst the wild beasts and the manifestations of Nature, created by the Beloved himself. And here," he points to an image of a man and a woman that is frankly profane, "is their meeting in the bridal chamber." To my surprise, he makes no comment on the openly erotic expression of consummation and, instead, reads the accompanying text aloud, almost chanting:

> *"The Bride now entering*
> *The lovely grove which she so much desired*
> *And rests as is her wish*

Her neck reposed
Upon the sweetest arms of her Beloved.

"It is very beautiful, is it not?"

I murmur my assent. *Lovely grove? Desire?* Doctor Enrique perceives my unease.

"I have always had an interest in poetry. A personal interest, that is, aside from my duties as an occasional censor for the Holy Office. Garcilaso is my favourite. And you can see that Fray Juan probably read him, too." His bony index finger hovers above one line and then another. "See this hendecasyllabic meter? Very Italian, straight out of Petrarch. Fray Juan has combined it with the eight-syllable line of our *villancico* tradition, the folk songs and Christmas carols of our own people. Most skilfully done. Wonderful."

"And then there is the..." I hesitate, lose my nerve, "the pastoral setting. Shepherds, nymphs, wild beasts and so on."

"Typical of the lyric poetry of his time," he agrees.

I feel slightly dizzy, as though I have wandered into some strange universe hitherto unknown to me. Why, on this fine spring day, in my well-appointed office in the monastery of Gerónimos, am I exchanging views on a subject of which I know little and care less? With an Inquisitor who confesses to a passion for poetry that borders on the profane? The thought emboldens me. "And of course, the lush sensuality. The erotic content. No doubt influenced by the *Song of Songs*," I venture.

"You are quite right." Doctor Enrique regards me with appreciation. How simple it is, to feign authority on a subject equipped with nothing more than a bare minimum of knowledge. I do not even like poetry.

"Fray Juan wrote this while he was imprisoned in Toledo." I am on unsure ground here, and so maintain that flat tone that could, if necessary, indicate a question.

"Composed it, rather, from memory. During most of his time there, as you know, he had no access to pen and paper."

I did not know. I maintain my politely neutral expression as he continues.

"You can see that many of these lines – *He whom I love best*, for example – are familiar phrases, common enough in popular songs at the time, easy to memorise for a poet composing his lines in the dark. And these frequent internal rhymes help, too."

"And he wrote it all down after – when his period of detention ended?"

"Probably. Or, at least – possibly. It is also possible that he recited or sang it and that the first transcription was made by a listener. We are not sure. What we have here," he sweeps his elegant hand across the surface of the vellum, "is a version of the *Canticle*. A beautifully crafted copy, obviously. But as things stand, there is no way of knowing how far this corresponds to Fray Juan's original composition."

His eyes have taken on a sly glint and I once again recall Crespo's casual reference to Fray Juan's papers, tossed as an afterthought into our conversation concerning my terms of reference. When the Reverend Doctor understands that I do not intend to speak, he clears his throat and continues. "It may be that this is not a very accurate copy. It is certainly somewhat inconsistent with other versions in circulation since Fray Juan died. Copies of copies, gradually altered by errors in transcription."

He looks closely at me and some instinct tells me that this is a time to maintain my questioning silence.

"Have you come across such versions? During your current investigation, perhaps?"

I hesitate. The truth is, I do not know. Strewn across the sill of my south-facing window, there is, I am chastened to see, the jumbled contents of a package that arrived for me yesterday from Oviedo. Old Prior Andrés kept his promise. A few of the pages are exposed to the full glare of sunlight. I left them there myself but an hour ago. At least they are sheets of common paper, not priceless vellum. Still, I feel a twinge of guilt. I must be sure to begin my inspection of them before I finalise my progress report.

"I have not yet scrutinised any of Fray Juan's poems," I admit. "Doctor Enrique, may I ask a question?" He nods once. I hesitate, not sure how to phrase this without either giving offence or revealing more than I wish. "I can understand that it would be interesting for scholars and those enthused by modern poetry," I make a little bow in his direction, "to find Fray Juan's original, definitive version and perhaps compare that with other, later copies. But, Doctor Enrique," I hesitate. "I struggle to understand the interest of the Holy Office of the Inquisition in this matter, which is essentially a question of literary technique."

The glittering eyes open wide, their cold gleam a little too close to my face. "Fray Martín," he murmurs, "read this again. Does it seem to you to be a simple account of a love story, daring only in the profanity and sensuality of its mode of expression?"

"Surely the erotic dimension…"

"The erotic dimension is troubling, Fray Martín. But not because we Inquisitors fear the spread of unbridled sensuality amongst readers of Fray Juan's poetry. We have ways of dealing with that. It troubles us for quite a different reason: for its expression of the relation between the individual and God. This work is a detailed, practical guide to spiritual development, written not for novices but for religious initiates – and represents Fray Juan's deeply interior version of spirituality and prayer."

He takes a deep breath, apparently ready to explain further but stops himself. He could say much more on this subject but has decided not to.

"Interior prayer?" I am aware that some of the contemplative orders and at least one heretical sect that I know of reject the communal prayer that is chanted aloud as part of the Office. A few fanatics, the *alumbrados*, even reject the holy sacrifice of the Mass, insisting that prayer should be unspoken, personal and…

yes, interior. Held within the heart and mind of the individual; and thereby, inaccessible to guidance, to authority. "Like the *alumbrados*? Was Fray Juan suspected of heresy?"

Immediately, I regret my words. My companion's brow creases and he looks away. I am suddenly furious that he has troubled to share with me his enthusiasm for Fray Juan's poetry and his reservations about the man. My opinion of Fray Juan, of his *Canticle*, of his life, is of no significance to my work. I no longer care what matters are of interest to members of the Holy Office of the Inquisition, provided their attentions are not directed at me. Doctor Enrique seems to understand that he is on the point of losing my goodwill, which, for some reason, he wishes to retain.

"You were very badly served in Salamanca," he says gravely. "My cousin has acquainted me with the details of your case."

I receive his comment stone-faced, silently repeating my habitual, internal response: that there never was any case.

"You were a convenient scapegoat, targeted by unscrupulous people of high rank who were determined to protect their own. You were in the wrong place at the wrong time. It is to your credit that you extracted yourself from the situation, and with honour."

I am unmoved by his flattery but some instinct bids me feign gratitude. "I was lucky."

"You were. But only because of your astute handling of the situation. I believe – though of course, I cannot be certain – that your diplomacy and restraint under those difficult circumstances recommended you for this delicate commission."

I struggle not to laugh. According to that logic, the real man for this delicate mission is Diego Clemente, former handyman and jack-of-all-trades in the University of Salamanca, now employed, I think, as a labourer on the demolition work being carried out in preparation for the rebuilding of the Plaza de Arrabal here in Madrid.

"However, under the right circumstances," the long, grey head swivels towards me and a bony hand grips my arm, "you may be certain of my support, and that of my cousin." He falls silent, that I might inquire what those right circumstances could be and what form the promised support would take. When I say nothing, he smiles. "Provided that you accomplish this mission satisfactorily, there is every likelihood that you will be restored to your professorship at the University of Salamanca. With full acknowledgement of your achievements, past and present. And a complete exoneration, possibly even a public statement, that you are innocent of any illegal or impure acts unjustly imputed to you."

When I speak, my voice is hoarse. "Satisfactorily?"

He raises his eyebrows.

"By locating the originals of Fray Juan's papers?"

"That would be part of it. If that archive has survived, of course. Also, by submitting a final report that is informed by the key points of our discussion today. Which we can elaborate at a later date."

So. I am to write a report to Doctor Enrique's specifications, in pursuit of a purpose as yet unstated, whether to support or oppose Fray Juan's beatification, I cannot tell. I swallow. My heart is beating fast, my thoughts are in a turmoil of excitement and panic. As though judging the exact moment to release me to my own thoughts, the wily Inquisitor removes his hand from my arm and, eyes returned to the texture of black stone, stands and extends his arms to receive my embrace.

"There is no need of words," he murmurs. "Your deeds will suffice." And then, a soft whisper. Or did I imagine it? "You know what to do."

The noonday light blinds me, my head is pounding as I open the door. He turns to me and raises one bony hand. "I do not wish to delay you any further in your work. It will soon be time to sing Sexts. I will find my own way."

The door closes and he is gone. For a few moments I stand, scarcely breathing, my palm pressed on the patterned oak, my vision hovering and unfocused. For the first time, I perceive the beauty of the wood – the delicacy of design, those vertical and horizontal ridges, intertwined in varying depths and shades across its entire surface – and when my normal sight returns I see it there, unmistakable, a shadow or a beam of light or a slight hue in the grain, tints deep in the wood, shining and clear: a bold, gleaming, most radiant, cross.

Monastery of San Gerónimo, Madrid,
Thirteenth day of March in the Year of Our Lord, 1616.

It is understood that my status as special investigator accords me the right, should other matters detain me, to keep people waiting. Yet I hate to arrive late for any appointment, and always feel at a disadvantage whenever I do. On such occasions, I offer neither apology nor explanation. Now, as I make my way along the light-pooled corridor that overlooks our enclosed orchard and the open fields beyond, I deliberately slacken my footsteps to a measured stride.

I am surprised to see my office door is ajar and beyond, a slender, brown-robed figure seated on a low stool that someone has placed beside my desk, for I gave no permission for the visitor to enter in my absence. Madre Carmela de la Luz was a novice in the Convent of Encarnación in Ávila during two of the five years when Fray Juan served the community there as spiritual director and father confessor. As I close the door, she rises and bows her head in greeting.

"Fray Martín de Sepúlveda?"

My guest takes a step forward and in that instant, a cloud

drifts across the sun. For a few moments, the harsh light softens, so that the contours of her face are as smooth and fresh as that of a young girl. I open my mouth to speak. No words come out. The cloud passes, noonday brilliance floods the room once more, illuminating dust motes floating in the air and fine lines around those full lips. Her smiling, hazel eyes are speckled with flecks of gold and glow with a luminosity I do not think I have ever seen before. The white headdress entirely covers her forehead and neck, designed to cover the hair, but also to disguise any vestige of beauty or grace. Yet here, now, that stern garb creates just the opposite effect. This is the face of a woman close to my own age, yet only lightly touched by time. When she speaks, furrows in her brow deepen to reveal the wisdom of years but in repose, her expression is ageless. This is a moment I will not forget.

"Forgive me for keeping you waiting, Madre. Archbishop Crespo…"

She shakes her head and one slim hand brushes the air, as though flicking a mosquito. "It is no matter, Fray Martín. I have passed a pleasant hour in contemplation of these fine paintings. Your colleague, Prior Ortiz, most kindly brought me refreshments."

My superior, my tormentor. I make no reply but indicate the chair in front of my desk, for it is higher and more comfortable than the little stool she has occupied while waiting for me. Alongside it, someone has placed a small table that bears the remains of a light meal: bread, olives, dates and a pitcher of water. Carried there by Ortiz himself? I cannot believe it. But she has travelled from Andalucía, a difficult journey of several days, and endured many hours rattling around an uncomfortable carriage and still more hours of broken sleep in those cheap inns where the poorer travellers making their way towards the capital are obliged to lodge. Some enquiry concerning her journey – how many days and nights it took, whether she has other business in Madrid – would not be out of place. But I find

I am unable to hold those gold-flecked eyes for more than a second or two. Was there a subtle rebuke in her words? I think not, for I perceive no guile in that frank gaze.

I look down at my hands folded in my lap, then at the floor where I make a study of Madre Carmela's modest hemp sandals, before fixing on the painting of St. Jerome holding the sacred scripture. It is said that our King Felipe's father brought it here from Flanders.

"You are no doubt aware, Madre Carmela, of the nature of the questions I have called you here to answer?" This introduction is brisker than I intended. Madre Carmela nods, unperturbed. "You were received into the Carmelite Order as a novice in the year fifteen seventy-four?"

"It was fifteen seventy-five, Fray Martín. In the spring of that year."

I glance down at the list of questions on my desk. When I start to speak, she holds up one hand.

"Before we begin in earnest, Fray Martín, I wonder if I might first trouble you to clarify one or two issues concerning the nature of your investigation?"

Now I do meet her eyes. Some flash of annoyance must have crossed my face, for she intones her next words as though placating a child.

"I wish only to be sure that I am covering the kind of ground you expect, Fray Martín. In the interests of relevance."

This woman reminds me of myself. Small wonder that I was such a source of irritation to Ortiz and Crespo. The thought makes me smile. Madre Carmela's light brown eyebrows almost disappear beneath her headdress. She is displeased.

"Have I said something witty, Fray Martín? Or perhaps merely foolish?"

I cannot help myself, I burst out laughing. Madre Carmela surveys me with a frosty mien.

"Neither, Madre, and please forgive my levity." Unlike Crespo and Ortiz, I have nothing to hide. Except, perhaps, the mesmerising effect of those gold-flecked eyes. "You remind me of myself at the very start of this investigation, hence my amusement. I, too, attempted to seek clarification on 'one or two issues'. Your words almost exactly echoed my own." I sweep my arm in an extravagant gesture, not at all my customary demeanour. "Ask me whatever you wish."

She smiles and my mood lightens. It seems I am forgiven. "I am wondering, Fray Martín, about this investigation you are conducting. What manner of story are you hoping to construct?"

Keep to the facts. We are not interested in your opinion. "Well…" I do not want to discourage my witness in the way that Ortiz's response to a similar question from me punctured my own enthusiasm. Nor do I wish to be over-cautious or evasive. "For the most part, my superiors are interested in obtaining an objective account of Fray Juan's life, as distinct from some of the… mythology… which may have obscured the simple facts."

Madre Carmela grimaces and her face squashes like a little girl tasting something unpleasant for the first time. It is quite charming. "Please do not think me obstructive, Fray Martín, when I tell you that in my experience, there is no such thing as a fact. Much less, a simple fact."

For once, I am lost for words. And a little amused. "Indeed?"

"I mean, if you are seeking an objective account of what happened in Encarnación during the time I was there, I cannot guarantee to provide it. Everything that I will tell you was viewed through the innocent and rather fearful eyes of the young girl I was then, ignorant and credulous. And of course, overlaid now with the patina of many years."

Brava, Carmela! I should like to set this interesting mind to debate with my two superiors. I must take careful note of her commentary and decide later how much of it, if any, I will convey to Ortiz and Crespo in my progress report.

"I will be more than satisfied to hear any of your recollections from that time, Madre. Do not worry about distortions, if that is your concern."

She nods. "That is precisely my concern."

"All that is required is an account of your recollections, what you saw and what you heard in Encarnación which may pertain to the life of Fray Juan, as far as you are able to remember. The distortions, you can leave to me. I will compare your version with accounts from other witnesses, many of whom I will ask, or have already asked, similar questions as those I now put in your particular case."

That clear brow furrows briefly. Madre Carmela does not care to be referred to as a 'case'.

"My hope for this meeting," I continue, "is that you will be well placed to illuminate Fray Juan's views on physical and mental mortification, whether as an aid to his own spiritual development and that of the members of your community at the time, the sisters whose souls were in his care; whether he actively sought out hardships and discomforts; how he responded to those which came his way without the intervention of his own will."

Madre Carmela nods, looks down and smooths the folds of her habit, an unconscious gesture that draws my attention to her hands. They are small and brown and slender, the palms a little calloused, as though accustomed to the demands of physical labour. Now they are clasped together, quiet and still.

"Austerities?"

I nod and remark, with some hesitation. "There are those who would say that accepting the position of confessor in Encarnación at a time when Teresa and her reforms were, shall we say, unwelcome, could be considered an act of mortification in itself."

"Perhaps," she says, non-committally. "I cannot speak to that, for Fray Juan's arrival at Encarnación was before my time. Most likely, he did not have the choice, being bound by his vow of obedience."

She sits a little more erect, her demeanour brightened, having received permission to speak freely rather than accurately, or rather, without excessive heed for precision. I have observed a kind of paralysis in certain individuals who are temperamentally disposed to the quest for perfection, which, at its most extreme, may reduce a fountain of inspiration and activity to a mere trickle. I wonder if Madre Carmela may be such a person and consider reminding her of St Thomas Aquinas's observation that 'the perfect is the enemy of the good'. But before I can speak, she launches into her recollections.

"I arrived in Encarnación in late spring of fifteen seventy-five, just a few days after my fifteenth birthday, by which time Fray Juan had been the spiritual director of the community for two or three years. In any case, he was well established and the initial reluctance of some of the nuns to have a Discalced friar as a father confessor had been long overcome."

I do not interrupt her but, in fact, Fray Juan had joined Encarnación three years before the young Sor Carmela began her novitiate. So she was born in the year fifteen sixty. This surprises me, as it means that she is about a year older than I. These internal calculations have caused my attention to waver and I am obliged to ask her to repeat her last few words. She looks at me oddly, those two lines furrowing her brow again.

"On the day of my arrival, I was conducted to a little cell at the end of a long corridor on the ground floor of the main building. It was tiny," she pauses, glancing around her, "about one-tenth of the size of this office of yours."

She tilts her head and regards me sideways. Is she teasing? I perceive my surroundings through the eyes of an outsider, the stranger I was at the beginning of the year, not a little awed by my new circumstances. I now take such pleasure in this room, such pride: those two tall windows, one which I often keep shuttered, for it faces south and I cannot endure the glare of the sun for very long; beneath those shutters, the oaken chest I received from Crespo shortly after my arrival; wood-panelled walls; polished flooring, which is waxed every other day before I begin work; and three paintings, one of them rather fine, Vincenzio's Resurrection, which Madre Carmela has already remarked; a carved chair; a pair of low stools; and my own desk. Sparse enough furnishings for such a large room. Still, the effect of the whole is opulent and redolent of ancient authority. For a moment, I feel a little embarrassed.

"I have not always enjoyed such well-appointed surroundings, Madre Carmela. In Salamanca..." I check myself just in time. "Forgive me. Your little cell in Encarnación?"

"The walls were whitewashed and unadorned save for a simple wooden cross above the narrow bed. I had a desk and a single chair and a window that looked out on to the vegetable garden. This would be my home for almost two years. I would soon grow to love the place, but on that night, I wept until dawn and barely slept."

I had not expected such a personal account of her first days in the convent. To ignore it would be churlish but I have no practice in this kind of talk.

"I am sure that many young girls...perhaps most...having taken such a decision..."

"It was not really a decision. I had never wished to devote myself to Christ. But nor did I want to marry. Becoming a bride of Christ was an honourable alternative."

She turns towards me and I become aware that the sleeve of her tunic has slipped along her raised arm. The skin is smooth and toasted light brown by the southern sun.

"You are shocked."

I am. However, as my voice has deserted me, I am unable to utter a word. I gaze into those hazel eyes and shake my head, conscious that the fewer words I stammer out at this moment, the better. "Please. Continue."

She hesitates, as though unsure of her subject, which I sense is not a habitual state of mind for this determined woman. "During my first weeks in Encarnación, Sor Dolores de Jesús, who occupied the cell next to mine, was most kind to me. Especially on those nights when I cried myself to sleep, which, for a time, were many."

At this revelation, this intimacy – for surely, Madre Carmela de la Luz does not share such confidences with everyone – my mind and my body are flooded with sensations I have never before known, or perhaps once have known, but are long buried and forgotten. These longings both perturb and reassure me. It is a pity I cannot confess them to my accusers in Salamanca but that would merely substitute one heinous tendency for another which is considered only slightly less heinous. My breath has deepened and I pray that my cursed fair skin remain free of the dreadful rush of blood that so tormented me as a young man. I am sure that my voice will tremble should I attempt to speak, so I remain silent.

"'Everyone has doubts,' Sor Dolores said, 'even brides on the day of their marriage and likely, in the days after.' The best thing, she said, was to pay such thoughts no heed. I was sure that her counsel came not from hearsay, but from some events in her own life. But if that were so, she never spoke of them."

Despite being immersed in the uneasy thrill that Madre Carmela's low, sweet voice sends pulsing through my thoughts, I wonder what bearing the personal history of this Sor Dolores could have on Fray Juan, and on my investigation. But I cannot bring myself to interrupt the musical flow of those words. Soon, Madre Carmela herself begins to look uncomfortable. She glances around the room, at the pictures, through the window, at her hands, anywhere. But not at me.

"I soon understood that Sor Dolores had a… a… friend."

The word lingers in the air, brimming with unspoken meaning. I find I am less disposed to clarify terminology than I was while in conversation with old Prior Andrés. Madre

Carmela is speaking quickly now, her slender hands no longer in repose but fluttering like little birds.

"Perhaps that was why she took care to make me her companion – to be assured of my discretion, should I discover her secret. Our cells were at the very end of a corridor, close to a door that led to the vegetable garden and was kept locked and bolted at night. Only the prioress, Madre Teresa, had the key. But I found out by chance that Sor Dolores also had one."

"How did you discover that?"

"Not long after I joined Encarnación, I heard a door opening in the middle of the night. Too frightened to look into the corridor, I moved my chair to the window, stood on it and peered out into the dark. The moon was covered with cloud but the night was quite warm. At the end of the pathway, between the rows of peas and beans just coming into flower, I caught a glimpse of my neighbour, Sor Dolores."

"What made you so sure that she had an assignation with a…" I force myself to say the word, "… lover." It is no use. The dreadful, familiar warmth is tingling the base of my neck and already has risen to my earlobes. Soon, my entire countenance will be the colour of a blazing fire. All I may do is ignore it, refuse to allow the agitation to rattle my voice.

"Because she was wearing her habit, but no head-covering," Sister Carmela continues rapidly.

Well, that settles it. What else would a beautiful young nun be doing in the middle of the night, stealing out of the convent, into the garden? I say nothing, but there must be something in the story that connects to the work of Fray Juan. Anticipating my next question, Carmela shakes her head.

"She did not visit the garden every night. For some weeks, I heard her door open on two or three nights and then for a whole month, nothing. During those times, she became melancholy. I imagined that they had some signal but I never knew what it was."

Fascinated though I am, I feel obliged to feign indifference, concerned to elevate our conversation above the level of gossip. "Do you think Fray Juan was aware of this? As her confessor?"

"He became aware of it. But he was not her confessor. Fray Germán, Fray Juan's Discalced colleague in the convent, had that role."

I must check this. Though I think she is probably right. It was widely believed at the time that some of the Encarnación sisters never quite forgave Teresa for imposing not one, but two Discalced friars on the community as father confessors – to Carmelite nuns who continued to adhere to the unreformed Mitigated Rule. Teresa herself had followed that same Rule for many years, in that very convent, before she embarked on her mission of change.

"Once they understood that the mother prioress was not going to impose her reforms on anyone who did not want to do things differently, I believe the atmosphere improved. For everyone experienced the tranquility and peace of mind that flowed from the changes some of the sisters made – engaging in much longer periods of silence, for example, deep meditation and hard physical labour, too, in the garden or the kitchen. After a time, many of the older and most entrenched of the sisters relaxed their opposition to her."

While she speaks, I reflect on how pleasant it would be to take a turn around the cloisters and the herb garden, feel the sun and air on my skin and inhale the scent of the budding blossoms, in the company of this woman who brims with an intensity I have rarely encountered, a simmering energy pent up in the fluid stillness of her delicate frame. Unaware of my failing concentration, she continues.

"I do believe that Fray Juan's sweetness of temper and his gentle nature, as well as the kindness of his spiritual guidance, won over many of the most resistant sisters. I remember well many of the little unnecessary kindnesses he showed us."

"Indeed?"

"Most certainly. He once gave the last of the asparagus crop to Sor Úrsula, the cook, to put in the soup even though we all knew he himself was partial to asparagus. And he was especially gentle with Sor Dolores. I remember one day she was sweeping the terrace. Observing her bare feet and the sharp stones and thorns scattered around, so many that she could not avoid stepping on them and cutting her feet, Fray Juan fetched her a pair of sandals with his own hand.

"'But Fray Juan, in summer...' she protested. She had begun to observe the Discalced practice of going barefoot in good weather. But he hushed her. She had a task to finish, he said, and it was pointless and unwise to inflict unnecessary pain or discomfort, especially if it meant that our dinner would be delayed. That was at a time when we had as much food as we needed," Madre Carmela adds. "No doubt you are aware that that was not always the case."

I am. In fact, I find it difficult to understand why the Prior General continued to allow novices to join that convent when at times there was no bread and the sisters were starving, not in compliance with strict rules of fasting, but because there was nothing to eat.

"So Fray Juan took pains to spare Sor Dolores unnecessary suffering?"

"Not only Sor Dolores. All of us. He was quite firm on the theme."

My countenance must convey disbelief, for Madre Carmela's tone becomes more vigorous, her index finger tapping out the rhythm of her words on my desk. I notice the skin of her right hand is marked by a slight graze that has not quite healed. She watches me observing her.

"I was digging out the root of a sapling," she explains, and once again the blood rushes to my face. "Above the ground, it looked to be a tiny thing. But beneath the surface... well, it became much deeper and more complicated once we started. You know how these tangled roots…"

Our eyes meet. Silence falls between us. I can think of more than one meaning for her words. I allow my gaze to linger on that luminous skin, the arched brows, the full lips that often seem to suppress a smile, those eyes. At this moment, my safest response is surely no response at all. Yet I do not look away.

"I am told that the gardens of the south are very beautiful. Though I have never seen them for myself." My voice is hoarse. My breath has stopped. I am balanced on the edge of a high, craggy mountaintop, surveying the foaming rapids and rivers rushing below. The air has thinned and I fear – I wish – that I might fall.

Carmela is silent. Her lips are parted in a half-smile, eyes turned towards the cloisters through the west-facing window. Her eyelids flicker shut and she inhales, as though savouring the scent of a lovely flower, and for a moment, I think she is about to turn towards me.

Instead, she nods once. "It is true. There is great beauty and great healing in nature."

And that is all.

Is that all?

The moment, brimming with intensity, has evaporated. A great, hovering change has been averted. My skin tingles with excitement, disappointment, relief.

"And Sor Dolores?"

"After Fray Juan made her his gift of the sandals, in her eyes he could do no wrong."

This entire episode puzzles me. It conveys the opposite meaning to what I had expected to hear. Madre Carmela surveys me for a moment, eyes narrowed, glinting slyly. "Goodness, Fray Martín, did you believe all the tales of grinding self-mortification which we Discalced Carmelites are reputed to practise?"

I shrug, feeling a little foolish without knowing why. After all, the physical and mental demands endured by the Discalced sisters and friars are well known.

"When I was a young friar in Burgos, we heard many stories of how the nuns and friars of the Discalced Carmelite order lived. Of course, it was then but a few years since they – you – had been declared a separate Province and the feuding between the Carmelites of the Mitigated Rule and Teresa's Discalced reformers was still very bitter."

"Quite so." Once again, that long index finger taps the edge of my desk. "Did it never occur to you, Fray Martín," – who does this woman think she is talking to! – "that some of those tales might have been fuelled by ambitious opponents, adherents of the Mitigated Rule?"

I survey her, but she does not flinch. The skin around her eyes begins to crinkle. "Not really." Even to my own ears, I sound like a sulky schoolboy. I am irritated to notice that she is trying, with limited success, to hide a smile.

"I am convinced, Fray Martín, that most people believe what they want to believe. The notion that carefully assembled facts – such as those you seek – create a true image of reality is no more than a fiction. All of us carry our reality within us, selecting the facts – and only those facts – that support it."

"Indeed." I have turned frosty and pompous but the truth is, Madre Carmela's observations have caused me great discomfort, though I know not why. The strange excitement I felt at the start of our meeting is now coursing through my whole body. It is rare that I have the opportunity to debate with a mind so fine-tuned and brave, even if wrong-headed.

"What of the novice master in Pastrama who was known to have subjected the young friars in his charge to the most humiliating of practices? Such as extreme fasting, days and weeks without being permitted to wash, screamed insults that reduced these young men – boys, really – to a state of terror that left some novices disturbed? To say nothing of the noxious effect on those who inflicted the humiliations. What of those austerities?"

At this moment, I seek no response to my questions and raise my hand, palm out, to halt her intervention. "In what way does such behaviour enrich spiritual practice? Does this represent the original vision of the Desert Fathers? When the conditions they endured – fasting, interrupted sleep, silence, lack of possessions and yes, even lack of cleanliness – were proper to their time and place? But not to our own? In short, might not opponents of the reforms enacted by Blessed Teresa and Fray Juan, the followers of the Mitigated Rule, have had good cause for their fears?"

The gossamer thread that had bound us together is broken; we are two rocks now, immobile, separated by the light of a harsh sun. I am aware that such people in our own day do penance not just for their own sins, but for those of us who are too frail or worldly to do penance for ourselves. I can even accept that in such mortification, the flesh is purified; in subordinating the body to the spirit, in granting the spirit dominion over the physical self, a door to some of the stranger manifestations of holiness may open; and that the body may thus become an open channel to receive the Divine.

Yet did not the Discalced Carmelites take suffering, and the love of suffering, to great heights? Lack of sleep or interrupted sleep. Fasting and abstinence. Disciplines. I have never approved of those garments or implements that the most zealous wear next to their skin. And it is true that many friars are in a constant state of pain. Though in later life, Fray Juan had no need to inflict such suffering upon himself, for the beatings he received from his captors in Toledo were said to have seared wounds and weeping sores upon his skin that afflicted him for the rest of his life. Such was the legacy of his decision to remain captive, when the innkeeper and his son begged him to make his escape.

Are these the consequences of simple-minded idealism? Or perhaps some people – perpetrators of suffering and those who endure the actions of the perpetrators – simply enjoy it.

When I eventually fall silent, Madre Carmela's smile has vanished. There is an awkward silence.

"Your understanding of the nature and purpose of the rigours of our way of life, Fray Martín, is…" she casts around for a word that sufficiently expresses her displeasure, for there is no doubt that I have displeased her, "…primitive. You are perhaps unaware, Fray Martín…"

"Please enlighten me, Madre Carmela. I would welcome your instruction."

"In the first place, the novice master of whom you speak – yes, his excesses, his cruelty, were well known – was severely reprimanded. In fact, his subsequent behaviour was monitored and subjected to intense scrutiny. By Fray Juan himself."

This, I did not know. My companion surveys me and only when she is satisfied that I am resolved to remain silent does she continue.

"Fray Juan was appointed to investigate the practices of austerities in that monastery and it was he who put a stop to them. At least, to those excesses you describe. Furthermore," that tapping index finger again, "the practice of austerities, and their intended impact, Fray Martín, is a great deal more nuanced, more subtle, than you allow. You give us little credit."

I shift uncomfortably in my chair, surprised to see that I have really offended, perhaps even hurt her. I feel a little ashamed. We sit in silence for a few moments and even though I remain unconvinced that the excesses of austerities are a useful path to spiritual development, or indeed that they are practised with such circumspection as Madre Carmela describes, I am loath to quarrel with her.

"I beg your pardon, Madre Carmela. Please forgive my impetuousness, my levity. You are quite right, I do sometimes speak with great authority and occasionally I am unencumbered by the necessary knowledge. I am more than grateful that you should share your intelligence with me," I add humbly. Perhaps I even mean it.

To my amazement and also my relief, she bursts out laughing. "Self-knowledge is a wonderful quality, Fray Martín. One that is essential for the pursuit of our practice. We will make a Discalced Carmelite of you yet."

Feeling a little sheepish, I attempt a smile, accepting the rebuke. "So, neither her confessor nor Fray Juan imposed penance on Sor Dolores, once her transgressions became known?"

"I did not say that. What I am sure of, is that any penance imposed was private, of a spiritual nature, and did not involve any physical disciplines. Or at least, the most demanding of them."

"She renounced the man, I assume. Her lover."

For the first time, Madre Carmela's pale skin takes on a slight flush. She nods. "Soon after she began conversing with Fray Juan, her nocturnal visits to the garden came to an end. Not straight away. First, they became less frequent and, after a time, I noticed that she had stopped visiting the garden by night altogether. I assumed that the man – her lover – had discarded her. Until the beating."

Madre Carmela is surprised to learn that I know nothing of a beating. I am sure that there is no mention of any such incident in the files I was given by Crespo and Ortiz.

"You are aware that Fray Juan did not share our quarters in Encarnación?"

This, I did know, for at least two of the documents I have scrutinised draw particular attention to this circumstance, it being specifically forbidden. According to the Rule of the Order, the confessor of a community is obliged to lodge within the confines of the convent or monastery grounds. Fray Juan and Fray Germán must have interpreted this rule rather broadly, for they were quartered in a small house located a very little way outside the convent walls, at a distance of less than a single field.

They called it *el torrecillo*, which must have been a joke for it was no tower, small or otherwise. By all the accounts I have read, it was little more than a hovel consisting of one room with barely space enough for two blankets and a desk for working. Located no more than a minute's walk from the gates of the convent but still, technically a transgression that would later be thrown in Fray Juan's face.

"It was fortunate that the assault happened when he was on his way to hear our confessions. If it had occurred on his return, he might have lain in the field all night, bruised and bleeding. Who knows how it might have ended."

I listen in growing amazement as Madre Carmela recounts her memory of the crisis: Fray Juan, carried into the convent, cut and bruised from blows received from a heavy stick, wielded by a man well known in the town.

"A random attack? I presume the rogue fled."

"It was not random, and the man did not flee. Quite the opposite. He continued to beat Fray Juan, even after he had fallen to the ground. Were it not for the intervention of two passing farmhands, he might have killed Fray Juan, such was his fury. And all the while he bellowed that the lily-livered priests should mind their own business and stay out of his affairs."

"Sor Dolores?"

"Exactly."

"The ruffian referred to her by name?"

"He did. He even accused Fray Juan of taking his place."

I put down my pencil and remove my spectacles. So, Fray Juan stood accused of having sinned against his vow of chastity. But by a source that could hardly be deemed credible. I decide not to pursue this line of enquiry. "So, by guiding Sor Dolores away from the path of sin, Fray Juan had deprived this man of his lover?"

"Of course. But not because he..."

"That goes without saying. I assume Fray Juan was above reproach in such matters."

"Certainly. Without a doubt. All the same..."

I look curiously at my companion who, for the first time, is struggling to find the words to express her thoughts. Or perhaps her thoughts pertain to those unsayable circumstances which everyone knows, but of which no one speaks.

"The role of confessor, of spiritual director, carries with it dangers of a particular nature," I offer.

"Exactly." Relieved not to have raised the topic, my Carmela is nevertheless willing to elaborate on it. "In the giving and receiving of spiritual guidance, in confessing weakness and struggles within the soul to another human being, there is a...closeness...between the confessor and the confessed that can be..."

"Misinterpreted?"

"Just so. And may occur within the convent walls, or without."

I lean forward, my pencil at the ready. This, I had not expected. "And did it? Did Fray Juan's spiritual ministrations give rise to such misunderstandings?"

"Not within the Encarnación, of that I am sure. Not even on the part of Sor Dolores, who had come to love him greatly. As one would love a father. We all did, for that is what he was, our spiritual father."

"Then...?"

Madre Carmela looks down.

"There was a girl in the town. Very young, very beautiful, of a good family. She fell in love with Fray Juan. But not as a father. She desired him as a...as a man."

"And how did this come to be known?" I pour Madre Carmela a cup of water from the pitcher on my desk. "May I?" She nods and takes a sip. I have been inconsiderate. This woman, who, I must remember, is no longer young, has been travelling for days and I am sure is in need of rest. Blue shadows have appeared beneath her eyes. I resolve that we must finish our work here as quickly as we can.

"She visited him in his quarters," Carmela says. "Visited is perhaps not the correct word. She forced her way into his *torrecillo* when he was, unfortunately, alone."

I lean back in my chair and whistle through my teeth, a habit I was cured of long ago by my father. I must be careful not to make too much of this. Carmela echoes my sentiments.

"It was not a scandal, by any means, for Fray Juan made light of it. Few people know exactly how the situation was resolved, in fact. Some said that he threw her out into the darkness. Others, that he spent the whole night talking to her and persuaded her of the error of her actions. You must remember that our vow of silence meant that even before Teresa's Discalced reforms, the increasing piety of the ambience she created left us little inclination for idle conversation. So I am not exactly sure how this matter was solved. Only that it was."

"What was the outcome of the assault? The criminal was apprehended and prosecuted, I assume?"

"By no means. Fray Juan never protested. Not then, while he was receiving the blows, nor afterwards, while we treated him. No, Sor Dolores kept away or perhaps was kept away, I do not know. I did not minister to him myself but I assisted those who did. I brought hot water and herbs to treat his wounds. Wounds which he smiled over and indeed, from which he derived no anger nor pain, but rather, satisfaction. He seemed to see this incident as a kind of test that he had passed, and that gave him joy. We all thought he was a saint."

Disciplines. Austerities. I have never approved of them – and not only from a distaste for the personal discomforts they inflict, both physical and mental. My experiences of such practices are well within the outer limits required by my own Order, which is far less exigent than others. In truth, despite Madre Carmela's rebuke, I confess to a degree of suspicion concerning the purpose and motivation of the most rigorous austerities. The contents of my case files reveal that I am not alone: many others – the officials of the Carmelites of the Mitigated Rule, among them –

believed that in this respect, the Discalced reforms enacted by Teresa and Juan went much too far.

But how far is too far? Impossible to know, without first considering the purpose of such practices and what they are thought to accomplish. Moreover, I believe that the mental relationship between the individual's capacity for suffering, and the nature of the suffering itself, is decisive. For myself, the fast between Christmas and the end of Lent, when meat is forbidden and nourishment is confined to one meal a day, inflicts upon me little more than fatigue and a mild discomfort. I cannot claim that this is due to any particular strength of will on my part; rather, to my general lack of interest in food, which has never been the greatest of pleasures to me but mere fuel that equips me to carry out the work of the day. Fasting, therefore, inflicts no great suffering on me. After a day or two, hunger passes, often followed by strange and far from unpleasant mental states. Deprive me of sleep, however, and I am demented, a raging bull. I confess that in my little monastery in Salamanca, I frequently absented myself from Matins, an indulgence that, for reasons I never questioned, my brother friars and prior permitted, thus often allowing me to luxuriate in a full night's sleep.

My commitment to personal mortification, therefore, has always been half-hearted. I have never been convinced of the underlying motivation: the desire to emulate the trials of our founding saints and, ultimately, of Christ himself. But to what end? Of what benefit is it to us, or to the world, to expose our flesh and our minds to unnecessary and even harmful privations, whose effects are determined by the physical and mental dispositions and capacities for endurance of each person?

Strolling with my fascinating companion through the garden, I decide against sharing these thoughts, sure that giving voice to them will simply reveal the skill with which I justify my own weakness. So we converse on matters of no consequence: Madre

Carmela's forthcoming visit to a sister convent here in Madrid, her long journey back to Andalucía, and my own fervent desire to see the gardens of the south for myself, one day.

Monastery of San Gerónimo, Madrid,
Twenty-third day of March in the Year of Our Lord, 1616.

I t is widely and mistakenly believed amongst people acquainted with such matters, that those of us born under the sign of the Balance are blessed with an enviable sense of equilibrium and tranquility of spirit. Nothing could be less true. Those scales, as I have good cause to know, are calibrated to gauge the merits of wildly fluctuating opposites, antithetical impulses forever in flux: emotions and desires, understandings and interpretations. One moment, fully persuaded of an argument or a preferred course of action; the next, equally convinced of the opposite. It is exhausting.

On this occasion, my reasoning has led me to an impetuous outburst. "She invited him into the lion's den. In the midst of a rebellion. A request to which he willingly acceded."

Ortiz recoils as though I had raised my hand to strike him. My observation has hit a wrong note. Without looking at me, he settles himself into his chair and steeples his bony fingers. Too late, I realise that some of my commentary in this first progress report could be construed as criticism of the recently beatified

Teresa, who no doubt will one day be elevated to sainthood. Crespo, who has been standing with his back to the room, gazing out at the slender young saplings swaying in the distance, turns and fixes me in the relentless blue beam of his glare. But his words are mild. "Not so dramatic, Fray Martín."

The geniality of his tone disturbs me more than Ortiz's unbridled scorn. "Sit." Crespo lumbers to his feet and approaches my chair. I accept the goblet of purple wine he pours from an exquisitely fashioned decanter. The last rays of the sun catch a filigree pattern traced across the surface of the glass and for a moment, I immerse myself in contemplation of its beauty. This is no pale imitation. It is a piece straight from the hands of one of the masters of Murano and I wonder which prince of the Venetian Church owed Archbishop Crespo a big enough favour to make him such a handsome gift. He continues to survey me, a shrewd glint in his eye. I could swear he is reading my mind and that we are about to embark on a discussion of the latest modes in Venetian glassware and how they compare to those of the past. Instead, he inclines his head and motions that I should drink, his stubby fingers splayed in a courtly fashion, as he returns to his post by the window. I take a sip. The wine is excellent, of course, but in the present company, I must keep my wits about me. He invites me to begin.

"Fray Juan de la Cruz: born Juan de Yepes, in Hontiveras, Ávila, Old Castile, to Gonzales de Yepes, a nobleman, and Catalina Álvarez, a weaver. Upon the marriage, the de Yepes family disinherited their son and Gonzales was obliged to earn his bread as a weaver, like his wife. A very great fall in status, from minor nobility to near poverty." I pause. In truth, I have little to say that is not already documented in the bundles of files Crespo gave me himself. Nothing arising from the witness interviews – with the authorised witnesses, that is – to justify my work of the last two months.

"I can confirm that the father died when Juan was barely three years old. The extended de Yepes family declined to assist his widow and her young family, which additional misfortune plunged the mother, Catalina, and her three sons, into dire poverty. The second son, Luis, died but a few years after his father. For a long time, the family lived on the edge of starvation."

Crespo moves away from the window and returns to his desk. "All this is well known, Fray Martín."

Yet I hear no real rebuke in his tone; rather, a tremor of anxiety. I keep my eyes lowered on my notes but when I glance up, I see that both he and Ortiz are watching me intently. For the first time, it occurs to me that they may be more interested in determining which facts I have failed to uncover, rather than those I have. Not that I am telling them all I know. Far from it, for I have decided to defer reporting on my recent and most interesting findings. These concern the documents I received from Oviedo almost two weeks ago, which require a more detailed examination than I have yet carried out. Only when I have completed my inspection of Prior Andrés's archive will I summarise their contents for Ortiz and Crespo's benefit.

Although young Fray Francisco could not have guessed the contents of the bundle, he carried it towards me with an air of ceremony and hovered whilst I untied the string. My curiosity must have alerted his interest, for he edges closer to my desk and cranes his neck over my shoulder until I tell him to leave. I do not want him, or anyone, to observe my excitement.

Might not old Prior Andrés have buried one or two of Fray Juan's originals in his archive? My fingers brush the cover of an aged pamphlet, two hand-spans wide and twice that in length. This is an entire file composed of about two dozen leaves sewn together, the whole bound by a thick board whose surface bears the blemishes of a working document, sprinkled with light stains, as though someone had spilled a few drops of water on it. Though water would have dried without leaving a mark, would it not? Perhaps it was wine. One margin is secured by three double stitches inserted at regular intervals along the vertical edge, from top to bottom. I raise the file to my face, inhale the scent of old paper, stroke the rough, bulky surface of the cover as though it were a living thing, wondering how many other hands have caressed it over the years.

Very gently, prepared to find something of great import, I open the cover. The interior pages are thick and roughly textured. They crackle to my touch. The first leaf is blank except for a date inscribed at the foot, underlined with a dramatic flourish in faded black ink.

Only a few months after Fray Juan escaped from his Toledo prison. I dare not hope, but my heart beats a little faster. I turn the page.

A table of contents, set out in alphabetic order, the 'a' and 'b' drawn with perfectly executed serifs, the tails of the 'f' and the necks of the 'h' and 'b' and 'd' all embellished with delicate flourishes in a gracious hand. I cannot resist comparing the penmanship with my own scrawl, which, I am told, resembles the meanderings of a drunken spider that has dipped its feet in ink and scuttled across the page.

Income and expenses. Distracted by the beautifully formed letter 'y' whose jamb underscores almost a full line, I am all but blind to the content and the meaning that this lovely script conveys. I turn another leaf and another. The list continues. The same litany, relentless letters of the alphabet marching down the pages.

A set of accounts. Meticulously ordered, verified on the final page with the seal of a Sicilian estate, dated the month of December in the year fifteen seventy-eight.

Disheartened, I put the folio aside and set about sifting through the dozens of accompanying documents, many of them single pages, only a few secured and gathered together. I am soon disappointed. One glance at the quality and type of paper and ink tells me that most of these documents were created within the last decade; and that the very few older files amongst them concern trivial matters with no relation to Fray Juan or his work.

I will have to examine every page in detail. But this first rapid inspection yields no other documents with the aged appearance of the Sicilian accounts, no lines in faded ink, no rough-textured paper that might be the manuscript of a poem written out almost forty years ago. Hope yielding to irritation, I gather the pages into two unruly piles which I heap upon my windowsill.

One file, smaller and thicker than the others, attracts my attention and although I should be working on my report, I cannot resist taking a quick look. The cover is dark red and although the individual leaves are of uniform size and texture, the entries are written in many different hands. Some are mere scribbles. I am intrigued to see that the pages are ordered according to two different numbering systems, both inscribed at the top right corner of each page, one digit in ink and another different number pencilled beside it. I surmise that at least two people have worked with this material, and that both arranged the sequence of pages according to their priorities and interests. Though I am pressed for time, I begin to skim through the leaves:

I am Sor Ana de San Josef and I present this testimony in fulfil-ment of the requirement explained to me by the Visitator General and although my memory is not very good I set down here what knowledge I have of the holy man Fray Juan de la Cruz with whom I was acquainted when he was vicar of Segovia and Fray Doria was Definidor General of our Order... Fray Juan confessed the nuns in my convent every week and I knew him well...

There follow eight pages of Sor Ana's meandering thoughts, written in her large, cursive scrawl, extolling the great sanctity and virtue and kindness of Fray Juan. On the ninth page, the script transforms to long, slanted lettering:

I am Fray Pablo de Santo Hilarion, and I knew Fray Juan de la Cruz when he was rector of the College in Alcalá de Henares and he was a very holy and spiritual man.

Fray Pablo was a man of few words, for his observations, which are set out in the form of a list of unadorned comments, occupy a little less than a single page.

It takes me some moments to understand that I am reading original witness testimonies, gathered within the last few years, written in the witnesses' own hand. So, this is how earlier investigators gathered and recorded their information. I had wondered why, amongst all the letters, minutes of meetings, draft reports and rough notes crammed into the chest that Crespo gave me at the start of this commission, I found not one single transcript or note of an interview with someone who was acquainted with Fray Juan. This file proves that at least one of my predecessors did speak to some of those who knew him and persuaded some of them to commit their statements to paper. How these records came into the possession of an aged prior in Oviedo, I cannot fathom.

As I turn the pages, I have the strange sensation of being observed, as though another reader were peering over my shoulder, directing my attention. Perhaps that early investigator, the person who gathered these witness statements, provided the old friars and nuns with paper and pen, and sat in front of them while they wrote also prompted them, collected, ordered and numbered the precious sheets, and later had them sewn together to create this folio?

I do not think so. My companion reader, whose shade hovers by my side, has a different purpose. He is not only gathering this information, he is making meaning from it; and his presence is visible only when serving that goal. Many of these pages are free of his attentions, but in others he reveals himself. He lingers. He imposes his thoughts, sometimes in the form of a firm, black, vertical stroke that marks out three or four lines in the margin; sometimes a bold line that underscores a few words, even a whole paragraph. Now and then, he records his thoughts in a phrase or two that hints at the path his attention seeks out:

> *prophecy*
> *foretold hour of his own death*
> *appeared after death*
> *miracle of the sheets*
> *resplendence of his tomb*
> *heavenly scent in room at time of his death*
> *healed women who suffered pain in head for three years*
> *food appears in El Calvario*
> *incorruptibility of body*
> *asparagus appeared at wrong time of year*
> *calmed storms*   *exorcisms*

Guided by my predecessor's notations and emphases, I retrace the steps he takes, as he navigates the dense thickets of handwritten evidence. He shows himself also in his absences, the many anecdotes and observations that escape the beam of his attention. Without a doubt, he is on a quest. More than that: he is creating a story, a certain type of person. Acts of simple kindness are of no interest to him. Nor are tales of jesting, teasing, the singing of joyful songs and prayers. One playful scene recalled by an old nun makes me laugh aloud:

> *The mother prioress Teresa prostrated herself on the ground to receive his blessing, as was her custom. Fray Juan blessed us all and bid us rise, but not the mother prioress. So we asked him would he not bid her rise. And he smiled at us and said, 'I think we will leave her down there, she seems to like it.'*

My shadowy companion has taken no special note of this. He seeks a certain type of anecdote, tales of special gifts and miracles, and discards all else. I take a moment to ponder this, then make a note of my own.

Much of this writing is too small to read with ease. My eyeglasses give insufficient amplification so I will probably need a magnifying lens. I gather the documents together, wrap them up in the cloth and string in which they arrived, resolved to store them in my sleeping quarters rather than my office, that I may examine them in spare moments, uninterrupted. This brief inspection provoked many thoughts and questions. None of which I am ready to share with the Archbishop and his minion just yet.

Crespo has turned back to the window and an uneasy thought occurs to me. I am confident that he knows nothing of so trivial a matter as the arrival of a parcel from Oviedo. But he may have learned of other activities I would, for the moment, prefer to keep private. I shift in my chair while Ortiz casts his eye over my report, holding the pages between finger and thumb. There are only two sheets but they are closely covered, the tone deliberately dry. Objective.

As he scans the text in continued silence, I regret that I am seated in a chair which, though comfortable, is rather low, whilst my superiors have remained standing. Perhaps this summary of my findings, which contains a formal account of meetings with about a quarter of the designated witnesses, is less dispassionate than I had thought. Might the liberty I permit myself in this private journal, where I record my thoughts, uncertainties – and also, notes of meetings with unauthorised witnesses – have spilled over into my official communications, both in the written testimony and in the words I have just spoken? That reference to the convent of the Encarnación as a lion's den might be considered an impertinence. Or worse. The genial tone of Crespo's next question as he turns to face me does not reassure me.

"Can you confirm that you have followed all the procedures for this commission that were stipulated before you began your investigation?"

I hesitate, wondering if I should disclose the names of the few unauthorised witnesses I added to Ortiz's original list. Both he and Crespo insisted on discretion, but not on total secrecy. It must have been clear from the start that an investigation on the scale they envisaged, to include interviews with more than thirty people in less than a year, however quietly done and however lowly the individuals questioned, could never hope to remain secret.

"Of course."

In truth, I have been discreet. As to procedures, well, that is a different matter. The greater part of our first meeting had been devoted to the niceties of how I should, and should not, carry out my duties.

"You may inform your prior in the monastery of San Salvador when your task is approaching completion and you may also supply him with occasional progress reports, in the form of a verbal account – and only verbal – of how you have spent your time."

Crespo continued writing while he was speaking, I standing before the two of them, like a schoolboy receiving his homework.

"And that, only concerning the process," Ortiz intervened. "The contents, your actual findings, you will bring to this room and this room only."

With that, he handed me a list of names and the summary of conditions which Crespo had just completed and signed. In addition to the identities of the people I should meet, it set out detailed procedures for the conduct of my work. There should be regular reports, verbatim where possible and when written, in Latin only; a detailed quarterly conference – of which today's meeting, a little delayed by my other commitments, is the first. Listed in no order that I can discern are names of identified witnesses who had either known Fray Juan, or been close to people who knew him or who had lived through significant occurrences.

"What manner of occurrences?"

Ortiz enunciated his answer word by word, as though for the benefit of a small and not very intelligent child.

"You've heard the rumours. Use your initiative."

At that very first meeting with Ortiz and Crespo, as I recalled my own experience in Salamanca, the strategy of constructing the life of a man on a foundation of whispers which have outlived him, filled me with foreboding. Nevertheless, I made no remark and simply took the three pages proffered, which set out a list of the questions I must ask all witnesses; a further series of questions to be put to particular individuals; a warning not to deviate from the supplied script; the length of time each interview should take, although some flexibility in this condition is permitted, to accommodate uneducated witnesses who might be less articulate than others and likely to require more time in which to express themselves – an observation that made me smile, remembering my father's coachmen and our old cook, neither ever having had difficulties with self-expression. But then, neither Ortiz nor Crespo ever speak with members of the lower classes, that invisible army of underlings whose discreet labours provide them with the meals, pleasant surroundings, transport and clean clothes that befit their station.

"I do not recall," Ortiz glances down at my report, then sidelong at Crespo, "any agreement that your personal experience, your boyhood recollections," he pauses, as though unsure how to express his next thought without giving insult, thereby multiplying it, "should contribute to the process in which you are engaged."

I breathe a sigh, which I hope conveys distress rather than relief and explain in some detail to my superiors the relevance of my own recollections.

Given the location of the Carmelite convent of Encarnación, outside Ávila city walls, it is easier to make the approach from my village by the road that skirts the town and cuts through the fields, in preference to guiding a carriage through the narrow streets and cobbled squares of the town centre. Besides, the road slopes steeply from the ancient Roman gateway whose contours may yet be seen embedded in the newer, honey-coloured structure of the *murallas*. On that day, more than forty years ago, I was a boy of eight or nine years old – yes, nine, for this was just a few months before Pepita died. And it was the last time we made our monthly visit to the city, when my mother would visit Catalina, her cousin.

La tía Catalina, as I called her, event though she was not my real aunt, was quite a young girl in those days, of marriageable age, a little over twenty. Beautiful and difficult, she had just rebuffed the advances of various suitable young noblemen of good family and insisted on her love for a dancing instructor who had had to be paid off to disappear. Catalina's father had resolved to teach his unruly daughter a lesson by placing her for a time in one of the convents in Castile. For reasons of convenience, he chose the Encarnación in Ávila. All this I heard during playful arguments between my parents about whether my mother should visit Catalina so often. My father thought that those pleasant visits undermined the parental authority that Catalina's father was trying to exercise. Nevertheless, my mother was determined. Catalina was a good girl. She had done nothing wrong except to allow a silly boy to fall in love with her. How was she to blame for that?

My father never could deny my mother any wish and so, once a month, on the Saturday following market day, we three would rattle our way in our carriage along the winding road to Ávila from our village of Montecastillo del Río. We called it the *pueblo de las tres mentiras*, three lies in one name, as it boasted neither castle nor river, nor was it perched on a mountain top but, rather, nestled in a valley.

I remember those visits as being amongst the happiest days of my childhood, for my parents always left Pepita with her nurse and I would have the whole afternoon alone with my father while my mother visited Catalina in the convent. Sometimes he would take me to see a cock fight in the company of humble people of the town, or pay a visit to old friends from his days at the university of Salamanca. I would sit listening to them talking and watching them smoking, at that time a new and rather disreputable habit that a friend of my father had brought back from the Americas. Before sunset, we would return to the Encarnación convent and my mother would spring into the carriage, slim and dark-haired, her fair skin a little pink, animated by her afternoon of conversation and gaiety with my aunt.

In truth, being sent to a convent to be taught a lesson was not the worst fate that could befall an unruly young woman like my mother's pretty cousin. If her father had reflected on the matter a little more, he might have preferred to keep his young daughter at home where he at least could have supervised her behaviour. In those days, if Catalina's experience was a good example, and my later experience has persuaded me that it was, life in a convent could be pleasant for a young woman of noble birth. She could expect to be permitted her own servants, have special meals cooked for her and engage in daily chatter with nuns who were cloistered, yet often found in conversation and merrymaking with their continuous stream of guests, such as my own mother.

It was even said that in some convents, these aristocratic lodgers were visited by lovers. And that some of the nuns themselves were suspected of receiving young men from neighbouring towns and villages, who scaled the convent walls and took their pleasure. Even though Madre Carmela's account of Sor Dolores's conduct confirms this, I do not believe such immorality was habitual in the Encarnación in Ávila. All the same, there is no doubt that the life the sisters lived, if free from the vice imputed by some critics, nonetheless had drifted very far from the silent devotion, contemplation and austerity that had originally imbued the primitive Rule, before the mitigations of various popes had so greatly softened the demands of their religious practice and their lives. It is perhaps not surprising, then, if the sisters of Encarnación, Teresa's former religious companions, were less than pleased when she brought her reforms to their door.

On that day, long before our carriage arrived at the northern fork in the road leading to Encarnación, it was clear that something was amiss. My father always insisted that this visit to Catalina be arranged to avoid market day. He could not bear the noise and the throngs in the square. Hence, he always sent his steward to sell a calf or buy a ewe, unless it was an especially significant purchase that required his expert attention. So, when we turned onto the northbound road and our coach was suddenly surrounded by an unruly mass of townspeople, my father exclaimed in annoyance. Either market day had been moved, which was unthinkable, or some other festival or event had brought the townspeople outside the city walls, far into the fields and the countryside.

A few shallow steps lead up to the main convent door of the convent of Encarnación and on the highest of these stood a squat little fellow who was attempting to address the crowd. My father recognised him as the mayor. As we drew closer to the convent, the speaker was joined by a long-limbed *padre* in a black habit who, my mother murmured, was the provincial of the Carmelite Order.

"What is a provincial?"

Both my mother and father at once told me to hush.

"And the civil guard," my mother breathed.

Unable to move backwards or forwards, our carriage came to a standstill. Raised voices filled the air and there was a relentless surge towards the convent. Even so, my father assured us there was no danger. Something was happening at the

Encarnación which the townspeople surrounding our carriage were straining to see. That was all.

When one of our horses began to whinny and tremble, his eyes rolling in fright, my father jumped down from his place and pushed his way towards the flash of a silver breastplate glinting in the sun. At the same time, we heard the strangest of sounds carried on the warm summer air, mingled with shouts and catcalls from noisy townspeople swarming through the fields. The better to see and hear the strange hum, my mother drew back the curtain and leaned out.

"They are singing a *Te Deum*," she whispered.

The sound swelled and a group of singing women more than a hundred strong, wearing black tunics and white veils, made their way around the convent garden. Advancing towards them were another group of women who were not singing but shouting. It was not a decorous gathering. Soon, the singing group lost formation, broke up and mingled with their opponents, jostling and pushing. In the midst of the melee, a tall lady with strong features and an aquiline nose, stern of brow, her face set like stone, made her way up the convent steps, accompanied by two large men clad in silver breast-plates and helmets, who kept the mob of rowdy nuns and townspeople at bay.

"They don't want you!" shouted one ruffian, who was quickly clapped about the head by a guard.

The tall lady made no response, save to glare at the offender with a frightening eye. The little mayor tried to assert his authority but could not be heard above the shouting and the remnants of the *Te Deum*. "This is the prioress and she will effect entry to the convent of Encarnación, whether these unruly nuns will have it or no."

As he spoke, one voice emerging from the group of singing nuns called out: "The choir! Let us enter by the choir!"

And there came another great surge, as the singing nuns pushed forward and the others blocked their way. Most puzzling of all, the nuns in the two groups looked the same, the only difference being that some of these women wanted to get into the convent, while the others were determined to keep them out. After a time, the tall lady accompanied by the singing nuns finally succeeded in reaching the porch, entered through the main convent door, and disappeared.

By the time my father managed to elbow his way back to us through the throng, he was mightily irritated. We would have to wait here until the disturbances had passed.

"Will we not be visiting Catalina today?" my mother asked.

"Not today," my father declared, with some satisfaction, "In fact, I doubt there will be many more visits to the parlour at Encarnación for a very long time."

He was right. After Teresa had taken over as prioress – for it was she, with her supporters and her opponents scuffling in a most indecorous manner, in the grounds of the convent of Encarnación outside Ávila's city walls – the visits to *la tía* Catalina and those pleasant afternoons with my father ended. Less than a year later, Pepita was dead of a pain in her head that began in her ear and could not be healed. Just a few months after that my mother succumbed to a fever brought on by the frequent soakings she got while out walking in the rain, a habit she took up after Pepita was gone.

That day, when she returned to her old convent, now prioress and no doubt burning with reforming zeal, Madre Teresa did succeed in gaining access to the convent at Encarnación. But it took the mayor, the civil guard and over a hundred of her staunchest followers to achieve it. How she won the support of her community, when she put a stop to the merrymaking and the parlour visits that the nuns had always enjoyed, I do not know. Yet within a year or two, she had won over the hearts of many of those who had been her fiercest opponents.

And she did not do it alone, but with the help of Fray Juan de la Cruz.

So that was how it happened: she summoned him to Encarnación, to a community of Carmelite nuns who wanted nothing of Teresa's Discalced reforms. She installed him as their father confessor, whether they liked it or not. That was the start of his trials, where the worst of his troubles began.

When I have finished explaining all of this to Crespo and Ortiz, they fall silent. Ortiz has turned away. Crespo favours me with a quizzical look.

"I included this account of mine – this eyewitness account of a crucial episode in the Carmelite reform, which pertains to subsequent events in the life of Fray Juan – because I am endeavouring to uncover the reasons for Fray Juan's later tribulations, and whether they had their roots in the dissent and rebellion in the convent of Encarnación."

Crespo nods without looking at me and taps his short, pudgy fingers on his desk as he carefully enunciates each word. "Uncertainty? Yes. Resistance? Perhaps. But dissent? Open rebellion?" He shakes his head and fixes me with a look of concern. "The Holy Office of the Inquisition advises that in this endeavour of ours, we must take care to avoid the malign influence of unfounded rumour."

His comment hovers in the air and the grey, grave face of Doctor Enrique, my visitor from the Inquisition, rises in my mind. For the first time, the unease I have felt from the very beginning of this commission assumes the vertiginous contours of fear. Is this advice from Doctor Enrique himself? Or merely a vague threat from my superiors? Certainly, Crespo's words remind me that there is a direction which this story must – and one which it must not – follow. Certain authorities of the Church, perhaps with the support of the Inquisition, have commissioned an independent report into the life and work of Juan de Yepes, known in Christ as Fray Juan de la Cruz. The work to be conducted by an outsider, in the apparent expectation that a stranger could discover truths that would remain hidden from

– or be concealed by – an investigator within their own Order. They have scented something on the wind and they are preparing for it. Using my investigation. My report. Even so, they do not make it easy for me.

What are they really after, these two? Why do they think I am the man to get it for them? When I turn to shut the door behind them, I glance up and intercept a hard look that passes between them. Crespo is nodding and Ortiz is wearing a half-smile of satisfaction.

Desperate to breathe air and feel daylight on my face, I step out of the stuffy, opulent room and make my way towards the garden. Careful to maintain the decorum proper to my station, I hurry through the cloisters, stride past the trickling fountain and the roses in bud, aware that I am shivering, in spite of the heat of the sun.

Convent of Encarnación, Ávila,
Third day of April in the Year of Our Lord, 1616.

As I draw near the convent of Encarnación, my mood simmers in agitation, seasoned with annoyance. This unhappy state of mind is due to the intelligence imparted to me by Ortiz just before I set out, while I waited for the stable boy to prepare Caminante for the long ride to Ávila. By then, of course, it was too late to object. I am to meet a Sor Úrsula, who did not observe the events which she has undertaken to describe for me, and not Sor Beatriz, who did. In what sense, then, can the person I am ordered to meet be considered a witness?

Not for the first time, I wonder at the logic, if there is a logic, behind the processes of investigation so meticulously prescribed by my two superiors. I must choose to believe that some coherent strategy, designed perhaps to serve a hidden purpose, is at work; for the alternative – that their chosen methodology serves neither rational thought nor elementary competence – is too disturbing to contemplate.

It being many years since I visited Ávila, I elect to approach the convent of Encarnación from the east, whence Caminante and I might pick a careful path around the city walls. In my mind's eye I plot a route through the narrow streets that will allow us to avoid stairways and take the shortest way towards the old Roman gate.

Soon we reach the city walls, whose curved towers and crenellations I often drew as a child. The surrounding landscape has changed little since then, yet I am shocked at how much I have forgotten. Those *verracos*, great hunks of granite that keep vigil over the fields of this region, each boasting the heft of massive haunches and the bare suggestion of a head, as though our ancient ancestors knew that the hint of form was enough to invoke the spirit of the bull or the pig which their handiwork created.

The town square is just as I recall, its gracious Roman arches and reddish stone unaltered, each side elevated by two storeys of long, slender windows embellished with wrought iron balconies. In the centre is a fountain which I do not think was there before and on the south-west corner, a covered market. Otherwise, everything corresponds exactly to the pictures in my memory – but for the scale. The wide expanse of ancient cobbles has shrunk to the dimensions of a compact little square which I cross in fifteen strides. The town hall and the offices of the mayor around the perimeter are not much taller than the height of two men. I might easily scale those walls myself, if I had a mind to. I have entered a miniature version of the Ávila of my childhood, scorched and still. The only living creature about is an ancient dog stretched out in the shade. On hearing the clip-clop of Caminante's hooves he raises his muzzle and surveys us, then lets his big head flop back onto his paws, closes his eyes and snuffles his way back to slumber.

Caminante is docile today and allows me to lead him along an alleyway that winds towards the cathedral. Soon we reach the ancient Roman gate. For a moment I pause to gaze upon the gentle curves of the warm, honey-coloured walls that embrace the city, cast my eyes across the sloping fields and the convent of Encarnación nestled in the landscape before me.

I hesitate, wondering whether I should tether Caminante here and walk across the fields instead of taking the road. As though reading my mind, he nuzzles my hand. "Very well, Caminante. The road it is. Let's see if we can find you a drink." He butts his head against my satchel and I pull out an apple. Others may mock, but I fancy he does not like to be left alone. Out here there is not a soul and no sound but for the buzzing of bees and the chirruping of crickets. I rub his smooth, shining flank and inhale the pleasing scent of his coat.

Together we pick our way down the stony track that meets the north-bound path to the convent, stopping first at the crossroads to let Caminante drink from a trough that looks to have been there since Roman times. On one side, the granite is carved with the curlicues and flourishes typical of the Arabic script. This convent was constructed on the site of an old Jewish cemetery which, in even more ancient times, my mother said, had been a *mezquita*. The sisters must have had a good reason to move to this old mosque outside the city walls – though their Hebrew and Moorish predecessors would have had no choice in the matter.

Instead of approaching the convent by the main porch, I enter, as instructed, through a little circular courtyard tucked away to one side. The strict rules of enclosure observed by the sisters require that guests obtain special permission to visit, which is granted only in very limited circumstances. All this, of course, has been arranged for me by Ortiz. I am not sure of the conditions under which I will meet this Sor Úrsula, whether I will be obliged to address her through a double grill, in compliance with usual procedures. But in that case, how will she conduct me around the building, as I have requested? I loop Caminante's reins through an iron ring set into the wall, taking care to ensure that he is but loosely tethered and within reach of a half-filled water trough close to the gate. I slap his haunches and strike the bell. The echo fills me with melancholy.

"Do not fret, my old companion. I will not delay too long."

The dark wood of the door, blackened by years, is fashioned from three imposing panels bolted together with metal studs. A hinged section at head height may be opened separately, allowing the nuns to inspect callers before deciding whether or not to admit them.

I take a step back and survey my surroundings. The building itself is large enough – at one time more than a hundred and fifty sisters lived here – but there is an air of defeat about the place. The few plants straggling along the wall, tired geraniums and herbs I do not recognise, are wilting. Spindly foliage clings to broken canes, some of the stems about to bend and break. Perhaps the community has dwindled, leaving only a few elderly nuns who are unable to maintain the place.

Lost in my musings, the scraping of hinges returns me to the present. A pair of light eyes surveys me through the grill. Even though I am expected, I must introduce myself. "I am Fray Martín de Sepúlveda, sent by Prior Ortiz and Archbishop Crespo to speak with Sor Úrsula." The eyes disappear and the door creaks open.

The vestibule I enter is no more than a narrow corridor lit by beams of sunlight filtering through a few small windows that look over the courtyard. To my left, an interior wall is punctuated at regular intervals by imposing double grills which afford a glimpse of the rooms inside. The sisters receive their very few guests here: they in the inside room, barely visible behind the grill, their visitors seated outside. The ceiling, low and heavily beamed, bears down upon me and the clatter of my boots on the stone floor startles me – of course, the young sister's footfalls are silent, as the members of her community usually walk barefoot, or in winter shod in plain hemp sandals. I wonder if she will bid me be seated on one of the chairs alongside the double grills. But we pass instead through another door into a somewhat larger vestibule, from which a staircase rises alongside another door. This, I take to be the main entrance to the building. The young novice indicates a second double door straight ahead.

To my relief, this opens onto a real parlour. The room is sparsely furnished but has all the necessities that permit the sisters to receive official guests. While I await my witness, the novice, who does not speak or meet my eye, flits from the room and returns bearing a cup of cool water which I sip gratefully. She holds out her hand to receive the straw hat I have begun wearing, on the advice of Madre Carmela, to protect this fair skin of mine from the sun. Like me, the young novice has blue eyes, her light brows and lashes suggesting blond hair, also like mine before it started to turn grey.

We are of so many types, the people of this peninsula of ours. Pale or rosy skin in the regions of the north, luscious olive complexions and velvet-contoured features like those of Madre Carmela amongst the people of Andalucía. Perhaps her family tree, like that of Fray Juan, conceals some *converso* ancestor or *morisco* grandfather. So many were expelled or went into hiding when the edicts of our great Catholic monarchs of the last century made traitors of both our Arab and Jewish brethren. Still, their beauty of countenance continues through their bloodline. The clear oval disc of Madre Carmela's face appears to me unbidden and brings a smile to my lips.

Sor Úrsula shows none of the reticence I have come to expect from those of her Order. She is a garrulous little woman who has evidently been greatly flattered to have become a centre of attention, through neither fault nor merit of her own, often called to give testimony concerning certain events in the lives of her celebrated superiors which occurred in her extreme youth. She bustles into the room and sets before me bread and a generous portion of cheese, which, she assures me, is made from the milk of the convent's goats and churned by the nuns' own hands. From an ancient earthenware jug, she pours another cup of water. The cold, crystalline stream that spills from the lip of the roughly hewn ceramic comes from the well behind the choir, the same choir where Sor Úrsula's predecessors attempted to bar Teresa's first entry to the convent as mother prioress.

No, she admits, I have guessed correctly, she herself is a little too young to have witnessed those disturbances. She does not recall exactly when she entered the convent but is certain that she took her first vows in the year before Fray Juan left Encarnación under mysterious circumstances. I do not think that this Sor Úrsula, with her round, innocent face, will be equipped to enlighten me about those events. For the moment, I do not ask. She is eager, however, to tell me what she does know and I realise that this fluent, practised delivery is the hallmark of a story that has been told, and no doubt embellished in the telling, many times before.

"It was the day before Sor Constanza died." My unease mounts. I begin to despair of hearing a version that in the slightest measure approaches the limpid, balanced account I require, if I am to have any success in reaching a reasoned judgement on the reality of the matter. I stifle a sigh. However, there is nothing to be gained by conveying my scepticism to this little woman who, no doubt, is breaking one of the vows of her Order by taking such pleasure in speaking to me of things that occurred almost forty years ago.

"And why is this of significance?" I ask, mildly enough. But I have offended her. Sor Úrsula purses her lips and makes a slight wriggle in her chair that reminds me of nothing so much as a plump little bird ruffling its feathers, affronted at this encroachment on its territory. Clearly, no one has ever questioned the accuracy of the little nun's account of these matters. She inspects me, head tilted, and under the guise of slow and apparently helpful speech, endeavours to put me in what she imagines to be my place.

"Had it not been that Sor Constanza was in her final agony, the mother prioress would never have been disturbed." I do not follow her reasoning. My puzzlement must show in my countenance.

"One of the farm boys came running from the hospital, having received a message that Sor Constanza would not last the night and that the father confessor should come at once to hear her last confession and give her the Last Rites."

"The father confessor being Fray Juan?"

Sor Úrsula nods.

"So he was Madre Teresa's confessor, too?"

"Of course."

I find it strange that although Fray Juan was barely thirty years old when Teresa summoned him to Encarnación, she should have appointed him to guide her and her community in matters of the soul, she herself being then almost twice his age. But then the 'mysterious circumstances' carried him off. Crespo and Ortiz have made it clear that they will not discuss any possible connection between Teresa's reforms in Encarnación, and the imprisonment of Fray Juan, who was at that time her most favoured colleague and friend. Yet I cannot rid myself of the suspicion that herein lies the source of many of Fray Juan's later tribulations.

The thought reminds me of the fate of the unfortunate Fray Jerónimo Gracián, who later became Teresa's confessor and perhaps her most intimate friend of all. It is a name I hear mentioned by several of my sources, including that cultured Inquisitor, Doctor Enrique. Apparently, the fate of Fray Jerónimo was even worse than that of Fray Juan. I believe he was stripped of his habit, and for many years endured the most dire circumstances, at whose hands and for what reasons, I do not yet know. Later. I must not allow myself to be distracted.

"And was Fray Juan also your father confessor?"

"I knew him, of course, but not well. That is, I had no direct contact with him in the short while between my arrival at this convent and his departure. I took my preliminary vows only a few weeks before he left, that is…" she hesitates and I wonder if perhaps she is better informed on this subject than I had thought, "…before he was… moved."

Moved. Well, that is one way of putting it. In spite of the seriousness of her tone, I am tempted to laugh, but I maintain my air of gravity with a restrained smile, hoping to convey encouragement sufficient to the sharing of confidences, but not so much as to invite outright embellishment.

"The mother prioress had insisted that she should be kept informed of Sor Constanza's condition. That is why Sor Beatriz persisted so, even when it was known that Fray Juan was hearing Madre Teresa's confession."

"Persisted? In what?"

"In searching for her. In knocking on the door of the *locutorio*, even knowing that she most likely was at prayer. Or in conference with Fray Juan."

Naturally. Confessions, like meetings with people from outside the community, are conducted in privacy, confessor on one side of the *reja*, that double grill which separates the nun from her spiritual guide or her visitors from the outside world. I should like to see that room.

"There was no answer, even though Sor Beatriz knocked again and again. She was first cousin of the mother prioress, entrusted by Madre Teresa with the most delicate of commissions."

Of course, I know who Sor Beatriz is. Had I known that she has been dead these three years past, I would not have consented to waste my time on a second-hand account of events that has already been accepted as the unquestioned truth. And I really have no wish to encourage Sor Úrsula's undoubted talent for storytelling. I compose my features into a motionless mask, determined to show neither interest nor admiration, however anxious the little glances she casts up at me. The lusty

Sor Dolores was fortunate to have shared a corridor with the young Carmela – whose laughing, tawny eyes have more than once illuminated the misty moments between my sleep and my waking – and not this little gossip. I force my attention back to Sor Úrsula's contented chirpings.

"What happened then?"

"Sor Diamana ran out to the orchard thinking that the father confessor and the mother prioress might be walking there. But they were nowhere to be found. Madre Teresa was not in the orchard, nor in her cell, nor in the kitchen so Sor Beatriz knocked on the parlour door one last time to be absolutely sure, for poor Sor Constanza was in her last agony and needed the ministrations of the father confessor, and the mother prioress had expressly ordered that she be kept informed..."

"Yes, yes."

"And that was when she saw."

Sor Úrsula stops speaking. This is a well-practised, dramatic pause. She must discern in my eye a glint of intolerance, for she hurries on with her account. Perhaps she will learn soon that truly sensational events require no gilding.

"Who saw? Saw what?"

"The mother prioress. Kneeling by the confessional grill, hands folded in prayer, her head thrown back, unnaturally immobile, scarcely breathing, her eyelids mere slits showing the milk of her eyes which had rolled up in their sockets. And her body entirely enveloped in a pale white glow."

Unnaturally immobile? Mere slits? Sor Úrsula recites these details as though reading from a list imprinted inside her own fluttering eyelids.

"An ecstasy?"

"Of course. A rapture. She was enraptured with the Holy Spirit."

This is what I have been expecting. Rapture. Ecstasy. Words brimming with significance, replete with an energy that one might almost call magical, were not that term itself heretical. The visitation of the Divine upon the human, the triumph of the spiritual body over the corporeal. Swooning. The loss of normal senses, yet the heightening of those same senses, raising the self out of the self.

If that is what it was. For who can ever tell what happens within the heart and mind, much less the soul, of another human being?

"How did Sor Beatriz know it was a true ecstasy? A rapture, and not simply an intensely prayerful position?"

The little nun is momentarily stunned into silence, amazed that anyone would doubt the veracity of her report.

"For we had seen it before, Padre!"

I am not sure how to point out that this does not answer my question.

"You mean, surely, that others had seen something of the kind. You yourself said that this…" I search for the most neutral word I can find, "…event was observed by Sor Beatriz, who then recounted it to you. And to everyone else in Ávila," I add. But Sor Úrsula is beyond the perception of mockery.

"There were others, Padre, many other raptures that the mother prioress experienced. Quite often, sometimes even in Church, when people, fine ladies, were present. Once or twice she even had to ask us to sit on her."

I have heard this tale before but I would like to hear it from one who was actually present. "Because of…?"

"Her levitation, Padre. She would find herself raised from the ground, not much, just so that her feet would touch the seat, but enough that others outside our community might notice. Members of the public congregation. The mother prioress did not wish to set tongues wagging in the town, for such happenings can cause misunderstandings."

Indeed they can. The gravity and sanctity of Teresa's raptures and levitations are now verified and well documented. What I need to know now is how much all of this can illuminate my understanding of the life that Fray Juan led during the five years he served as father confessor to this community. First, however, Sor Úrsula must finish her story.

"Besides, Madre Teresa really did not like such elevations, Padre. They frightened her sometimes and when they did not frighten her, they embarrassed her. She told us that she often asked the good Lord please to desist from the elevations, although she did not mind the raptures, or if he could at least desist from raising her from the ground in public. Whereupon he told her – for mother prioress had direct conversations with the Lord – that that was what he did for his friends. And she told him she was not surprised, then, that he had so few friends."

We both laugh. This is a good story, well known and moreover, according to other accounts of Teresa's demeanour, the personality that emerges from her writing and from the words of those who knew her, it rings true.

"And the father confessor? Was he also in the parlour on that day?"

"Fray Juan was also there, Padre. They were imbued with the rapture of the Holy Spirit, both of them together, mother prioress on this side of the grill and he on the other. But Fray Juan was very greatly elevated, much above the ground. Almost to the ceiling."

"Tell me, Sor Úrsula, exactly what Sor Beatriz told you, with respect to the father confessor. As much detail as you can remember."

She hesitates for a moment and looks at me somewhat fearfully as she struggles to recall words she heard almost four decades ago. She does not find it easy to express her thoughts when required to depart from her customary script. A glimmer of compassion flickers within me.

"Could I, perhaps, see the room where this took place? You can point out to me where these momentous events occurred. It cannot be easy to remember such precise details, after all this time."

Such broad brush strokes of a story will not suffice for my purposes: they never have. In order to pursue any line of enquiry, I must immerse myself in the myriad details, sink into my subject, its surroundings, which in this case is the room where Fray Juan heard Teresa's confession on that day. I wish to see what he saw and what those who observed him saw, that I might absorb the reality and the truth of it. How strange that sometimes, particularities that are at first sight unimportant, may later prove to be critical in achieving a robust under-standing of events. Or exoneration from accusations. Not that I always know which detail to seek, or where I might find it. But I will recognise it when I see it. As my tormentors in Salamanca did, in the end.

We traverse the oak-panelled corridor by which I entered and mount the narrow staircase that rises from the front of the house. At the top, I step out into a spacious room with plain, gleaming white walls, a high ceiling and a small, square window that looks on to the courtyard where Caminante awaits me. The harsh Castilian light casts a dense shadow across the floor. Against the far wall, directly in front of me, a low pew occupies the space beneath a wide-meshed grill set into an interior window. This was Teresa's office during the three years she lived here as mother prioress. In this very room, Fray Juan received her confession, she on this side of the grill, he on the other. The interior room beyond is broad but low-ceilinged and dark. A door in the far wall of this outer room leads to the main staircase used by the few visitors who had occasion to parley with Teresa; and no doubt, by her father confessor.

"And has this room been changed since your earliest days here, Sor Úrsula? This pew, for example, this grill? Perhaps it has been widened. Or moved."

"The only changes, Padre, and they are not really changes at all, are made every year or two when the farm boys come from a nearby estate to do the jobs we sisters cannot or prefer not to do. One of them always whitewashes this room and makes any repairs needed to ensure that the place is fit to receive guests. The rest – polishing and sweeping – we sisters of the community take care of ourselves."

I make my way around the outer room, Sor Úrsula an uneasy presence behind me. The place is bare of embellishment but for a simple wooden cross hanging on a nail above the grill, and a bunch of tall, pale lilies arranged in a pitcher made of reddish clay. Their perfume pervades the room, weighing heavy on the air, in spite of the open window and a light breeze floating in from the courtyard. Since my little sister's funeral, I have never cared for lilies. Their ostentation seems vulgar to me. And they remind me of death. Pepita. My mother.

"Lilies were the mother prioress's favourite flower," chirps Sor Ursula, misunderstanding my glance. "In the month of March this year, we had them every day. Tall, white ones, in honour of the hundred years since her birth. Since her elevation to Blessed, we place fresh lilies here every week."

"Very appropriate," I murmur. Of course, the beatification of their founding mother two years ago was an important event but this community does not seem to have prospered since the death of their most celebrated prioress. Notwithstanding the cleanliness of the original building, there is an air of poverty about the place. I recall the bread and the cheese with discomfort.

Sor Úrsula continues to hover by the door but she seems eager to speak. I wonder if she begins to understand my method.

"Sor Beatriz was standing by this doorway, having just knocked for the eighth or ninth time before she entered. And that was when she saw the mother prioress." She points towards the pew.

"Who must have had her back to the door," I murmur.

"She was looking upwards, her shoulders arched and her head thrown back."

"So anyone standing here," I position myself in the spot she has indicated, "would have a clear view of the interior room beyond the grill. Where Fray Juan was sitting to hear Madre Teresa's confession."

"Exactly!" The little nun's cheeks are pink with excitement, that together we have confirmed her vague recollections by means of careful examination of the surroundings. I understand her pleasure, for I share it: the delight of interrogating knowledge, not necessarily in order to dispute it, as Sor Úrsula had first thought my purpose, but rather, to test it.

My experience in Salamanca proved that the scrutiny of evidence is too often discouraged. The notion that we must take everything on trust, including the strangest stories of improbable happenings, has always amazed me – as if our deepest beliefs could be shaken by a few questions born of reason! I even dare to think that faith and yes, loyalty to those individuals who profess it, is the most over-exalted of the virtues. What merit can there be in extinguishing the very light of reason with which the Lord endowed us, the power of thought which raises us from the beasts of the field? Might not the absence of such reflection, rather, endanger the institutions of the faith? Unexamined beliefs must surely leave the Church Temporal open to superstition, to bizarre and ungodly practices. Hence the rigour of my questions, which poor, simple Sor Úrsula had least expected.

I must take care, though, for this kind of interrogation was not what Crespo and Ortiz had in mind when they asked me to verify facts that are known to be miracles, plain and simple, to which the application of reason is not required. However, Crespo and Ortiz are not here today.

"And in the alcove, the room beyond the grill, Sor Beatriz could see... what?"

"Fray Juan's feet, Padre, just his feet. Unshod, of course, and slightly extended from the chair."

"His chair? What do you mean?"

"He was seated, Padre, and he was elevated almost to the ceiling. On this very chair. You see?" She points to the corner behind me and indicates a small, squat chair, the worn leather pinned to the wooden frame with plain brass studs, long discoloured. It is rather low and would be an uncomfortable height for one of my stature. But it is sturdy. And heavy.

I stifle a sigh. I am convinced, up to a point, by the plausibility of the details presented to me here today. I can believe in Fray Juan's bare feet, yes, for it is only in the deepest winter that the community of the Discalced Order wear sandals. But the chair? I try to maintain an impassive countenance that conceals my scepticism concerning this last detail. It is a most significant elaboration, to claim that the infusion of the Divine ecstasy may elevate not only the enraptured body, but inanimate objects as well. My head begins to ache and I look around for my cup of water. Sor Úrsula hastens to fetch it. When she returns I have somewhat recovered.

"Did Sor Beatriz say what she could see of Fray Juan from her position at the door? Perhaps his throat, too, was bared, or there might have been a bright light about his forehead."

"That, she did not say," Sor Úrsula is firm. "All she could see were his feet, and the lower part of his habit, its folds draped around the chair."

The little nun crosses the room and motions me to join her in a spot beside the door. We take a few silent moments to survey that part of the interior room beyond the grill that can easily be seen from this position. If things happened as she has just described, it is true that only the very lowest part of the body would be visible from the door.

My mind drifts to another time, long gone. I am about eight or nine years old, it is a hot day, I am playing down at the river with some of the children from the village. My father has forbidden me to consort with them, sons of the blacksmith, the shepherd, the small farmers, the baker; for he worries that I might learn rough ways and become unfit for society and the position that he has already planned for me, marriage to a daughter of one of his wealthy merchant friends. But my mother simply laughs at him and whispers to me to be sure there is no mud on my shoes when I come home. After Pepita died and my mother followed her to the grave I stopped frequenting those playmates, innocence and childhood now in the past, my father reduced to a querulous, frightened old man who no longer cared about his young son's muddy boots and unsuitable friends.

But on that day by the river, all this sadness was yet in the future and I spent long hours making sport with playmates of many different stations. Sometimes, the women and maids of the village would carry their household linen down to the riverbank and when they had finished the washing, some of the thick, milky substance they used to clean their clothes, which in our village was a paste made of olive oil and ashes, would melt into the water into a thick, frothy scum. Dissolved to a certain consistency, smeared on a hollow reed – the kind that is long and strong enough to make a whistle – you can create the most beautiful, glassy rainbow spheres of many different sizes that go floating off in the air; and there is a delicacy and skill in the making of them, for your breath must be just strong enough to form the little globe from the watery paste, but not so strong as to shatter it before it floats away.

Some of the boys, I amongst them, are blowing and bursting dozens of the little spheres before they ever have a chance to be carried off into the air, but one survives. Its brilliance gleams against the azure of the summer sky. I am determined to create another, even larger and stronger, so, long after the other boys have jumped into the cool water I remain there on the bank where I try and fail and try and fail again and soon my breathing steadies, mounts to the crown of my head, descends to the soles of my feet, my vision is both sharper and softer than before, colours glow, I meld with them and with all things around me, my playmates, too, their laughter and their cries take on the same glow, for how long I know not, an hour, a minute, I gradually dissolve into them and they into me, there is no Fernando or Jaime or Alfonso or blacksmiths or shepherds or lawyers, there are no bodies and no boundaries, all is a wondrous globe, a marvellous rainbow sphere that glimmers in the sky, floats into the sunlight and we are all part of it, blended, merged, one.

And then the lovely globe bursts, a tiny drop of cool liquid falls upon my brow and returns me, in sorrow, to the frontiers and boundaries which form once again, solidify, separate us from the heavens, from this world and the next, from each other, from us all.

Coruela, Old Castile,
Fourteenth day of April in the Year of Our Lord, 1616.

No man is a brute in his own eyes. It is a rare being indeed who, in full knowledge, commits actions of great inhumanity and evil without the sanction of a great leader or cause. And what better cause than the glory of our Lord Jesus Christ?

Such was the way of my father's uncle Ginés, who denied the presence of souls in the native people of New Spain because, as he wrote, *"those whose condition is such that their function is the use of their bodies and nothing better can be expected of them, those, I say, are slaves of nature."* No better, then, than beasts, born to serve the will of our monarch, to slave for our empire and for our God. My great-uncle Ginés was convinced of the justice and piety of his own actions. Just like this Fray Alonso, whose words and demeanour have today so unsettled and troubled me.

I had not intended to break my journey from Toledo to Madrid for a second night. There is time enough to reach my destination before darkness falls. But Caminante is weary and, as I discover when we stop for water at this *mesón* in the tiny hamlet of Coruela, I am myself in need of rest. Only now, seated on this upturned wine casket in the little garden behind the house, as I lean on a makeshift bench to write my journal and contemplate the *sierra* that encircles all of Castile in the dusty evening light, do I permit myself to own how much this last encounter has perturbed me.

I reach for the pitcher of wine that the innkeeper's wife has set before me, accompanied by a glazed bowl filled with stew whose aroma – lamb, rosemary and other herbs I cannot identify – nourishes my senses and my spirit, even before I have taken a single mouthful. But this hand that pours the wine is not quite steady. So, yes. I will lodge here for the night, where I am unknown and blessedly unremarked. The vista of the arid plain and the blue mountains rising in the distance calms me; and the knowledge that for the next few hours, no one in the world knows where I am, is a comfort. Caminante is happily stabled and rested, the rich stew and heavy wine begin to restore me. Little by little, I feel equal to reflect on the error of judgement that has led me to this place.

During the course of my interview with old Fray Alonso – and perhaps in having met with him at all – I made a bad mistake. Not only did I misjudge his temperament, I seriously underestimated his resolve. Misled by the softness of his voice and the delicacy of his manners, I allowed myself to believe that the hardened gaoler he must have been four decades ago had softened, that he had repented of his iniquitous treatment of Fray Juan, that the wisdom and, perhaps, vulnerabilities of great age might have led him to feel shame for the actions of his middle years. But can a person change so much? Is the patina of old age enough to absolve the savageries enacted by younger selves and permit a person to put on a different character, like a new coat? I used to think so. When my great-uncle Ginés was failing, when his powers of intellect and oration had faded and his body shrivelled to a withered husk, the shame and disgust he aroused in me mingled with pity for the brittle shell he had become.

But this Fray Alonso is of another type altogether. Granite-eyed. Unrepentant, without a shred of regret for past actions, believing them to be just and with merit.

Our interview begins coolly enough, I cultivating my usual manner of aloofness, which Fray Alonso matches without effort. He is a tall, thin old man, agile and still able to work the fields and the orchard where he has spent the morning inspecting the young pomegranates. They are just starting to put forth tiny bright orange blossoms that cover the sloping terrace with a carpet of fire. In no hurry at all, he removes his boots and places his wide-brimmed hat on the windowsill of his cell where he has insisted on receiving me. It seems that I have interrupted his labours.

At last, having taken his place behind a small bench which seems to serve him both as dining table and desk, he is settled. The single window commands a dramatic view of the river Tagus and the old Moorish fort on the crest of the hill. It is not quite noon. A golden glow from the rays of the sun warms the bare stone and brings cheer to the cell, though I would not like to spend many hours here in the deep of winter. Having no other choice, I wait while he arranges some loose papers on his desk. Once satisfied, he leans back in his chair and surveys the ceiling, giving no sign of having heard my question. I put it to him again.

"Correct. I had the immense good fortune to be assigned to Toledo very early in my religious life. Mostly spent in this very monastery, which I joined many years ago."

"Thirty-seven years ago." Having troubled myself to make a careful study of most of the documents in Crespo's oaken chest, I want my host to know that I have taken particular note of his file and am aware of his history. He rewards me with a curt nod.

"If you say so. I will not disagree."

His answer is an affectation and I admit that his manner of studied indifference irritates me. I plunge in. This, I now see, is my first mistake.

"Fray Juan was brought to you in chains?"

Some sharpness in my voice or in my choice of words alerts him to the presence of a judgement: an unfavourable one. He glances up at me and this time his dark eyebrows arch in surprise.

"Of course. He was a prisoner. Though the chains were removed when he was inside his cell. He was shackled only when escorted from it."

"For what purposes did that occur?"

His gaze returns to the ceiling. Fray Juan, in the decades that have passed since his death, has been so much venerated that this man cannot have forgotten his most illustrious role in life: as gaoler to one of the most pious of men of Christendom who will soon, like Teresa, become Blessed of the Church. Perhaps even a saint, one day. This silence, this feigned uncertainty, begins to raise my temper.

"How often was he taken from his cell?"

Fray Alonso's eyes close and his brow puckers in mock concentration. "Once, perhaps twice each week."

"Each day, surely? To perform his..."

"The prisoner was facilitated in meeting his bodily needs within the confines of his cell."

I make no comment and endeavour to show no reaction. The space that Fray Juan occupied during those nine months could not really be called a cell. It was an alcove, rather, a recess in the wall, which in earlier times had indeed been used as a privy. But to serve as permanent living quarters as well?

It was perhaps unwise of me, when I arrived the day before, to have insisted on viewing the room where Fray Juan was confined during those months of imprisonment in Toledo. On my arrival I was greeted by a young novice who showed me to my dormitory before disappearing into a maze of stone corridors. For the next two hours, I strolled through the cloisters and met not a soul, all the friars being occupied in silent meditation or in preparing for the singing of the Office of None. I profited from the solitude to prepare my questions for the man who had been Fray Juan's gaoler within these walls, so many years ago.

My perambulations soon led me to the kitchen. There, I encountered an ancient friar who, by a stroke of luck, has lived in the monastery almost as long as Fray Alonso. Having explained the purpose of my visit, I requested that he escort me to that part of the building where Fray Juan had been confined. My credentials, and the importance of my task, left him unimpressed.

"I am sure that Fray Alonso will show you, when he is freed from his obligations."

Was that a flicker of unease at the particular nature of my request? Or a simple, habitual reflex to obstruct the slightest request for assistance?

"Fray Alonso and I have an appointment to meet at noon tomorrow. I do not think that he will be available before that time."

"I must prepare the vegetables for the soup. Else dinner will not be served on time."

The old friar glared at me. The occupants of menial positions in any Order can wield influence far beyond that which their station would suggest, often acting as covert gatekeepers who may grant, or deny, access to people and favours. Still, I had not arrived a day early to be put off by the preparation of soup. But this wizened little cook had a stubborn set to his jaw that warned me against further reference to the importance of my mission here.

"I have no wish to delay your brother friars' meal," I answered, in humble tones. "And if you will allow it, I will be glad to assist you in the shelling of the peas and the chopping of the carrots."

I approached the table where the vegetables were scattered and picked up a small-bladed knife. The little friar, who had so far declined to tell me his name, snatched it from my hand. "I came here a day in advance of our appointment on purpose," I continued, smiling and undaunted, "in order to prepare for my conversation with Fray Alonso. I am sure that he will expect me to be acquainted with all aspects of the subject we are bound to discuss."

In truth, I was sure that the topic of Fray Juan's accommodation during his time in this monastery was the last subject that Fray Alonso would wish to discuss with me. But the little cook did not need to know that. He hesitated, weighing his reluctance to oblige a troublesome stranger against the possibility of incurring Fray Alonso's wrath. That his ruminations ended in his covering the bowl of half-shelled peas with a muslin cloth and removing a heavy key from the windowsill, muttering under his breath all the while as he beckoned me to follow, gave me some insight into the character and influence of the absent Fray Alonso.

Across the courtyard he led me, along one side of the arched cloisters and down a windowless corridor, towards a stairway set in the wall behind a low oaken door. I followed as he climbed, step by weary step, his gnarled fingers clutching at an iron rail curved around the walls, for we were ascending and turning, mounting a narrow tower. Was this the only entrance to these quarters? The little friar made no answer. It occurred to me that he might be hard of hearing.

At last, the staircase opened onto a bright, airy room which I judged must occupy a large part of the second floor of the building, lofty and gracious in construction, the principal storey which the Italians call the *piano nobile*. One entire wall comprised a line of wide arches overlooking a terrace with a spectacular view of the river and the undulating hills of the Kingdom of Toledo. Not such a bad place of confinement, then. But the old cook did not linger there and instead hobbled toward a low door set into the farthest corner of the room, out of sight. He stopped in front of it and stood to one side as I approached.

"It is not locked."

I leaned on the door, which swung open to reveal a dark interior. A few broken benches and three wooden trunks, rather like the one in my own office, were pushed back against one wall. This was evidently some kind of storeroom. I looked at my guide in puzzlement.

"Long ago, when I was young, this was a dormitory." He waved his hand to indicate the wide-arched room behind us. "And this," he pointed to the dank little store-room, "was used as a latrine."

"And Fray Juan was quartered…?"

Without speaking, he pointed into the darkness. I took one step across the threshold and turned back to face the little cook.

"Here? In this… cupboard? Fray Juan was kept here, in the dark, for nine whole months?"

The little friar gazed at me, shrugged his bony shoulders and muttered something that might have referred to the preparation of peas.

"Leave me here a while." I waited until the painful shuffle of his sandals receded, one step at a time, down the stone staircase. Only when I was left in silence, did I venture into the interior of this… alcove, cupboard… which was Fray Juan's prison for nine whole months, almost four decades past.

Although it was just after noon, it was not at first easy to discern the shape and dimensions of the place. There was no window, nothing more than a slit of an opening in the wall close to the ceiling, about three fingers wide. Just enough to permit an arrow of sunlight to spear the darkness and pool on the opposite wall. In order to profit from this shaft of sun, I edged my way towards the largest of the wooden chests and stamped hard on the lid to check if it would hold my weight. Reassured, I clambered onto it. Once upright, I felt the warmth of the narrow sunbeam, first upon my forehead, then across my eyes and face, until I stood at my full height, when it came to rest at the base of my throat. According to Teresa and others who knew him, Fray Juan was not a tall man, perhaps a full head shorter than I. So, he must have raised himself at least by the height of the trunk upon which I was standing – on top of his bed, perhaps? – and lifted his breviary or his papers, so that a spear of light would fall upon them. Excluding this splash of illumination, the room was in such deep shadow that without a candle, reading would be impossible.

I stood there for a few moments, my feet planted on the wooden chest, without moving my head, while my vision adjusted to the dimness. This sliver of light would soon slip away. If I dragged the trunk along the wall I could follow it for a little while, but then the laws of nature would compel that ever-weakening beam to retreat into the blackest corner, where it would soon fade and disappear. The notion expanded and floated through my mind like a poisonous miasma. I closed my eyes, leaned against the cold wall, inhaled. A dank smell made me cough. Perhaps the crack high on the external wall, which seemed to be dripping slime, was new. Perhaps the air was not so fetid forty years ago. Voices, and the lowing of cattle in the fields rose from the working farms below.

Disorientated and unsteady, I clambered down from the chest and, placing one foot in front of the other, heel to toe, paced out the cell. Ten tight steps brought me from the doorway to the external wall. A jumble of old benches and pews piled against one wall made it difficult to measure the cell's width but I estimated it to be about half its length, perhaps a little more. Were I to lie down and stretch out my arms, my fingertips might just graze the walls. Fray Juan, being shorter in stature, would have had a handspan or two to spare.

So, when Fray Alonso assures me of the wisdom of confining a man within such a space, for such a length of time – or any time – I cannot repress a shudder.

"What of the washing of his clothes, how was that managed?

Did you have charge of that?"

"You are no doubt aware that some of the most pious of the desert fathers inflicted certain austerities on themselves."

"Of course. Extreme fasting, lack of sleep..."

"And there were some who ignored the... hygienic... needs of the body. Who eschewed washing or changing their clothes from one season to the next. That was yet another mortification of the flesh, conceived to bring the person closer to the sufferings of Christ. As it was known that this prisoner had a taste for austerities, the conditions you describe were considered suitable for him. After all, Fray Juan and Teresa and Gracián and Ana de Jesús," he spoke the names with a spitting contempt, "insisted upon the need to reject the more relaxed practices of the Mitigated Rule."

"Mitigated by Pope Eugene. In fourteen fifty-two."

"Indeed. But Teresa and those other misguided reformers were determined to restore the earlier Carmelite practices and return to the purity of the Ancient Rule, as they saw it. Fray Juan's detention here gave him an opportunity to put those beliefs into practice."

I am silent for a moment, in part distracted by the mention of those names – Gracián, Ana de Jesús – which I have seen mentioned in some of the documents I have studied in recent weeks, in part shocked that Fray Alonso should present the torture of Fray Juan as some kind of spiritual gift.

"So, he was brought from his cell, once or twice a week, to the refectory? To take his meals with his brother friars?" I am aware of the absurdity of my next question. I know the answer. Fray Alonso fastens me with his grey, granite look.

"Not to eat," he answers without flinching. "To be disciplined."

Whippings, then. I do not falter. "By whom?"

"By his brother friars." Exactly as Fray Angelo reported. The old man's gaze does not waver. "His offence was most serious."

"And that offence was what, Fray Alonso?"

The silence lengthens. I resist the impulse to fill it. After some minutes, the old man rises from his chair. Three firm strides take him to the window where he remains, immobile, his back turned towards me. Then, a deep sigh. An extravagant raising and falling of the shoulders. Meaning: how can any reasonable man answer such foolish questions? His voice, when he speaks, is light, almost jocular. "I am not sure I understand what you mean."

I am determined that he will not provoke me. "The offence. You said it was most serious. What was Fray Juan's offence? The cause that justified his abduction?"

Fray Alonso wheels around to face me. "Arrest. Fray Juan was not abducted. He was arrested."

Well, that is a matter of opinion, I do not say. Apprehended by strangers in black robes who had lain in wait for him near his living quarters for days, perhaps weeks; his humble lodgings invaded and ransacked; brought by force in the middle of the night to a secret location that no one, not even Teresa, could discover. Not a normal arrest. So many irregularities, the only sliver of hope remaining that this could not, therefore, have been the work of the Inquisition. An internal matter. A Carmelite solution to a Carmelite problem, orders handed down from on high. But from whom? Fray Alonso is not about to tell me. Perhaps he does not know.

Since the word 'abduction' passed my lips, his eyes have not left my face and in the rigid stillness of his posture I sense the alertness of both predator and prey. In my mode of expression, my choice of words, I have revealed too much. His silence, also, tells me that I have hit my mark; that I may have gone too far.

"Very well. 'Arrest,' if you will." I leaden my voice with mockery. "When Fray Juan was pursued, manhandled in his own quarters, beaten and dragged across Old Castile in the secrecy of the night, removed from his post as father confessor to the Encarnación nuns and detained in an unknown location for the greater part of a year. To live under conditions that were somewhat uncomfortable."

Fray Alonso's clenched jaw warns me that once again I have hit my mark or overstepped it. But it is too late to withdraw.

"And not for the first time. Is that correct? Is it not true that both Fray Juan and his fellow confessor Fray Germán had both been under surveillance by agents of your monastery for months? That the townsfolk had mounted a vigil to protect him, to ensure that he would not be abducted – beg pardon, arrested – as he had been the previous year and conducted to Medina del Campo, to the distress of his aged mother and brother who lived there? And that he was released on the orders of the highest authority, the papal nuncio?"

His gimlet eyes narrow as he moves from the window and brushes past me to retrieve a paper and a plume from his desk. "On whose authority did you say you are conducting this research?" He dips the tip of the plume into a small glass dish half-filled with ink. "And for what purpose?"

For the first time, it occurs to me to wonder why Fray Alonso is not on the list of witnesses supplied by Crespo and Ortiz, even though he is named by several sources as Fray Juan's first gaoler in Toledo. I added his name on my own initiative, assuming the omission of such a central witness from the investigation to be an oversight. Perhaps it was not.

"This investigation is taking place by Royal Decree, with the collaboration of the Holy See." Even if he dispatches a messenger on horseback to Madrid as soon as I leave, it will take at least four days to verify my declaration, if he has a mind and the authority to do so. Better a big lie than a small one, then, as the consequences of either, if there are consequences, will be much the same.

"In short, Fray Alonso, all you need to know about me is," I pause to take a sip of water, "that I am here."

Fray Alonso nods once and raises his eyebrows, a faint smile playing across his lean, still handsome features. He seems to have reached a decision. When he finally speaks, his tone is conciliatory.

"I did not apprehend Fray Juan. Nor did I give the order for his apprehension. I merely carried out my duties, in accordance with my vow of obedience."

"Fray Alonso, I repeat: what was the charge?"

"To my knowledge," his voice is level and without emotion, "the prisoner had violated the Rule of the Carmelite Order: the Mitigated Rule of Pope Eugene which stipulated the conditions under which the religious brethren of the Carmelite Order vow to live. You know this."

I know that he is once more evading my question.

"Teresa's insistence on returning to the Ancient Rule of twelve forty-seven was a direct violation of the Carmelite practice and therefore a deliberate challenge to the authority of the vicar general of all Spain. Anyone who aligned himself – or herself – with these rebellious and contumacious influences in the Order could be subjected to such disciplines as Fray Juan experienced. It was all quite legal, you know. The prescribed punishment for disobedience and rebellion."

Of course, he is right. The actions of Prior Maldonado and Tostado and those Toledo friars during the winter of fifteen seventy-seven and the months that followed, were indeed in accordance with canon law, and also with the law of the land. Fray Alonso seems to perceive an advantage over me in this, which he presses.

"Fray Juan and Teresa's other acolytes, Gracián and Ana de Jesús among them, as you know…" I do not know, but I nod. "In many matters, again and again they refused to follow the orders of the Carmelite vicar general of Spain." One index finger marks off their transgressions on his other outspread hand. "In setting up unauthorised convents and monasteries that followed Teresa's interpretation of what the Rule should be, and not what it was; in unauthorised travelling, to promote those illegal and most unpopular reforms; in the case of Fray Juan, refusing to submit to the order to desist from all duties as father confessor in the convent of Encarnación, whose community had never embraced Teresa's reforms; and, most of all, in carrying out practices which aligned them with the heretical *alumbrados*."

"But those practices you mention had nothing in common with the extreme and heretical practices of *alumbrados*," I object. "Theirs was an approach to interior prayer which others chose to interpret as *alumbrado* heresy. And the Carmelite reformers, Fray Juan included, answered to, and were bound by, a higher authority, were they not? That of the Vatican. Neither Fray Juan nor Madre Teresa nor any of their associates took any step or action that had not been authorised by the papal nuncio: Bishop Ormenato, the representative of the Pope himself. He not only gave permission for the establishment of Discalced convents of both friars and nuns, but recommended them, urged them on! I have in my possession copies of such authorisations, signed by Ormenato himself."

"Pah!" Fray Alonso flings his plume onto the bench. "You have been convinced by the voices of powerful personalities. Ambitious individuals who exploited confusions in the Carmelite chain of command for their own purposes. Pure strategy."

"But the Vatican's representative, Ormenato…"

"The Vatican does not command the Spanish Orders in this land!" He raises one palm to forestall my interruption. "You, a Dominican, of all people, should know that. The supreme authority of the Carmelite Order in Spain is the vicar general, who is under the authority of his majesty, the king. Your Dominican vicar general would not tolerate interference from Vatican officials in the internal matters of your order. Nor would King Felipe himself, and they would be right."

"But the king favoured many of Teresa's reforms."

"Up to a certain point. But do you think our monarch would give unqualified support to foreign influences from the Vatican, favour them over our own religious authorities in Spain? And if he did, why did Teresa's influence with the king suddenly evaporate during the period of Fray Juan's detention in this monastery?"

I make no reply. This is a question that has preoccupied me. Why did the king not respond to any of the frantic letters that Teresa sent him after Fray Juan was apprehended, when just a short while before, her access to the royal court had been almost unlimited? Two competing chains of Carmelite command – the Vatican hierarchy, some of whom supported Teresa and Juan's reforms, and many of the Spanish, who resisted them – with the king himself in the middle, unwilling to endorse or alienate either camp.

"And with such skill those Discalced ruffians sowed confusion!" Fray Alonso's voice seethes with bitterness. "They dazzled the Vatican inspectors with their piety, by sweeping away any display of human frailty in our monasteries and convents, with their aspirations to sainthood, their austerities and ecstasies. Seduced them with tales of levitations and direct communion with God. If the Lord himself tells you to set up a monastery here, a convent there, which Vatican inspector is going to argue? All the more so when many members of the nobility support them. The Duchess of Alba. The Countess of Badajoz.

"Small wonder, then, that Teresa was able to set up her little empire, an Order within an Order, install her own people to run her convents – and impose her chosen father confessors on communities who wanted no truck with the excesses of those Discalced fanatics, her rabble of misfits. Teresa and her acolytes – Antonio de Herrera, Ana de Jesús – all dangerous rebels, inflamed by personal ambition. With no chance of ever rising through the ranks of their legitimate Order, they did what second-rate people, supported by superstition and half-baked mysticism, have always done: they created their own movement, populated by outcasts and the simple-minded, led astray by those few cunning, unscrupulous climbers, quite lacking in purity of blood yet determined to manoeuvre themselves into positions of influence. I was obedient to my orders, and happy to be so."

He is shaking with anger now but I do not relent. "And if your superiors had instructed you to kill him outright, would you have complied?" In spite of his great age, I feel some satisfaction at having disturbed his composure. I keep my voice cool. "There was no formal offence, Fray Alonso, was there? In which case, there could have been no formal arrest. The procedure of choice was abduction and torture first, ask questions later, was it not?"

Fray Alonso looks at me quizzically, his temper having calmed as soon as it had erupted. "Are you acquainted with the name Evangelista? Diego Evangelista?" The sudden change of topic disorientates me.

"He was prior of the convent in Úbeda, where Fray Juan died," I venture. "I have with my own eyes seen copies of letters from Fray Antonio de Herrera. He was summoned to Fray Juan's sickbed when Prior Evangelista removed the nurse from the care of Fray Juan, even though he was in his final agony. The cruelty of Prior Evangelista's treatment of a dying man was beyond understanding and condemned by all."

"Perhaps he had his reasons. They might cast a different light upon your investigations. Your Archbishop Crespo could enlighten you."

Another evasion. When I stand to take my leave he does not offer me his cheek nor extend a hand.

"I should point out that I had charge of Fray Juan for only six months of his detention. When he escaped, he was not under my supervision. If he had been, he would never have been able to abscond."

Twilight has faded, darkness fallen over the vast plains of Castile. Fray Alonso is an individual of the most fearsome type:

one who has never suffered a moment's self-doubt, who was born with and nurtures the conviction of the righteousness of his own interests, and succeeds in conflating them with any actions he wishes to perform, however distasteful, to protect that advantage. But the quiet hours here have calmed me, I have finished my stew and this cup of harsh red wine has made me mellow and drowsy. I gather my papers, certain that I will sleep well tonight and awaken tomorrow refreshed, ready for the journey back to Madrid, to face whatever awaits me.

Monastery of San Gerónimo, Madrid,
Thirteenth day of May in the Year of Our Lord, 1616.

For the second time this month I am obliged to rely on information which will be recounted at second or even third-hand. Given that most of the people who knew Fray Juan are now dead, taking testimony on the basis of hearsay is sometimes unavoidable. This creates special problems, for it is not always clear whether the witness who recounts what he is told, rather than what he saw, is a credible source. Did events unfold as described? Did they happen at all? My students and former friends in Salamanca taught me that some people are capable of embellishment and outright invention for no particular reason, or just for the pleasure of having a stranger listen to them with interest and attention. Are we so impoverished in our intimacies that we are no longer capable of telling each other the simple truth, even when it concerns events in which we have no involvement and nothing to lose or gain by telling one version rather than another?

Then again, I begin to suspect that there are people for whom the truth is not so straightforward; who, uncertain of the independent reality of a situation, view events through the prism of their own wishes, fears and desires, including the simple longing to be admired or, at least, not to be despised. Might that be the true meaning of St. Paul's maxim that now, we see through a glass, darkly? Perhaps this darkness is not the shadow of evil as I once thought but rather, the splintering of reality by our own thoughts, which distort each version of events as it passes from one person to the next: a fracture that may lead to any number of calamities. The loss of a man's position and livelihood. The destruction of a reputation. The ending of a life.

Fray Ezequiel's niece was a girl of about fourteen or fifteen when she last saw her favourite uncle, her father's youngest brother. She is now a matron of perhaps fifty years, the mother of several sons and one daughter and, so she tells me, a grandmother of three. I can see that she was once a beauty. Her olive skin is unblemished by the wrinkles and pouches common to women of her age; her light brown hair is free of grey and is burnished with streaks of copper that suggest Celtic origins. She tells that her name, Lorea, means flower in the Basque language, and I recollect that one of the Franciscan missionaries who died in Japan may have been Basque.

"My uncle's given name was Gaizka, which means saviour. When we were children, my father, who was almost a decade older, often teased him and joked that a man with such a name would never be content to remain close to his family in Guipuzcoa, or even on the Spanish peninsula. Later, when uncle Gaizka declared that he wanted to become a missionary and save the heathens for God, no one really believed that he would go so far away." Lorea's voice trembles and her eyes grow moist but she does not falter.

"'If we had not given you that big name,' my father said, 'you would not have had such big ideas.' Perhaps he was right. And if my dear uncle Gaizka had listened, he might be with us still."

We met but a half hour ago, yet I judge that Lorea Iturburua is not a person who craves the admiration of a stranger whom she will never meet again, nor is she disposed to invent or embroider the facts. She appears to have been fond of her long-dead uncle and at this moment, her recollections are less concerned with the young man's brief acquaintance with Fray Juan, than with the tragic ending of the young missionary's life in a distant land.

"Was your uncle Gaizka one of the twenty-six martyrs of Nagasaki?"

Taking a handkerchief from within the folds of her gown, señora Iturburua dabs her eyes and shakes her head. "He did not have that distinction. Many Christian missionaries were killed in the months and years leading up to the crucifixion of the twenty-six. My uncle was one of those earlier victims."

I nod gravely. It was a dreadful martyrdom, but not unprecedented, as señora Iturburua herself knows.

"In truth, I do not believe that my uncle Gaizka – Fray Ezequiel, as he was called in Christ – would have been so happy to travel to Japan, had not the Franciscans been convinced by the welcome they received in the early days of their work there. But times change. In fact, when he received his posting, he no longer wanted to leave Spain – he had thought rather to continue his teaching in Valladolid for a year or two. But he was ordered to go. An unexpected decision was taken to found a monastery north of Nagasaki and he left soon after."

That was a grim time and for young Fray Ezequiel, the changed position of the Franciscans and how the warrior lords of Japan viewed them, was fatal. Mass conversion to Christianity was a particular kind of invasion which those canny rulers could accept, if it meant opening valuable trade routes with our peninsula. But wholesale colonisation, such as that which occurred in the Philippines and brought our faith to those islands – well, that was quite different. Unlike the natives of that archipelago nation, or even more, the unfortunate indigenous peoples of the lands we call 'New Spain,' the warlords of Japan had some knowledge of what to expect when our Christian soldiers arrived bearing gifts, such as promises of eternal life or trinkets to adorn the body. I think of my father's uncle, Ginés de Sepúlveda, and feel my face grow hot.

"I must not burden you with the ancient troubles of my family!" Lorea has perceived my discomfort and misunderstands its source. I should like to reassure her, but having an uncle whose most notable achievement was his treatise defending our colonisation of the New World and declaring the natives to be natural slaves, is not something to boast about.

"My uncle Gaizka – Fray Ezequiel – was a very young man when he was ordained. He was dedicated to his studies of philosophy and theology in the university. No one in our family had ever studied such elevated subjects; my father had never learned to read. He went to work in a baker's shop when he was eight years old so that his youngest brother could stay in school."

This matron has a mischievous smile and her memories are untainted with drama so I am inclined to believe her when she reflects on the questions I put to her, gently, so as not to interrupt the fluency of her utterances. She frowns, not a customary expression, I am sure, because the two small lines that crease her brow disappear almost immediately and the olive skin of her brow is smooth again. This woman has had a happy life.

"No, I do not think he recognised Fray Juan when he met him. In fact, I am sure of it. They became acquainted when uncle Gaizka had arranged to give a lecture in Alcalá de Henares. He had planned to make the journey on foot when Fray Juan heard that they were bound for the same destination and arranged for a farmer to lend them a second mule. Their conversation must not have impressed my uncle at the time, for we only heard the story some years after Fray Juan had died, when his remains were carried through the streets bound for Segovia."

I confess I am surprised that this matron should speak of that strange pilgrimage in such a matter-of-fact way, for it occurred under cover of night and in great secrecy. No doubt the literary meanderings of disreputable soldier-scribblers who describe peregrinations of dead bodies have made it common knowledge, and also the subject of much mockery, in that ridiculous tale of the knight and his servant and his sorrowful countenance. I must not allow exasperation to distract me from the essentials of señora Iturburua's recollections.

"Did Fray Juan make any reference to the conflicts between the Carmelites who followed the Mitigated Rule and the Discalced reforms that he and Teresa – Blessed Teresa – expounded?"

It is an ill-judged question and I am not surprised when señora Iturburua hesitates and frowns again, this time in puzzlement. This is a subject of no interest to her. Nor to her martyred uncle, it seems. I smile, hoping that my misplaced interruption has not interfered with her recollections.

"To be honest, I had the strong impression that uncle Gaizka did most of the talking. Perhaps that is why he never referred to their meeting until after Fray Juan had died. I guessed that he was embarrassed to have spent the whole day discussing his lecture and explaining his thoughts on theology to this quiet little man, without knowing that he was in the company of a famous scholar, practically a saint, loved and venerated. Gaizka had heard of him, of course. But he didn't know that this was his travelling companion, and the little friar did not enlighten him. He just listened while Gaizka educated him in all manner of philosophies."

She laughs a deep, throaty laugh. Her words confirm the love and respect in which Fray Juan was held long before his death, even before he was imprisoned in Toledo. No wonder Crespo and his associates are wary of him still. Such veneration, if not moderated by the authority of the Church, can produce saints by proclamation, a most dangerous phenomenon, when piety is established by common accord and not independently verified through the proper channels. The Vatican's rigorous procedures are designed to avoid the creation of saints by declaration of the mob. But young Fray Ezequiel was not one of that number or, if he was, Lorea knew nothing of this and so has no new information on the struggles that led to Fray Juan's imprisonment. Yet I am not quite ready to terminate this interview, for I feel a quiver of anticipation: my instincts are alert, certain that she has more to say which will illuminate some corner of this great canvas I am endeavouring to restore to the light.

For the moment, I resist the temptation to question her further. We sit in comfortable silence that drifts into conversation on matters of no consequence. I pour her a cup of fresh water. She exclaims on the beauty of the bright ceramic goblets I take down from the shelf where I keep my personal belongings. I explain that these were a gift from my mother, brought from Granada, the design copied from the intricate mosaics of the Alhambra. This leads to a few guarded comments on the great achievement of our Catholic monarchs in having united Spain and, with the fall of Granada, putting an end to the Arab kingdom of Al-Andalus. Just in time, I stop myself from musing aloud on the beauties we lost when all Moorish culture was banished from our land, with the destruction of all those Arabic documents, the suppression of the Moorish language and dress, and the final expulsion, just a few years past, of the *moriscos*, those who had converted so that they might be allowed to stay. In the end, their efforts were in vain.

Gaining confidence, Lorea tells me a sad story of neighbours she knew as a girl, an Arab family whose grandfather had converted to Christianity long before she was born.

"They were very great with my mother. She never believed the things that were said of them. My uncle Gaizka, who lost his best friend as a result of what happened, spoke of the tragedy often. They were denounced by someone from another part of the city, a person who did not even know them."

I make no reply, for reporting on the fate of innocent *converso* and *morisco* families is far outside my terms of reference. That kind of thing happened in those days. I suspect it still does. I linger while my companion finishes her tale, reluctant to bring our meeting to an end. I have observed how the outpourings of thoughts and memories that arise in response to my questions can sometimes produce surprising results. Formless ramblings may contain precious nuggets of knowledge, unanticipated and therefore unsought, that might otherwise never have surfaced.

In this way, I heard from señora Iturburua the story of how, as a very small child, Fray Juan almost drowned near his home in Hontiveros and how, in later life, he became convinced that the Blessed Mother herself had saved him.

According to Fray Ezequiel's account, the two men made the journey from Madrid to Alcalá de Henares on mules that carried them across wide, open plains under a harsh sun. The young professor was brimming with pride at his achievements and the mild, unassuming older man was content to listen to the prattlings of his companion. On the second day, they came to a few scraggy trees on the edge of a little pool, almost a lake, its water not very deep but clean and cool. Both men dismounted to allow the mules to drink. Fray Ezequiel, having filled his *botijo*, offered it to his companion. While Fray Juan quenched his thirst, the younger man immersed his head in the cold waters of the lake. Refreshed and exhilarated, he urged his companion to do likewise, the water being sweet and cold. But Fray Juan laughed, shook his head and contented himself with sprinkling a few drops on his face and neck. He had no taste for the water since the day he almost drowned when he was a little boy.

Lorea pauses, not sure whether I am interested in the trivial details of an idle conversation.

"Did he have an accident?"

"So said my uncle. He – Fray Juan, I mean – was no more than five years old, perhaps even a little less. It was a quiet day in late spring, unusually hot, with not a breath of wind. The children of Hontiveros were forbidden to play near the lake, especially at that time of year when the banks of the laguna were mostly mudflats, often hidden by the greenery, not yet parched by the heat of the blazing summer. You know the harsh climate of Castile."

I smile. *"Half a year of winter, half a year of hell."*

"On such days, no one chooses to be out of doors in the middle of the day. But high-spirited little ones care not for the warnings of their elders. The oldest of their group shouted to his playmates to come and see the saltworts growing in the mud. He reached out and plucked a few of them from the edges of the lake where they were growing, half in water and half in the silt, and challenged the others to see which of them could gather the most. The other boys were younger than him and smaller, so it was not surprising when the tiniest of them leaned over too far and fell in. That little one was Juan."

All at once the world changes and he finds himself immersed in the water of the lake which had looked so blue and clear from a distance but really is foul and pestilential, and he sinks to the bottom where the mud churns as he kicks, thrashes about in terror and although he has not learned to swim, his writhing propels him to the surface where he makes a desperate gasp and he hears the cries of his playmates but does not know how to stop himself from sinking again, so down he plunges, the muddy water of the *laguna* in his mouth, pond weeds floating, gathering around his limbs, his head moving from side to side, a tightness behind his eyes, in his chest, his whole body, he opens his eyes, all light dimmed, filtered through slimy ripples and floating strands of green and the churning of his panicked, thrashing limbs.

At that moment, the faint glint of the sun takes on an incandescent, silvery glow, stillness descends upon him and a beautiful lady with the sweetest face appears, smiles, reaches out her hand to him. Understanding, he extends his little hand to grasp hers but when he sees his fingers covered with mud and slime he knows he may not sully such soft white hands so he withdraws his own, ashamed. But the lady laughs, reaches for him again, this time holding both hands out to him yet still, he resists.

Just then, a long, sharp stick with a hook on the end appears through the mud and the slime. The lady has vanished. He grasps the stick and finds himself hauled to the surface and safety. The other children had set up such a squawking that a passing labourer waded in and saved the day.

"Fray Juan said that the little child – himself – refused to take the offered hand because he was convinced that the beautiful lady was our Blessed Mother, the Virgin Mary. He and uncle Gaizka both laughed at the innocence of children and at his own child-like piety, at the notion that he was so awed by the vision that he would rather have died than sully the hand of the Mother of God. He believed that she sent a labourer along the right path with just the kind of stick suitable for a boy to grasp and allow himself to be saved. Ever since, he had no desire to immerse himself in still water. They joked that it was fortunate he had been baptised as a baby for he would not like to be plunged bodily in the Jordan like John the Baptist, who was the patron of Hontiveros and greatly venerated there. Gaizka said that Fray Juan was a jolly companion," Lorea adds, "that is, when he himself had ceased talking and allowed his companion to speak."

When she has finished, we are both silent. I ponder the strangeness of this story, which is so singular that it does not occur to me to doubt her. Some of those who wish to see Fray

Juan beatified would make much of such a story: childhood piety, seasoned with the whiff of a miracle. But Lorea Iturburua is so far removed from the priorities of our Mother Church that I doubt she even understands the significance of what she has just told me. Young friar Ezequiel, by his own admission, attached little importance to the story until after Fray Juan had died. I must take care in how I present this episode, for it lends credence to some of the less rational explanations for events that took place later in Fray Juan's life. For that reason, the saint-makers from the Vatican and from the royal court, too, would dearly love to hear it.

Yet I am glad to have heard this story myself, for it might explain something that has puzzled me during these last weeks since I began my reading of Fray Juan's life. How, and why, did the young Juan de Yepes come to be admitted to the Jesuit college in Medina del Campo, where he received those four years of study that allowed him entry to the illustrious University of Salamanca and set him on the path to erudition? It is not surprising that his brilliance, once noted, should have attracted the interest of his teachers. But how did he come to their attention in the first place? What unlikely sequence of events enabled an undernourished child from a desperately poor family, shunned by their immediate relatives – perhaps also tainted with some unspoken blemish on the honour of their ancestors – to be selected to attend the school at all?

The journey of the sad little family – or the remnants of the family, after his father and brother had died – as they made their way to Medina del Campo, is well documented. However, those same records fail to explain why his dead father's family denied succour to the young mother and her children. Yes, it was harsh, though not surprising, that the family disowned Gonzalo when he insisted on a love marriage so far beneath his station. But to refuse aid to his widow and her starving children? That is not so easy to explain, for in such circumstances, provision of some kind of assistance would surely be the Christian response. Unless charity were inhibited by some significant doubt concerning the reputation of Catalina's family, such as a stain on *limpieza de sangre*, or perhaps some history of criminality.

Or there may be a more straightforward reason. I have observed that for prosperous nobles of a certain type, there is no crime more heinous than poverty.

Monastery of San Gerónimo, Madrid,
Seventh day of June in the Year of Our Lord, 1616.

As I raise my hand to knock, the door to Crespo's office swings open and Ortiz's reedy voice bids me enter. Despite this sultry air, I feel myself surrounded by a frozen wasteland, like the great expanses of ice and snow in the Italian maestro's ninth circle of hell. He had his own difficulties with the authorities and it pleases me to think that perhaps he was no stranger to the likes of Crespo and Ortiz.

I approach the centre of the room and wait, head bowed. The tall, graceful windows are unshuttered and a light breeze carries the faint scent of bougainvillea on the air, trailing dreams of other times and places. When this is all over I might visit that poet's native land, so much renowned for the beauty of its cities and landscapes and people. But I must not allow my thoughts to wander. For the next hour, I need to justify how I have spent my time during the weeks and months since first I was summoned to this room.

They have been waiting for me. Both men are standing: Crespo by the window, a little to my left and Ortiz in front of me, leaning on the side of Crespo's massive carved desk. He takes a step forward. "We understand that your second progress report is now ready."

As Crespo does not move from his position when he speaks, I am obliged to turn and crane my neck. "Together with an assessment of your sources," he adds.

It seems that today I must parry questions from two hostile interrogators. If I confess to my departures from their prescribed method, they will make short work of me. Perhaps they already know of my transgressions. Before I can reply, Ortiz leans over the desk and stabs a bony finger on one of the pages spread out in front of him, covered with dense writing. I recognise it. I wrote it.

"You have completed but a dozen interviews from the original list of thirty-one."

It is a statement, not a question. I must be careful. I may not answer *Beg pardon, you are mistaken*, even though he is. Especially because he is.

"In fact, Reverend Father, you are correct in stating that I have furnished you with reports of twelve interviews, whose main findings you have seen already, summarised in the document you have in front of you. However," I draw a thin sheaf of papers from the folds of my habit, "I can report that since we last met, I have interrogated a further eight of the named witnesses." I do not add that I have also seen at least the same number of unauthorised witnesses. "Therefore, having completed twenty of the required thirty-one interviews, my progress is on schedule. Eleven witnesses remain, and I have ample time to conduct those meetings before the autumn. That will allow me to draft my final report before the Christmas festival. Meanwhile," I hold the file out into empty space, "I am pleased to offer my original notes on each of those most recent meetings, for your perusal."

Crespo, who today has abandoned his habitual role of mollifying and tempering Ortiz's hostility, turns back to the window. I do not think he is simply admiring the garden. The prior has planted himself in my line of sight but makes no move to take the papers from my outstretched hand. The bodies of these men, if not their words, are speaking to me with great urgency, warning that I should retreat from the foolhardy strategy of probing their motives with yet more questions. My hand falls limp to my side.

Continuing his inspection of the roses, Crespo nods once. "A brief summary will suffice."

I make a rapid mental inventory of all the unauthorised witnesses I have met and can think of only one who was unhappy enough and connected enough to cause me serious trouble. But I am sure I can justify my meeting with Fray Alonso: bewildered surprise at his omission from the list, accompanied by humble apologies, should suffice to extract me from that difficulty. But if I should be further challenged?

Crespo seems to read my mind. "Speaking of original notes, Fray Martín, have you had any success in locating the personal papers of Fray Juan?"

As I shuffle through my file, I consider whether I should mention the archive I received some weeks ago from Prior Andrés and perhaps summarise my initial thoughts on the various documents it contains. In fact, against all my expectations, I did find something. Not original manuscripts, but several pages that I am sure will be useful, when I have examined them in more depth.

At first glance, I did not recognise the closely written lines in those twenty-two pages as not one, but two, versions of the same poem that Doctor Enrique showed me, for neither version contains the word *Cántico*, not in the title nor in any part of the text. Ten of the leaves are covered in a small, close hand that is not very easy to read. The twelve remaining pages are recognisably distinct, inscribed with a most exquisite calligraphy, cursive and rounded, embellished with many adornments.

This second copy is the work of a scribe of great skill. Notes in another hand – in tiny lettering that is yet legible – are inscribed in the margins. This writer has used an ink that is somewhat lighter than the rest, the way with the quill being quite different from that wielded by the creator of the copy he has annotated.

On that ten-page version, I counted thirty-nine stanzas, of which one bears the introduction, *Songs of the Loves between God and the Soul*. I read on, ever more certain that the pastoral scenes described here tell the same tale of a girl in search of her lover as that depicted in the old Inquisitor's illustrated vellum manuscript. Unaccountably excited – for I understood that neither copy could be an original manuscript – I placed the two documents side by side. The second version, copied out in the beautiful calligraphy that so entranced me, contains forty stanzas, not clearly separated but each new grouping of lines indicated by a mark in the left margin, made with the sharpest point of the quill.

As a quick scan of both documents failed to reveal the location and content of the extra stanza, I decided to make a close examination of both copies, and of the entire contents of Prior Andrés's archive, as soon as possible. Not in time, though, to include my analysis in this second progress report. In any case, these are not the original manuscripts to which Crespo refers.

"I have not found them yet, Your Grace," I answer truthfully. "In fact..." I hesitate. Ortiz's Inquisitor cousin stressed the importance of Fray Juan's original texts, especially the *Canticle*. But had Doctor Enrique spoken only on his own behalf? I should very much like to know whether he shared our conversation with my two superiors. "I had formed the impression that locating Fray Juan's original manuscripts, if they still exist, was a secondary task."

If Ortiz had heard of Doctor Enrique's visit, he does not say. Crespo turns from the window and claps his hands, as a musician signals a change of tempo.

"I have a question, Fray Martín."

"Your Grace, I will do my best to answer."

"Why did Fray Juan join the Carmelites? Why not the Jesuits? After all, they educated him."

I make no attempt to answer. Given their earlier prohibitions against my interpreting facts instead of simply reporting them, I do not see how I may. Perhaps this is a trap, designed to induce me to reveal my deviation from their instructions. Yet Crespo's question intrigues me, for it had also crossed my mind.

"Speak, Fray Martín. We are interested to hear your impressions. With or without firm evidence."

It is a question that has been little probed, mentioned only in passing and answered in platitudes: that Fray Juan was devoted to the Virgin who had saved him from drowning as a child; that the Carmelites had an ancient tradition of veneration of Our Lady. But this explanation does not satisfy me. I do not understand why, having studied for four years as a young man with the Jesuits in Medina del Campo, where he was recognised as a person of unusual piety and intellectual ability, his studies did not lead him to the obvious path – to the Society of Jesus. The malicious glint in Crespo's eye persuades me that he well understands my reluctance to cast doubt on the reputation of Fray Juan's own family, much less on the Jesuit Order, or any individual within the Order.

"It is possible," I venture, "that there was some cloud, some… taint… in the mother's lineage."

"You mean a question concerning *limpieza de sangre?*"

"Perhaps, though not necessarily. In itself, a Jewish or Moorish ancestor need not have impeded Fray Juan's entry or even his progress through the ranks. As you know, many of our most venerated princes of the Church and grandees of the Empire are of *converso* stock. The Blessed Teresa herself had a Jewish grandfather."

We both know that my cautious response, and all other theories that might answer Crespo's sudden question, are pure speculation. Until more information becomes available to us there is simply no way of knowing whether the young Juan de Yepes rejected the Jesuits, or if they rejected him.

Ortiz takes up the interrogation. "Supposing some ancestor of Fray Juan's had resumed his Jewish practices, encouraged others to follow, attracted the interest of the Inquisition…"

"I think that unlikely. After all, you have just described Blessed Teresa's family secret – an open secret. Even during her lifetime, it was quite well known that her Jewish grandfather was a *converso* who had fallen back into Jewish ways. The whole family were brought as penitents before an *auto-da-fé*, including her own father, when he was a small child. They were lucky not to burn," I add, perhaps a little too bluntly. This brutal observation is met with silence.

Crespo clears his throat. "And nothing of the kind has been discovered in Fray Juan's family tree?"

"Not to my knowledge, Your Grace. At least, not yet. There may be nothing to discover."

It is also possible, I do not say, that Fray Juan's family were of too lowly a social standing to suit the Jesuits. Pious, brilliant, admired, yes, but not the right… type… for a new Order whose ambitious founders are bent on achieving intellectual and political influence. Some things are best left unsaid.

"Or there could be something altogether different," I muse. "An ordinary criminal in the family tree, perhaps."

"You may be right." Ortiz's acquiescence surprises me but I make no comment. For a few moments, the three of us look at each other.

Crespo takes a deep breath. Is that a sigh of relief? "What can you tell us concerning the circumstances of Fray Juan's first acquaintance with Teresa?"

"None of the witnesses I have met was acquainted with Fray

Juan at that crucial time in his life, Your Grace. I have hopes that at least two of my remaining witnesses might have information on this subject. But at the moment, I can tell you very little that is not already in the files."

"Then tell us that very little, Fray Martín."

Determined not to rise to Ortiz's provocations, I consult my notes. The truth is, I have learned not very little, but absolutely nothing, concerning that first meeting between the two people who would be the driving force behind the foundation of the Discalced Carmelites, in defiance of the most virulent opposition from the Carmelites of the Mitigated Rule, many of whom had been their erstwhile companions.

"One thing we do know is that they met in fifteen sixty-three, in Salamanca, either just before or just after Fray Juan completed his studies at the university there and sang his first Mass in Medina del Campo."

"How can we be so sure?"

"Because Teresa travelled to Salamanca with the aim of founding a reformed Carmelite convent for men, all her previous foundations hitherto being for nuns. She had finally received permission…"

"Or what she chose to interpret as permission," Ortiz interrupts, sotto voce.

"…to establish a reformed foundation for friars. She was actively seeking male collaborators to assist her. Of course, the long-term survival of her reform needed father confessors with views similar to her own to sustain it. At that time, Fray Juan was thinking of leaving the Carmelite Order for the Carthusians. Teresa persuaded him to work with her instead."

Crespo leans forward. "Why the intention to leave the Carmelite Order? What did the Carthusians have that the Carmelites lacked?"

I shrug. "This is another area that I have not yet been able to clarify, Your Grace. Perhaps when I complete the remaining interviews…"

"Is it not obvious?" Ortiz waves his hand. Crespo regards the dismissive gesture in surprise.

"I beg pardon, Your Grace," Ortiz insists, unaware of having incurred Crespo's displeasure, "but there is no mystery here. The practices of the Mitigated Rule of the Carmelites were not sufficiently rigorous for Fray Juan's temperament. The Carthusians, by contrast, had held aloof from society and managed to avoid the worst excesses of the decadence that had befallen so many of our Orders during the last century."

"We cannot know Fray Juan's motivation for certain," I object. "Besides, I think it unfair to impute lax conduct to all Carmelite communities, or others, for that matter. It is just as likely that the poverty of Fray Juan's early years or his experience ministering to the sick in the hospitals in Medina del Campo and Salamanca gave him a preference for a more demanding practice of religious life, than that chosen by others who had not known such early privations. We should not infer criticism of others from Fray Juan's choices."

My words are sharper than I had intended but I cannot abide careless reasoning. Ortiz colours a little but says nothing. Crespo also holds his counsel. I sense that they are waiting for me to reveal myself further.

When he realises that I am not going to speak, Crespo breaks the silence. "Is that all the information you have concerning the circumstances of the first meeting with Teresa?"

"Regrettably, yes, Your Grace. Little more than the bare facts contained in the notes left by previous investigators. They confirm that Fray Juan did indeed join Teresa and that he founded the first convent for friars."

"In Doruelo, was it not?" Ortiz is already almost as well informed as I. Perhaps more so, if he has been discussing the case with his cousin. Crespo extends a hand and beckons.

I pass him a single page of my notes. "You are right, Prior

Ortiz. After Doruelo, Fray Juan founded several other convents throughout Castile, where he held positions of increasing responsibility, including that of novice master, prior and even rector of the college in Alcalá de Henares. Until Teresa summoned him to her convent, the Encarnación in Ávila. A deeply unpopular…"

"Yes, Fray Martín, your last report included an account of that situation. In full and luxurious detail. Clearly, it was an unapproved appointment."

I hesitate. I would prefer not to correct Ortiz again but he is only half right. "It was not approved by the vicar general of the Carmelite Order in this country," I agree cautiously. "But it was certainly approved by the Vatican. By the papal nuncio, Archbishop Ormenato, who even intervened to secure Fray Juan's release the first time he was abducted from Encarnación."

"Hardly abducted. He was detained for a few days, I understand."

"That is not the point, Your Grace." Once again, my passions are running away with me. I make a supreme effort to compose myself. "For at least some of his time as confessor in Encarnación, unnamed officials of the Carmelites of the Mitigated Rule kept Fray Juan under surveillance. They took him into custody not once, but twice. On the first occasion they returned him to Medina del Campo, the town where his family had put down roots, and paraded him, in disgrace, before the townspeople and his own family. Like a common criminal. Had it not been for the intervention of the papal nuncio Ormenato, there is no knowing when or how that detention might have ended. We know what happened the second time he was detained. In Toledo."

During the silence that follows I take care to keep my head bowed and my eyes on the threadbare, faded carpet I noticed on my first visit to this room. Crespo is planted on the edge of his chair. I feel his gaze penetrate my temple. Ortiz has begun to pace the room, advancing towards me and retreating, as a hunting dog seeks the scent of vulnerability or fear. This is inappropriate behaviour towards one of my station and he knows it. He is playing on what he imagines is my respect for his office and his person, of which he has an inordinately high opinion. He knows not how my experiences of recent years have altered my view of authority: that I no longer see in him a prince of the church but rather, a shabby little bully garbed in a habit of the finest wool. I must take care that neither Ortiz nor Crespo senses this.

"If you have no further intelligence…"

"Intelligence, no." I take a deep breath.

"In that case…"

"But I do have a number of questions concerning a few matters that puzzle me. Firstly, the nature of Fray Juan's escape from the monastery in Toledo."

"Is not the sequence of events well known?"

"An agreed sequence of events is indeed well known, Your Grace. That Fray Juan prised the hinges from his door whilst the guard and a few guests slept in the dormitory outside his cell. That he climbed down from a high, arched window using a sheet he had torn and fashioned into a rope."

"And that he made his way to the convent of the Discalced Carmelite sisters, where he sought and received succour." As he speaks, Crespo heaves himself to his feet and moves heavily around his desk. "I see no cause for puzzlement," he concludes.

"I see many, Your Grace." That exchange of looks again, this time unconcealed. I plunge on. "To remove the hinges from his cell door, such a manoeuvre would require a degree of physical stamina and strength impossible for a man in his physical condition at the time. Also, he would have needed tools of some kind. Perhaps, over a period of many weeks or even months, in the dead of night, he might have fashioned some such implement. From a spoon, for example, if he was allowed a spoon. It is a very slight possibility.

"However," I mark off each argument on my fingers, "to climb down from a high window using a makeshift rope…" I am careful to omit the detail of its dimensions and location, for it is just possible that they do not know about my unauthorised visit and that I have seen this window with my own eyes, "…a rope that, by all accounts, was not quite long enough, so that he was obliged to drop to the ground from some height…This is simply not credible. Such acrobatics would be no small feat for a man in the full of his health. For one deprived of food, light and movement for nine whole months…I am sorry, Your Grace, I do not believe it."

"Perhaps it was a miracle," Crespo murmurs.

I incline my head. "Indeed, Your Grace. And that is how Fray Juan explained it himself. However, let us allow that this… miracle… plucked Fray Juan from his prison of nine months and placed him at the foot of the monastery on the banks of the Tagus in the middle of the night. It is well known that effecting an exit is but the first step in a successful escape. Everything depends on what happens next."

"We know what happened next, Sepúlveda." Ignoring the mollifying tone of his superior, Ortiz has now abandoned any veneer of courtesy towards me. "Fray Juan made his way across the town, to the convent of the Carmelite sisters, his own and Teresa's people."

"Yes, Your Grace, but how? Leaving aside the question of his weakened bodily state, how did he find his way from the place of his detention to the sisters who granted him succour?"

"By skirting the city walls, I imagine. That convent is easily found. It is near the Gate of the Hebrews, as everyone knows."

I hesitate. Once again, Ortiz is both right and wrong, and I wonder whether he himself is aware of this. The convent of the Discalced sisters is indeed located near the city walls, exactly where he says, but it has only occupied that site in recent years. If Ortiz is as acquainted with the city of Toledo as he seems to be, I cannot believe that he does not know this.

"That is all very well," I respond, with caution, "but there is no reason to suppose that Fray Juan was familiar with the location of that convent or how to reach it. Especially when he did not even know the name of the town where he was being held."

Ortiz gives me a hard look and I find that I am unable to recall from whom I received this information, whether from an authorised source or not. I recover quickly. "If Teresa was unable to discover his whereabouts during the nine months he had disappeared, it is most likely that Fray Juan himself did not know where he was. How, then, could he make his way through lanes and courtyards, traverse narrow streets, climb steps and alleyways, all in the depths of night? Impossible. Not without significant assistance. Fray Juan had help. Both in his escape, and in finding the one place in the region where he could find shelter."

I am sure of my ground, for I attempted that journey myself, in full daylight, after my meeting with Fray Alonso in Toledo. I had not anticipated the difficulty of retracing the route Fray Juan would have taken, from the place of his detention outside the city walls, to the convent of the Discalced sisters within them. The monastery is perched on the crest of a hill, overlooking the river, and the route in daylight was clearly visible. I simply had to follow those *murallas* of golden stone that coil around the narrow streets in tightly wound terraces, leading all the way from the new city gates, up beyond the ancient Moorish *mezquita*, past the proliferation of new churches and palaces, many in various stages of construction, the whole nestled in the red plains of Castile. By night, this terrain is black as ink, the *murallas* mere looming shadows. Even in the full light of day, I managed to get lost.

Caminante and I set out from the rear porch of the monastery, my face and eyes shaded by Madre Carmela's straw hat. Animated by my dispute with Fray Alonso, I strode on, elated, animated by the sliver of danger I felt in the company of Fray Juan's old gaoler.

Soon we reached an ancient Roman gate. Having passed beneath its imposing arch, we made our way alongside a recently reconstructed *palacio*, staying as close to the interior *murallas* as the winding laneways of the city would permit. The next archway, which we reached less than a quarter hour later, was the imposing Gate of the Hebrews. Almost directly in front of it, stood the convent of the Discalced Carmelite sisters of Toledo.

I knew at once that this could not be the place where Fray Juan sought shelter almost four decades ago, this building being of recent construction, barely five or six years old. For a few moments I hovered and contemplated the pewter bell set in grey stone alongside the main convent door. Ringing would be futile, for the sisters' vows of enclosure and silence would not permit a meeting without prior arrangement.

"Let us find you a drink, Caminante, before we set off home."

He nuzzled my shoulder and turned towards a newly installed pump in the centre of a courtyard a few paces from the convent door. I could swear that he often understands me, not only my words, but my intentions. Sweat trickled down my face as I worked the pump, glad to see it in good order. While Caminante drank his fill from the trough beneath, I mopped my forehead. Fray Alonso had not invited me to eat but I had pilfered a few dates and figs from the kitchen before leaving, and a muslin cloth in which to wrap them. The shadow of the convent wall fell on one side of the trough. There I perched, balanced on the rim, unwrapped the food and ate. Not very hearty fare, but it took the edge from my hunger.

I had just finished my modest meal when an old woman emerged from a laneway beyond the convent and shuffled towards me. I do not habitually give alms to street beggars but her frail, stooped form and her laboured gait made me think of Fray Juan's mother, trudging around the market towns of Castile. The crone approached me, palm outstretched and I found myself reaching for a few coins. Yes, she was a native of

Toledo and she remembered when the Discalced sisters took occupation of their new home, here, by the Hebrew Gate. Their convent in the centre of the city could no longer accommodate the growing community. Yes, she knew exactly where the original convent had been located. A quivering finger indicated a winding alley that rose from the street and plunged into the dim interior of the city.

Uncertain of what I might find in these dark laneways, I resolved to leave Caminante in the courtyard, near water and shade. I looped his reins through a wrought iron rail and scratched his ear. "Old fellow, you would not like what comes next. Stairways. Stony alleyways. You could lose a shoe, and then what would become of us?"

Before long, I found myself in a warren of lanes that twisted and turned, bounded by walls so dank and high that even on this bright summer's day they were deep in shadow. I stretched out my arms. My fingers almost brushed doors and walls on both sides. An occupant of these streets could stand on one of the narrow balconies of the upper floors, lean over and shake hands with a neighbour on the other side.

That day, however, there were no people about, all windows being shuttered against the sun. The defiant elation that had gripped me when I took my leave of Fray Alonso gave way to unease. The distance from the courtyard where I left Caminante to the shadowy square at the top of the laneway was not very great – for a person who knows the way. But I did not. That alley led to other alleys, flights of stairs ascending and descending, now narrowed to a lane that skirted past a parched fountain. Soon I found myself blundering along the same dark passage, climbing the same steep steps a second time, and then a third.

Out of breath, I paused to reflect upon my lack of progress. The old convent building should be here or hereabouts, but I had lost my bearings. The old woman's directions made no mention of this dark little square, bounded by forbidding walls on two sides and on the third, the massive door of yet another church built in the gleaming, golden stone typical of so many of the new buildings constructed during the last half century.

I had no heart to confront this steep, stony lane a fourth time. Admitting defeat, I approached the church door, opened it a crack and glimpsed an interior that was empty, but for an old priest kneeling at the railings of a side chapel, his head bowed, lost in prayer. Clearing my throat so as not to startle him, I crossed the stone floor. He did not look up. A few votive candles flickered in a candelabra to one side of the alter rail. I removed an unlit candle from a box underneath the stand and held the wick close to a live flame. When it caught, I pressed the candle into a trickle of warm wax. Reluctant to interrupt the old man at prayer, I knelt beside him, casting the occasional sidelong glance at his moving lips. After a time, he opened his rheumy eyes.

"Have you come to view the works of our master?" He nodded towards the altarpiece. "What a marvellous triptych," I murmured, not meaning a word of it. The subject matter, which depicted the figure of Christ resurrected, surrounded by angels, was unremarkable. But in execution it was most curious, all the figures elongated and shrouded in a cold, blue-grey mist. I did not like it. And I could not delay much longer.

"Our adopted son. He was a great artist, no matter the disfavour of the king."

I had no idea what he meant, beyond the obvious conclusion that he greatly admired the creator of this unpleasant image. It seemed impolite to ask, but nor did I feel able to remain silent, especially when I required assistance. "And this triptych is...?"

"The Resurrection of Christ. As you see, it is unlike any other," said the old man, with a touch of pride. "It was his first commission in Toledo. In the whole of Spain, in fact. Our church has that honour."

"And this is the Church of...?"

The old man looked up at me in surprise. "Santo Domingo el

Viejo." So there are people who come here on purpose to view these strange and disturbing images. "The master was buried in our crypt, according to his own wish. A little more than a year ago. Would you like to see it?"

"Unfortunately I cannot, Padre, for I must make haste," I said, immediately regretting my words when the old man's face fell. "I must return to Madrid as soon as I can."

The hour I had passed stumbling along these narrow, eerie streets and lanes had wearied me and I was no longer elated from my encounter with Fray Alonso but rather, enveloped in a thickening miasma of unease. I would make one final attempt to locate the original site of the Convent of the Discalced Carmelite sisters of Toledo.

"You will find nothing there but empty ground," the old priest warned. "So much building and rebuilding has gone on in recent decades, nothing is as it used to be."

He was curious to know my purpose and for a reckless moment, I considered confiding something of my mission to him. But prudence and caution prevailed, I am relieved to recall. I thanked him, genuflected towards the chapel and the unpleasant image of the risen Christ, made the sign of the cross and left. The old priest was right, though. My efforts to find the convent were futile. Although I followed his directions with care, once I arrived I found only a tiny cobbled courtyard and a water pump of the modern type from which Caminante had quenched his thirst in the square below. Losing patience, and with no small difficulty, I retraced my steps, lurching down the lanes and alleyways that I had climbed with such effort.

"Back to Madrid, my old friend."

We had wasted too much time and I had lost heart for the journey home and for whatever might await me there. Consequently, we lodged for the night in the village of Coruela and on the morrow returned to Madrid refreshed, bright and animated in humour, my optimism restored.

Monastery of San Gerónimo, Madrid,
Eighteenth day of June in the Year of Our Lord 1616.

D octor Enrique punctuates his words with a series of rhythmic knuckle raps on my desk, an even greater intrusion than his presence, which is both unannounced and unexpected. Weary after yet another journey, uneasy lest my absence had been noticed, this morning I hurried to my office to collect my draft report and make a few additional notes, arriving just in time for this meeting with Crespo and Ortiz. If the old Inquisitor had been sitting in my chair perusing my files, I could not have been more shocked. In fact, he is standing, head tilted, examining the copy of Vincenzio's *Resurrection* that had so impressed Madre Carmela.

He turns towards me and indicates a bundle of papers he has placed on the desk, apparently in readiness for my arrival. I take a moment to compose myself and arrange my features into a smile of inquiry.

"Examine, if you will, these commentaries on Fray Juan's poems," he orders without preamble, as though continuing a conversation interrupted but a few hours ago. I approach the desk, suppress the impulse to ask what he is doing here and why he has appeared without an appointment at the very hour when I am engaged to meet his cousin and the Archbishop. Suddenly, I understand. His presence, unconcealed and at this time, answers one of my questions: Crespo and Ortiz knew of his first visit to me, and they are privy to all his questions and all my answers. I give thanks that I spoke to him with such caution during our first meeting and resolve to be circumspect today.

"Is this text Fray Juan's own work?" I ask, judging that there is nothing to be gained by insisting on the usual courtesies in meetings of this kind. Instead, I accept his terms and plunge into the conversation.

"We are not sure. As you can see, these pages seek to convey that which cannot be expressed in mere words: the soul's journey towards a direct experience of, and union with, God. In this life, you will notice. Not the next. Which is the precise subject of many of Fray Juan's poems. I believe this is a commentary on specific sections of some of his works."

He passes two or three pages to me and, peering at me, points out a few passages. I resolve to remain silent until I hear what he has to say. At last, his patience gives way. "You must see that this is a profound threat to the authority, to the stability, of the Church. And, therefore, to the state."

I lean over my desk, the better to examine the text he has placed in front of me. It is not poetry but rather an extensive and somewhat rambling explanation of a different, absent text, which, judging from references to lines and stanzas, is a poem of significant length. As I read on, I begin to understand something of Doctor Enrique's concerns. The writer is preoccupied with his personal experience of God: a mystical union that indeed calls to mind the teachings of those *alumbrados* who were gaoled for heresy not long before Fray Juan's own tribulations began. There is not one reference to the sacraments, to ceremonies or rituals, nor even the holy sacrifice of the Mass, no exhortation to the faithful to follow the guidance of priest or bishop. Despite being a religious text, all mention of ecclesiastical oversight is entirely absent. For the writer of those pages, the Council of Trent might never have taken place.

"These commentaries most probably refer to Fray Juan's *Canticle*. Fray Martín, they express beliefs that are on the very edge of orthodoxy. Some of my colleagues think that the thought expressed herein has tipped over into heresy. In very recent years, others have been sentenced for writings that are far milder than this."

He pauses and we both listen to the quiet of the day. It is close to noon, the sun is at its height, the air is hot. All birdsong has ceased, and the silence gathers thickly around us. After a long moment, Doctor Enrique shakes his head with vigour, as though to expel troublesome thoughts.

"Is your concern, Doctor Enrique, that the original *Canticle* could express even greater heterodoxy of experience and thought? To the point of exhorting active opposition to the communal, ceremonial religious life that is properly subject to the laws and hierarchies of the Church?"

He does not answer but walks over to the window. "It is possible. It is also possible that other hands have slightly... rearranged... the words and thoughts to... create a particular effect," he says softly.

So, Doctor Enrique is struggling to decipher not only original documents, but to unearth possible falsifications in the work of a writer who died almost a quarter of a century ago. I consider how I may discover the wily Inquisitor's intent and decide to take a straightforward approach. "Why has it suddenly become so important to find Fray Juan's original version of the *Canticle*?"

The tapping, which had ceased while I was reading the text he had put before me, resumes. I struggle to conceal my irritation but he appears distracted, preoccupied, his gaze drifting towards the orchards and fields far in the distance.

"Not only the *Canticle*, Fray Martín, but yes, especially that work. And it has not suddenly become of interest to us. It has always been important, ever since Fray Juan's death. But in this last year, in the light of Teresa's beatification two years ago, it is now important that we find that manuscript. If it still exists. As you know, Blessed Teresa's elevation was achieved following rigorous interrogations by Vatican inspectors of her life and work; also, examination of all her writings, public and private. A similar process could be enacted with reference to Fray Juan."

"So, if the original *Canticle* exists still, it is likely that they will find it."

"Likely? I do not know. It is possible." Doctor Enrique is watching me closely, as though gauging how far I have understood his meaning. I think I do understand. If Fray Juan's original has survived, then I – or a new crop of Vatican inspectors – might succeed in finding it where others have failed. And if I should fail…

"If that manuscript is found – if I do manage to locate it – what will you do with it?"

His mild, amused look does not deceive me. My question is an impertinence, but he indulges me. "Well, Fray Martín. That depends. If that manuscript is found and if it expresses thoughts that are frankly rebellious, or even heretical, it could be…stored for safekeeping. Until better times."

"To ensure that no whiff of heresy should tarnish Fray Juan's reputation? To strengthen the case for his elevation to Blessed?"

"Exactly. Or at least, to avoid weakening it."

Immediately I am alerted to a conflict between the confidence of his words and a sudden wavering in his physical demeanour, his eyes shifting uneasily, his tapping foot. There is more to this question than he is willing to say.

"Or...?" I must take care, for I do not think he will tolerate my questions much longer.

"Or it could be made available. Judiciously," he answers.

To the Vatican inspectors? I am filled with confusion, unable to grasp in the moment the many uses such a manuscript could serve, but certain that any chosen action will depend on the motives and intent of those who have this precious document in their possession.

"I will be frank with you, Fray Martín. I do not have to tell you what crucial times these are in the life of our Church, not only in this peninsula but in the whole of Europe. At such a moment, the elevation to Blessed of one such as Teresa, who is widely renowned both for wisdom and sanctity, benefits the Church greatly, both temporal and spiritual."

"And Fray Juan?"

The haughty old fellow casts a sharp glance at me and begins to pace the room. Coming to an abrupt halt in front of me, he opens his mouth, closes it, then seems to make up his mind.

"To elevate a man whose thinking is poised on the edge of heresy, who promotes questionable practices, who encourages unmediated mystical experiences... That would be a disaster in every way. Not only for the internal control of the Order. It would confirm all the calumnies of the Lutherans and Calvinists who denounce our Catholic practices as primitive super-stitions."

I feel some agitation and almost regret having asked the question. Yet, having come this far, I must press on. "Do you truly believe that Fray Juan – and therefore, by association, Blessed Teresa – were charlatans and frauds? Or *alumbrado* sympathisers?"

"No, Fray Martín. Speaking for myself, I do not. Though that is not beyond the bounds of possibility. Did you know that Teresa herself on more than one occasion was summoned before the Holy Office to answer charges of *alumbradismo*?"

I did not know that, but Doctor Enrique's question is rhetorical, for he sweeps on without waiting for my answer.

"The charges were dismissed, of course. I am prepared to believe that Teresa and Fray Juan and their various followers were – are – pious people, sometimes misguided, but well-meaning. However, we must face the facts. Not only did the rigour of their practices alarm their religious brethren and lead directly to the great abyss that opened between the Carmelites who came to be known as Discalced and their brethren who rejected the reforms, they also frightened some of our more cautious Inquisitors who could not see a difference between their method of prayers, of contemplation, and the *alumbrados'* flights of mystical fantasy."

"Doctor Enrique, I think…"

He waves his hand. "What you think, Fray Martín, or what I think, is of no importance. What is important is the scholastic and spiritual legacy that Fray Juan has left us to… manage. It is not straightforward."

"But if his legacy derives from his piety and a true desire to serve the Lord most humbly, as you yourself admit, Doctor Enrique, I do not see…"

Once again, he raises a hand to halt my words. "Some practices are an infection, Fray Martín. They spread like the plague and, like the plague, they change their form and become impossible to treat. They are inaccessible to reason. Is not our peninsula infested enough by beggars and hermits, poor lost souls, unhinged cranks and, yes, frauds too, who tramp the highways and byways, live in caves, claim stigmata, see visions, experience levitations and conduct personal conversations with the Lord? The writings of Fray Juan, you must see, come very close to encouraging all manner of unhinged behaviour and making saints of those who claim to experience them."

"Indeed, but…"

"As you know, Fray Martín, heresy is not a personal matter for the individual, or even a religious matter of exclusive concern to the church. It is a matter of state. A threat to the state. Look at what happens when translations of the Bible into the vernacular are made available to the masses, when printing presses make hundreds, thousands of copies of the holy book. What is the result? The result is England, Germany, the Low Countries. Men – and even women – preaching in the streets, challenging the guidance of their priests and bishops. And a king who creates a new religion and declares himself Defender of the Faith."

Sighing, he closes his eyes. "Fray Martín, listen. We of the Holy Office of the Inquisition have a most undeserved reputation for the perpetration of injustices and brutality. I do not deny the occasional harshness of the measures we are sometimes obliged to take. But the extremity and frequency of these are greatly exaggerated in the popular mind. I can prove this. Are you aware, for example, that many secular prisoners actually petition to serve their captivity in the gaols of the Holy Office, in the knowledge that the conditions of our places of detention are more humane than the secular prisons of the state?"

I shake my head.

"As for torture. That is a strategy used very rarely and only under the most extreme circumstances. For the simple reason that it is only effective *in extremis*. Moreover, the period of physical coercion never exceeds fifteen minutes."

"Only fifteen minutes."

If he perceives my scepticism, he does not show it and continues his litany of justification and explanation. "Executions. Burnings. Again, these measures are by no means commonly used. A few prominent events – I am thinking of the *auto-da-fé* in Seville in fourteen eighty-one, almost a century and a half since – have tainted us with a reputation for cruelty which is in no way supported by the facts. In my jurisdiction, for example, fewer than forty sinners have burned during the last seventy years. Whereas, many more penitents who confessed and repented their transgressions were fined or imprisoned and returned to their homes to live normal lives."

Such as the paternal grandfather of Blessed Teresa, I do not say, for I prefer not to provide more fuel for the flames of Doctor Enrique's eloquence. The crime of her father's *converso* parents in relapsing to their Jewish faith is by now well known, although never acknowledged, as far as I am aware, by Teresa herself. According to law, this taint on her *limpieza de sangre* ought to have prevented her from joining any religious order, much less assuming such positions of leadership as she later enjoyed.

To my alarm, Doctor Enrique now reaches across my desk and gathers up a few of my own papers. They contain the rough draft of my next progress report for Crespo and Ortiz which I am due to present – a quarter hour ago.

"Fray Martín, if you are hoping to support Fray Juan's beatification, this…" he brandishes my report and smites the desk with it, "…will not do." He allows his words and actions to hang in the air as he surveys me, eyes glinting, curious to see what I will do. I make him a deep bow.

"I am an impartial investigator, Doctor Enrique. It is not my function either to promote or obstruct Fray Juan's beatification. I hope for nothing but to create a true and accurate account of the man and his life, locate his original surviving manuscripts, if I can, and thus fulfil the terms of my commission. To the best of my ability."

Doctor Enrique raises one eyebrow. I fall silent, wondering when I abandoned neutrality. Perhaps after my first meeting with Carmela. Or even earlier, when I spoke to Prior Andrés. Until this moment, I had not realised how far my objectivity had been compromised. It disturbs me to know that others have observed this in me, before I saw it myself.

He places the report back on my desk and alongside it, the pages he had brought with him containing the commentary of

Fray Juan's work. "We must see what we can do with this," he says slyly. "Perhaps you could help."

I do not immediately understand. When I do, a startling thought presents itself. I judge that his baiting has earned me the right to one more impertinence. "Doctor Enrique, forgive my curiosity. I cannot help but wonder…do you intend to rewrite all of Fray Juan's work?"

He laughs. "Rewrite? By no means. That would be a gross exaggeration. And of course, an abomination." He sighs and turns to contemplate the Vincenzio, subjecting it to minute scrutiny. "I would call it rather…retouching." He peers at the one section of the painting where the brushwork is a little less skilful than the rest. I remain silent. "School of, rather than the master himself?"

"A copy."

"Really? I would not have known. I am impressed." I wait a beat or two and he turns towards me, his thin lips set in that amused, knowing smile. "A line here. A stanza there. A single word, even. Just enough to make necessary adjustments to shades of meaning. As a professor of Theology, Fray Martín, you…"

"Former professor."

"…you are aware of the difference a single word can make in revealing the quality and meaning of an individual's thought."

I am distracted, for Doctor Enrique's words introduce an important possibility: that the editing of Fray Juan's work has already been started, and indeed, might almost be finished.

He continues. "There are many ambiguities in Fray Juan's writing that are open to different interpretations by different people. Not always unorthodox in themselves, but open to questionable uses by unsavoury people. Those *alumbrados* in Seville, for example. They are under surveillance and will come to a bad end. When that happens, the association of their practices with Fray Juan's poetry will do his reputation no good at all. It is in our interests to see that he is distanced from them."

Or else, if that is not possible, to cut him loose, he does not say. My face must have betrayed the horror I felt, for he throws his pencil on my desk in exasperation.

"Please do not regard me thus, Fray Martín. What do you think is our purpose, we of the Holy Office of the Inquisition? Do you think we take pleasure in parading families through the streets, clad in the robes and sanbenitos of penitents? In casting heretics into prison or even upon the pyre?"

I say nothing. Privately, I have indeed sometimes thought that the Inquisition was a magnet for the type of person who does enjoy such practices. People like Gregorio, the bloodthirsty steward employed long ago by the family of that Castilian innkeeper. Or Fray Alonso, Fray Juan's first gaoler. Perhaps even my own uncle Ginés.

"Do not answer that. Rather, cast your mind and your memory towards the North. Reflect on how a change of thought, the undermining of religious orthodoxy, can shake the foundations of the state. Remember Erasmus. Luther. People who knew better than their bishops, better than the pope. Think of the constant threat of treachery from our New Christians."

"Surely it is not feasible to regard with suspicion every *converso* family and every *morisco* that chose to stay behind when Ferdinand and Isabella expelled all the rest, those who refused to convert?"

"It is not only possible, Fray Martín, but absolutely necessary. It is our function as the Holy Office to protect the state from being hollowed out from within, by those whose allegiances are to other gods or to no god; or by freethinkers who deny authority and recast the holy practices of the Church for their own ends. Our constant vigilance is all that has saved this country from going the way of the Low Countries.

"And let us not forget that mad English king. Did he really believe that a daughter of Ferdinand and Isabella, a niece of the Holy Roman Emperor, would consent to be put aside, to make way for a concubine? Not to mention the threat posed by the so-called New Christians in our own land."

"But so many of those who converted and remained did great honour to our country. Blessed Teresa. Fray Juan himself, probably. Both came of Jewish stock."

The inquisitor waves his hand dismissively. "In my opinion, Fray Martín, and if you repeat it outside this room you will regret it, our Catholic monarchs made two mistakes. The first was in driving the Arabs and the Jews from our land. Had the decision been mine, I would have allowed them to stay and made it worth their while to pledge their loyalty to the new Catholic state of unified Spain, as grateful subjects of our Catholic monarchs."

"And the second?"

"The second mistake was allowing those who became Christians, or claimed to have done so, to remain, after their brethren who refused to convert had been driven out. Our New Christians are the sons and daughters of those who lost everything after they were expelled in fourteen ninety-two. No matter how loyal their descendants may seem, no matter how pious their outward display of our Catholic practices, some of them will never forgive us. I know I never would."

He gives me a crooked smile as though to invite my comment, but I know better than to answer. When I remain silent and expressionless, he sighs. "We of the Holy Office cannot monitor the workings of the human heart, the conscience. We can only make judgements based on behaviour. Leaving aside interrogation – which brings its own special problems – we must infer belief, or its absence, from the smallest of signs and symbols. What people eat. How they conduct their daily lives. What they write. Especially…" he rubs his eyes as though beginning to tire, "…what they write."

I wait in Crespo's anteroom for our meeting to begin, a half hour after the designated time, turning the words of the old

Inquisitor over in my mind. No doubt he is at this very moment conferring with Crespo and Ortiz on our conversation. Yet I am not troubled by the mercurial Inquisitor's unexpected arrival, nor by his casual references to the 'consultation' in which he hopes I will engage – with him, of course – whenever I am ready to draft my conclusions. He even gives me instructions on how I might contact him. There is a baker with a stall near the Plaza de Arrabal where I may leave a note for him. This bit of intrigue both flatters and irritates me. I promise him nothing. Nor do I tell him I would need to know a good deal more of what he expects, and how I might profit, before I committed to the action he proposes.

I hear footsteps approach. Crespo and Ortiz sweep in from the corridor and motion me to follow them. "Well?" The Archbishop settles into his throne-like chair, his squat frame almost hidden behind his desk. His aspect today is genial. Perhaps he has not yet heard of my visit to Fray Alonso in Toledo. "Have you any new information? Any revelations arising from your work in recent days?"

I bow my head and smile. "Perhaps not revelations, Your Grace. Impressions. From my discussions with your witnesses, coupled with my analysis of many of the documents you provided for my scrutiny." I bow again. "I have formed an impression of Fray Juan's character that is rather different from the usual."

"The usual?" Ortiz seems unable to ask a question without imbuing it with a sneer.

"Well, that of a rather severe person. He was an ascetic, of course, I have no quarrel with that judgement. But the harsh, joyless picture of a man whose life was not only frugal but bleak, is not the one I see. In fact, I see much to indicate quite different qualities."

Ortiz makes to interrupt but I speak over him. "In fact, much of the documentary evidence I have read, and not a few of the witness statements I have taken, reveal another side to him. He was fond of music and sometimes sang his poems for his companions, of whom several found his company agreeable and his temperament merry and joyful, rather than melancholic. And my own analysis of the events of his life..." Here I break off to consult my notes and am satisfied to observe that Ortiz maintains a surly silence, "... suggest to me that he was a person with flaws. Like any other."

I look up but neither of my listeners responds. "Item one: as a youth he was offered a permanent position in a local church. It would have given him and his family – his poverty-stricken family – a measure of financial security. He did not take it. Instead, he joined the Carmelites, almost overnight and without warning.

"Item two: he had frequent disputes with Teresa and refused to defer to her on matters of business, despite his youth and his inexperience in that field.

"Item three: he gained a reputation as a gifted exorcist, but in at least one case, he may have made a serious error. He declared a young nun possessed, even though she had been deemed infused with the spirit of God, not the Devil. The assessors who made that judgement were eminent theologians from Salamanca, amongst them Fray Juan's old tutor, the scholar and theologian Fray Luis de León. Whereas Fray Juan was quite a young man at the time and his judgement may..."

"What happened to the nun?" Crespo asks unexpectedly.

"She died. Soon after the exorcism. Shall I go on?"

Crespo nods briefly.

"Item four: he sometimes advised the sisters to refrain from confessing certain thoughts and experiences."

"What kind of thoughts and experiences?" Ortiz is no longer sneering.

"We do not know, Prior. But he was renowned as a most humane spiritual adviser who could be stern, though only when he thought it necessary.

"Item five: in later life, he supported the communities of nuns against the growing authority imposed by the vicar general Doria's new tribunal, the *consulta*. A decision that made him many enemies and probably contributed to his ultimate loss of office. Finally," I hesitate, unsure of how to put this without overstating my point, "his choice of human, profane love as allegory for the journey of the soul towards union with God was not the most neutral literary device he could have chosen."

"And what does all this suggest to you, Fray Martín?" I am not sure if the smoothness of Crespo's question conceals genuine interest or contempt.

"A more complicated personality than the usual idea of him, Your Grace. Most descriptions of the man put me in mind of those flat, sombre paintings of saints with halos and rigid faces and not a shadow in sight. When I hear people who knew Fray Juan speak of him, when I read the small, daily details of his life, I see a person composed of many shades of light and dark. A man, like others. Out of the ordinary, it is true. Above all, a brave man."

"Brave?" Crespo looks up, interested.

"He stood his ground, Your Grace, in the face of violent opposition and physical brutality. He resisted threats, both of physical harm, and of damage to his reputation. No doubt his opponents really believed that the theological differences he illuminated gave good grounds for their actions. Some may have thought they were protecting the Order from a heretic, that he was aligned with the *alumbrados*, and perhaps they feared he would bring the Inquisition down upon their Order."

Neither man speaks, which I take as permission to continue. "Notwithstanding such concerns – possibly even legitimate concerns – in one other matter I consider the conduct of his opponents to be deeply reprehensible." I pause, unsure whether I should stop or go on. "I refer to the investigation into Fray Juan's conduct that occurred towards the end of his life. Into accusations of improper conduct. Of a... Of his having sinned against his vows of chastity."

Crespo looks up sharply. "Those accusations were made against Gracián, you mean."

"They resembled those made against Fray Jerónimo Gracián, Your Grace, yes. Such calumnies were also made against Fray Juan, in the year before his death, not long before he was banished to Andalucía to wait for the ship that would take him to Mexico."

"Yes." Ignoring my observation, Ortiz casts a sharp glance at his superior. "Gracián was a casualty of circumstances."

"And of his own vanities and ill judgement." Crespo's florid colour has risen further. Mention of Fray Jerónimo Gracián, Teresa's father confessor after Fray Juan was imprisoned, has agitated him. Recalling that Gracián had held high office and positions of great influence in the Carmelite reforms, being Teresa's faithful friend and possibly her favourite, to whom she had even pledged a vow of obedience, I wonder at Crespo's distress.

"I am not speaking of Fray Jerónimo Gracián, Your Grace, but of Fray Juan de la Cruz. Who was a casualty, not of circumstances but of false accusations." Although my tone is reasonable, there is no gentle way to openly challenge an Archbishop. I resolve to press on. "Fray Juan was a victim of baseless calumnies that were invented by the same Discalced Carmelite official who investigated Gracián. An official whose methods were, to say the least, questionable."

Ortiz rises from his chair and strides across the room, his hand extended to take possession of the notes I am reading.

"Who are the witnesses who provided this information...?"

Unwilling to relinquish my papers, I clutch them. "That official was called Fray Diego Evangelista." At this point, I pause to leaf through two or three pages, conscious of Ortiz by my side, standing much too close. "He was assisted by an associate named Fray Crisóstomo. Together they invented a tall tale, or a series of tall tales they had concocted about Fray Juan and various nuns." I hold up two letters I found in Crespo's chest. "Some of those sisters made formal written complaints about Crisóstomo's methods to the vicar general. I assume you are aware of this, Your Grace."

Crespo looks straight head and makes no answer. I sense Ortiz stiffen by my side.

"It appears that Evangelista subjected some of the sisters to brutal questioning. He kept them under lock and key for hours without food or water or sleep, trying to intimidate them into making outlandish claims against Fray Juan's conduct. He even presented some of them with fabricated statements, which he demanded that they sign. Here." I stride across to Crespo's desk and place two letters in front of him. He does not look at them. Neither he nor his subordinate has anything to say.

"What I cannot understand, Your Grace, is why such persecution was visited on Fray Juan by amateur investigators determined to invent stories that were patently false."

A thick silence descends. Crespo and Ortiz remain quite still, the only sound the cry of a bird in the garden. Without knowing how, I have crossed some invisible frontier.

"Tell me, Your Grace. Please," I urge, "why did they – the new vicar general Doria, and his acolytes – engage those two men on a mission that was clearly designed to destroy Fray Juan's reputation?"

Crespo brings his fist down on his desk. It is an unprecedented display of emotion, all the more shocking for its rarity. "Your logic is deeply flawed!" I flinch. Ortiz does, too. "You have no evidence whatsoever that such was the purpose of Fray Evangelista's investigation. Nor that such was Doria's intention in having commissioned it. Fray Martín, you abuse your position and the privileged knowledge to which it has afforded you access."

"I am sorry to speak so bluntly, Your Grace," I answer, badly shaken yet resolved to stand my ground. "These are not opinions. The facts speak for themselves. Those two friars, Diego Evangelista and Francisco Crisóstomo, nursed a grudge against Fray Juan for years, possibly decades, since they were novices and he was their novice master."

Crespo's steady gaze shows no surprise. I am sure that he knew this, and much more.

"All because Fray Juan once chided their preference for preaching in the market place rather than engaging in solitary prayer and meditation in their cell. It was a reprimand that they never forgave and explains their rigour and enthusiasm in keeping their vow of obedience to Doria: it must have been a pleasure for them, as well as a duty."

Crespo attempts to interrupt but I raise my voice, conscious that this might be the last time I will have the opportunity to speak plainly in this forum, or to speak at all. "It is difficult to decide which of the two was the more reprehensible: Fray Crisóstomo, who used his position as prior of the monastery in Úbeda, where Fray Juan sought refuge in his last illness, to mistreat him, deny him nursing care, companionship and even bodily nourishment, to treat him more cruelly than any of us would treat a sick dog; or Fray Diego Evangelista, whose vile bullying of the sisters of Andalucía induced many of them to destroy all the papers and correspondence they had received from Fray Juan over many years."

Unable to silence me with words and angry looks, Crespo finally stands, his squat bulk outlined against the window. He lumbers across the room and plants himself in front of me, much too close, all the weight of his command directed towards silencing me. Still I do not flinch. In launching my final barb, I look him straight in the eye.

"Therefore, Your Grace, I lament to inform you that the task of finding any of Fray Juan's original papers will almost certainly remain unfulfilled. Most probably, they have all been destroyed, thanks to the disgraceful conduct of this Fray Diego Evangelista. Many of the sisters report that they burned Fray Juan's letters and poems and other documents by the sack load, precisely to ensure that they would not fall into Fray Evangelista's hands."

At that, Ortiz glides noiselessly to my side, grips my elbow and guides me to the door. His murmured assurances that my questions and concerns will be given due consideration, his unaccustomed, exaggerated courtesy, perturb me. But not as much as the look on Crespo's handsome, fleshy countenance – full lips pressed together, complexion pasty white and in the beam of those pale eyes, directed at me, a glare of pure, intense hate.

Monastery of San Gerónimo, Madrid,
Twenty-eighth day of June in the Year of Our Lord, 1616.

You are fording a river in flood, a wide, dark torrent rushing through a barren landscape. How was such a journey possible before now? How did you navigate these turbulent waters without knowing that they thundered all around, dragging you forward, inexorably, then into the deep? For such a long time you knew not that such turbulent waters were the element of your life, had never heard those roaring currents, as they eddied and foamed around hidden rocks. Somehow, without knowing, without wishing, you navigated. And now, no more.

You are on a faraway shore,

past frontiers and fountains

Turn, face back along the path that led you here. You will not gaze upon the arid landscape that remains. Half a century gone. Yet until now, before those darkening waters had been crossed, your gaze was fixed ahead, towards the future. No more.

The candle flickers, the fire is guttering down. Soon the flames will turn to ash for you will not rouse yourself to find another lump of wood, a few twigs nor even a log that would bank it up, you will not trouble to retrieve another candle, to keep the darkness a little way away another while. Immobile, you will stay here as shadows gather round. This cold turns flesh to marble. You are motionless, for this body, your body, is emptied of spirit. Of will. The flame dims a little, then more, now as the candle flickers you become weary, these limbs are heavy, these eyelids droop. There is no blood within, nothing but poisoned water courses through these veins. This heart. Vitality has drained away, through an open wound that empties on to darkness.

It is a small, high room. If you reached out your arms, which you cannot, such is their weight, but if you did, your fingers would touch walls. Is that a spear of light entering through a narrow slit high on the wall? If you stand, a little of that warmth will touch your face. It has been so long since you felt the sun on your skin. Weeks. Months. You no longer count the days that slip unbidden into night. How many have passed unobserved, since the soft breeze breathed on your skin, since you

cross these mountains and shores
pluck blossoms
brave savage beasts

You take a breath. A deep, deep draught of air that is not stale with the stink of your sweat, your vomit, your dirt and urine, air that is not rancid from the stench of the wounds on your skin, raw from the fleas, from filthy undergarments, from the fishy whiff of sardine heads the gaoler sometimes tosses on the floor. Voices. They speak your name. You are vilified by all. Abandoned, left for dead, and death will surely come. The leather of this breviary is rough, your palm caresses it, you cannot read for it is night, yes,

one dark night when
> *where did you hide, my love, and leave me to bewail you?*
> *like the stag you fled*
this wound

> *these wounds*

I follow
> *I set out calling after you*

It must be night, but the sky is moonless. If you die here, and you surely will, no one will remember your existence. Nobody will know. Or care. The candle struggles, wavers, is finally extinguished. You take care to keep these eyes tight shut. Even so, the glow that penetrates your eyelids starts to fade. The tiny glimmer that banished the darkness is almost gone. Now, it is truly gone, leaving nothing. Only this body, slumped in this chair. In a chilly room, every moment colder, for there is no flame, no fire to warm the air

> *living flame of love*
> It is no more alive for
> *warmth and light that joins with love*

are so very far away. No will for life. These twigs and sticks and, heaped at your feet, a basket filled with kindling, candles, flints, would do. No. A granite stillness. These eyes clamped shut give no protection from dark visions of how this life has been. You wait on a far river bank, all purpose fled. Despair. The only sin that can never be forgiven. In the deepest part of the night, when you know you nevermore will take Communion, never sing another Mass, no more transform the bread and wine to blood and body of Christ, you know that you will die here. You will die here and all that remains to be done, will fall. All, will fail.

Not for this did you survive

who will succour me,

>*how can this life go on when I not living where I ought to live*

this smile unbidden in the darkness

>*leave me dying*

>>*take these arrows*

these thoughts sensations,

>*through this heart are healed*

these eyes are flickering. You have no pen, no paper, no ink

>*this crystal fountain flows*

shows you

>>*drawn on my entrails*

This is a golden thread that weaves through the night, a bright guide weaving back to the world. It will save you. These lines forged in blackness. Your lips move in rhythm, these whispered rhymes soft on the night air. There is a girl who steals out to meet her lover and the lover is God and the girl is your soul. Very soon there will be succour and shelter and pears poached in cinnamon. There will be people who listen and hands to wash away the blood and souls to hear these lines.

But the truth of life lies behind, far in the past. You survey it in sorrow, in all the bitterness of small concerns that blind you. There is no solace in the darkness, only the deepest of shadows and the abyss ahead. Somewhere along the barren path that you now tread, on the farthest bank of this great river, the deep ravine that separates you from the self that once you were, and who you are. There is nothing. Squandered, all. A throng, a magnificent town square, the Plaza de Arrabal renewed, with rich columns, porticos, crowds all around. A line of penitents, heads bowed, covered in the shameful yellow *sanbenitos*, those penitents might be spared. The court proclaims its judgement on the rest, the flames are painted heavenwards. These accused will burn. It is a summer festival and a man of strange aspect takes the throne. He has the eyes of our Felipe but larger, enormous, protruding. Does he weep? Saliva dribbles down his enormous jaw. His tongue is thick and huge in his mouth. He speaks.

Will they repent?

Of what?

The creature leans, inclines himself and the flames leap, sizzle on skin and the stench of burning flesh. A grotesque, smiling face looms above.

"Fray Martín?"

The room is freezing. A log has toppled from the fire and smoke is rising from a smouldering twig.

"Fray Martín, are you ill?"

Young Fray Francis is leaning over me, his grimace a nervous smile. I open my eyes and remain motionless for a second or two, gathering my thoughts. At least it is not Ortiz or one of Crespo's secretaries. I judge that I can trust this young novice to keep his counsel.

"I was reading. I must have fallen asleep."

The young man looks around. I know there is no book for him to find.

"You have been here all night, Fray Martín. Are you sure you are well?"

His gaze is troubled. I reassure him and he pads away, promising to bring me an infusion of mint and rosemary. My neck aches, my bones are stiff and creaking. I stretch and try to stand. It will be another leaden day. My eyes swivel around the room for it is still too painful to move my head. It must be late, for the high summer sun has slipped across the polished floor, illuminating the scratches and stains on the oak, the fine film of ash that has settled over the mantelpiece. If I move too quickly I will tumble like a puppet to the floor. No one must know that I slept for the whole night in a chair, my habit and cloak gathered around me for warmth.

Must my thoughts ever return to my illustrious uncle? Must I judge myself as blood of the man who used his learning to take the light of humankind from other men and women, declare them inferior species of humans, fit to be used for the glory of King Felipe and of God, in bringing the wealth of the Americas to our land?

Why must I be blood of anyone?

Pepita. My blood. Her little life. I understand that if ever I can move from this place, it will not be force of will that drives me. Will has deserted me. I must seek help. And choose with care. Fray Juan chose his pain, he sought it out: the silences, the suffering. Pepita never chose and yet it came. Though almost half a century has passed I hear her cries, her whimpers penetrate the house, my father grips the armrests of his chair. The sickroom door is closed to us, where Pepita lies with my mother as she tries to soothe her. From time to time, the whimpers turn to screams.

"Please, God, make it stop. Not for always. Just for a minute, good little baby Jesus, just for a little minute."

The door creaks open. Your nurse slips out, a bloodied sheet in her hand. Our mother lies beside you on the bed, cradling your head. I sit on the stairs watching your nurse open the door again. It closes on my final glimpse of you. But your whimpering, your screams, do not end then. I hear them, all through the night. Before the end. Of childhood. Of innocence.

Spare your prayers, Pepita, there is nothing for it but to endure the final, searing agony that racks your little body and ends your tiny life. Do not waste your final breaths on cries for mercy, the good little baby Jesus is not listening. He is not there. No one, nothing, is.

Convent of El Carmen, Málaga,
Twelfth day of July in the Year of Our Lord, 1616.

E very morning since I came here, I have started the day with a special tea brewed by one of the novices, while passing a pleasant hour gazing over the narrow strip of sea that separates our peninsula from the coast of Africa. Sometimes I am alone, but more often Madre Carmela sits with me for a while. She recommends this infusion to calm a troubled mind and animate the body. Today, I feel the benefit of its effects. The time I have passed in the convent of the Carmelite sisters of Málaga, in the shadow of the ancient Moorish castle, the Alcazaba and the fortress of the Gibralfaro, has restored me. I feel my spirits revive and my will regain strength, due, in part, to the beauty and serenity of this place.

All around us, the work of the Arab civilisation casts its peaceful spell. Long, motionless pools of water reflect archways fashioned in the gracious *mudéjar* horseshoe style. Courtyards enclosed by slim columns brim with flowers and evergreen shrubs, most in full bloom, the aroma from their scented blossoms heady in the early morning. From a spring high in the hillside, a stream trickles and tumbles from the upper terraces to the lower, sprinkling its music on the air. The whole, a most beauteous legacy bequeathed by those whom our Catholic monarchs and their descendants expelled from our land.

"One of our nuns comes from a family of gardeners attached to the home of the Duke of Alba," Madre Carmela informs me as she pours a second glass of the delicious infusion. "One of the duke's homes, I should say. Sister Beata takes a special interest in our courtyards and tries to recreate the atmosphere of the original. We find it soothing and conducive to meditation."

I say nothing. Between us, there is no need for words. We remain seated, side by side, comfortable in this scented silence that is broken only by dark, screaming little birds as they swoop and dive in graceful arcs, wings almost grazing the still surface of the water.

"What are they?"

"Swifts. We consider their presence a great blessing. It is said that they left with the coming of Ferdinand and Isabella, when the Moors were driven out. During the last few years, Sister Beata made it her mission to try to coax them back. This is but their third summer in our little convent and we are charmed that they have returned to us. Many years ago, these gardens and courtyards were in ruins."

"Which explains why you were allowed to take over this site."

"At the time no paying tenant could be found. But as you know, we Carmelites have often been obliged to occupy the most derelict of places and from our struggle and labour, create an oasis of peace. The restoration of this place was much easier than we expected, because the underlying structures of the buildings were so good, even though they had been unused for almost a hundred years. Since the siege."

The siege of Málaga. When the last shreds of Moorish resistance to the armies of Ferdinand and Isabella capitulated, and the townspeople and soldiers, weary of starvation and terror, relinquished the gardens and fountains of the city, its orchards and palaces, to our Catholic monarchs.

"After that great victory, a royal garrison occupied the city for a while," Madre Carmela informs me. "But in the years that followed, this little corner of the fortress grounds fell into dereliction. As you see," the sweep of her arm embraces the sea before us and the gardens and cloisters of the convent behind, "that was to our great advantage."

The sleeve of her habit falls back to reveal smooth, glistening skin where tiny beads of sweat are rising on her arm, even though the hour is early and we are in the shade of a tall cedar that casts its protective shadow over us. I should like to taste the salt on that brown skin. I watch myself lean forward, bury my face in the delicate crook of her elbow, part my lips, rest my fingers on her wrist, run the tip of my tongue along her arm…

"But I confess I sometimes wonder at the wisdom of our Catholic monarchs in having expelled our Arab brethren from the peninsula."

Unaware of my discomfort, she spreads both arms wide. They are slim and muscular, accustomed to physical labour. I am sure they are firm to the touch. I avert my eyes and fix my attention on a bright red blossom that has the form and grace of a lily. I hope that my deep, contented sigh steadies my uneven breath.

"We may not always have lived in perfect harmony, we Christians, Arabs and Jews. But life was at least as harmonious as now. In the days before the constant scrutiny of the Holy Office of the Inquisition."

My own view is that the situation was far from being so simple. I decide to keep my opinions to myself, for the moment.

"That is heresy, Madre Carmela," I point out. "High treason."

"Are you going to denounce me, then? As if anyone would listen to you, now."

I burst out laughing, unable to help myself. This is an incorrigible woman. And she is right. During this investigation,

I have not only failed to distinguish myself, I have made no progress at all towards recovering my position in the university. Worse, after my calamitous attempt to meet Archbishop Crespo free of the watchful presence of his lackey Prior Ortiz, I may have placed myself in real danger.

"Why did the Archbishop refuse to meet you alone?"

I shrug. "Who knows? Perhaps he needed a witness to any discussions about Fray Juan. Or he may have wanted Ortiz to be present to keep me in check, to obstruct any difficult questions I might put to him."

Having weighed every word I uttered during that final dreadful encounter, having reflected on the nuance of their words, I think I have identified the moment when the temperature plunged from chilly to freezing. At least I now know the reason for Crespo's bitter rage, when he ordered me from his presence.

I should have treated Fray Alonso's suggestions with more caution. That wily old fox dangled the bait, and I tumbled straight into his trap. Still, my final misstep – to have imagined that Crespo would want to hear of my findings concerning the accusations against Fray Juan, and the ill-treatment he suffered at the hands of Prior Evangelista... Well, that was all my own.

"Had Fray Juan lived, Your Grace, there is no doubt that those investigators would have seen him stripped of his habit. Only his death robbed them of that victory. The unfortunate Fray Jerónimo Gracián was not so..." I left the thought unsaid. The trials and disgrace endured by Fray Jerónimo, who lived into old age, were a far worse fate than that of Fray Juan, who at the time of his death was greatly loved and deeply venerated. "Your Grace, I struggle to understand why these two men – Fray Juan and Fray Jerónimo, friends of Teresa who is now Blessed by the Church – pious friars who devoted their lives to the Carmelite reform, whose efforts finally succeeded in gaining a measure of independence for the Discalced Order – should have been so viciously slandered by members of their own Discalced community."

I paused, determined to say no more until one of them responded. At that moment, Crespo chose to launch his attack.

"Fray Martín. What was the reason for your visit to Toledo and the unauthorised interview you conducted there with Fray Alonso?"

I had long anticipated such a challenge. Yet, when it came, it caught me off balance. I grasped my papers, as though clinging to a raft in a sea of uncertainty. "I had been made aware of certain conditions that prevailed while Fray Juan was imprisoned in Toledo. I wished to verify the information and to see the premises for myself."

"That subject is outside your brief. Far, far outside it."

"But it emerged as a direct consequence of my work on this brief. Moreover, the meeting I conducted in Toledo," I could not bring myself to utter the old brute's name, "allowed me to confirm details of how Fray Juan was abducted, imprisoned, held without charge for almost a year, beaten, starved, made to live with his own..."

"You were not authorised to take testimony from that witness."

Aware that I was exceeding the boundaries of protocol but unable to stop myself, I pressed on. "There is more. Much more. The physical tortures that Fray Juan endured while held captive in Toledo were as nothing compared to the mental torment that his own Discalced brethren visited upon him many years later. In the form of that investigation," I allowed the word to dangle in the air for a moment, injecting it with all the contempt I could muster, "the mock investigation that sought to destroy his reputation by the simple stratagem of asking questions. The kind of questions for which the very act of denial implies culpability. Questions designed not to elicit truth, but to create an alternative version of it."

Crespo's pale eyes swivelled to meet the troubled gaze of his subordinate. Ortiz got to his feet. He is a tall man, almost as tall as I am. "That is all very abstract, Fray Martín," he sneered. "An alternative version of truth? I cannot imagine what that means."

"Then allow me to explain." At that moment, it was clear that neither Ortiz nor Crespo was listening. Rather, each was seeking an opportunity to silence me. But I had come too far to retreat. "I have only recently understood that the most bitter struggles in this saga were waged between members of the Discalced Carmelites themselves, after they gained a degree of independence from the Carmelites of the Mitigated Rule when they were accorded the status of a separate Province."

"Perhaps so. Perhaps not. But none of this has the slightest relevance to your commission."

"On the contrary, Prior Ortiz. The hostilities that erupted between the Discalced Carmelites after Teresa's death is central to Fray Juan's legacy, precisely the legacy that you have bid me probe. These very conflicts led to Fray Jerónimo Gracián's expulsion from the Order, by people who wanted him out of the way. The same conflicts contributed to Fray Juan's loss of office and final banishment. Decisions that were effected at the great Chapter meeting of..." Here, I paused to consult my notes.

"June fifteen ninety-one," Ortiz murmured. I looked up at him in surprise. I had long suspected that Ortiz, no doubt kept informed by his Inquisitor cousin Doctor Enrique, had little to learn concerning Fray Juan and the turbulent history of the Discalced Carmelites. Was he thinking now to share his knowledge with me? Unlikely.

"June fifteen ninety-one, yes." I repeated. "At the instigation of..." This time, neither man spoke, but they continued to survey me, their blank gazes an affectation. "Doria. Niccolà Doria. The new provincial of the Discalced Order." I paused, awaiting a response. "A late vocation," I added, "favoured by Teresa and also by the king, for whom, I believe, he arranged a significant loan when he was still a Genovese banker."

Crespo cleared his throat. He did not speak but neither did he bid me be silent. I pressed on. "I do not yet understand Niccolà Doria's opposition to both Fray Jerónimo Gracián and to Fray Juan," I observed and immediately regretted my words, for Ortiz and Crespo may have heard in them some defiance, the threat that whether they liked it or not, I would very soon know all. "Perhaps, having achieved the status of a separate Province, bound by Teresa's Constitution, this loss of a common foe drove the leaders to squabble amongst themselves."

"Those were far from simple squabbles." Crespo's voice was low, his brow furrowed.

As I spoke, a strange, parallel line of thought began to surface in my mind, as though my words to Crespo had penetrated my own confusion, plumbed its depths and finally grasped a hitherto formless thought that was now taking shape.

These men do not seek a coherent outcome to my investigation. They already know everything I have reported to them, and much more besides. They plucked me from the obscurity of my little convent of San Salvador, damaged reputation and all, not in recognition of my special talents, but for precisely the opposite reason: for the inertia, the bitterness of my being during these recent years. That was my recommendation for this job.

The understanding struck me with the force of a physical blow to the chest. I fear that my final, strangled words betrayed my anguish. "Thus are the fates of the great sealed by the petty preoccupations of the mediocre."

I do not know why it took me so long to understand that I had gone too far. No doubt my dismissal was certain from the moment I had entered Crespo's office for that final meeting. When I finished speaking, reeling from the force of the brutal illumination just visited upon me – of how I am viewed by my superiors, perhaps by many others – it seemed impossible that my situation could be any worse.

"But it was. Much worse than I knew."

Carmela's gold-flecked eyes open wide. "That scarcely seems possible," she remarks.

"I know. But it is true. For, as I learned shortly afterwards, Fray Diego Evangelista – the vicious young pup, Doria's minion who sought to bully the Discalced Carmelite sisters of Andalucía into making false accusations against Fray Juan – was a brother of Archbishop Crespo's father. He was Crespo's uncle."

Carmela draws a sharp breath, bites her lower lip. "Forgive me, Martín. I am not... It is just so..." A deep, hearty laugh bursts forth from her throat.

In truth, this is no laughing matter. But again I shrug and smile, disposed to forgive her levity. "I know. I was so pleased with the results of my discoveries. Well, my vanity has been punished. As I deserved."

Carmela rests her hand upon my arm. The warmth of her touch sends a jolt through my body. "You are not to blame. You carried out your given task to the best of your ability, with no help from those who were responsible for the commission. Your tenacity is rather to your credit."

I frown. "Perhaps. I prefer not to delve into my motivations."

"Very well, Martín. But is it possible that Evangelista's role in persecuting Fray Juan at the end of his life explains why Crespo wanted to limit the scope of your work?"

"I suppose it is possible. Overall, I think not, however. The family relationship between Crespo and Evangelista is not a secret. I do not understand the intricacies of these webs, but Crespo and Ortiz probably assumed that I did. No doubt they interpreted my insistence on Evangelista's conduct as a brazen challenge to their authority."

Carmela breathes a deep sigh and stands, gazing out across the bay where the sun is dancing on the waves. I miss the touch of her hand on my arm. "Did Fray Juan make no attempt to defend himself against the campaign those people mounted against him?"

"As far as I can ascertain, he did not. He advised others to ignore Evangelista's accusations. Convinced that the truth would save him. Until that last Chapter meeting in Madrid, when he lost his position." I allow my fingers to trail in the pool of water alongside my chair. "I think that Fray Juan did not understand the seriousness of the situation. He trusted too much in the courage of other people to stand with him, and against Doria."

Carmela turns from her contemplation of the sea and resumes her seat at my side. "At that last Chapter meeting, you know, he tried to have the votes for elections and policy conducted by secret ballot. He tried to support us sisters in our struggle against Doria's new regime."

I look up, startled.

"Martín, much of this is well known amongst the Discalced sisters. Doria's new procedures – that new tribunal, the *consulta* – was a disaster for us. The rules and regulations he introduced, hundreds of them, no doubt suited the business of an Italian bank but they completely distorted the administration of the Order. Above all, the *consulta* stripped away the independence of our convents. Fray Juan alone tried to stop him, to maintain the spirit of Teresa's Constitution for our Order. If a secret ballot had been permitted at that Chapter meeting, he might have succeeded."

Her observation gives me pause. I have always opposed secrecy in votes concerning matters of great importance, convinced that it is nothing more than a breeding ground for the noxious weeds of calumny. I am sure that the whispered rumours that blighted my life in Salamanca would have gained no purchase at all, had my accusers been forced to speak out and be held to account.

"Carmela, you have shown me the other side of that coin: how dealings conducted in the open can be used by a powerful leader…"

"Doria was a tyrant, not a leader."

"…to identify and reward his allies…"

"…and punish his opponents." Carmela's sombre words fall on silence. I yearn, and dread, to feel the touch of her small hand on my arm once again.

"Your own… difficulties… in Salamanca did not go so far, Martín. Did they? Your enemies withdrew their accusations?"

When I make no answer, she misunderstands my silence. How could she not? "Beg pardon, Martín, please forgive the intrusion."

"There is no intrusion, Carmela." My voice is hoarse. "I owe my liberty, perhaps even my life, to Diego. Diego Clemente, one of the workers attached to the university. Had it not been for him and his understanding of the situation…"

"How could a menial labourer have understood the danger, when you yourself did not?"

I shrug. "Diego has a more practical view of the world, I suppose. Also, I suspect that he has education above the usual for one of his station. I have sometimes wondered whether his humble position in the university might not have been the result of some calamitous decline in status."

"You did not inquire?"

"Often. At least, until he told me to my face that such questions were unwelcome and to mind my business."

Carmela laughs again. "I like him already."

I am silent a moment, ashamed to remember that I have not seen Diego, nor sought him out, since I left Salamanca. "Whatever the source, Diego had notice of the lies being whispered about me long before I heard them myself. I dismissed them, of course, assuming that my reputation, the respect in which others regarded me – as I thought – would protect me. I assumed that nothing evil could befall me, because I had done nothing wrong."

"Fray Juan's mistake."

"Until then, I had no idea of the power of innuendo. What need is there of open accusations, when questions and hints can gather momentum and create a reality that in no way corresponds to the facts?"

Carmela leans towards me. "Might this explain the very great risks you have taken during this investigation? Forgive me, Martín, but you admit that you have pursued it in a manner most disadvantageous to yourself."

I sigh. "That is not quite true, Carmela. I have pursued it in a manner which, if I am honest, I considered would be advantageous and would display my abilities in the best possible light. It was a mission born of vanity, if you will. The desire to shine."

"Or to uncover the truth?"

I shake my head. "How can I understand the depths of my own motivations? Yes, from the beginning I have had a profound resistance to the very idea of this investigation. The absence of boundaries. The vagueness of purpose. The use of questions as an instrument. To do what? I do not know. To set boundaries on the quest for truth. Perhaps to destroy a reputation. Such methods can do that."

"As you have good cause to know."

"As I have good cause to know."

"Martín, you have gone beyond what Archbishop Crespo asked. By adding your own witnesses and asking your own questions, you have complicated the matter."

"I have. But I am not sure what I have accomplished in the process. I may have done no more than unearth fragments of Fray Juan's life and work that were hitherto ignored or dismissed. Details that could make it possible to construct an alternative to the version authorised by Crespo and Ortiz and the others."

"These fragments, have you documented them?"

"Of course." I hesitate and for a moment consider revealing the existence of this journal. But if things go badly for me, then it is better that she know nothing of these scribblings. "Documentary evidence can make all the difference to how things turn out."

"Did that make all the difference to you? Is that how Diego helped you?"

I find myself chuckling. Perhaps I have learned something of strategy from my old servant and friend after all.

"Tell me."

I had just returned to my cell, shocked and trembling, following my meeting with the vice chancellor. There was significant evidence – a 'web of circumstances,' the vice chancellor called it: dates, sightings, places – that supported the young man's accusations. Although only minor nobility, he was a nephew by marriage of the Duke of Alba and, therefore, under his protection. The boy's dissolute ways were well known but had hitherto been overlooked. Something must have happened to change this, some scrape or assault that was too public to be kept quiet.

On that day, I did not call for Diego as I usually did but slumped into my chair, allowed my eyes to wander over my bookshelves, the many parchments and folios, wondering how much longer I would have the pleasure of living amongst them. Footsteps echoed in the corridor and stopped outside my cell. A gentle knocking was easy to ignore, but when a heavy fist started to pound on the door I gave up and flung it open.

"Fray Martín." It was Diego. Outraged at his persistence, I waved him away. He stood firm. To my astonishment, he inserted a foot – a large foot – in the space between the threshold and the door. "I am deeply sorry for what is happening to you, Fray Martín. If I may, I should like to suggest…"

"Diego, I cannot discuss this with you. They will realise their mistake soon enough."

Diego's acquaintance with my situation horrified me. A discussion with a university servant on the subject was the last thing I wanted. My only wish was to return to my desk, read the scriptures and prepare my lectures for the coming week. I was about to remind him of the differences in our station and chide him for his impertinence, when, to my astonishment, his eyes filled with tears.

"Fray Martín, you have always treated me with great understanding and compassion." Had I?

"When my daughter was ill, you made me a gift that allowed me to leave the university for almost a week to be with her. The two reales you gave me that day paid for the doctor and her medicine."

I had no memory of this. At least... Yes, something of the kind had occurred several years before.

"And you allowed me to attend your classes with the apprentices."

To carry my books and accompany me to a part of the town that is not always safe. I frowned, wary of what was coming next.

"Fray Martín, those kindnesses were trifles to you, but they made a great difference to my life. I am in your debt. I cannot bear to see you place yourself in such danger, through blind trust in those who would see you burn, to save their own skins."

Burn? Hands trembling, I stood aside and motioned him to enter. When I resumed my place at my desk he sat, unbidden, on the edge of my bed. "I am listening, Diego."

Dark eyes blazing, he leaned forward. "Fray Martín," my visitor steepled his fingers. Diego was not a timid man and his success in gaining entry to my cell seemed to have unleashed in him even greater reserves of confidence than the usual. "You are a man of great wisdom and learning. You have much knowledge and understanding of the life of the mind. About ideas, books, the thoughts of philosophers and saints."

I frowned. I knew all this to be true; I did not need a minion of the university to tell me. "It is my profession."

"But you are a poor judge of character. And a bad tactician." I blinked, lost for an adequate response. "Those final year students of yours…"

This could not be. Those five young men, whose intellectual and spiritual progress I nurtured for more than three years… "They would not. Never."

"They have, Fray Martín."

I stared, not even trying to hide my shock. "How can you know this? I cannot, will not, believe such a thing."

"I know it from their servants, Fray Martín. They do not accuse you." His tone was gentle, as though trying to soften the impact of a terrible blow. "But they do not support you either, and in circumstances such as these, that is almost as bad."

"But this is impossible! I have never been seen abroad with the… participant," I could not think of another word to describe him, "because I have never been alone with him!"

"Fray Martín." Diego's voice took on a new urgency, as though he feared that the shock of such betrayal by my few protégés, and worse, by those whom I had considered my friends, would extinguish my will to fight. Until that moment, I had not known that I would need it. "You are looking at this in the wrong way. You are thinking about truth. Justice. You know that these heinous accusations are untrue and believe that the facts will support you, clear your name, expose the true wrong-doers. I am sorry, Fray Martín, this may be life in the world of books and ideas, but the world of the human heart is very different. People who are threatened – and the appetites and indiscretions of that young nobleman have put his future in great danger, for as you know, sodomy can be a capital offence – will do anything, to protect themselves."

"But how does accusing me save him?"

"If he can show that he was not an instigator, that he was corrupted by an older man in a position of authority, things will go better for him. Much better. The fact that he is telling a pack of lies affords you no protection. Rather, the opposite. The supporters of the Duke of Alba's young nephew cannot now disbelieve him. They cannot allow themselves that luxury, for there are too many fortunes bound up in that family. Besides, the king needs the money from the alliance with that Duke. His coffers are almost empty."

The economics of the situation ring true, for it is an open secret that our state is bankrupt, or will be soon. Profligate spending on the wars in the North have devoured the riches our *conquistadores* brought back from the Americas during the last century. All squandered, the feudal lords complain – but never too loudly – whenever new taxes are raised on them. If my accuser really has a connection to King Felipe, however tenuous, then the destruction of an obscure university professor, a mere Dominican theologian, will be a small matter.

I must have paled, for without asking my permission, Diego went to the shelf where I keep a small jug of red wine for saying Mass. He poured two fingers into the cup on my desk and handed it to me, before settling back into his place on the edge of my bed, to explain how I might be saved. Or save myself.

Item: I must forget about the truth, which is a dangerous distraction, and concentrate only on strategy.

Item: I must discard notions of justice and concentrate on finding information that discredits my accuser.

Item: I must not trust in my peers or superiors, but rather, make myself as troublesome to them as I can. Let them know that their plan to use me to extricate this young count from his predicament will cause more problems than it will solve.

"But what, in plain terms, am I to do, Diego?"

At those words, my old friend – for now, I think of him thus

– heaved a sigh of relief, the sallow skin at his eyes crinkled and his mouth twisted in a sly grin I had never before remarked. "There is a way, Fray Martín."

Entranced by the clear chimes of a bell floating on the air, for a moment I drift into silence, until the cracked voice of Sor Eugenia calls us for lunch. It has done me good to speak of this. I feel my spirit lighted, relieved of a burden.

Madre Carmela tugs at my sleeve. "What was Diego's plan, Martín? What did he do?"

Already the sisters are emerging from their cells, making their way to the refectory. "Let us speak more of this later," I murmur. Side by side we stroll, both of us in contemplative mood.

"If Fray Juan had not died so soon after that Chapter meeting in Madrid when he lost his position, there is no telling how the whole dreadful story would have ended," Carmela reflects. "He might have gone to Mexico, as Doria ordered. He might even have been stripped of his habit."

"They would have expelled him from the community he helped to create. That is what happened to Fray Jerónimo Gracián much later. Fray Juan would not be remembered. We might never have heard of him."

"Except for his poems."

"Yes." I recall a beauteous, illuminated manuscript in a vellum scroll and two disordered sheafs of pages, some numbered, some not, piled high on the windowsill of my office.

The *Canticle*. Therein, I will find the key to Fray Juan's past. And, if I am fortunate, to my own future.

Convent of Carmen, Málaga,
Thirteenth day of July in the Year of Our Lord, 1616.

O n this, my final day amongst the Discalced Carmelite sisters of Málaga, I make a discovery that is both puzzling and unwelcome. Madre Carmela has concealed from me the presence here in Málaga of a member of her own community who has first-hand knowledge of Fray Juan's escape from his Toledo cell. I learn this quite by accident. Weary of all the talk of my own troubles, I decided to show Carmela copies of a few of Fray Juan's short poems which I had gathered up in haste before I left Madrid, hoping that I would feel disposed to study them in the tranquil ambience of Andalucía, where Fray Juan lived for so many years.

"I received these from an old prior in Oviedo who was Fray Juan's companion during his student days in Salamanca," I tell her. A few of the pages are covered in widely spaced lines, grouped in couplets, some followed by a refrain: a dozen stanzas in all.

Carmela scans the pages. A broad, sweet smile illuminates her countenance. "I have heard this poem before." Some faltering in her voice alerts me to an unusual discomfort in this self-possessed woman. Her lowered head fails to conceal the light flush that has suffused her face.

"You have *heard* it before? Not read it?" I do not think my tone is sharp, but she colours even more deeply. Instead of answering, she takes a breath and begins to chant, her voice an incantation of words and tones, soft and deep, in strange contrast to the brilliance of the day:

> *How well I know the gushing, flowing spring*
> *   Even though it's night.*

> *That everlasting spring is well-concealed*
> *How well I know the place where it's revealed*
> *   Even though it's night.*

> *I do not know its source, for it has none*
> *Yet from it, I know everything must come*
> *   Even though it's night.*

> *I know nothing more lovely can exist*
> *And from it, earth and heavens quench their thirst*
> *   Even though it's night*

> *And I know well those depths are bottomless*
> *Without a ford, impossible to cross*
> *   Even though it's night.*

> *The lustre of its brilliance never dims*
> *I know that every light from these depths comes*
> *   Even though it's night.*

> *I know those waters are so bountiful,*
> *They flow through nations, through heaven and hell,*
> *   Even though it's night.*

The stream whose waters brim forth from this fount
Is filled with grace, its powers paramount
Even though it's night.

From that fount and stream a torrent flows
Which I know neither fount nor stream foreshadows
Even though it's night

That everlasting spring is well-concealed
Within this living bread and our lives healed
Even though it's night.

This water calls out here to all creatures
Who from it drink their fill, even in darkness
Because it's night.

That living spring which I so much desire
I see alive within this bread of life.
Even though it's night.

The echo of the final words drifts on the breeze, mingles with the music of the flowing fountain and the chiming of bells in distant churches. When her last whisper fades, so profound is the silence that it lingers in the air, as a fragile perfume trails a blossom carried on the wind.

"Carmela?" Perhaps the softness of my voice, or the magic that the fading poem has sprinkled on the air, touches her. "There is something on your mind, Carmela. Speak to me."

She reaches out. My skin burns in anticipation of her touch, but she will not meet my gaze. I am ready to grasp her wrist, draw her towards me, but the slim fingers falter, curve towards the palm and come to rest at her throat.

"Please, Carmela." There is a tremor in my voice. "There is something you wish to say. Something I may not wish to hear." Is that a sigh of relief? Or disappointment? "Even if your words go against my inclination, I have an interest in knowing your mind," I urge. "Especially if those words go against my inclination."

She laughs, ill at ease but the tautness in the air is broken. "You are right. There is something I have not told you, because…" Once again, her voice falters. "I feared…" She checks her tumbling words, her countenance burning.

"Continue. Please."

She makes a great effort. "Our Sor Eugenia – you have not met her. Like most of our community she observes the enclosed life and does not receive visitors. As a young girl she completed her novitiate in the convent of the Discalced Carmelite sisters of Toledo. In the year fifteen seventy-seven."

I open my mouth to speak, close it again, pondering the import of her words. "And did she…?"

"Yes. She met Fray Juan. And spoke with him on the very night he made his escape from the monastery. It was she who answered the door when he arrived at the convent and begged shelter."

I do not understand. Did Madre Carmela feel obliged to protect the sisters of her community from me? From the possible consequences of speaking to an investigator whose credibility has been compromised? I endeavour to keep my voice steady. "Carmela, we have spoken much of these matters. I have been your guest for many days. Why did you not tell me this before?"

She looks away, misunderstanding – perhaps choosing to misunderstand – the urgency in my voice. "Before you ask, yes, I can vouch for Sor Eugenia's truthfulness. At that time, she was a girl of sixteen. She has been with us for many years and has been an invaluable support in establishing our little community, in spite of her physical afflictions and the constant pain she endures."

I am not interested in the physical afflictions endured by this Sor Eugenia. "Why have you not spoken of this before now?"

She looks down. "If I am honest…"

"Please, Carmela."

"I do not doubt Sor Eugenia's truthfulness. Nor do I fear for her welfare, should she confide in you." She raises her head and looks at me, almost in defiance. "It is your own well-being that concerns me."

I draw closer to her.

"You have been with us but a few days, Fray Martín." Why this retreat to formality?

"Almost three weeks," I murmur. "And you have all been most kind. Especially as I arrived without warning."

"You were very welcome even so." She looks up at me, her gaze steady. "Martín, this investigation has never been a straightforward mission. I understood this the moment I met Prior Ortiz, before you and I spoke for the first time in Madrid. And when you came here to us, in need of rest and southern warmth to assuage your troubled spirit, I resolved that you should have time to gather your strength, after your troubles with Crespo and Ortiz."

This is tactful. I have revealed too much of the black melancholy that brought me here, seeking shelter from the scrutiny and machinations of my masters.

"Your community has been more than generous, Carmela. The simple kindness and care of your community has been a healing balm. I have discovered here a balance, a serenity of spirit I have not known for a very long time."

She smiles. "I hoped to see you thus restored, Martín. Especially now that your work on this mission is over. Or very soon will be."

I look down, conscious of her hand in mine. "I am sure of it. The only question is the circumstances of my removal: whether they will send me away or…"

"This is why I did not speak to you of Sor Eugenia. If your work on this mission is all but done, what is to be gained by continuing your research? Why subject yourself to more uncertainty, more worry?"

I reflect on the good sense of her words. Although the formalities have not yet been completed, at our last meeting, Crespo and Ortiz made their intentions clear. Officially, there is now nothing for me to investigate.

"I understand your concern, Carmela and I am grateful for it." All at once I am overcome by an emotion I cannot, dare not, name. I stand, turning my face away from her, towards the sea.

"Sor Eugenia's story concerns Fray Juan's escape from Toledo, rather than the sorry details of his imprisonment there, is that not so?"

"Yes."

"Surely that would be a happy tale, more likely to lift my spirits, than to plunge me into melancholy?"

This is the closest I have come to admitting, in my own voice, how much the story of Fray Juan and his sufferings has disturbed me. The frightening dreams, that office where I slept in my chair, the saddest memories of my childhood and how the whole has infected my spirit with darkness. All this, accompanied by none of the joy that Fray Juan was able to forge from his sufferings. Thus far, my darkest nights have remained dark.

"Very well. But first… As this is your last day with us, will you finish your story of how Diego saved you from your accusers in Salamanca?"

I laugh, a little embarrassed, for if the telling shows Diego at his best, it does not flatter me.

When Brother Ignacio first asked me to teach some of the apprentices in the town to read and to write a little – at least enough to permit their master craftsmen to expand their workshops – I insisted on being paid. The sum I requested was small but I believed then, and still believe, that handing over a portion of their wages, however small, would impress on these young men the value of their lessons, strengthen their commitment and ensure their continued attendance at my class. I was proved right, for at the end of five months only one youth had left, and that because of illness in his family.

But from the very beginning, Brother Ignacio and I had done battle on the subject. As I refused to yield, he agreed that every apprentice would make a small payment each week. It was to be channelled through his own parish; and a portion of the whole would be deducted.

"For expenses," he said, without specifying what those might be. As I am – was – in receipt of a salary from the university, and had won my point, I did not press the matter. But when he insisted that I present him with a receipt, signed and dated at the end of each class, stating the number of hours' tuition, the starting and finishing times, the whole countersigned by himself, I was irritated. This was a ridiculous arrangement, designed to inconvenience me, for I could not leave the premises until Brother Ignacio himself had arrived to check my entry and verify my claim with his own signature.

I could not have known then that Brother Ignacio's love of bureaucracy would save me from my accusers. Those very receipts, countersigned by that annoying little priest, would prove beyond doubt my movements on certain days, at certain hours. Some of which coincided with the very days and hours when the dissolute young nobleman claimed to be alone in my company. But I did not think of that myself. That distinction belongs to Diego, both in conception and in execution.

When he proposed this strategy, my first exclamation was relief, my second, despair. "Diego, I do not have those receipts. I have no idea where I filed them, or even if I kept them." I saw my redemption crumble before my eyes. "I think I have thrown them away. How could I have known...?"

Smiling, and with the air of a magician making ready to retrieve some marvel, he reached into a woollen pouch fastened around his waist. From this, he drew out a crumpled bundle of papers and placed them on my desk. "When you explain the situation to the vice chancellor, you might not even need these."

I wanted to throw my arms about him, embrace him. I closed my eyes and gasped. "Diego. You have saved me from disgrace. Or worse."

"Probably worse, Fray Martín. These documents have spared you from a plight much worse than disgrace."

As I finish my tale I hear my voice lose strength and trail into silence, as I wonder how, and why, I am once again in such a precarious position. Carmela shakes her head and sighs. "He was right, Martín. He saved you from the Inquisition's gaol, at least. You are in his debt."

Dusk is falling. The scent of evening flowers drifts on the air. A soft mist descends over the sea and the last of a golden light glimmers on the horizon. Tomorrow, I must set off for Madrid. I turn towards those amber-flecked eyes, glowing in the twilight. Carmela's voice is low and sweet. "Diego must be a remarkable person. I would like one day to meet him."

"I hope one day you will. Soon."

"I think I will be posted to Madrid during the autumn. For a few weeks, at least. Sor Eugenia is not well, she will soon return to the capital to be near her family and someone must accompany her on the journey."

"Then we will surely meet again. And Diego, too. Count on it."

"I will." She bows her head in farewell. "Sor Eugenia is waiting. I think you will enjoy her company."

Sor Eugenia is a shrivelled little woman who looks older than her years. She walks with a stoop and her hands are misshapen in the way of the gnarled limbs I have often seen amongst farmers and washerwomen whose harsh lives keep them out of doors in inclement weather.

"It is a sickness of the bones," Sor Eugenia explains, easing herself onto the pile of cushions I have arranged alongside me.

"Have you suffered this affliction long, Sor Eugenia?"

Her eyes flash and the sweetest smile suffuses her wrinkled features. "It came upon me when I was much younger, not yet forty. My mother was struck down with the same complaint at the same age."

"I am sorry for your suffering, Sor Eugenia."

She waves a claw-like hand. "This is but an affliction of the body, Fray Martín. It is true, I experience pain most of the time. But that does not necessarily mean that I suffer."

"Begging your pardon, sister. I would have thought that pain and suffering were two sides of the same coin. That the first of necessity leads to the second."

She wags a twisted finger. "Then you would be wrong, Fray Martín. Pain is part of life, experienced by all of us. Whether it is pain of the body or pain of the mind."

Her penetrating look unsettles me. Has Carmela discussed my troubles with her? A ridiculous idea. What could she have said? That on a balmy summer's evening I arrived here unannounced and requested shelter; that my investigation is about to be terminated; that my reckless actions and questions have exposed me to a danger that I do not comprehend myself. I think not. I recall that puzzling scrawl I deciphered on the back of a scrap of paper buried deep in Crespo's oaken chest: 'Work and be silent.' Neither Carmela nor Sor Eugenia would indulge in idle chatter. Their vow of silence prescribes not only when they are permitted to speak and for how long, but also, the quality and content of the thoughts to which they give utterance.

"But pain of the mind is the same as suffering of the mind, is it not?"

"Perhaps. Though it need not be, Fray Martín. The cause of suffering is not pain, but the flight from pain."

"I am not sure I understand."

"Consider, for a moment, that none of us may escape pain, no matter how perfect our physical form. I do not refer to pain such as mine, that is an extreme case, an unfortunate legacy of my mother. But consider: you may occupy the most comfortable chair or cushion in the world, yet if you sit or lie or recline for long enough in the same position, you will experience discomfort. And then, pain. Is that not so?"

I recall that dark night when I dozed off in my favourite, most comfortable chair, warmed by the pleasant crackle of the untended fire, as I sat for hours, immobile, too despondent to cast kindling upon the embers, much less rise and take myself to bed. I will not easily forget my aching limbs and the stiffness in my back when I awoke late the following morning. "Agreed."

"And what is the usual response under such circumstances?"

"To move, Sor Eugenia, if one can."

"Indeed. To remove the discomfort, or move away from it. To flee."

"If you like. Yes, you are right. We – I – am inclined to respond to pain or discomfort by seeking to escape it."

On that dark night I did not flee the pain. It engulfed me.

"What then, Fray Martín?"

I laugh. I fancy I begin to catch her meaning.

"I suppose it never ends. When we have found another, more comfortable position, sooner or later the discomfort returns."

"From which we again flee."

"From which we again flee. But does not this mean that pain – and suffering – are therefore inescapable?"

"Pain, yes. But suffering? Perhaps not."

She struggles to her feet and stands for a moment, stretching her arms above her head. "You must forgive me, Fray Martín. Sometimes I find it difficult to practise what I counsel. I am indebted to Madre Carmela for bringing me here, so many years ago. I would probably be bedridden now had I remained in the chilly plains of Castile."

She has aroused my curiosity. "So, what is your counsel, Sor Eugenia? How is it that pain and suffering are not as one? How can they be uncoupled?"

"That is not too difficult." She smiles and eases herself back onto her cushions. "It requires strength – strength of the mind, that is, rather than the body – to take the opposite action to that determined by the most natural impulse."

"So instead of fleeing discomfort..."

"We may approach it. Investigate it. Enter it."

I remain silent, unconvinced.

"If you do not believe me, try it. No, do not move. If there is pain in any part of your body, bring your attention to it."

"My back," I murmur, "my lower back." It has not been right since that night I slept in the chair by the fire.

"Explore the discomfort, Fray Martín. Is it sharp? Dull? Does it move? Throb? Is it on the surface or deep within?"

As instructed, I guide my attention according to her directions and very soon a strange sensation suffuses my consciousness. The ache in my back remains, the urge to move, to relieve it, has not departed. But my irritation has dissipated. The pain is still in my body. It is of me. But it is not me. A small crack has opened that separates my self from the ache in my back; a narrow fissure, it is true, but deep as an abyss and quarried by the simple act of observation, of examining the sensation with interest, even curiosity. But without judgement.

"Suffering arises from the refusal to accept or to understand that which cannot be changed," Sor Eugenia murmurs. "But if I remember to approach and explore my pain, instead of taking flight from it, it becomes a neighbour with whom I share my life. It may even become a friend. So I have found."

I cannot help but smile. "I think it would take a stronger soul than mine, Sor Eugenia, to make friends with my afflictions as you have with yours. But remembering your wise counsel, I may one day learn to tolerate them as a neighbour."

She throws up her poor, misshapen hands. "Then that is a start!" she cries. "And speaking of suffering, I am distracting you from your investigations of Fray Juan and the torments he endured."

Carmela is right. My work on this investigation is nearly at an end. All that remains to be done is my final report, which I am sure will end up in Crespo's oaken chest, with all the rest, probably unread. Why, then, am I troubling this elderly woman with my questions? Perhaps it is time to leave it all behind.

"If you are willing to share your memories with me, Sor Eugenia, I would be most grateful. I believe you know something of the night of Fray Juan's escape, when he sought shelter in your convent in Toledo."

She settles herself in her seat and closes her eyes, a faint smile playing over her shrivelled lips. "What would you like to know? Better that you question me, otherwise you will have to endure the ramblings of a tired old woman. Which you will also find painful."

We both chuckle.

"I am sure your words could never be called ramblings, Sor Eugenia. I would like to hear anything, everything, you saw and heard that night."

She opens her eyes. They are bright and black, most startling, like chips of basalt in a long, brown countenance.

"He must have reached your convent deep in the night. How did he gain entry? Were you and the other sisters awakened by his arrival?"

The little nun shakes her head. "He came to us in the morning. It is true, he had escaped in the middle of the night, but he did not arrive at our door until just after dawn. Which broke early, of course, for it was summer, July or August, I believe."

"It was the end of August, sister. You opened the door to him at six o'clock? Seven?"

"Earlier, much earlier, Fray Martín. I had already started my household duties, which that morning included polishing all the wooden floors. I was hard at work in the parlour, alongside the main entrance where visitors were received, although unexpected callers were rare, Fray Martín, our Discalced Order being enclosed. When people do visit, we speak to them from an adjoining room connected to the parlour by a small iron grill that allows for conversation but no physical contact. Not even with close relatives. You know all this."

"Of course. But Fray Juan was not a visitor."

"That much was clear from the moment I set eyes on him," Sor Eugenia agrees.

"The parlour was close to the street, which is how I came to answer the door. Young and inexperienced though I was, I recognised an emergency when I saw it. The man standing before me in the pale morning light... I can see him now..." she closes her eyes, "... was skin and bone. His tunic was torn and matted, his face dark with a filthy beard and his eyes glittering. A fever, I later learned. He leaned on the doorway as though he was about to collapse."

"How did you know who he was? That he was not some beggar who might turn violent and dangerous?"

"Fray Martín, the man who knocked on our door that summer's morning had difficulty standing. Besides, I noticed straight away that he was wearing a friar's habit – not the brown habit of our fellow Discalced friars, but the black one worn by our brethren on the hill who followed the Mitigated Rule."

"As at that time your convents belonged to two branches of the same Order."

She nods. "You are well informed. Our Discalced reform only gained some measure of independence many years later."

I cannot resist displaying my knowledge. "Eleven year later, Sor Eugenia. Fray Juan made his escape in August of seventy-seven. The Discalced reform was granted the status of a separate Province in fifteen eighty-eight."

"Yes, we achieved a degree of independence at that time. Sometimes I think that that was the start of our greatest troubles."

I hesitate, recalling that Madre Carmela had said something similar. I would be interested to discover Sor Eugenia's view of those unhappy events, but I fear that she will tire so I decide to avoid any further digression from my subject. "And your first sight of Fray Juan that morning?"

"Forgive my digressions, Fray Martín. At the sight of this scarecrow of a man in a friar's garb, I became alarmed. And confused."

"Why confused?"

"Because he identified himself with an authority that was at odds with his ragged appearance. 'Daughter,' he said, though his voice was so low and weak, I could barely hear him. 'Please do me the favour to inform your prioress that Fray Juan de la Cruz, of the Discalced Carmelite brethren, begs shelter.'"

My heart begins to race. "Did you understand the import of what was happening?"

"I was aware that something momentous was afoot, when a scrawny beggar dressed in a torn habit of the Mitigated Order announced himself as the famous friar who, everyone knew, had been missing for more than half a year." Even now, almost forty years after the event, her eyes glitter with animation. I hold my breath. "I admit, I did not straight away understand the danger he was in. And the danger we risked, in receiving him. By a happy chance, one of the older nuns, Sor Juana, was passing and came to my aid. I began to tell her about the strange visitor and as soon as she heard his name, she ordered me to fetch the mother prioress immediately. Instead of showing the visitor into the parlour, Sor Juana brought him straight down to the kitchen, even before the mother prioress had arrived. By the time we arrived in the kitchen, a great commotion had broken out."

"Did everyone present know who he was?"

"Everyone knew him by reputation and a few of the sisters knew him in person. He had been father confessor to some in Valladolid and Segovia."

"So he hid in your convent, amongst your community?"

"Yes. The first odd thing was that the mother prioress told Sor Juana to take him to the sick bay where one of our companions, Sor Ágata, was very ill with a disease of the lung. Even before he had taken something to eat, the mother prioress insisted that Fray Juan should be kept away from any part of the convent that could reasonably be visited. Or searched. The sick bay, of course, would be out of bounds."

"So your prioress was expecting a search party?"

"She was. And she was right. But Sor Juana had been posted at the front door by the time they arrived."

"Did you see them? Hear them?"

"By then, Sor Juana had ordered me from the kitchen and instructed me to return to my task of polishing the parlour floor. As though nothing unusual had happened. I confess I left the parlour door ajar on purpose. Quite soon, not more than a half hour after Fray Juan himself had appeared, more visitors arrived. They ignored the bell and pounded on the door. I recall remarking the violence of their blows, which seemed to me a discourteous approach to an enclosed community of pious nuns. I watched Sor Juana hesitate and gather her habit around her before opening. She had arranged her face into a picture of the most innocent surprise."

"Was it Maldonado? The prior of the Carmelite monastery where Fray Juan had been held captive?"

"I am sorry Fray Martín, I do not know. I never met Prior Maldonado, though of course I came to know him by reputation.

At that time, I was a postulant, only recently arrived in Toledo from my home in Madrid and not yet acquainted with the names of the different participants in the conflicts between the Discalced Carmelites of our Reform and those who followed the Mitigated Rule. All I know is that three friars clad in black habits hammered on the door in great agitation and demanded to know if a friar of the Discalced reform had come amongst us that morning."

"I assume Sor Juana said no."

Sor Eugenia throws back her head and laughs. "She did not, for she would not tell a direct lie. She opened her eyes wide in amazement. 'Brothers,' she said, speaking very slowly, as though she had all the time in the world, which seemed to agitate them further. 'What do you mean?' They answered her with great impatience, even roughness. 'Our mission is urgent. We are in pursuit of a Discalced friar, an escaped criminal detained by our prior.' 'Well, my brothers,' she answered, 'if such a thing had happened, if we had such a person here, it would be a great miracle indeed.'"

I cannot help smiling, for Sor Eugenia is an accomplished raconteur. "How did they respond?"

"Not well. They forced their way in. And insisted on searching the place."

"That is an outrage!"

"I know. It is hard to believe, is it not? I myself would have made a simple denial. But later we laughed about the wisdom of her reply. And it was a miracle that Fray Juan found his way to us. If his pursuers went away persuaded that he was not here, it was only because of their own lack of faith in miracles!"

Not for the first time, I marvel at the cleverness of those innocent-looking sisters, and their ways of getting the better of the craftiest princes of our Church. "He was hidden in the sick bay, then."

"Hearing Sor Ágata's confession. Just in case."

"And what happened when they left? When your prioress was satisfied that his pursuers had gone?"

"I had the task of drawing water from the well for his ablutions while the other sisters prepared some food. He was in such a state of starvation that he could not eat. Sor Juana gave him a small dish of warm cinnamon pears that he managed to force down. I did not think he enjoyed them, though he was grateful for our ministrations."

"Did you hear anything of how he made his escape? How he found your convent?"

"He said that it was a miracle. Our Lady had appeared in his cell and told him what to do, offering him succour on his way."

I consider asking the elderly sister if she thought that Fray Juan had received other help of a more temporal kind, but not wishing to draw attention to my doubts concerning divine intervention, at least in this case, I remain silent.

"He told us that he had wandered through the streets in the deepest part of the night. That he found an open doorway and slipped into the patio to await the dawn. The owner of the house was returning from some assignation and allowed him to sleep there. It was a blessing that he also locked the door behind him. Had it not been for that happy chance, his pursuers would have found him, for I do not think that they waited till morning to begin their search."

"Did he stay with you in the convent for very long?"

"Not with us, no. The mother prioress was afraid that the black-clad friars might return so she arranged for him to be sheltered by a nobleman from the city who was sympathetic to the Carmelite reform."

"And he remained in Toledo?"

"Yes, and under the noses of his former captors! Just for a few weeks, until his strength returned. For a time, he was too weak to travel, though his spirit had remained undimmed throughout his ordeal. In some ways, it was even strengthened by the torments he had endured. Or so he said."

I wonder at the difference in temperament between those whose spirit is elevated by sufferings and those who are crushed by them. "Can you remember anything more of what he said, Sor Eugenia? After all this time, no doubt…"

"In fact, I do remember, Fray Martín. Some events are so momentous, they are seared on the soul. On the evening he first arrived, despite his exhaustion, weakened though he was, he recited some poems he had composed during his time in that great darkness, lost and abandoned. He had brought with him a little notebook. He did not read from it but recited his verses from memory."

A notebook. Before I can question her, the little nun has begun to recite. I do not have the heart to interrupt her.

> *"O night, o guiding night!*
> *O night that made us one!*
> *O night more lovely than the dawn!*

"Are you familiar with Fray Juan's *Dark Night of the Soul*, Fray Martín?" I nod.

"Sor Maria transcribed his words while he was speaking. When he had finished, he gave her his *cuadernillo* so that she could verify her version against his original."

I take a deep breath and make a very great effort to couch my words in an unconcerned tone. "And this notebook, Sor Eugenia, what happened to it? Did Fray Juan leave it in your convent for safekeeping?"

"Alas, no, Fray Martín. After that first night I never saw or heard of it again. I believe he lent it to another sister in another convent and that it was lost."

A wave of disappointment engulfs me. That was my last flickering hope.

"But the loss of his notebook was of no consequence, for many of us learned his poems by heart, from the few copies that Sor Maria made that night. We often recited them, as if they were prayers created to remind us that even in the midst of abandonment and sorrow, the dark night of the soul brings joy that can lead us to the greatest bliss: to union with God."

Sor Eugenia is not only a wise woman, she is good company. I take my leave of her a little better for her words and her piety, though not at all convinced that I will ever be equal to her teachings. This night, when I rest my head on one of the blocks of wood that the sisters use for a pillow, I know I will sleep the whole night through.

No matter the hostility of Crespo and Ortiz, I am determined that my journey in the company of Fray Juan is not yet over. I do, after all, have spirit enough to continue the search – for what, I am not sure. Even now, I continue to hope that some new fact, some lost document will emerge, make everything clear and turn the tide in my favour.

Before I go any further, though, there is one person I have neglected, to whom I must make amends. It has been too long.

Plaza de Arrabal, Madrid,
Eighteenth day of August in the Year of Our Lord, 1616.

It is not much past sunrise, yet the busy life of the Austrias neighbourhood has long been animated by craftsmen and labourers hard at work. Since the middle of the last century, when the father of our present king declared Madrid the capital, the population of the city has greatly increased, many of the newcomers being homeless beggars who have failed to find work, now obliged to spend their days loitering in the streets demanding alms. As we make our way along the calle de la Huerta, besieged by artisans calling out orders, carpenters sharpening their tools, boys dragging carts piled with rubble from the demolition works, a few of these unfortunate paupers jostle us. Such is the difficulty of passage, I am obliged to dismount.

It is no easy matter to navigate this uneven ground. Caminante could lose a shoe here, so I take care to guide him around the stacks of building materials that obstruct our path towards the main plaza. My mood is troubled. Each uncertain step reminds me of the fantasy by which I have long justified the conduct of my life: that my sins of omission, however many, are fewer than my acts of wrongdoing; and although I have rendered little assistance or succour to others, nor have I inflicted upon them any great evil or harm.

As I survey this warren of streets and alleyways, the fine mansions of the rich and the pitiful dwellings of the poor huddled side by side, I must own that I am wrong. A foul dust sullies the air and stings my eyes, contamination rising from the demolition and reconstructions that will, we are told, transform this neighbourhood into a quarter fit for a capital city. I cannot delude myself that Diego's departure from his pretty house on the edge of Salamanca to this noisy, dirty situation, was born of any motive but necessity. That I myself caused this reduction in Diego's circumstances, a consequence of his support for me when all my colleagues and friends had disappeared, afflicts me. I am ashamed to admit how little thought I gave him, my own worries having driven all else from my mind.

I hope he is not living in destitution. I am not sure how I can face him.

This part of town has greatly changed since I was last here. Twice I stop to seek directions. Passing along the north side of the square where a friend of my father had a house many years ago, I pause to contemplate an edifice of great magnificence in the final stages of construction. The handsome porticos and elegant wrought iron balconies remind me of the palace of El Escorial and I recall that old Don Pedro's house had to be demolished to make way for this handsome new Casa de la Panadería. Of course, a grain depositary was deemed more important than the home of a merchant, that the people of Madrid might never again want for bread. So many old places demolished, so many new ones rising in their place – I feel light-headed, disorientated, my familiar bearings crumbling.

I no longer recall which corner of the square opens onto the calle de Ciudad Rodrigo, so we are obliged to skirt the entire perimeter before we find it, opening from the south west side into a narrow, twisting street that slopes down, towards an old toll gate. According to my directions we should go no further than a church half-way along, distinguished by an ornately carved bell tower. I take a moment to consult the map Fray Francisco drew for me.

By chance, we are stopped at a doorway facing that very church, on the opposite side of the street. It is a low dwelling, overshadowed by taller, more imposing neighbours. Diego's landlord must be one of those sly Madrid builders who made sure to construct houses of only one storey. The king might decree that the upper floors of every house must provide lodging for the multitude of nobles now thronging the city and the Royal Court. But it is, after all, a simple matter for a clever builder to construct a single-storey house – or one of that appearance from the street. The king might make all the laws he pleases but in the absence of an upper storey he decrees in vain.

Having no further cause for delay I rap the door and start to count to twenty. The sun does not penetrate these packed streets at this hour and the full heat of the day has yet to descend on the city. Even so, a few drops of sweat trickle down my temple. The clamour of the demolition works on the Plaza de Arrabal is louder than ever but in the room behind this door there is only silence. I knock again and repeat my count in a low murmur, trying and failing to steady my breath. Again, I reach twenty. My heart pounds and I wonder if I should smite the door a third time. Perhaps my information was wrong or the map badly drawn. I am not convinced that Fray Francisco knows the city as well as he claims.

Just as I am about to turn away, light footsteps echo from within. The door opens, and I submit to the scrutiny of a pale girl of about fifteen. This must be Josefina, the child who was ill with measles some years ago while Diego was in the employ of the university. When I introduce myself she makes no response.

I fear I may have erred in coming here. The dreadful thought occurs that I may be too late, that Diego...

"Your father...?"

She casts a glance into the dim interior. "Papi! You have a visitor. Come and see."

An unintelligible growl emerges from the shadows. I stand a little taller and brace myself. The voice must have conveyed permission, for the girl's regard softens and she manages a smile. "He is in the patio."

I follow her down a narrow, low-ceilinged passageway between dark walls of unadorned brick. Though new churches, public buildings and mansions for the nobility are constructed all around us, the dwellings of the poor are little changed. I almost trip on an uneven flagstone. Perhaps Diego and his motherless daughter occupy a single room. The girl directs me to a door of dark, fresh-sanded wood at the end of the passageway, barely visible in the weak light that filters in from a narrow window set high in the wall.

We enter a wide, broad room, bright and pleasant, despite the low ceiling. Walls are whitewashed, the floor is strewn with fresh rushes that infuse the air with an agreeable aroma. A rough wooden table flanked by a bench and two stools stand in the centre of the room. One corner is occupied by a stove whence emerges the scent of baking bread. A humble home, but far from destitute.

"Fina! Bring him here at once, for I cannot come to him. Whether he be the archbishop or the Pope himself, I must finish tying up these tomatoes, else the stems will break!"

Fina beckons and a dozen paces take me to the far end of the room, where a narrow door opens onto a patch of greenery. A broad-backed figure is stooping over a triangular structure of sticks and string, the head covered in a straw hat rather like the one I am holding in my hand. A few red and yellow tomatoes at different stages of ripeness peep out from the foliage. It does not surprise me that Diego is growing these strange fruits with such apparent enthusiasm. Others have cultivated them in Castile for some decades, but I have heard too many stories of poisonings to be persuaded to eat one.

He turns towards me. How long has it been? Why, after all this time, should my old help-mate welcome me into his home, when I repaid his loyalty with such lack of care? Not that I did not wish to help him. I did. But not enough to stop thinking of myself.

For a moment he stares at me, his eyes moist. Before I can speak, he has pushed his way through the profusion of greenery and enfolded me in his embrace. In Salamanca, I do not think we ever shook hands but here, in his home, where I am a visitor and a supplicant, the old divisions of station have fallen away. My eyes sting.

"Fina, my chicken. This is Fray Martín, the man who helped us when you were so ill and bought us your medicines and even paid for his own physician to attend you. He was one of my masters at the university."

"I remember, Papi. He brought the doctor to our house himself."

I am amazed that the girl remembers an event that occurred so long ago. "You were a very little girl then, Josefina. No more than five or six."

"I was six. I remember the fever I had. And the potion the doctor made, which you tried to get me to drink. I spat it out. It went all over your white habit."

Diego and I exchange glances and smile. I am grateful for the distraction, for it is difficult for me to look at him. "Diego…"

He raises one hand and leads me to the far corner of his patio where we stand in the shade of a large shrub. He has made a great deal of this tiny space. All around the perimeter, pots and containers of various kinds spill their bounty, some blossoming flowers but most vegetables of various kinds. I recognise feathery asparagus fronds, sharp leaves of pepper plants and a cluster of deep green stems that taper and blossom to purple blooms. Diego has made better use of the last three years than I.

"Fina, dearest," he calls, "Fray Martín and I will talk out here."

"Will I bring cold drinks, Papi?"

"We can get our own drinks, my petal. Finish your studying."

The girl smiles and disappears into the shadows of the house.

"She is still at school?"

"No. She is in service with a noble family whose villa is close to the Casa de Campo, by the river, beside the old site of the Gerónimos monastery. She helps a servant to tutor the children of the house and their cousins. If the mother finds Fina's reading and writing and drawing to be satisfactory, she will perhaps recommend her to relatives to take care of their own children."

"That would be a good position."

"It would. She is a clever girl. And beautiful, as you see. Like her mother, may the Lord rest her."

"With her mother's looks and your brains, Diego, she will go far."

His smile is tinged with melancholy and I regret my levity on such a serious subject. "But where, Fray Martín? It is not easy in these times to be father to a motherless daughter. As she has grown, I have noted many troubling things in the way women must live that I had never before remarked. What kind of life can there be for a girl of our station who is blessed with intelligence and beauty and a little too much ambition?"

I do not answer, for I have no reassurance to give him. Even a good position in service is no guarantee of security. Too many noblemen or even mere merchants consider servant girls as their personal property, to do with as they will. I know of more than a few houses in Salamanca whose masters sent servant girls back to their home villages, carrying babes who would bear no name or future patronage.

"Did you ever consider that she might take the veil?" I am avoiding the subject that I came here to discuss, and Diego shows no desire to press me on it. He raises his palms, helpless before the uncertainties of the years ahead.

"Of course. But I should not like to see her deprived of... I do not know if she would want... Yet I sometimes think that those women in their convents have the best of it. To be in charge of their own affairs. Not bound by the bidding and caprices of their menfolk."

Only up to a point, I do not say, for I have come to believe that we are all bound by the biddings and caprices of another, whoever fate or God or man has deemed our superior. The constant battles Blessed Teresa fought with the opponents of her reform, the bitter struggles of her successors to maintain the spirit of that reform to rescue it from the stranglehold of rules and regulations Niccolà Doria introduced, have convinced me that a state of quiet, uncontested autonomy is a mirage; that the sovereign will inhabits border country, the frontier of a besieged city under constant threat of encroachment by stronger or craftier invaders. I sigh. I cannot bear to look at him.

"Diego, it was very wrong of me to leave Salamanca without enquiring about your welfare, or what my departure would mean for you. Please forgive my..."

He takes my elbow and steers me towards a wooden bench that looks as though it was once part of a church pew. "There is nothing to forgive, Fray Martín. You were right to depart as soon as the lies of that vicious young pup were exposed. You could not have done anything for me. It was better for us both that you left as you did."

Head bowed, elbows on my knees, I continue my inspection of the ground. Diego might be right, perhaps I could have done nothing for him. But I should at least have tried. Looking for the right words to pose a delicate question, I clasp and unclasp my hands. "And how are you managing, Diego?" At last I meet his eye. I would almost prefer a rebuke than this cheerful mercy.

"We are getting by. Fina earns a few *reales* from that family, enough to help. And I am employed most weeks on the demolition works around the plaza." He waves his arm in the direction from which I came. "The rebuilding is due to start next winter, but who knows? They have been saying that for more than fifteen years."

All this demolition and building has been going on for much longer, since our present king's father resolved to transform the lively, chaotic marketplace of the Plaza de Arrabal, for centuries home to traders and small businesses where the people could buy olive oil, wine, basketwork, into an imposing Plaza Mayor, fit for a new capital city.

"This neighbourhood will be a good place to live, once work on the Plaza Mayor is finished, especially being so close to the Puerta del Sol. There may be fewer markets but no doubt, many more festivals suitable for such a grand city space. I am sure they will continue to celebrate the Corpus Christi processions here."

Diego grimaces.

"And public executions. And *autos-da-fé*, should the Inquisition wish it, I'll wager."

There is a gloomy silence while we both ponder the images his words have conjured up. He shakes his head as though to banish unpleasant thoughts.

"But what of your own fortunes, Fray Martín? I have heard that you are doing important work here in Madrid for Doctor Enrique of the Toledo Inquisition. And in the Monastery of the Gerónimos! I can see that you are doing well."

"Not as well as appearances suggest, Diego. And I have not been working for the Holy Office but for Archbishop Crespo."

"I have not heard of him."

"No matter. But I must soon leave Madrid, for they are about to terminate my investigation. I am to return to the monastery of San Salvador by the end of October."

He sighs deeply. "Are you in trouble again, Fray Martín?"

I cannot help laughing. "I fear I am, Diego. At this moment, I am not sure how much trouble. Things could get worse. But they might also, perhaps…"

"Get better?"

I nod. "Even at this late stage, I might find a way to improve my situation. With a result that could benefit us both." A shrewd glint ignites his narrowed eyes. "If you have the time, Diego, I would like to tell you the whole story."

He opens his arms wide. "I have nothing but time, Fray Martín. Tell me all."

For almost an hour we sit in the shade of Diego's shrubs. As the sun moves higher and the shadows become longer and blacker, I recount everything that has happened since I took up my position at the start of this year, to the most recent disastrous meeting with Crespo and Ortiz.

"Do you know their reason for terminating your commission?"

I stand, stretch my limbs and inhale deeply. "No reason has been stated, for my dismissal is not yet official. But I am sure it is coming. I suspect they no longer trust me to provide the information they seek, the documents and conclusions they want, in the manner that they require."

Diego peers up at me. "Are they right?"

I shrug and reclaim my place on his pilfered church pew.

"Fray Martín. Why do you endanger yourself in this way? Why not simply give them what they want? It is just a report, after all. Mere words. And you have much to lose."

And much to gain, for although I have told him of Doctor Enrique's veiled threats, I omitted to mention his inducements. I hesitate, but caution prevails.

"Diego, there is no such thing as 'mere words'. It is Salamanca all over again. The creation of fictions by the simple use of innuendo, selection of facts, the posing of certain questions in a certain way."

"But to what end, Fray Martín? What kind of fictions do Archbishop Crespo and the Inquisition wish to create? And for what purpose?" When I make no answer he glares at me, irritated. "Another question, Fray Martín. If you have been

240

removed from this investigation, or are about to be removed, your final report will no longer be required."

"It will be required, Diego. Ortiz asked for it. I must finish it before the end of October."

"But how can anything you say or write now influence the thoughts or actions of your masters? Will your work sway them to support or oppose Fray Juan's beatification? Can you do anything more than you have done already? Should you even try?"

Many times in recent days I have asked myself the same questions. In truth, I have no idea how any recommendations I make will be received by the Archbishop and his associates, as they have been careful to conceal their motivations and priorities – whether to support Fray Juan or discredit him. The only certainty is that Doctor Enrique's skilful combination of flattery and threats dangled before me the prospect of a return to my old life, my reputation and my position – on condition that I write my report to his specifications.

As I remain silent, Diego casts his eyes towards the heavens and sighs. He stoops and pulls up a few tiny weeds just visible in the earth. They yield to his practised hand.

"My onions are doing badly this year," he murmurs, shaking some of the dark earth from a stem. "But at least they'll keep the carrots safe from pests." He glances at me from under his brim. "I begin to understand your place in this conundrum, Fray Martín. You are like this feeble little onion, not very substantial in itself, not enough to put into a good stew, for example. But its very presence here in the ground, alongside the other vegetables, stops the slugs and the other pests from turning our future dinners into mush. That is what your report will do. No matter how you write it. If you write it."

He grins. I am not sure I care to be equated with carrot fly or feeble onions, but I assume that his general intention is well meant. And there may be something in what he says. If I write what is in my heart and not what Doctor Enrique orders me to write, my final report, however insignificant, might expose the malicious attempts to drum up calumnies against Fray Juan towards the end of his life. Moreover, it will offer an alternative view to the rather stern portrait of him that others have created. Perhaps bear witness to the truth, or at least, another version of it.

"From what little you have told me, Fray Martín…"

"I have told you all I know myself, Diego," I assure him, which is almost true.

"… it is my guess that these people have not yet decided which side to support – whether to declare in favour of Fray Juan and his future beatification, or against him. You think that they have been spurred into action by the recent investigations into Teresa's life, before she was beatified last year?"

I nod. "I am certain of it. The beatification process has been greatly intensified. Those Vatican inspectors spoke to many people who had known Teresa and they examined every scrap of her writing, both personal and public. Not only her books but private letters, notes, anything they could find. Including an autobiography that was banned by the Inquisition during her lifetime."

"I see. Then your superiors, and the Inquisition, this Doctor Enrique, expect that Fray Juan's life will come under the same level of scrutiny."

"Without a doubt."

"What is there to find? What have people said or written about him?"

"There is no shortage of references to miracles. Healing the sick, casting out devils. Conjuring bread out of thin air."

"Enough to make a realistic case for beatification?"

"I think so. But the support is not unanimous. And it is far from unequivocal."

"I am not surprised. Until those original manuscripts of his writings are found, there is bound to be uncertainty"

For my own part, I think it unlikely that Fray Juan's manuscripts will ever be found. Too many people witnessed the destruction of his papers, sometimes in very specific circumstances. Especially, as I told Crespo and Ortiz, as some of the nuns with whom he had lengthy correspondences over a period of years burned his letters by the sack load.

"But why, Fray Martín? Why would his intimates destroy his written legacy?"

"The intention was not to destroy, Diego, but to protect Fray Juan from rivals within his own Order who tried to concoct a scandal that would damage his reputation. His friends were afraid that some of his writings could be misinterpreted and used against him."

Diego frowns.

"Is it possible that your investigation was commissioned for a purpose that is similar, but more subtle in execution: to identify any practices in Fray Juan's life, or beliefs expressed in his writings, that would render him unfit for beatification?" I hesitate. "Might that explain the visit from the Holy Office of the Inquisition? Perhaps they want to put an end to the process, before it begins," Diego suggests.

In truth, I do not think so. Notwithstanding Doctor Enrique's anxiety about certain aspects of Fray Juan's poetry, I did not form the impression that his intention was malign.

"Perhaps. Doctor Enrique did make his expectations clear to me," I muse, though this is not quite accurate. True, he attempted to insist that I consult with him when I am ready to produce the final version of my report, before I draft my conclusions. But he has said nothing, yet, about what those conclusions should be. I do not doubt that he will, though.

"What I do not understand, Fray Martín, is why any of these priors of the Discalced Carmelite Order would oppose the beatification of one of their own. Did the piety of his life reflect so badly on them?"

Once again, I am not at all sure that the story is so simple. Reluctant though I am to allow Fray Juan's granite-eyed gaoler credit for insights, one of his barbed comments rang true. Teresa, he said, had a talent for alienating her allies. Among them, high ranking officials such as the papal nuncio, at that time an Italian, one Rossi or Rubeo, I no longer recall the exact name. A supporter of her ideas at first, he, too aspired to reform the entire Carmelite Order, and believed that Teresa would help him. But that hope did not last long. When she began to act on her own initiative, opening new convents outside the permitted jurisdictions, putting her own people in charge of them, he became alarmed and withdrew his support, fearing that her leadership would not reform the Order, but divide it. He was right, for that is exactly what happened. But none of this explains the urgency of finding the original manuscripts of Fray Juan's poems, at this time.

"No, Diego. I do not believe that either the Carmelites of the Mitigated Order or the other Discalced friars and nuns who followed the Reform were themselves lacking in piety." I muse. "I think it more likely that their true opposition was to the nature of Fray Juan's teachings. Crespo and Ortiz and the Inquisition are anxious to know how he thought, his theology, his approach to prayer itself…"

"Fray Martín, you have lost me. Prayer is prayer. We attend Mass and the other sacraments, we recite the litany of the saints and you friars and monks sing the Holy Office at the appointed hours and on the appointed days. There is nothing more to be said on the subject."

"There is a lot more to be said, Diego. The ritual you describe is conducted in a manner that allows priests, bishops, cardinals and the Pope, too, to guide the faithful."

"The priest sings the Mass, the faithful recite their prayers."

"Aloud, yes. And in reciting those familiar words, prescribed by the Council of Trent, they are under the supervision of a priest or other superior. Communication with God is thus mediated by priests and their bishops, by archbishops and in the end, by the Pope." It is only now, as I speak, that the audacity of San Juan's *Canticle* begins to dawn on me.

"But surely the prayers recited by Fray Juan and Blessed Teresa were no different?"

I close my eyes, take a deep breath and for a few moments, delight in the murmur of a breeze rustling through the foliage, the scent of damp earth around the tomatoes which Diego has just watered, the warmth of the sun on my skin. When I open my eyes, I raise my hand to shield them from the glare.

"Their conduct was very different, Diego. Prayer, for them, was not only a means to worship, to communicate, with God – it was a path towards achieving union with God. Which they believed was attainable through a very particular practice – interior prayer. Prayer that is not chanted with one voice in the Mass or recited as part of the Holy Office or the rosary, or the litany of the saints or spoken aloud at all. Prayer that is silent. Internal. Unspoken."

"And thus, beyond the reach of external rules and regulations. Of supervision or control." Diego's eyebrows almost disappear beneath his unruly mane. "Yes, I can see why some people would not like that."

"To say the least. Interior prayer was more than suspect, Diego, it was outright rebellion. For all the reasons you have said. It was a practice which the Discalced Carmelites put at the heart of their reform, hand in hand with their practice of bodily austerities."

On rare occasions, the practice of severe austerities is something I can almost understand. That the spirit, bound to the body, tied to a dying animal, must be emptied, to be filled with the grace of God, and God Himself. A state achieved through physical discomfort, suffering the pain of fasting, lack of sleep and all the rest. Diego interrupts my mediations.

"That is all very well, Fray Martín. I can understand that the holy officers of the Church Temporal do not want friars and nuns thinking that they are in direct communion with God without their help. But was Fray Juan really exhorting the faithful to rebel? To dispense with the authority of the clergy? You make him sound almost like a Lutheran! What proof do you have for that?"

None. For, as I remind him, it seems likely that all definitive documentary evidence has been lost. I wonder aloud if Fray Juan himself divined dangerous interpretations in his own writings; or even, if he destroyed some of his own manuscripts.

"No poet would discard his own writings," Diego objects.

"Fray Juan might have been the exception. Not only if he thought they were dangerous, but even more so, if he was proud of them. For it was his way to seek to overcome such worldly attachments and pleasures. At least once he burned a bundle of letters he had received from Teresa, because they were so precious to him. Ridding himself of his own manuscripts would be no different."

Diego frowns. I am sure I can guess his thoughts, which he is too polite to voice: that the stripping away of comfort or pleasure is a barren, austere way to live, which baffles him; that the more reasonable of Fray Juan's opponents and yes, the Inquisition, might have had good cause to curb the greatest excesses of the Discalced practices, expressions of a virtue too clear and brittle for this world.

Since returning from Málaga, I have thought often of Sor Eugenia and her method of living with pain, both physical and mental: to approach and investigate the very tribulations and discomforts that trouble us, instead of trying to flee them; to accept that our trials will always be with us, that flight or respite will be fleeting and are sure to be replaced by others. It is a noble path and, I do believe, a skilful and generous way to live. Perhaps the reforms created by Fray Juan and Blessed Teresa were always intended to follow this path. I know that if I wished, I could govern my feelings and my thoughts in the way Sor Eugenia described.

Why, then, do I not? Because the effort is beyond my will. When I think of renouncing those actions and thoughts that cause me pain, I wonder – might I, perhaps, at heart – enjoy them? No. 'Enjoy' is not quite right. I am accustomed to them. I am a little attached to them, these recollections of trials and disappointments, of furies and griefs. I reflect on them often, caress and refine them. In some strange and not unpleasant way, they tell me who I am. I am not yet ready to give them up. I am not yet ready to be that better, happier, person. Which is, perhaps, another way of saying that I just prefer to be miserable.

And yet, and yet. Although I will myself never follow Sor Eugenia's path, I sometimes catch a glimmer of the purpose of the pious men and women who live as Fray Juan did. Enduring, even seeking out pain, determined to overcome the dominance of body over spirit. The raptures and strange bodily sensations, as the physical self opens to the plenitude of the divine and struggles to contain it. And the final consummation, a bliss rarely attained, though much sought. Fray Juan never urged this path on people outside the communities who had freely chosen it and was said to have prohibited the most rigorous practices that lead to those states of being.

I hope to include all these reflections in my conclusions in a way that might satisfy Crespo and Ortiz as to my competence and good faith; and perhaps impress Doctor Enrique too. But I will need help to finish it all on time.

"I am forbidden to do any more work on this mission, Diego. There are, therefore, people I cannot question myself. I have need of your sharp and steady eye. Your wisdom."

He looks away and for the first time it occurs to me that I may be placing him in danger. I lay my hand on his arm.

247

"Are you with me?"

He sighs, casts his eyes around his garden, his humble little house where his daughter awaits him inside, their comfort hard-won, through honest toil. For a moment I think I have lost him but when he turns back to me, a crafty smile is playing about his lips and I am sure I can count on him.

"Fray Martín. You know I can never resist a scrap."

We grasp hands in mock solemnity, two conspirators sealing a pact, our gravity dissolved into mirth.

"Then, my good friend, I have a job for you." We raise our cups in a toast to our forthcoming endeavours. "But first, there is someone I want you to meet."

Church of San Pedro el Real, by the Puerta Nueva, Madrid,
Twentieth day of September in the Year of Our Lord, 1616.

San Pedro el Real is distinguished from neighbouring structures by its slender tower whose horseshoe windows, fashioned in the Arab style, recall the ancient *mezquita* that once stood on this site. This honey-coloured edifice is planted in the centre of a busy plaza and encircled by a narrow pathway where workers and peddlers, housemaids and craft-workers go about their business, jostling and weaving their way between the numerous market stalls that so animate this neighbourhood. If I should have the bad luck to be spied by any of my colleagues from the monastery of San Gerónimo el Real, I could with ease invent a reason to be in this part of the city.

Diego turns the parchment towards me and a sliver of sunlight falls on the official stamp of the Holy Office of the Inquisition that verifies the declaration inscribed beneath: a mere two lines, followed by an embellished signature.

"You were right, Fray Martín."

It is not easy to decipher the whorls of script in this dim light. This ancient church of San Pedro el Real has many deficiencies, but it enjoys the merit of being situated close to the convent where Madre Carmela will be posted for the next few weeks. And it is but a few minutes' walk from Diego's place of work on the Plaza de Arrabal.

"What was I right about, Diego?"

"Fray Juan's detention by the Holy Office. Your visitor, Doctor Enrique from the Toledo Inquisition, spoke true. I consulted the public records, as you asked. There is no notice that Fray Juan was ever detained. No records at all that any case was ever brought against him. All the files bearing his name are lost."

All? Notwithstanding my two reliable sources – Doctor Enrique and Diego – I find this beyond belief.

"How do we know that there were ever files on him to begin with?"

"I found a master list of the names of any person in the district of Toledo on whom the Holy Office ever opened a file. This supplies a serial number which indicates the location of any records pertaining to each individual. I looked up Madre Teresa's number to start with, to check that the system worked."

"And? Did you find anything?"

"Several cases against her. The Holy Office kept a close eye on her activities, and her writings. They even withdrew her autobiography, which offended them in some way."

"But nothing on Fray Juan?"

"I told you, his name was on the master list. Which indicates that he was at the very least a person of interest. But there were no case files corresponding to his serial numbers. Someone must have removed them."

This news disturbs me. I take a few steps into the nave and cast my eye over the altar. The floor is littered with blocks of wood and workmen's tools, the ambience is silent, the air is cool. Despite the advanced state of dilapidation of this little church, soon to be reconstructed, I am pleased to have found a refuge where we can meet, far from prying eyes. It disturbs me to learn that not only his own manuscripts, but official documentation concerning Fray Juan have an unfortunate tendency to vanish.

"I suggest we wait until Madre Carmela arrives before discussing this further. She may have a useful opinion to offer."

Diego raises his eyebrows and surveys me from under his heavy brow. "I am looking forward to meeting her. She has been of great assistance to you in these difficult times."

"You both have, Diego." To my surprise, and his, I grasp his arm, my eyes swimming. He does not speak but rests a big hand on my shoulder. Glad of the excuse to disengage, I point to an old wineskin I had the foresight to pack. I raise my eyebrows. He grins and nods, no doubt guessing that I filled it from the well-stocked cellar of my Hieronymite hosts. I offer him first draught. He holds the skin aloft, tilts it to a certain angle and a thin stream of purple liquid arcs through the air, flows into his mouth and into his throat, for what seems like a rather long time. When his thirst is quenched, he gasps, wipes his lips and hands me the wineskin. I raise it to my lips and content myself by swallowing a mouthful or two.

For a few moments, we remain lost in our thoughts until a rattling of the external door disturbs us. Diego leaps to his feet and sprints down the aisle, his gait light and noiseless for such a big man, one finger pressed to his lips. I know that this is no intruder, but Diego's caution is infectious. He presses his body against the wall so that he is out of the line of sight from the door. I, however, am positioned in front of it, in plain view. The visitor pushes twice, thrice, before the door creaks open and a faint footfall steps into the transept. Diego springs forward and plants himself in front of a small, slight figure clad in a rough brown habit, white cape and cowl. I cannot conceal my amusement.

"Madre Carmela, allow me to present my associate, rescuer and friend: Diego Clemente. Diego, this is Madre Carmela, prioress of the Discalced Carmelite convent in Málaga. Another saviour and…friend?" I had not meant that note of interrogation to enter my voice and hurry on. "She has come to Madrid to nurse a sick companion. How is Sor Eugenia?"

Carmela stares at both of us and Diego looks down at his boots. He bows, uncertain of the etiquette in these unusual circumstances. She nods, cool and unsmiling.

"Forgive me, Madre Carmela. I did not mean to startle you. I did not know who..."

"Who else could it have been?" There is a sharpness in her tone I have not heard before. "Who would come here at this hour of the day?"

"Madre Carmela," in Diego's presence I suddenly feel shy, obliged to observe some semblance of formality, "we cannot be too careful. If we must err – and being human, it seems that we must –" a playful sparkle has returned to her eyes and she purses her full lips, trying not to smile, "then this is the side on which I prefer to err. Diego's caution has already saved my skin once. It may yet do so again."

"You are quite right, Fray Martín," she answers, her dancing eyes belying the formality of her words. She turns to Diego and offers him her sweetest smile.

"That is the second time this afternoon someone has told me I am right. I must enjoy this while it lasts, for I am sure that it will not." My companions exchange a look. I am relieved to see a hint of complicity mingled with mutual appraisal.

"I do not have much time," Carmela says. "One of the novices is caring for Sor Eugenia and I do not want to be away from her bedside for too long."

"I will pray for her. Will you tell her so? Please say that I am grateful for all I learned from her."

"I will. Fray Martín, we should begin."

Diego concurs. "If the workmen return before we have finished our task, we will not be able to explain what we are doing here." He stares at Madre Carmela, who affects not to notice.

I open one of my leather saddlebags and draw out a large bundle wrapped in a woollen shawl. It contains the papers Prior Andrés sent me from Oviedo at the start of the summer. My companions look on while I unwrap the cloth. "I wish to thank you both for the assistance you have given me until now, and for having agreed to assist me with this final onerous task. We will not complete it today, but at least we can make a start."

In truth, without their help I would have to present these documents to Crespo and Ortiz, some of them unread, before I leave at the end of the month. This would reflect ill on me and confirm Ortiz's poor opinion of my abilities, so I am determined to scrutinise every page of them before I leave and be sure to reference them in my final report. It is always possible that something useful might be hidden amongst these papers, something more significant than the pages I perused after Doctor Enrique's visit. Something that might allow me to maximise the impact of my final progress report and redeem myself.

"Diego, you said that Ortiz's cousin did not simply refuse to inform you of whether Fray Juan had ever been arrested or questioned by the Inquisition; but that the files on him have been removed."

"No to the first, Fray Martín and yes to the second. I do not know if Doctor Enrique told you everything he knows on the subject but there are no files on Fray Juan; none that either confirm or deny an arrest by the Holy Office of the Inquisition."

"Does this not prove that he was never detained and that no file on him was ever opened?" Carmela puts in. "How do we know that such files existed?"

"We did not know," I explain, "until Doctor Enrique referred to them. In saying that they had been lost, he admitted their existence. Which suggests that the Inquisition had at least taken some interest in Fray Juan and his activities. But we know nothing specific. No details of how far this went."

"Is it possible that they kept him under observation, monitored his writings, took soundings, subtle or otherwise, from people who knew him?" Diego wonders. "But found nothing that warranted further action."

"That is one possibility," I admit.

Carmela's eyes darken. "It is also possible that they did arrest him, or at least bring him in for questioning, but were obliged to release him for lack of evidence of any offence." I nod. "But who would want to remove that information from the record? And for what reason?"

Ever since Doctor Enrique's visit, those same questions have troubled me.

Carmela touches my arm. My skin tingles and I cannot suppress a shiver. "Have you considered, Fray Martín, that whoever lost or disposed of those files could be the same persons who set in motion your investigation of Fray Juan's life and your search for his original manuscripts?"

We regard her with interest, Diego's brow furrowed in a deep frown. I spread my hands. "I do not see... How would this benefit...?"

"Let us reflect. You receive an unexpected commission to conduct research – much of which has already been carried out – by superiors who are unable, or unwilling, to explain the rationale or the target audience for the final report. They limit whom you must meet, the questions you must ask, the manner in which your findings are recorded and who has access to your notes. All of this could be understood, to some extent, as sensible precautions – if somewhat exaggerated – on the part of the superiors of an Order whose reputation has been greatly enhanced by the beatification of one eminent founder."

"Blessed Teresa," Diego murmurs.

"It could be further enhanced by the elevation of another: Fray Juan." Carmela frowns. "For that very reason, Martín, I find the reactions of your superiors to you and the work you have conducted, most puzzling. And interesting. You have expanded the scope of your investigation by meeting witnesses who were not on the supplied list, whom you identified by your own research. Such diligence should merit reward, congratulations at the very least. Not hostility. Certainly not dismissal from the case."

A draught blows in from a gap in the roof tiles and almost topples the flickering candle that Diego has been trying to light while Carmela spoke. He steadies and tilts it to one side, so that a little stream of melting wax pools onto the stone ledge. There, he presses the base until the liquid has set and the candle holds firm. For a few moments, the three of us contemplate the guttering flame in silence.

"It is obvious that their choice of witnesses was made with a specific outcome in mind," he says. "They might not be interested in the discovery of new information or insights. Does that sound strange, Fray Martín?"

"It does not sound strange at all, Diego." I am relieved to hear my own misgivings echoed. "At the start of this mission, I thought that Crespo and Ortiz wanted a report that would evaluate and summarise the existing material, incorporating new insights from additional witnesses, with an appearance of depth and objectivity. Since then, it has indeed crossed my mind that they wished me to add nothing to what is already known about Fray Juan, his life and his writings. But I cannot understand what purpose such a futile exercise could serve."

"I can think of two." Diego leans forward, marking off his arguments one by one. "In the first place, should your interviews yield no new information, your final report would be a valuable resource in any communications with the Vatican inspectors concerning Fray Juan's life and work."

Is this possible? Would the vicar general of the Discalced Carmelites in Spain dare to withhold original notes, witness statements and Fray Juan's manuscripts, if they are found, knowing that scrutiny of original writings by independent

Vatican inspectors is a required part of the beatification process? I select a few pages from Prior Andrés's files and glance over them, thinking of the many hundreds of other papers in the ancient oak chest in my office.

"That is a possibility," I acknowledge. "Given the amount of material to consider, which includes, at least, two substantial reports carried out in the last ten years, the superiors of the Order might feel justified in presenting an in-depth summary, in place of the actual source documents. That would certainly be an efficient strategy."

"It would save the Vatican inspectors a lot of time. They might even agree to it," Carmela adds. "Which would allow Crespo and Ortiz to oversee – more, to determine – the extent of the Vatican's access to first-hand information about Fray Juan's life and work. That would also explain why they insisted on such a precise methodology for your own work, Martín."

"From which I have departed many times," I mutter.

"Exactly. By deviating from the strict conditions they stipulated for your work, by asking your own questions and interviewing additional witnesses, you have expanded the source material – and therefore, any conclusions that may arise from it – beyond their control."

"Madre Carmela is right," says Diego. "Even though it was not your intention, you have undermined the Order's entire strategy for controlling what the Vatican inspectors see and hear concerning Fray Juan. Little wonder that Crespo and Ortiz are so furious with you. It would not surprise me if they responded by trying to discredit or otherwise silence you." He regards me with a sombre mien, that 'otherwise' suspended in the air like the sword of Damocles dangling over my head. If he is right, I have placed myself, through my own actions, in an invidious position. Perhaps even in danger.

"And the other potential benefit of my investigation, Diego? You said you had thought of two."

"Your work gives advance warning, Fray Martín. If you were to uncover any surprises, reveal any unexpected facts or insights, the superiors of the Order would have time to create an explanation for the Vatican that would serve whatever priorities they wished to promote."

"But my investigation has produced unexpected insights!" I count them off on my fingers. "Item: the doubts I expressed about the public face and character of Fray Juan, and the very different personality I discovered. Item: my conviction that other investigators sought to emphasise so-called miracles, discarding all other information that might suggest a flawed, less than perfect character. Item: my scepticism on the miraculous nature of his escape from a Toledo prison, convinced as I am that he had outside help. And most especially, the association of Fray Juan's thinking with that of the *alumbrados* and the..."

"You are missing the point, Martín." Carmela is doing her best to disguise her irritation. "Your power of analysis and insight is not in question. But all those conclusions you have just mentioned arise from the information you obtained from additional witnesses and documents you met on your own initiative, not from those prescribed for you by Crespo and Ortiz."

"Fray Martín, I think Madre Carmela is right. The superiors who commissioned your work, whoever they are, cannot be sure that your private sources are amenable to their influence. But now that those people have been consulted, it will be impossible to ignore their witness statements."

I gaze into the flickering candle. I am inclined to agree with the line of reasoning my friends have just outlined. It could explain the hostility I encountered from the moment I arrived in the monastery of San Gerónimo el Real, the efforts of Crespo and Ortiz to intimidate me and their fury whenever they discovered my slightest departure from their instructions. However, I am not convinced that this theory casts any light on the reason for my being summoned to conduct this investigation in the first place. Did my superiors – do they? – plan to use my conclusions to reaffirm Fray Juan's reputation for piety, to encourage the Vatican to recommend his elevation to Blessed and, thereby, enhance the standing of their own Order? If such is their intention, then my questioning the accepted biographies and versions of events would certainly interfere with their plans.

Yet a prickling unease convinces me that this is not the whole story. Are the intentions of Crespo and Ortiz, of the Discalced Carmelite Order towards Fray Juan's future status, so benign? For the first time, a glaring question looms. I wonder why I did not think of it before.

"Carmela. Diego. Why has no formal edition of Fray Juan's work yet been published? After all, he is renowned as co-founder of the Order, as Teresa's associate and confessor, well known as a gifted spiritual director and as an eminent poet. Yet, in almost a quarter century since his death, no edition of his works, official or otherwise, has appeared."

"Because there were no original manuscripts on which to base them?"

I shake my head. "Not a valid reason, Diego. There are multiple copies and versions stored in convent records and amongst the papers of his lay followers, more than enough to produce an edition of his work. Why has the Discalced Carmelite Order not yet taken this in hand?" I think of the hundreds of dusty pages of notes, records and half-completed dossiers in Crespo's oaken chest. No doubt my own report was always destined to join them.

"That is indeed odd." Carmela's tawny eyes rest on mine. "The Order would as a rule publish writers of such eminence, if not in their lifetime, at least within a few years of their death."

"They don't want people to read his poetry," Diego declares. "Or at least, no more than those who are already acquainted with it: that is, people who already understand his teachings. It seems obvious to me," his eyes take on a sly glint, "that if they don't want anyone to read his poems, then we need to read them. With particular attention."

"*The Dark Night*. And the *Canticle*, of course. Diego, find the copies, please, they are at your elbow."

While he is riffling through the papers I move closer to Carmela. "I do not disagree with your theory. I have indeed disrupted Ortiz and Crespo's strategy to influence the Vatican's inspection into Fray Juan's life. That explains their hostility to me, at least in part. But I am guessing that if they intended to support Fray Juan's beatification, their intention was – is – provisional. I do not believe that they are committed to that course of action."

Diego interrupts his search. "If you are right, Fray Martín, then their final decision on how to use your report – whether to enhance Fray Juan's reputation or to undermine it, to support or oppose the case for his beatification – may well depend on what information, if any, comes to light during your investigation."

"Exactly. Perhaps they are also influenced by other priorities we know nothing about. But I do believe that they expected my research to recount nothing more than accounts of miracles and sermons and evidence of qualities considered proper to the life of a saint."

"And that you would suppress everything else? I find that hard to believe." Carmela's voice is trembling. Diego and I look at each other, and at her. "It is not likely that the superiors of our Order would seek to falsify evidence in this way."

"'Falsify' is a strong word, Carmela. We are talking about emphasis and focus, not outright invention. Lies are crude things, blunt instruments, easy to expose. And unnecessary, when the weapons of interpretation and innuendo are so much sharper. And almost invisible." The three of us fall silent and for a few moments. My companions regard me, uneasy. I am tired of being pitied as the sad victim of a stifled scandal at the

University of Salamanca. I sweep on. "Not only is it possible that other investigators selected which details to highlight and which to discard, in the way you describe, it is certain. I can prove it."

I skim through the sheaf of papers Diego has compiled and select the oil-stained folio of the two dozen or so testimonies written in the witnesses' own hand, which some earlier investigator had collected and filed between stitched covers. It is not difficult to find the pages that prove my point, as the lines and paragraphs of interest to my predecessor are clearly marked. I point to six or seven highlighted phrases. It is obvious that they were selected to support a single goal – to advance the case for Fray Juan's beatification. Carmela frowns, engaged in a wordless struggle with warring thoughts. Meanwhile, Diego sifts through a few pages I have fanned out on the bench in front of us.

"Fray Martín, have all of Fray Juan's other papers, these letters and notes and poems, been marked in the same way?"

"I do not know, Diego. This folio of witness statements and a few poems are the only sections of Prior Andrés's archive I have had time to analyse in detail. I had hoped to examine the rest of it today." I look from one to the other. "With your help. That is why I asked to meet you both."

Diego nods. Carmela gives no sign she has heard but leans forward and plucks at the corner of a single page covered in a small, cramped hand. She turns it over and holds it aloft. A single shaft of light spills over it. "Is this the poem you were looking for? The *Dark Night of the Soul?*"

I nod, reach out to take the page from her. Did I imagine a resistance as she released it from her grip? "This is one of the few texts I have had time to examine closely. I am convinced that some of Fray Juan's poems will reveal motivation for the persecution he suffered during his lifetime. I am sure that the reasons are deeper than institutional rivalry with the Carmelites of the Ancient Observance."

"Then what? What other reason could there be, Fray Martín?"

"That is a good question, Diego." I get to my feet and take a few paces, back and forth along the aisle to assuage my restlessness. "This single poem reveals a most unorthodox view of religious observance and practices. In this version, Fray Juan's view of the relationship between God and man was very close to heresy. I suspect that his original versions might go even further."

Carmela's luminous eyes rest on mine and, seeing those full lips tremble a little, at that moment I am convinced that she understands my meaning. For a few moments she holds my gaze, then turns her regard to the paper in my hand.

"Fray Martín? Madre Carmela? What does that all mean?" Diego takes the page from me and casts an eye across the closely written text. "This *Dark Night of the Soul* is a love poem. A girl, the *amada*, steals out of her house by night in search of her beloved. If you had not told me that the *amada* is the soul and the beloved *Amado* is God, I would have thought this a very explicit description of profane love. Your talk of heresy baffles me."

"I will explain the details by and by, Diego. Just for a moment, let us assume that I am right. If the theological foundation of the *Dark Night* really is so nicely balanced on the line – the very fine line – that separates orthodox belief from heresy, it is possible that the *Canticle* is, too. Perhaps even more so, for that poem has attracted a great deal of attention from the superiors of the Discalced Carmelite Order, including Crespo and Ortiz."

"And from the Inquisition," Diego reminds me. "Might this whiff of heresy explain the interest of so many people in recovering Fray Juan's original manuscript? The definitive version, the one that reveals what he really thought and believed?"

I nod and sink back into my place on the bench, conscious that Carmela has said very little. My own voice trails off to a murmur. "I am sure it would explain their unease, in particular if the *Canticle* expressed a view of faith and an approach to religious practice that did not conform to the tenets laid down by the Council of Trent. Those principles are non-negotiable. They are a protective web of precepts created to protect both laity and clergy from the abuses of position that have corrupted our Church for centuries past."

"Also, to protect our mother Church from the reformers of the north," Carmela adds suddenly, her voice shaking, "who deny the Pope and the sacraments, who distribute translated copies of the Bible, who deny the mediation of the relationship between God and man by the chosen hierarchy of bishops and priests."

She falls silent, one hand flying to her lips as though to call back the words she has just spoken.

"Exactly. You see the problem, Carmela?" When I turn towards her, those tawny eyes are cast down.

"Fray Juan's work does not challenge the precepts of Trent," she murmurs. I have touched a nerve.

"I am not so sure." She remains silent, but I cannot retreat now. "What is certain, Carmela, is that he does not support Trent, either – the rituals, the sacraments, prayer which is communal and vocalised. Fray Juan makes no reference at all to those precepts. Look at this poem." I hold before her the copy of the *Dark Night*. "In forty-eight lines – eight stanzas, each composed of six lines – there is no priest or bishop in sight. No reference to a mass or a sacrament of any kind. Not a single prayer. The cornerstones, the foundations of our practice of the Christian faith – where are they?" Carmela makes to take the parchment from my hand but I will not be silenced. "Only hear Fray Juan's own words and you will see that this dark night of the soul is not in the least painful. Listen:

"O blissful destiny...
blazing with desire for love...
my house being now at peace..."

Alarmed at my own vehemence, I pause for a moment to compose myself. I take a deep breath and continue. "Do Fray Juan's words describe a path strewn with trials and tribulations that the soul must navigate, in its battle with good and evil, with temptation and sin? No. In its struggle towards salvation, the journey of the soul on this dark night is very far from being a soul writhing in agony. It is joyful!"

I pause but still she remains silent. "And where does he speak of guidance from spiritual leaders, priests and bishops and our Holy Father the Pope, who administer sacraments and thus separates us from the heretics of the North...?"

"Like Luther?" Diego asks, startled.

"Luther, Erasmus, Calvin. All those who insist on a personal relationship between God and man, unmediated by religious authority. Here," I retrieve my spectacles from the folds of my habit and bow my head over the copy of the *Dark Night of the Soul*. "This is how Fray Juan describes the journey of the soul towards union with God." I declaim, almost chant the words.

> *"And I, not heeding anything*
> *No other light nor guide*
> *Than that which blazed within my heart...*
> *...that light showed me the way*
> *More clearly than the midday sun."*

I fall silent, waiting for a reaction from my companions. There is none. "Carmela, you insist that Fray Juan did not challenge the orthodoxy of Trent. You must agree that in this poem, he did. And not only by omission. The lines I have just quoted state that the individual has no need of guidance from without. That the goal of prayer is not redemption, which he never mentions, but rather, unity with God, which is attained by following the light within. He could not be clearer."

My words fall like stones into the silence. A sliver of light pierces the gloom, falls upon my eyes, dazzling me for a moment. I raise a hand to fend off the glare.

"You must try to understand." When Carmela speaks, her voice is soft, but insistent. "This poem is not a formal declaration of belief. Fray Juan was not a poet who wrote of spiritual matters. Rather, the opposite: he was a spiritual director who communicated with us, his daughters and sons in Christ, through his poems. They were an aid to his teachings, a means of complementing his sermons, his letters, the words he spoke in the confessional; intended to be read within the confines of the convent walls, where the nuances of his thinking were clear to those who knew him well. It is only when his words are removed from that setting and exposed to the harsh glare of judgement that there is a real danger some will misunderstand."

I am determined not to waver. "Carmela, you are unjust. I well understand that Fray Juan's writings were intended for his intimates, for those initiated into the practices associated with advanced spiritual development. That they are, for the most part, read by them – by you. Their limited exposure explains why he was not challenged – by the Inquisition, for example."

"We do not even know for certain that the Inquisition did not summon him," Diego reminds me.

"True, but if they did, nothing came of it. And if any of his works had been censored, you would have found a record of it. Remember, the Holy Office recalled several of Teresa's works. Yet these words of Fray Juan, went unremarked." I pick up the parchment again.

> *"And I forget myself…*
> *…all my senses suspended.*

"You know what this means, Carmela. He is referring to the gathering in of the senses. The suspension of the powers of the mind to allow the presence of God to flood the soul. *Recogimiento*. A practice regarded with the greatest suspicion by the Church hierarchy. On the very edge of orthodoxy." As I speak, a troubling thought crosses my mind. "Perhaps your Sor Eugenia knows something of this?" I stammer.

Carmela suppresses a smile. "Do not worry, Fray Martín. The meditation practice you learned from Sor Eugenia was not *recogimiento*. You did not stumble into a nest of *alumbrado* heretics in Málaga, whatever you might suspect."

Her levity irritates me. Having made a study of Fray Juan's *Dark Night of the Soul*, I am not at all surprised that the Seville *alumbrados* adopted it almost as their anthem. But I am amazed that the Inquisition did not censor this poem outright, and I am bemused that Fray Juan managed to evade the serious attention of the Holy Office during his lifetime. I keep these thoughts to myself, but Carmela reads my mind.

"Martín, as a theologian and an academic, you know that sometimes there is little to distinguish orthodoxy and outright heresy. A single word can separate one from the other." I nod. "And you know that so many of Fray Juan's words, such as you have just quoted, can be interpreted in different ways. They can be twisted this way and that. To fit a particular reading, or another, perhaps even a contrary meaning. In this way, certain readers whose minds are less finely tuned, or else disposed towards a specific goal, could misinterpret them. Or choose to do so."

I say nothing, though I think that what she says is true. This poem of Fray Juan's is the perfect double-edged instrument. Wielded in certain hands, it is an ideal tool that will proclaim Fray Juan's piety; in others, it is a weapon that reveals the heterodoxy of his vision and, thereby, condemns him.

"It seems to me that the very poems that are so greatly loved, that give us Fray Juan's written legacy," Diego observes, "are the ones that create the greatest difficulties, both for him and for his Order. If he had never written a line, none of these worries about dark nights or *recogimiento* or interior prayer would matter. All would be forgotten and he'd be a saint by now."

Carmela looks at me and I am unable to suppress a smile, in spite of our differences.

"There is merit in what you say, Diego. Fray Juan's thoughts on the most contentious questions of his time are preserved in his poems. In those versions which have come down to us."

"Diego, I agree with you," says Carmela, leaning forward and leafing through a sheaf of papers. "And you speak true when you say that many people are anxious to find the originals of Fray Juan's work. They are desperate to see the definitive versions. Or else, to determine once and for all that those originals are forever lost."

I glance at the copy of the *Dark Night* and ponder the implications of her comment.

Diego's eyes follow my own. "Is there any possibility that the version you are holding now, Fray Martín, is Fray Juan's original manuscript of that poem?"

"Out of the question," I declare without hesitation. Carmela nods in agreement. "The type of paper is relatively recent. I estimate that this is a copy, probably made from another copy sometime within the last ten years."

"So there is no way of knowing," he probes, "if those departures from orthodoxy, as you put it, are Fray Juan's own words?"

"That is correct, Diego. Without sight of the originals, we do not know if his own words might have departed even further from orthodoxy. To the point of religious rebellion."

"Or the opposite," Carmela puts in. "His original expression might be well within the bounds of orthodoxy."

"True," I agree. "Without the original manuscripts, we simply do not know. Some of his supporters – those who wish for his beatification – might prefer that his papers remain lost. Whereas his detractors…"

"…could use his own words against him, to prove that he was a borderline heretic, fanatic, and generally unfit to be elevated to Blessed," adds Diego.

"I do not think that the original manuscripts ever will be found," Carmela declares. I have come to the same conclusion. Other investigators have followed the same path that I now tread, sifting through the hundreds of files and thousands of pages crammed into the oaken chest in my office. If the originals of Fray Juan's manuscripts had survived, they would have been found by now.

"It seems that Fray Juan's reputation and that of his Order is safe, as long as the original of the *Canticle* is never found."

I shrug. "I wish I could agree, Diego. But even without the originals, many copies are already in circulation. If the themes and language of the *Canticle* go as far as those in the *Dark Night*, who knows what use could be made of them. People who are now Fray Juan's most staunch supporters might become his greatest opponents. I do not know."

I cannot banish the weariness from my voice. I wonder if I have erred in bringing my companions together, to carry out work whose purpose is so nebulous and uncertain. But I cannot leave Madrid without one final attempt to achieve some insight, make some discovery that will satisfy Doctor Enrique enough to restore me to favour and to my old life in Salamanca.

My companions observe my despondency and try to restore my good humour. "I recommend we begin by sorting the rest of these papers into documents according to type – letters, personal notes, poems, longer commentaries and miscellaneous," Carmela suggests. "Then we can decide which of us will examine each set of documents in more depth."

Her enthusiasm restores me to action. "We can meet here one week from today," I suggest. "This will be an onerous task. But together…"

"Whatever can be done, will be done, Fray Martín," Diego declares. "You may count on us."

Church of San Pedro el Real, by the Puerta Nueva, Madrid,
Twenty-seventh day of September in the Year of Our Lord, 1616.

Carmela's lips are pursed in concentration as she unpacks a faded velvet pouch containing the papers she selected for scrutiny at the end of our meeting last week. For a prioress of the Discalced Carmelite Order, the opportunity to examine documents that illuminate Fray Juan's life and work must be as enthralling as it is for me, though for different reasons. In silence, she hands me a batch of about thirty individual pages.

"This will take some time." Her allocated sample of Prior Andrés's archive includes documents of several types comprising papers of varying sizes and textures, some fastened together with string. In the few hours that remain to us, we must examine all of them, for this is our last but one meeting. Next week, I will finalise my report for Crespo and Ortiz in preparation for my return to the remote convent of San Salvador. Unless some unforeseen discovery provides me with the means to retrieve my position at the university, it seems that I will, after all, be obliged to go. If there is something to be found in old Prior Andrés's archive that could alter the course of my immediate future, there is no time to lose.

Dragging my thoughts back to the present, I see that Carmela has selected one page for inspection. "I believe that some of these documents explain the struggles that arose within my Order after we had gained some measure of independence, when we were declared a separate Province. I have often lamented that we Discalced Carmelites were riven with conflict at the very moment when we should have been most united."

This is not the moment to explain that the death of a strong, charismatic leader such as Teresa would of course reveal internal fissures and rivalries that the force of her personality had repressed or concealed during her lifetime.

Yet I wonder must it ever be thus? Is the struggle to achieve our heart's desire – great wealth, status, even freedom from an oppressor – a unifying force only while we are in pursuit of the goal? Does success in achieving our aim then splinter, rather than strengthen, the very unity that made success possible, thus creating another goal, another dream, until the battle itself becomes the destination, and peace is but a distant memory? The history of the Discalced Carmelite Order convinces me that this is so, blighted as it was by such great rivalries between its founding members – Jerónimo Gracián, Ana de Jesús, Fray Juan, who all supported Teresa's Constitution – and the newcomers. These later incumbents, ambitious bureaucrats, were determined to apply to the religious life all manner of controls and regulations derived from the previous occupation of their Italian leader, Niccolà Doria, the banker who delivered more than one impoverished bishop and nobleman, perhaps even the king himself, from financial ruin. Doria's earlier vocation had taught him how the skilful use of procedure, wielded in certain hands, can be more effective than brute force in the pursuit of dominance and power.

Diego has turned his attention to a document some four or five pages in length.

"These are minutes of a meeting, Fray Martín, of the Grand Chapter of the Discalced Carmelites, held here in Madrid in the month of June fifteen ninety-one. Just a few months before Fray Juan died. Here." He places five creased pages on the bench and smooths them out, pointing to a few lines on the last page. "Do you see these conclusions?"

The final paragraph contains three lists, all names: those who were nominated for office during the meeting, those who were elected to office and those who were defeated. He runs his finger down the third column: "Fray Juan de la Cruz."

"We know this," Carmela murmurs. "He was nominated for office in the Chapter, as he always had been, ever since he and Teresa instigated the reform more than twenty years before." She raises her hands to the rim of her wimple. "But in June fifteen ninety-one, he was defeated."

"It was a coup." Diego's voice is hoarse. "He was ousted. Stabbed in the back. And not by the other Carmelite faction..."

"Carmelite Province, Diego. By the Carmelites of the Ancient Observance," Carmela breathes.

"...but by his own people, the Discalced. Your people," Diego continues, nodding towards her. "Members of the reform he had founded and nurtured and defended and suffered for during all those years."

"According to this motion," I indicate a few lines in the middle of the second page, "Fray Juan tried to force a secret ballot in the election of office-bearers."

"Which was defeated," Carmela reminds me. "He proposed a secret ballot on all important questions, Martín, not only for the election of office bearers. The vote on Doria's proposals for new procedures in the organisation of convents was most significant. An open ballot would ensure that Doria knew who had supported his measures and who had opposed them. He was not about to let Fray Juan deprive him of that intelligence."

Diego turns to the next page and whistles in surprise. "They sent him to Mexico!" he exclaims, incredulous. "To work as a missionary? What had he done that was so bad, that drove them to banish him to the other side of the world?"

I turn to Carmela.

"It was because of us," she whispers. "At least, that is what we sisters believe. Because he continued to support us, in our individual convents, in maintaining control over our own affairs against the wishes of the new man, Doria. Who was determined to put the *consulta*, his own hand-picked committee, in charge of us. A governing council with the power to appoint our prioresses, our father confessors, they could even decide where each sister would be posted. In total contravention of Teresa's Constitution."

"But he failed."

"No, Diego. The new vicar general succeeded, though Fray Juan fought him on it. He begged his colleagues to challenge Doria, to defend Teresa's legacy, to stand firm against the intimidation and manipulation of this encroaching authority. That was why the secret ballot was so important. But he couldn't push it through. Instead, Doria got rid of him."

The three of us sit in silence.

"Did Fray Juan live out the rest of life in Mexico?"

Carmela shakes her head. "For a few months after the Chapter meeting he lived in a remote monastery in Andalucía but fell ill before he could make the journey to the Americas. The prior sent him to the town of Úbeda for medical attention. Where he died."

Not for the first time, I reflect that Fray Juan's death was a consequence of that Chapter meeting in June. Had he been elected to office in Madrid, he would never have gone to that little convent in Andalucía and might not have contracted the leg infection that inflicted an agonising death upon him in that monastery of Úbeda. Where the prior made it clear as soon as he arrived that he was an unwelcome guest and a burden on the community.

"Was old Prior Andrés on the official list of witnesses Crespo and Ortiz gave you, or did you identify him through your own researches?" Carmela is poring over a few lines sketched in the margins of one of the letters.

"He was on the official list," I answer. "Why?"

"I am not sure. Look at this little drawing." She unfolds a single page which is covered in a fine, spidery hand, not very easy to read, the writing ending in mid-sentence at the bottom of the page. And, close to the top right-hand corner, is a tiny sketch of Christ on the Cross. The figure is viewed on the diagonal, from above, as though an angel had hovered over the final agony of the Saviour and traced the outline of his sinewy arms stretched to their limit, hands driven through with nails and fastened to the cross, His head bowed. Carmela's hand lingers on the page without touching it. "I wonder if this drawing was made by Fray Juan himself," she murmurs.

Diego picks up the leaf and holds it to the light. "If so, then the entire letter is most likely written by him." I agree that this is a strong possibility. Amongst the various documents stored in my office, I have found two accounts, both written between ten and fifteen years ago, of Fray Juan's drawings. One describes a sketch of Christ on the Cross depicted from an unusual vantage point. It must be the same drawing. Or at least a copy.

"Perhaps the ending of this letter is somewhere amongst the other documents," I mutter. "The signature page would tell us for certain if this is a sample of Fray Juan's own hand. We must try to find it. It would be a most precious resource for our work. Meanwhile…" I lay two separate sheafs of pages on the wooden bench. Neither set bears a title but it is clear that they are two copies of the same text – two of the documents I inspected closely after Doctor Enrique's last visit. Diego picks up the page that bears an introduction: *This is a draft, from which the fair copy has been made.*

"Is that the *Canticle*?" Diego asks. "Two different copies?"

I nod. My examination of these manuscripts has led me to some preliminary conclusions, and also, to a number of questions I am hoping my companions will help me to answer.

"Is this one the first draft and the other the fair copy referred to in the heading?"

I press my finger to my lips and nod towards the documents. Diego's question goes to the heart of the matter and I do not wish to anticipate or influence any insights my companions may reach.

For the next half hour we each examine both copies of the poem, the only sound an occasional rustle of the paper we are handling with great caution, taking care not to tear or smudge the leaves. Carmela passes each page to me as she finishes reading, and I hand it on to Diego, until each of us has examined, word by word, these twenty-two pages on which are inscribed two versions of the *Canticle*.

Diego looks away. "For a religious text, this poetry sounds... unusual."

I grimace. "That it is."

"In truth, although these are two different copies of the poem, I do not see much difference between them."

"Nor I," Carmela agrees. "And, as you pointed out, Martín, we do not know how close these transcripts are to Fray Juan's original version of his *Canticle*. Are these similar to the text of the illuminated scroll that Doctor Enrique showed you?"

I have been dreading this question. "I do not recall." I cannot believe I did not have the wit to ask the Inquisitor permission to make a copy before he left. "The poem in that manuscript was certainly called *Cántico*. But it was much longer."

"The text itself, you mean? Even allowing for the illustrations?" Carmela presses.

"The text. I am sure. There may have been as many as... oh, ten different sections, each comprising six or seven stanzas."

"That would amount to seventy stanzas in total, then," she murmurs. "Almost twice the length of the versions we have here."

It is possible that the copies in our possession are incomplete. Or, that Doctor Enrique's is an expanded version of the original. Without sight of Fray Juan's first draft, there is no way of knowing.

"Fray Martín, what exactly do you want us to do with these two manuscripts?"

Diego's question reminds me of how little progress we have made.

"One of the few things we can be sure of, is that this poem has aroused great suspicion and unease. Given that we do not have the original, the only strategy open to us at present is to compare these two versions, in detail. The process might yield insights."

"We are looking for differences between these two copies of the *Canticle*, then. Which will tell us...what, exactly?"

"I do not know, Diego!" I throw my pencil on the bench. "Some revelation concerning Fray Juan's teachings that explains the hostility – and the veneration – he aroused. Some reason why this poem is of such interest to the Discalced Carmelite Order, and to the Inquisition. I do not know what I am seeking. Only that I will recognise it when I see it. If I ever do."

My companion raises both hands in mock surrender.

"It is not a bad plan, Martín." Carmela hands one of the *Canticle* manuscripts to Diego. "But given the uncertainty of our aim, we must be systematic in our approach."

After some discussion, we agree on a method that allows us to identify and classify every variation between the two transcripts, which, for want of any more original epithet, we call *Cántico One* – the 'draft from which the fair copy has been made' – and *Cántico Two*. We agree to work line by line: Carmela reads aloud a line from *Cántico One*, Diego follows with the corresponding line from *Cántico Two* and I ask questions and make notes as we go along.

In this way, I can record differences in spelling, punctuation, substitutions, the occasional deletions and other, more substantial differences that defy classification. Some variations, which I call 'minor', are most likely due to slips of the pen or to a mistake of the copyist. Of greater interest are the differences that a writer may have introduced on purpose, to achieve a specific effect. These, we call 'major' variations. In addition, we endeavour – but with only limited success – to propose reasons for the differences; and, with even greater difficulty, to assess their potential impact and consequences.

Proceeding thus, it takes us more than two hours to examine all the stanzas in both versions. By which time, I have amassed a dozen pages of scribbled notes.

"Can we draw any general conclusions?"

"Did you bring that wineskin with you today, Fray Martín?"

I look up in exasperation. "Diego, we have no time to waste."

"A moment's pause, Fray Martín. This reading aloud is thirsty work."

"I brought this as a reward for work completed," I grumble, retrieving the wineskin from beneath the pew where I had stored it. "Not as a distraction from our labours."

Diego grins and takes the pouch from me. When he has quenched his thirst, he offers it to me but I decline. Carmela, who is paying no attention to either of us, carries on reading my notes and, reaching into the folds of her habit, produces a set of eyeglasses. I raise my eyebrows. "Your handwriting is quite difficult to read, Martín," she explains. "And the light here is very dim."

Does my unworldly Madre Carmela not wish to admit to failing eyesight? Were Diego not of our company I would have teased her a little, but her tone is brisk and busy so I resist the temptation and set about summarising from memory the patterns I have discerned in our comparison of the two versions of the *Canticle*. "As we anticipated, some of the differences are straightforward errors – a letter misplaced, or a word substituted, perhaps because the copyist was tired or could not read the original or did not understand the word. Fray Juan's poems sometimes contained terms that could surprise a reader unaccustomed to poetic idiom."

"And if the copyist came from a different part of the country," Diego added, "some words might sound strange. In which case he – or she – might insert another that made more sense."

Carmela looks up. "A very good point, Diego. I think you are right. For example, judging from the formation of these letters," her pale fingernail points out two or three crooked scrawls, "and some irregularities in spelling, I would guess that this version was copied by someone who learned to write in the eastern part of Andalucía." She spends a few minutes itemising other differences that appear to fall into the same category of changes.

"You are both of the opinion, then, that some of the differences in these two copies of the *Canticle* are without any real significance. These are not deliberate, thought-out alterations but simple errors or at most, innocent substitutions influenced by the personal experience, background, even the speech of the individual copyist. Is that correct?"

Both nod their agreement. Before I can continue, Carmela interrupts. "I would include in this category a different type of error – perhaps we should not call these alterations errors: rather, edits."

"What is the difference, Madre Carmela?"

"Intention, Diego. An edit is not a slip of the pen or a misreading of an unfamiliar word. It is a conscious decision of a reader who decides to venture what she or he thinks is a slight improvement on the original text. For example, by substituting a word that makes the line read a little better or makes the meaning a little clearer. At least, in their view.

"These references to 'land' and 'horizon,' for example. In our *Cántico Two*, the words used in the same position in the same lines are 'air' and 'breeze.' I suggest that this alteration was made by someone unaccustomed to poetic imagery, someone who judged that the words 'land' and 'horizon' made better sense in this context. Which, according to a literal reading, they do. Whoever altered these words did not understand Fray Juan's use of those images to evoke the Holy Spirit. This is not a major change. More a matter of literary technique."

I am appalled. To my mind, the variation Carmela has just described is far from minor or insignificant but, rather, indicates a troubling intention: to recast, embellish or otherwise improve on meaning; to make it conform to a way of thinking that departs from the original intention of the text. I am convinced that such variations, however trivial they seem, could have significant consequences. But Carmela is immovable on this point.

In the end, Diego loses patience with us both. "Is there anything we do agree on? Are there any differences between these two versions which we can agree are major rather than minor?"

I consult my notes and mark off several of my most important observations. "I do believe we can identify some edits, changes, whatever you wish to call them, of a more purposeful nature: revisions that alter shades of meaning in ways that could make a substantial difference to how the text might be interpreted."

I take a few minutes to summarise these. The most obvious difference between the two versions is the length: *Cántico One* has thirty-nine stanzas, each of six lines. *Cántico Two* includes an extra verse, inserted as a new stanza fourteen, the contents of those six additional lines being wholly absent from *Cántico One*.

"And the order of this longer version, Fray Martín, from stanza fourteen onwards, is different."

In truth, this was something I did not remark when I read both versions separately. Only in reading them line by line, side by side, is it clear that the arrangement of the stanzas in the two versions is quite different.

To my great surprise, Carmela again dismisses this divergence as being of little significance. "This is a literary matter," she insists. "And to my mind, an improvement. You can see how the thought, the progression of the narrative, flows so much better in *Cántico Two*."

I am perturbed that she views this in terms of poetic technique. It is clear to me that these changes are decisive. For even though the content of both is almost identical, the overall effect of each version is quite different.

"Carmela, the insertion of this stanza into *Cántico Two* changes how the journey of the individual soul towards union with God is viewed. *Cántico One* foregrounds the immanence of God – that God is in all creatures; all creatures are in God. As you know, this is a heretical precept, for the soul cannot be at one with God, not in this life. But in *Cántico Two*, this same idea is greatly diminished. Not because anything has been removed – that would be too obvious – but because the modified order of the stanzas foregrounds other precepts, which as a consequence, pushes the idea of immanence into the background! A literary technique, yes, very subtle and very clever, which guides the reader towards quite a different interpretation of the poem!"

"I see what you mean, Fray Martín." Diego is intrigued. "How words that are almost identical can be arranged to produce such different meanings. Is there any other…?"

"Yes, Diego, there are many other examples. Here," I point to a line in *Cántico One*," we have a clear reference to *impecabilidad*, whereas…"

"I am sorry, Fray Martín, you will have to enlighten me."

"The impossibility of sin," whispers Carmela.

"One of the *alumbrado* beliefs that caused the most trouble," I add.

"Exactly." Madre Carmela leafs through the two copies of the *Canticle*. "It is an extension of the belief that the human soul can become one with God. An idea which itself is on the edge of heresy. If the soul is unified with God… well, it is easy to argue that the soul is therefore incapable of sin. A soul that is united with God cannot desire anything that God does not desire. *Impecabilidad*."

Diego lets out a low whistle. "Which would make anything permissible."

"For some of the *alumbrados*, that is exactly what it did, Diego," Carmela shakes her head in sorrow. "Some members of that sect engage in the most licentious of practices, which they justify with the notion of *impecabilidad*."

"We are agreed then, that the belief in possibility of the human soul's union with God – in this life, not the next – is neither innocent nor harmless. It is a dogma that can legitimise any manner of heinous actions," I put in.

"There is no question that Fray Juan's teachings encourage this heresy, or the behaviour that stemmed from it." Madre Carmela's voice trembles.

Diego jumps to his feet and points a finger at no one in particular.

"Well, it is obvious to me that *Cántico Two* has been tampered with. Someone got hold of *Cántico One*, worried about the way some parts might be interpreted and decided to…tidy it up. Get rid of a few of the most troublesome elements."

I find Diego's reasoning persuasive. But I am struggling to see how I might present this discovery to Crespo and Ortiz in a way that will be to my benefit.

"Unless Fray Juan did it himself," Carmela interjects. "What if *Cántico One* is indeed the first draft, and *Cántico Two* the revised copy? After all, the sub-heading of *Cántico One* even states that there is a fair copy. Our *Cántico Two* could be that copy."

"There is merit in what she says, Fray Martín."

Carmela presses the point. "Furthermore, Martín, we have no evidence that these changes were inserted by an alien hand. Both copies could have been penned by Fray Juan himself."

"I do not think so, Carmela. The two manuscripts are written in very different hands. Whether one is the poet's, we do not know. But look, here, in the margins of *Cántico One*."

I hand her my own eyeglasses, whose lenses are stronger than hers. "These annotations. They are too small to read without a magnifying glass." I indicate the minuscule lettering on the pages. "But I'll warrant that these are corrections, penned by Fray Juan himself. If *Cántico Two* is indeed the second draft – the fair copy of the corrected *Cántico One* – we would expect to see the corrections indicated here, made in that later version."

Diego makes no answer but looks intently at the annotations. For a moment, he sits very still then turns to the sheaf of papers on the bench. From it, he retrieves the single page embellished with the little drawing of Christ on the Cross.

"Fray Martín. Madre Carmela." His voice is shaking. "There is something else. But I need…" Madre Carmela hands him my eyeglasses, which he positions above the annotations in the margin of *Cántico One*. "This lens is not strong enough to allow us to read the annotations, but it might allow us to…" He moves the glass across to focus on the illustrated letter. "We guessed that this letter, and the little sketch of the Christ, are both the work of Fray Juan." Making a series of smooth arcs across both pages, he sweeps the lens back and forth, between the illustrated letter and the annotated margins of *Cántico One*.

He looks up, eyes glittering. "This is the same hand, is it not?" He warms to his theme. "And who would annotate this draft, if not the poet himself? Madre Carmela, Fray Martín, there are coincidences and there are strong probabilities. I think we can assume that all three – letter, drawing of the Christ, annotations – were made by Fray Juan himself."

Carmela and I exchanged looks. The evidence, if not definitive, is persuasive. But I am not sure how this discovery will advance our task. Carmela's flushed cheeks reveal her agitation.

"I think you are right, Diego. But where does that leave us? Does it prove that the version we call *Cántico Two* was the result of Fray Juan's own work? Or the result of interference from an alien hand? We still do not know."

I ponder her words. It is possible that Fray Juan, perhaps crushed by persecution or persuaded by his supporters, decided to soften his mode of expression in *Cántico Two*, authorising changes that couched his thought in more ambiguous terms, in case the Inquisition decided to take an active interest in him.

"Do you believe that a poet such as Fray Juan would change his mind thus, from one draft to the next?" Diego scoffs. "I cannot believe it. *Cántico Two* is a fabrication."

I do not answer, but I know that a change of mind and heart while writing would not be so strange; that the business of composition, even writing a lecture or a sermon, takes the path of a meandering river, not an arrow. Often, my final version reverses the thoughts of my earlier drafts, as though the act of thinking and reasoning travels a subterranean route between my brain and my quill.

"Let us not lose sight of our purpose, Diego. We must keep an open mind on the presumed motivation and consequences of these revisions. It does not seem odd to me that Fray Juan might have made them, or authorised them himself, as part of the process of poetic creation."

I can see that Diego remains unconvinced whereas for Carmela, this conclusion would be a kind of solution. For myself, I do not believe that *Cántico Two* is a later version made by the poet himself as part of a process of revision. I think that Diego's first instinct was correct: *Cántico Two* has been retouched to present a more favourable image of Fray Juan's thinking to the world. As to the author of these revisions, we cannot be sure who that was. The important thing is the intention behind them: which, I now believe, whether made by Fray Juan or by another, was to bring his writing into the fold of orthodoxy.

At last, we reach an agreement that will satisfy all our priorities. My report for Crespo and Ortiz will summarise the main conclusions arising from our joint readings of the two versions of the *Canticle* last week. I am keen to highlight my two main findings. First: that these, the only versions of Fray Juan's poems currently available to us, contain no real taint of heresy – and that any whiff of unorthodoxy is corrected in *Cántico Two* – and that his work, therefore, admits no impediment to his beatification. My second conclusion: according to the information supplied by the witnesses I have interviewed and my analysis of the different handwritings on the texts we have examined, Fray Juan's original manuscripts are almost certainly lost forever.

This strategy, I am convinced, will reassure Crespo and Ortiz that my conduct of the investigation has been both rigorous and productive. It will also deliver them from the fear of some un-welcome surprise concerning Fray Juan's work arising in the future.

And of greatest importance, for me, is the effect of all this on my own future. I am hopeful that my work will persuade Doctor Enrique to keep his promise and restore me to my position in the university. It is true that my final report will not be exactly what Crespo and Ortiz wanted, but given the complex nature of my terms of reference, coupled with the vagueness of the overall purpose, I do not think that they can expect more. They should all three be happy that I have assembled evidence enough to argue that the earlier, more troubling drafts of Fray Juan's poems expressed a line of thinking that was later corrected in revised copies that express what he really meant to say. If I make a convincing case that these improvements were made by Fray Juan himself, so much the better. It might even be true. Certainly, it sounds as though it could be true, and that is what matters now.

Church of San Pedro el Real, by the Puerta Nueva, Madrid
Eleventh day of October in the Year of Our Lord, 1616.

A t last, my work here is done. Our final meeting is almost at an end and soon I will return to my office in the monastery of San Gerónimo el Real, ready to put the final touches to my report for Crespo and Ortiz. Perhaps Diego and his daughter will accompany me when I take up my old position in Salamanca. But this is not the moment to suggest it. Trying to suppress my excitement, I cannot help wondering when, or if, Madre Carmela and I will meet again.

As my mood is now a peculiar mixture of elation and sadness, I resolve to push these questions to the back of my mind and prepare for our departure. In order that I may transport Prior Andres's archive in a manner that maintains our system for classifying the contents, I decide to sort and organise the documents into two bundles, according to their relative importance as references for my final conclusions. In one file I place those which are of little or no interest for my purpose. These include notes of a domestic nature, including the estate accounts for the Sicilian manor which attracted my attention when I first received this archive from the old prior.

The second, much slimmer, dossier contains my important source material. This includes texts which relate to Fray Juan's writings, or else reveal something of his thinking. Into this binder I place the two versions of the *Canticle*, a few pages of commentaries on that same poem and several short poems and fragments we have not yet had time to examine in detail. The folder fits comfortably in one of my two saddlebags. Relieved to see this important material safely stored, I set about securing the other, much larger, batch of files with a length of twine.

"Fray Martín, should I blow out this candle?"

"Not yet, Diego, I…" Distracted, I let the string slip through my fingers and send the entire stack of papers cascading to the ground.

As far as I can see in this dim light, none of the documents has been damaged but the largest folio in the bundle has fallen face down on the stone floor, its pages splayed open. Some of the stitching on the spine has snapped and a few of the leaves have come loose. From the size, colour and the stain on the cover, I recognise the accounts document for the Sicilian manor.

I am about to return it to the rest of the bundle when some sensation in the texture and weight of the cover stays my hand. How careful, really, was my first inspection of this file? I recall the lists of names, the graceful way with the pen. But the object, the thing itself, did I really look at it? When I press upon the back cover, an unusual thickness yields to my touch. The first and last pages have been overlaid with a protective paper, almost in the manner of a sleeve, glued around the edges with paste.

"Martín?" Carmela approaches. I do not look up but concentrate on prising a small part of the inner cover from the outer without doing damage to either. Beneath the rudimentary binding, in texture quite different from the rough leaves of the folio, peeps out the flimsy, yellowed corner of a single page. I tug, but it resists my coaxing. This is more than one page. If I am not careful I will tear, and perhaps destroy, whatever is concealed within.

"You will have to remove the entire sleeve, Martín," Carmela breathes. With great caution, I insert my pencil into the small gap between the inner and the outer covers, move it along the lower edge of the file and work the tip around one corner and along all four sides. Now, I can brush away the last dusty remnants of the paste. Taking a deep breath, I peel away the outer cover.

Within the space framed by the traces of the paste nestles a thin sheaf of paper, no more than a few leaves, folded in two and secured with three or four stitches along one margin, fashioned into a crude notebook. Whoever concealed this document must have been counting on the entire file remaining unnoticed, hidden amongst dozens of other similar files. Not such a bad hiding place. All three of us missed it.

"May I?" Carmela takes the little notebook from my hand and raises it to the light. The yellowish hue of the pages and the faded ink indicate a much older document than the others in Prior Andrés's archive. While Carmela is leafing through this little notebook, I turn to the last page of the folio within whose pages it had remained hidden for so many years. How many years? A stamp. A signature. The date: Sicily, April, Fifteen Seventy Nine.

Seven months after Fray Juan escaped from Toledo.

A thick, palpable silence charges the air.

"More housekeeping accounts?"

"Not housekeeping, Diego." Carmela's voice is trembling. "Fray Martín, may I trouble you to bring me the first *Canticle*, the version with annotations in the margin?

I retrieve the file from my saddlebag and extract the pages. I think she will need a magnifying glass to verify her theory. But my prickling skin tells me what she is thinking. And that she is right.

Scarcely breathing, I lay the manuscript of *Cántico One* alongside the little notebook. Diego points to the inscription at the top of the second page: *Declaration of the Songs which concern the love between the Soul and the Bridegroom Christ.*

A glance is enough to verify that the text scribbled in the little notebook is the same work as the text of our *Cántico One*. There is the same opening line: *Where did you hide, my love*; the same five-line stanzas, alternating with seven syllable lines; the hendecasyllables imported from Italy by the poet Garcilaso that Doctor Enrique pointed out to me so many months ago; the same images of searching and wild beasts and profane passion. Carmela picks up the notebook.

"But this version is incomplete," Diego murmurs.

"Yes." I remove the *cuadernillo* from Carmela's hand. "Only thirteen stanzas."

Carmela points to the third page of our *Cántico One*.

"The last stanza of the poem in this *cuadernillo* begins with the line *O nymphs of Judea*." I observe. "Which is just over half way through the poem in our *Cántico One*."

Carmela looks closely at the two versions. I am sure that the same thought has occurred to us both.

"Madre Carmela," I whisper. She looks up at me, lips trembling. "Did Sor Eugenia, or any of her companions, ever receive letters from Fray Juan? Would she recognise his hand?"

She bows her head and returns to her scrutiny of the little notebook.

"She did. And I am sure that she would. But I would prefer not to ask her."

I give her a sharp look. Perhaps she does not wish to trouble the elderly nun in her final days. Or judges that the fewer people who know of our find – if it is a find – the better.

"I think we may not need to trouble Sor Eugenia." She holds out one hand and Diego, anticipating her wish, passes her my spectacles. "Remember the annotations, here, in the margins of *Cántico One*? We are sure – almost sure – that they were written by Fray Juan himself. Likewise, the letter with the little sketch of Christ on the cross. It seems to me that this *cuadernillo*," she lays her hand gently across it, "is written in the same hand. Look at the thin, spidery letters. The tops and tails on the b's and g's and d's. The general way with the pen."

Diego and I lean forward, our gaze following her fingertip as it traces the letters. Diego sighs and rubs his eyes. "How did Fray Juan's *cuadernillo* first come to be lost?"

"A young nun in one of the convents where Fray Juan lived for a short time, not long after he escaped from Toledo, was told to make a copy of some of his poems. He gave her a little notebook in which he had written them down while he was in prison. His second gaoler pitied him and sometimes allowed him paper and ink."

"Was that the same nun who lost Fray Juan's *cuadernillo* before she could finish her task?"

"Martín, you are unfair. Sor Magdalena did not lose Fray Juan's precious notebook through simple carelessness. It was removed from her cell, stolen, a little while after Fray Juan lent it to her."

Diego and I remain silent, shocked by her vehemence. "You can see that this *cuadernillo*," she holds it up to the light, "is exactly what you would expect to find in the possession of a man who has spent almost a year in prison. Fray Juan did not receive a present of a dainty little notebook. At best, he must have begged for the occasional scrap of paper, pages that he later gathered and fastened together in this rough fashion." She runs her fingers along the spine. "I honestly believe that this settles the matter."

Diego glowers. "So even at that time, there were people who wanted to keep Fray Juan's writing in the dark. Who were prepared to make his poems disappear."

I had attributed the loss of the *cuadernillo* to bad luck and, yes, to the carelessness of one person. Now, as I leaf through these pages, I can believe that Diego is right. Many of the troubling statements I had noted in the *Dark Night* and the *Canticle* are here, expressed in even greater detail. Here, the path towards a mystic union with God is explained, without ambiguity. And I am alarmed to see more than one reference to matters of dogma that were of great concern to the Church during Fray Juan's lifetime. In one stanza alone, the writer of the *cuadernillo* text builds an elaborate poetic image around a single phrase: *because the earth moves around the sun*. Heliocentrism. I shiver, recalling the Inquisition's condemnation of Galileo not six months ago. Had Fray Juan written '*if the earth moves around the sun,*' the Inquisition would have been satisfied and the blushes of the Carmelite Order spared. But he insisted on '*because.*' As though Copernicus were right, and the Pope and all his cardinals, wrong.

In silence, I point to this and other phrases that challenge orthodox practice and belief. In truth, the charity of Fray Juan's second gaoler, by supplying him with paper and ink and the means to record what was truly in his heart, allowed him to bequeath us this most troublesome legacy.

"This is very hot soup," Carmela admits.

Long ago, Blessed Teresa jested that more tears are shed over answered prayers than those that went unheard. Well, I have got what I wanted. For so long, my most ardent wish was to find Fray Juan's lost manuscript of the *Canticle*, even though I thought it well-nigh impossible, convinced that it had been cast into the flames by friends who wanted to protect him. Now, I wish only that one of them had finished the job and disposed of this *cuadernillo*, too. During his lifetime, this little notebook would have given his rivals, and the Inquisition, all the evidence they needed to destroy him.

And if it were brought into the light today? What then?

A few months ago, I would have cared nothing for damage to Fray Juan's reputation, whether he was beatified, vilified or forgotten. I would have handed this *cuadernillo* over – to Crespo or to Doctor Enrique – without a second thought, my only concern being whether the old Inquisitor would keep his promise to return me to my position in Salamanca. Which might yet be possible.

"As I see it, there are several courses of action open to us," I begin.

Carmela lays a hand on my arm. "Martín, you must see that only one course of action is possible."

Diego raises his eyebrows and glances towards me. Carmela continues as though she has not observed our exchange. "If a verifiable original of Fray Juan's *cuadernillo* has been found here today – and I believe that it has – everything is changed."

"I agree. Up to a point." My words are rapid, too urgent. "Fray Juan's notebook will be recognised as the major discovery that it is. It will permit the authentication of any number of other manuscripts. It will verify, once and for all, Fray Juan's fundamental thinking on key issues of religious practice and belief. Those same issues that we discussed here, which I have included in my final report. This new material will allow me to…"

"Martín. What you suggest is out of the question." Carmela's voice is soft but there is a hard edge to her words that I have not heard before. "If this text is examined by the Vatican inspectors, or by the Inquisition, or even by members of Fray Juan's own Order, he will never be elevated to Blessed of the Church."

"I do not see…"

"Reflect on it, Martín. Please. The edited versions of the writings already in circulation, some of which are now in our possession…"

"Our?"

She sweeps on, ignoring my disquiet. "They are already open to interpretations that align Fray Juan's thinking with the beliefs and practices of the *alumbrado* heretics. You said so yourself. The focus on individual pursuit of unity with God, the role of the senses in achieving that unity, the profane expression of the encounter that recalls some of the most blasphemous sensual practices of some *alumbrado* sects, the complete absence of the community of the Church, of the sacraments."

"I did say that. I said more, Carmela: that Fray Juan's writings were a double-edged sword, one side employed by his faithful followers for guidance on their path, the other brandished by his enemies, to exaggerate those *alumbrado* links and brand Fray Juan a heretic. But I thought we also agreed that the unedited expression of his thought did not align him so definitely with heretical doctrine such as *alumbradismo*. You said so yourself," I take the *cuadernillo* from her hand. "How would the circulation of his work have such a damning effect on his reputation?"

Her skin is flushed and I am puzzled to see that she is now really angry. "Fray Juan is not and never was a heretic. His thinking is more subtle than you allow. When he refers to practices such as *recogimiento*, their context and meaning are very far removed from the world of the *alumbrados*. Whom he detested."

"Then why not simply hand over his original manuscript of the *Canticle*, this notebook, and explain those different uses of similar concepts and practices, as you have just explained them to me?"

She gets to her feet, all neutrality abandoned. "The nemesis of certainty!" She rests her hand upon the notebook. "Do you really not understand the havoc that would wreak? Evidence such as this would put a weapon in the hands of those who wish to taint Fray Juan's reputation beyond repair. It would inflict a blow from which the Discalced Carmelites would never recover."

I remain seated, my eyes cast down while I consider the implications of her words and try to divine her intention. All may not yet be lost. My report for Crespo and Ortiz, which I am sure will recover their favour, can remain unchanged. I need make no reference at all to the original version of the *Canticle*, or at least the first half of it, scribbled in this old notebook. I begin to warm to the idea of keeping the *cuadernillo* in a secure place – in Carmela's convent in Málaga? – until the day, sometime in the future, when it can be revealed.

"I do not see why the conclusions of my report need to change at all. No one knows we have found Fray Juan's manuscript. We can simply decide not to hand it over to Crespo and Ortiz, or to anyone else who would use Fray Juan's original manuscripts for their own ends. Then we can proceed as we agreed last week."

"Madre Carmela, I agree with Fray Martín. And even if Fray Martín did give them the *cuadernillo* – please, Madre, hear me out – they would wish to conceal it as much as you do. At least until Fray Juan's beatification is secure. And then, perhaps release it at a future time, when it is more advantageous to the Order." Diego leans back, spreads his arms wide. "That would be the logical course of action if they are so committed to gaining another Blessed for their Order."

"If, Diego!" Carmela's tone takes on a new urgency. "That little word conceals a multitude of dangers. We do not really know the true intentions of Crespo and Ortiz, only what we have been able to divine from their behaviour towards you, Martín. Perhaps they do support Fray Juan and intend to protect his legacy. But we cannot be certain that their superiors agree with them. Some might prefer to dismiss Fray Juan as a fanatic and a heretic, best forgotten. Do not forget," she adds, turning towards me, "that the few feeble attempts over the past twenty years to publish his work have come to naught." She pauses. "No, Diego, we cannot, must not trust to logic. Not without knowing the intentions, the interests that these people pursue."

Diego turns to me and frowns. For a few moments he is silent. When he speaks, his voice has lost some of its certainty. "I do not share Madre Carmela's worries, Fray Martín, but there is much to ponder in her words. Perhaps, in concealing Fray Juan's original manuscript, you will give Ortiz and Crespo exactly what they wanted. They commissioned you, among other things, to find it. As far as they are aware, you were unsuccessful. They are now secure in knowing that either the manuscripts were indeed destroyed long ago, or else they are so well hidden that foreigners from the Vatican will never unearth them."

"As long as Fray Juan's originals are in safekeeping, but out of reach, Crespo and Ortiz may shape events according to their own advantage," Carmela urges. "Today, that may be in support of Fray Juan's beatification, but tomorrow…"

"You cannot have it both ways!" I throw my pencil on the bench. "First, you say that having the manuscripts would allow the princes of the Church to shape Fray Juan's legacy, his future standing, so that they might pursue their own advantage. Then, you suggest that not having the manuscript would allow them the same freedom! Which is it? It cannot be both."

Diego sighs and rests his head on his hands. "I fear that it can indeed be both, Fray Martín." I am becoming tired of his riddles and do not try to hide it. His voice gathers strength. "Madre Carmela hinted at the dangers inherent in a particular kind of certainty. I would go further and ask: which certainty is most advantageous, and which is most dangerous, to all the parties involved? Given what little we know, what are the possible consequences of yielding up the *cuadernillo* to Ortiz and Crespo? Or of hiding it for some time? Or of destroying it?"

I instinctively lay a protective hand upon the precious notebook.

"You are right," the hard tone has returned to Carmela's voice. "We cannot foretell the outcome of either of the first two courses of action. Fray Juan's legacy could be enhanced or destroyed in either case. The only certain outcome derives from the third option."

"It is the only way to maintain the status quo," Diego agrees. "Fray Juan's reputation might not be improved, but neither would there be evidence that could be used to damage him further. Perhaps Madre Carmela is right and there is, after all, only one possible course of action."

Carmela eyes me without flinching. "Such is my reasoning, Martín."

I sometimes think that the greatest difficulty in navigating a course between right and wrong lies, not in remaining on the true path, but in knowing where its borders begin and end. Too often, the way ahead rises as a twisting, turning trail through high, rocky mountains, where today's virtue is tomorrow's evil and there is no telling where, or when, or even if one has slipped from one side over to the other. Perhaps there are no such borders or path, naught but stumbling steps judged in the flickering light of competing interests and struggles, whose consequences only become clear long after the journey is over. And sometimes, not even then.

"Fray Martín, are you listening? We must decide what to do with this *cuadernillo*. At once." The mounting panic in Diego's voice jolts me out of my reverie. "You were charged with finding the originals of Fray Juan's work. You must decide if you are going to comply with your obligation to your superiors or not. And if not…"

If not, I lose a certain route back to my old life in Salamanca.

"If this original version of the *Canticle* is provided to Vatican inspectors, Fray Juan will never be beatified," Carmela declares.

"But we know that these lines are no true evidence of heresy. You said so yourself, Carmela."

"That does not matter. They can be made to masquerade as evidence," Diego persists. "And you of all people should know that if something is said often enough by people who are important enough, the truth does not matter. Whatever is said becomes the truth."

"Given everything we have thought and agreed, Martín, you must see there is only one thing to be done."

I look down, hoping to find an answer in the pages I hold in my hand. "Our goal then, is to ensure that no definitive evidence survives – no words written in Fray Juan's own hand – that could be twisted to create the most damaging interpretation of his thoughts." I raise my voice, as though performing a formal ceremony. "Is this our agreement?"

"It is." Carmela nods.

"Diego?"

"I fear so. We cannot be certain that those who stand to gain from tainting Fray Juan's legacy will refrain from using his original words to misrepresent his thinking. All we can do is ensure that their efforts are based on copies and copies of copies. Not on lines written in his own hand." Ever practical, he glances at us both, his voice lowered. "There is no time like the present. Fray Martín?"

I gaze into the flickering candle and breathe a deep sigh. "Very well."

At that moment, a rattling on the external door to the street startles us out of our contemplations. Carmela slips the *cuadernillo* into the folds of her habit. "Later," she whispers. "We must leave this place before the workmen return."

Diego looks at me. "Which of us will carry out the task?"

No one speaks.

"I have been called to meet the foreman after sunset. To find out if I will have work next week," Diego says, staring at the ground.

"I must return to the convent to nurse Sor Eugenia. We do not think she will live more than a few days."

Both my companions regard me with compassion, no doubt believing that they understand my reluctance to take this final step. I hear my own voice echo, as from a great distance.

"I will do it."

It seems that this certain path to recovering my old life really is lost to me. And if my work does not satisfy Doctor Enrique, I must learn, after all, to be content with life as an obscure novice master in the little convent of San Salvador, grateful at least to live unencumbered by venomous superiors, unmolested by the Holy Office of the Inquisition.

We agree to meet here for the last time seven days from now.

"Is it safe for you to travel to the monastery with these papers,

Martín? Where will you conceal them until you can burn them?"

"I have hollowed out a secret compartment in the stables at the rear of Caminante's stall. That is where I store..." I falter and stop myself from mentioning this journal, "...my various personal papers. I will hide Fray Juan's *cuadernillo* there. Do not worry, it will never be inside the monastery." I am shocked to hear a quaver in my voice. "I will burn it tonight, if I can. If not, tomorrow at first light."

Carmela looks up at me, her tawny eyes soft again, glowing in the dim light. "This is the right thing, Martín. What you see as an act of destruction is the only way to protect Fray Juan's legacy from those who would misuse his words for their own advancement. What Diego said is true: there is very little we can do that will bring about a certain outcome. Yet we must do the little that we can."

She raises a slim hand in farewell. My skin prickles under her gaze. "More powerful than mere words or thoughts, is the power of Fray Juan's spirit. His soul will echo down through the ages," she whispers. "When we are all forgotten, when the Holy Office of the Inquisition has ceased to be and the dynasty of our kings is no more, the fire of Fray Juan's words will light the centuries, comfort and gladden the hearts and souls of those as yet unborn, illuminate their minds with the joy of the soul's dark night on its quest for union with God, his words transformed to flames of love, to live forever."

She bends her head to mine, the warmth of her breath on my cheek. "Remember: *muero, porque no muero*. To make Fray Juan's words endure, we must destroy them, now."

I die, because I do not die. I look upon those golden eyes and smile. It is enough. She turns from me, nods once and is gone.

Twilight falls like a veil across the day as I make my way across the Plaza de la Puerta Cerrada, feeling a little calmed by the measured clip-clop of Caminante's hooves on the earth. Everything I see around me – the deepening blue of the dusky

sky, lamps flickering in the doors of taverns and the mean dwellings of the poor, the glimmer of stars that begin to stud the air – all has taken on a glowing intensity, as though I am seeing these things for the first time.

In spite of my worry, I feel my spirits rise, soar in exhilaration and at this moment I wish for nothing more than to know that the words I held in my hand were no mere dictations transcribed from recitals or written from memory by tired or confused scribes, but the work of Fray Juan's own mind and hand: his thoughts, crackling, smouldering, transformed, ablaze. A living flame of love.

Monastery of San Gerónimo, Madrid,
Eleventh day of October in the Year of Our Lord, 1616.

I do not know why I have chosen to spend these last few hours of my commission at my desk, papers strewn around me in disarray, when very soon I will be summoned to an uncertain fate. Perhaps this final entry maintains the illusion that, set down in this private journal, my thoughts remain my own, beyond the grasp of those who would probe and judge them. Or is this no more than a final, futile effort to justify myself? But to whom? Only to myself, for no one else will ever read these pages. Still, it soothes me to sit here in the hours before Matins and the dawn, my room bathed in the flickering fire of candles I have placed along the windowsills and mantelpiece, every surface dappled in light and shadow. I have yet to gather up the books and papers that lie scattered across the floor, which rough, probing hands seized and cast from the shelves.

It does not matter, now. Events have unfolded regardless, our plans to influence how Fray Juan's story would be told all swept aside. I left my companions with a clear course of action in mind: to destroy Fray Juan's papers. Especially the *Canticle* and his little notebook. But since this last, brutal confrontation, I know that the consequences of our actions can never be fully understood, and that the desire to determine or even influence the course of events is but an illusion: our intentions are leaves, fluttering on the wind. Whatever happens will come to pass despite what we do, not because of it. To think otherwise now seems like perilous hubris.

Such thoughts were very far from my mind when I left my companions. It was a beautiful evening, the sky fading blue-black as the twinkling stars came out, one by one, a fingernail moon suspended above the shadows of the growing city. Breathing deep of the cool night air, I dismounted and led Caminante at an easy pace up the hill past the Puerta Nueva. Together we circled the Plaza de Arrabal, avoiding the builders' blocks and tools that would obstruct our progress in the dark. A warm light glowed in a few windows in the high, narrow buildings along the calle de la Huerta, but many more were in darkness, for these are homes of labourers and craftsmen who would be awake and working at first light. The road from the calle de Atocha to the Monastery of San Gerónimo el Real slopes gently downhill and together we ambled, enjoying the pleasant stroll. When we reached the little bridge at the Carrera de San Gerónimo, the darkness dispersed, the glowing embers of a small street brazier suffusing the night. The scent of roasting chestnuts drifted on the air. For once, I yielded to temptation and handed over two *maravedíes*. The vendor's eyes opened wide to see a pious, white-clad friar thus indulge himself. We exchanged a few words while I ate, before I resumed my journey along the Paseo de Atocha, homewards.

Soon the dark archways of the Puerta de Alcalá rose up, the lines of poplars beyond looming against the sky. A wave of melancholy engulfed me as I paused to lean on Caminante's warm flank, my arm across his back, the saddlebag where I had stored Fray Juan's papers pressed against my chest. Unbidden, the image of Doctor Enrique's long, thin countenance swam into my mind's eye and I wondered what fate lay in store for me. Despite my efforts, the sadness intensified to a profound sorrow, born of the knowledge that my one certain chance to regain the world I once knew – lectures, students, the streets of Salamanca – could turn to ashes in the very flames that would consume Fray Juan's *cuadernillo*. Sensing my mood, Caminante whinnied. I reached into the little burlap bag I keep tied to his saddle and extracted an apple.

"Here you are, my faithful travelling companion. Who knows where the next months and years will lead us?"

He nuzzled my neck and I felt comforted. The scent of horsehair, the smell of the leather, the aroma of the few chestnuts I had wrapped in a cloth and tucked into my belt calmed my mind and carried it back to a time long ago, before reports and lectures and vows had begun to crowd my thoughts.

It occurred to me that the stable boy, Mario, might still be about, tending to his evening tasks, so I quickened my step to ensure that we would reach the monastery garden before the gate was closed. We moved in the shadow of the perimeter wall but there was no disguising the clip-clop of Caminante's hooves on the cobbles. Just as we reached the stable door Mario burst forth, holding aloft a sharp implement that almost grazed Caminante's ear. All three of us started. Caminante snorted in protest.

"Beg pardon, Fray Martín, I had to fetch this," in his left hand he clutched a three-pronged fork, "if I am to finish clearing the courtyard." He nodded towards the poplars that surround the perimeter, starting to shed their leaves.

"Do not let me detain you, Mario." I stood back and allowed him to pass.

The boy touched his cap and grinned. Caminante likes him, perhaps because he always has a carrot or a handful of oats about him. But already the boy was busy raking up the dead leaves and when I followed his steps to the clearing behind the stables, he stooped and gathered a pile atop the fork, raised and tossed them into a shallow pit where he had set a fire. Sparks crackled and drifted upwards, shimmered and fanned out across the darkness, adding a shower of fiery little stars to the silver pin-pricks winking in the night sky. This was a stroke of luck, for I had not thought of how I would kindle a fire unnoticed. Thanks to Mario, Fray Juan's *Canticle* would burn with the ashes of the leaves.

"Perhaps we have chosen the best way forward after all, Caminante. What do you think?"

Without my leading him, he butted wide the stable door and made his way daintily to his stall, where he turned and gazed at me with liquid, mournful eyes. Despite my worries, I burst out laughing.

"Mario has disappointed you, poor fellow. Well, let us see if we can find something to cheer you up."

Pleased that I had had the foresight to enlist him as the guardian of my hiding place, I edged into the stall, alongside my old companion. This little niche can only be negotiated with Caminante's co-operation and I am sure that he would not make it easy for any stranger who might want to search the inner reaches. I dipped my hand into the bag of oats I keep on a nail in the furthest corner and drew out a handful. While Caminante munched, I disentangled the string and removed the sack, careful not to spill any of the oats, for I should not like Caminante to injure himself trying to reach a tempting morsel in such a confined space.

"Easy, boy." I stroked his mane, glad of the brightness in his eye. He was in a placid mood and did not object when I leaned over to push on a panel of wood in the stable wall behind him. Whenever I carry out this manoeuvre I feel a shiver of anxiety, lest my hiding place has been discovered. Tonight, as always, I was reassured. The space within is difficult to reach – I chose it for that reason – and requires an awkward twist of hand and arm to penetrate the gap between the wood and the outer stable wall. I eased my arm into the space, almost to the elbow, for the only way to retrieve the cache is by touch alone. There it was, snug and safe. This journal, in its leather pouch. I drew it out, placed it on the ground and again pushed my arm into the gap, as far as I could reach. There would be just space enough for the two leather satchels containing Fray Juan's papers, but not enough to contain this journal as well.

For a few moments I sat on my heels and pondered. Caminante looked down on me. There was nothing for it. This notebook, being small and portable, would have to be concealed elsewhere. Later, I would hide it in my sleeping quarters or my office, but for the moment it would have to stay fastened to my girdle, hidden in the folds of my habit. At least it would be out of sight, should I have the bad luck to meet anyone on the way back to my study.

Concerned that Mario might return at any moment to fetch some other implement necessary to his labour, I made haste to unbuckle the saddlebags while Caminante stood by, in meek submission. Crammed into the bulkier of the two satchels were the least important of the documents from old Prior Andrés's archive: the folio containing the accounts of the Sicilian manor – without the *cuadernillo*, of course – various notes on the practicalities of housekeeping, a few letters and poems which at first glance appeared to be of little significance for our purposes.

In the smaller satchel I had placed the two copies of the *Canticle*, along with Fray Juan's precious notebook containing the draft – the original version, I am now convinced, written in Fray Juan's own hand – of the first thirteen stanzas of that troublesome poem. For a few moments, I held the notebook in my hands, weighed its shape and heft, raised it to my cheek, breathed in the musty scent of old paper, transported back to my father's study. The thought of consigning these pages to the flames filled me with dread, as though I were gathering my courage to toss a living creature on the pyre.

"Enough, Caminante. We have no time to waste."

I pushed both satchels into the gap in the stable wall, replaced the panel and returned the bag of oats to its nail. My task complete, I sidled from the stall and surveyed the scene from without. There was no sign of any disturbance. My habit of passing by Caminante's stall at odd hours no longer attracts attention, so I would have no difficulty in retrieving the satchels after Compline when the servants were abed, and I could profit from the smouldering ashes of Mario's bonfire. I reminded myself that Fray Juan's own supporters, the sisters who wished to protect him, burned his letters and probably his poems, too. No one would ever know that I had followed their example.

The thought did not console me. Gait slow and heavy, feeling as though a lump of stone was lodged in my breast, I trudged through the gardens. The scent of jasmine floated on the night air... *I went out, all unseen... my house being quiet and still...* The kitchen door was unlocked. I hesitated and for a few moments waited in the outer hall, peered around the oratory and at the cloisters, where I have taken my ease every day in these nine months since I began my commission. The destruction of Fray Juan's papers was not the only task that weighed upon me, for I would soon have to gather and sort my belongings in preparation for my departure next week.

No sooner had my thoughts shifted to that immediate task than I felt an involuntary heightening of awareness, all my senses on alert, rendering the darkness darker and the silence more alive. As I mounted the sweeping staircase and traversed the upper corridor that leads to my office, some habitual discipline beyond my conscious will maintained the steady pace of my steps so that any listener – and I was sure that somewhere along that shadowed passage, there was a listener – would perceive no faltering in my footfalls.

I should like to claim this certain knowledge as a gift from some supernatural source, some miracle bestowed, warning me that all was not as it should be, that I must prepare for the peril that lurked in the darkness, as the Holy Virgin inspired Fray Juan's escape from drowning and later from a Toledo cell. But I do not believe this. An excess of silence, the active silence of stilled breath, of movement arrested, of fingers placed before lips, infused the air with danger. As a deep patch of shadow in the wrong place, where some faint glow from moon and stars should glimmer, but does not.

The door to my study was ajar. For one insane moment I thought, *Run. Turn back to the stable, seize the precious files, saddle Caminante, gallop away. South, to Andalucía. Anywhere.* I know not how long this state lasted – a few seconds, no more – but the moments unravelled before me, as my body moved towards that which my mind sought to flee. Until the moment when, as suddenly and unbidden as they had arrived, all thoughts of flight departed, and I found myself hastening towards a silence that was too silent, darkness that was too dark.

In my office, all was in disarray. Documents littered the floor, some I recognised from the ancient chest of files I had inherited from earlier investigators. Others had been swept from their shelves. In a strange moment of elation, I gloated at the thought of my clever cache in the stable, overseen by Caminante's mournful eyes.

At that moment, the intruders made themselves visible. Concealed behind the door, Ortiz stepped forward when I crossed the threshold. I almost laughed out loud to see young Fray Francisco on his hands and knees beneath my desk, his long body folded in two, apparently checking for items attached to the underside.

Only Crespo stood square in the middle of the room, his squat bulk balanced on short legs in the stance of a street fighter ready to attack, reminding me of how little I know of these men, yet how much they know about me. I made no attempt to hold his gaze but turned away to survey the room, my jaw set and teeth clenched in a semblance of outrage and bewilderment, neither of which I felt. Fray Francisco uncurled himself from beneath my desk and stood up, brushing dust from his habit. Ortiz placed himself beside me, a little too close. I stood solid, arms loose and ready, a parody of Crespo's posture, though I did not think that any of these three would attempt to overpower me. The pouch containing this journal, secured to my belt, weighed on me. If my cape did not conceal it, the discovery would do me no good. I resolved to say as little as possible.

"Fray Martín," Ortiz's voice was polite and soft, the rough edges of his habitual tones smoothed away. "May I enquire where you have been?"

Had I been followed?

I have heard that those subjected to interrogations by the Inquisition are advised to keep answers as short and as close to the truth as possible, for one lie always borrows another and it is impractical, under difficult circumstances, to keep track of a complicated web of falsehoods. I raised my chin in defiance and allowed my eyes to swivel in disdain from one face to the other.

"I have been in the *barrio de los Austrias*. By the church of San Pedro el Real." I judged that this was the correct moment to display outrage and raised my voice. "Might I enquire what is going on here?"

Crespo glared. I resolved that I would not be drawn into a staring contest, so allowed my gaze to flicker across him, to the empty shelves, the papers on the floor, the fine oak desk which someone had stripped of all my personal items. In that moment, my feigned outrage became real.

Ortiz ignored my question. "For what purpose? What business did you have in that part of the city?" His tone remained smooth. I dislike Ortiz even more when he feigns politeness than when he is rude, and his rare courtesy has always disturbed me. Senses heightened, I became aware of the palm of my hand lying against the door, the smooth grain of the wood, the delicate patterned ridges I had often admired while I sat at my desk, thinking. A mist of sudden fury descended and, with all the force I could muster, I pushed hard on the door. It slammed shut with a bang as loud as a musket shot. Fray Francisco started. I was pleased to see that even Ortiz winced. Crespo alone remained unmoved.

"What is the meaning of this disgraceful intrusion?" My voice was steady.

Crespo raised his head, his little eyes glinting through the folds of his eyelids. "Answer the question, Fray Martín," he said in a low voice.

I frowned in puzzlement. "Your Grace, during our last meeting you made it clear that my services in your commission were no longer required. That I was – am – no longer in your employ and should make my preparations to leave before the end of this month. That is what I was doing."

Understanding that he would have to drag every iota of information from me, his little eyes gleamed like two pinpricks and his fleshy lips puckered. He opened his mouth to speak but I anticipated his question.

"I had two errands to undertake in that part of the town." I wondered if I really had been followed and if so, how much detail would justify my meeting with a nun and a former servant. "My superior in San Salvador asked me to pass on a message for an old servant of his from Salamanca. Also, I needed to arrange for the copying of certain documents," I held Crespo's gimlet stare, "to facilitate your work, and that of Prior Ortiz, after my departure. I will not have time to examine that file before the end of the week."

A dense silence followed. Somehow, they knew that documents had come into my possession, but they could not know that they were connected to Fray Juan's writings. Thanks to my quick thinking, neither were they aware that the precious archive was hidden not a hundred paces from where we stood.

"Fray Martín, do you understand," Crespo enunciated, with exaggerated softness, "that everything you encounter in the course of your work with us – every letter, every set of minutes, every scrap of paper – is the property of this Office?"

"Of course."

"Then kindly hand over to Prior Ortiz the package containing Fray Juan's personal papers."

My breath stopped. At least he referred to a package and not a file. I frowned, as though trying to remember, hoping to gain a few moments that I might unravel the contrary reactions warring within me. Shock, that he knew for certain that Fray Juan's papers were in my possession; yet relief, for in mentioning a 'package,' he revealed that I had not been followed, that no one had seen me assemble or store the two files containing those precious papers. If young Mario had finished raking and burning leaves, it was just possible that I might yet accomplish the task agreed with Diego and Carmela, and my interrogators would know nothing of it.

"Documents? Fray Juan's papers?" I shrugged. "In my judgement – as I explained in my most recent report – Fray Juan's manuscripts are long gone. Destroyed. By his supporters, and by Fray Juan himself. I am sorry, but I know nothing of the papers of which you speak."

Ortiz interrupted. "Fray Francisco says that you do."

The young friar began a close inspection of his shoes.

"Fray Francisco? Look at me, please."

He obeyed, his cheeks burning, but he could not hide the triumphant gleam in his eye. "A package arrived from Oviedo. A large package. You received it at the start of the summer."

He must have disliked me a great deal. Or perhaps he was a spy from the very beginning.

"From old Prior Andrés, yes. You examined its contents, then?"

The young man remained silent and would not meet my eye. I am sure that the Sicilian file where Fray Juan's *cuadernillo* was hidden had not been disturbed in decades, until I myself removed its cover, a few hours ago.

"It is a pity you did not inform me of your diligence, Fray Francisco. You could have spared me the entire day's work I devoted to seeking a reliable copyist so that Prior Ortiz could read those documents at his leisure when I am gone." I turned from him and smiled at my superiors.

"The archives of this investigation, Archbishop Crespo, comprised a full chest of material that you bade me examine and assess, did you not?" Eyes narrowed, he nodded. "That task occupied most of my time, when I was not collecting witness testimonies." I glared at Fray Francisco, who started to shift from one foot to the other. "This has left me little time to read the documents in the package of which you speak, which, as you know," I made a little bow towards the young man, "I received from Prior Andrés some weeks ago. In May, I think. But I did carry out a preliminary analysis, which satisfied me that the paper used is – to an experienced eye – quite new. And are therefore not Fray Juan's original manuscripts."

I looked away but was gratified to see from the corner of my eye that Fray Francisco's fair skin had turned crimson. "It is true that Prior Andres's archive contains one aged folio which dates from Fray Juan's lifetime. This contains the housekeeping accounts of a Sicilian manor." I shook my head and smiled. "Of course, it is possible there is some hidden significance in those numbers which my swift examination failed to detect."

Fray Francisco turned away, his eyes glittering, in dumb misery. I was not so sure that my interrogators were convinced. For an impromptu explanation, though, it was not a bad one. In any case, I had no option but to continue. "Much of the handwriting is cramped and difficult to read, even with a magnifying glass. I therefore arranged to have the papers copied. It was not easy to find a scribe sufficiently skilled to manage the task but a nun in one of the convents…" I allowed my voice to trail off, waved my hand and smiled at Crespo, as though such minutiae were beneath his attention.

The air thickened with expectation, the silence charged with the pulse of four hearts beating, not in unison, far from it, but each of us listening to his own internal rhythm. They did not believe me, of course. No matter. I had carved out some time, and that might be enough to allow me to accomplish my task – with luck, undiscovered.

Ortiz's voice was hoarse, all semblance of courtesy abandoned. "Where are they now? Those housekeeping records and minor poems?"

Time slowed down. A bare instant stretched to contain everything I know or ever knew: memories of my childhood, Salamanca, this commission, the dark, ominous shadow hovering over my future. Cold beads of sweat ran down my back. A vision of the dungeon of the Inquisition rose before me, I saw the rack and heard screams – my own? – Doctor Enrique, fifteen minutes of torture, Carmela's sweet, oval face framed by her white headdress, Diego's solid shoulders. All my thoughts, all my work, all our agonised discussions, leading to this moment.

"I have just told you. They are in the care of a nun whom I met this evening in the *barrio de los Austrias*. The sisters of her convent are skilled copyists and will have the file replicated within the week, before I leave for San Salvador."

Ortiz turned away and muttered something under his breath. "You have put these confidential, most secret papers into the hands of strangers."

"They are neither confidential nor secret," I ventured, knowing that my very meekness would enrage him further. "Nor is she quite a stranger, for I am acquainted…"

At that, Crespo stepped forward, a mere two paces but I wondered if he intended a physical attack. I did not flinch.

"Retrieve those papers," he snarled. "Go now."

"The hour is close to Compline," I objected, unable to believe my good fortune in being ordered from his presence. "The sisters will be asleep or preparing to sleep." Determined that he should have no inkling of my relief, I judged that eager acquiescence might arouse his suspicion. "They must rise for Matins, before the dawn."

"Then you had best make haste, Fray Martín. Prior Ortiz, will you come to my office in a quarter of an hour? We have much to discuss."

Before he could change his mind, as swiftly as I could while avoiding the appearance of hurry, I swept out of the room and retraced my steps along the darkened corridor. I could not resist looking back. But no, I had not been followed.

When I reached the door to the garden I paused for a moment on the step, gathering my senses, that I might perceive what awaited me out there. The confrontation had lasted no more than ten minutes, yet in that time, the temperature had fallen. A sharpness pierced the night air with the tang of autumn, which, together with the scent of burnt earth, heralded the year on the turn.

Mario was nowhere to be seen. I made my way to the stable door where I stopped for a moment and listened, before entering. Save for Caminante's easy breath, there was not a sound. He whinnied, surprised to see me at this late hour. Soothed by the scent of his coat and straw, I slipped into the far corner of his stall, crouched and slid the loose board from its place. In a few moments, I had extracted one of the two pouches hidden therein, and placed it on the packed earth. Caminante snorted.

"Easy, boy," I whispered and, gathering my habit around my knees, sat on the ground, my back against the stable wall. For a while I stayed there, absorbing the night scents and sounds, an owl hooting, the glimmer of moon through a crack in the wooden boards. When I could delay no longer I got to my feet, wrapped my cloak around the precious file and slipped out of the stall, into the courtyard, determined not to think of what I was about to do.

A cloud drifted across the moon and plunged the night into complete darkness. Fray Juan's words came to mind: *How well I know that gushing, flowing spring, even though it's night.* Those lines brought me comfort, and courage. The firepit beyond the stable smouldered still, a few blackened leaves crackled, curled in the embers. I reached into my cloak, slid a single page from the pouch and, without daring to look at it, cast it upon the glowing cinders. My head reeled as the paper crackled, turned yellow, blue and black while the edges flickered in tiny beads of fire struggling to breathe, fanned by a gust of wind, leaping into life, a flame dancing on the night sending sparks shooting through the dark. I felt the pages clasped to my breast pulsing as a living thing, not paper, but flesh and bone, and my senses began to swim.

After a time, my spirit stilled, suspended in the night air, thoughts of my companions drift by: Diego insists that I fight my accusers, a cool, slender hand is on mine, the brave sisters who burned his letters whisper, Crespo and Ortiz await me, the shade of Fray Juan hovers, as I clutch his material legacy in my hand. I cast another page upon the flame.

All at once, a sudden, stifled cry – my own – rent the air and I started back from the flames. A single spark had floated on the breeze and stung my cheek. The pages turned to lead in my hands. I grasped them, as a drowning man clutches on a passing branch, turned away from the firepit, my spirit quiet, suffused with a calm certainty, all my senses tranquil, my body leading the way through the night, stealing through the garden, unseen, the soft darkness my only guide back to the house, to face those who would soon confront me.

Time is against me. I had hoped to gather and refine the pages of this journal before Doctor Enrique's arrival, try to decide which of these musings and scribblings are lucid, which should be recast or rejected and from these many fragments, assemble a coherent picture to illustrate and illuminate the strange, sad events of Fray Juan's life. But Doctor Enrique will be here at daybreak and I have no more than a few hours to put some kind of order upon these pages and return them to my cache, in the hope that one day in the future, perhaps when I am established in Salamanca, I will retrieve them for some purpose that is beyond my imaginings now.

I am surprised to notice that I am not at all disheartened. Carmela was right: no matter what we do, the words and the spirit of Fray Juan will echo down the centuries. And my friends will surely forgive me. I hope that Diego will agree to return with me to the university, to an easier life. If he does not, I must not hold it against him. As for Carmela, I do not know. She may be disappointed, perhaps they will both despise me – for what I have done, for what I have failed to do. But I must not be discouraged. They will get over it. People usually do.

Acknowledgements

I would like to express my sincere gratitude to the many people who helped me in different ways and at different stages when I was writing *Canticle*.

The Irish Writers' Centre supports writers at all stages in their writing journey, one of their major initiatives being the annual IWC /Greenbean Novel Fair. In 2016, the Novel Fair judges, Martina Devlin, Anthony Glavin and Margaret Hayes, selected *Canticle* as one of the twelve winners for that year. Thank you, Writers' Centre and judges, for the encouragement and the injection of energy your nomination gave me, just when I needed it most.

The Arts Council of Ireland awarded me a travel grant to support visits to several places of significance in the life of San Juan de la Cruz.

I had the privilege of workshopping *Canticle* with fellow writers and friends in two different writers' groups: Anamaría Crowe Serrano, Ross Hattaway and Eamonn Lynskey from the Troika group (not that troika and yes, there are four of us); and the

Brooks group, especially David Butler, June Caldwell, Lisa Harding, Joanne Hayden, Julie Cruikshank, Ger Moane, Henry MacDonald and Manus Tobin. Your critiques were incisive, tough, always constructive and I am grateful to you all.

My friend Ana Constán guided me around the highways and byways of Castile on the trail of San Juan de la Cruz and gifted me some gems in the Spanish language that found their way into the text. Muchísimas gracias por todo, Ana, y ojalá que un día leamos *Canticle* en español.

Father Francis McAleese O.Carm. clarified the history and hierarchy of the Carmelite Order and corrected at least one potential howler. Thank you for that, Frank.

The resources of the magnificent Biblioteca Nacional de España in Madrid made the research process a delight. I am especially indebted to the staff of the Sala Cervantes and the Sala Goya for providing access to manuscripts and to maps. The staff of the library of the Museo de Historia de Madrid helped me to establish the topography of Madrid in the early 17th century.

In the process of writing *Canticle*, I drew on many primary and secondary materials to illuminate the life of Saint John of the Cross and the era of the Counter Reformation in Renaissance Spain. Some historical novelists provide a bibliography but I have decided against this. The historical novel is a strange, hybrid beast, based on historical events and imbued with the character of the time, but not in itself a historical or biographical text, which I think a full list of sources might suggest. *Canticle* is a work of fiction. It draws on, interprets and reimagines the historical and biographical details which the work of the experts in those fields has made available to us. That said, I would like to acknowledge José Vicente Rodríguez's superb biography of San Juan de la Cruz, and the work of Gerald Brennan and Peter-Thomas Rohrbach.

I have saved my most heartfelt thanks for two people who watched over and nurtured *Canticle* at crucial stages in its development: my editors and friends, Doug Kinch and Anamaría Crowe Serrano. For your four eagle eyes, your meticulous work and your unfailing support, I will always be more grateful than I can say.

To everyone I've mentioned – your help and support made *Canticle* better. Any shortcomings or mistakes are all my own.

Liz McSkeane
Dublin, 2018.

Extracts and translation

The extract from Dante's "Inferno" on page 36 is from *The Divine Comedy of Dante Alighieri*, trans. Henry Wadsworth Longfellow, Boston: Houghton, Mifflin and Co. (1867).

The extract from the "Song of Songs" on page 38 is Canto 7 from the Authorised King James Version of the Bible, *Pocket Canons: Song of Solomon, with an introduction by A.S. Byatt*, Edinburgh: Canongate (1998).

All translations from the poems of San Juan de la Cruz in the novel are by the author, based on the Spanish edition of works of Fray Juan de la Cruz from the Clásicos Ebro (Ed Blecua, J M) *San Juan de la Cruz Poesías completas y otras páginas*, Zaragoza: Ed Ebro SL. (1976).

Jordi Forniés

Jordi Forniés (born in Huesca, Spain) is an international visual artist and music composer. His work has been featured in exhibitions around the world and is in many private and corporate collections, as well as in the collections of the Office of Public Works (Ireland) and the Patrimonio Histórico Nacional (Spain). His paintings are also included in the collections of the Museu d'Art Modern de Tarragona, the Consorcio de Museos de la Comunidad de Valencia, and the municipal collections of Fraga and Monzon. The artist exhibits regularly in Spain, and in Ireland where he is represented by the Olivier Cornet Gallery, Dublin.

About the Author

Liz McSkeane was born in Glasgow and has lived in Dublin since 1981. She has worked in Ireland, the UK and Europe as a teacher and educational consultant specialising in curriculum development and assessment. She has a degree in French and Hispanic Studies from Glasgow University and a PhD in Education from Maynooth University. In 1999, she was overall winner of the "Sunday Tribune / Hennessy New Irish Writer of the Year Award" for her poetry. Her short stories and poems have been published in Ireland and the UK and she has three collections of poetry: *In Flight* (Lapwing, 1996); *Snow at the Opera House* (2002, New Island); and *So Long, Calypso* (Turas Press, 2017).

Canticle, her first novel, was a winner in the 2016 Irish Writers' Centre/Greenbean Novel Fair.

Liz tweets at @EMcSkeane and blogs on www.elizabethmcskeane.com